HUSBAND
AND LOVER

*Also by Lynn Erickson
in Large Print:*

After Hours
In the Cold
Without a Trace

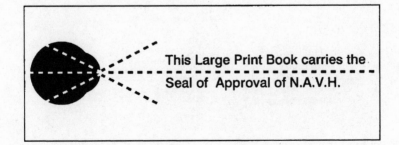

This Large Print Book carries the
Seal of Approval of N.A.V.H.

HUSBAND AND LOVER

Lynn Erickson

F
ERIC

WHEELER
PUBLISHING

Published in 2005 by arrangement with The Berkley Publishing Group, a division of Penguin Group (USA) Inc.

Wheeler Large Print Softcover.

The text of this Large Print edition is unabridged.
Other aspects of the book may vary from the original edition.

5/05   Gale Group $24.95

Set in 16 pt. Plantin by Ramona Watson.

Printed in the United States on permanent paper.

Library of Congress Cataloging-in-Publication Data

Erickson, Lynn.
  Husband and lover / by Lynn Erickson.
    p. cm.
    ISBN 1-58724-946-4 (lg. print : sc : alk. paper)
    1. Married women — Crimes against — Fiction.
  2. Police — Colorado — Aspen — Fiction.   3. Physicians'
  spouses — Fiction.   4. Remarried people — Fiction.
  5. Judicial error — Fiction.   6. Aspen (Colo.) — Fiction.
  7. Large type books.   I. Title.
  PS3555.R45H87 2005
    813'.54—dc22   2005000297

HUSBAND
AND LOVER

As the Founder/CEO of NAVH, the only national health agency solely devoted to those who, although not totally blind, have an eye disease which could lead to serious visual impairment, I am pleased to recognize Thorndike Press* as one of the leading publishers in the large print field.

Founded in 1954 in San Francisco to prepare large print textbooks for partially seeing children, NAVH became the pioneer and standard setting agency in the preparation of large type.

Today, those publishers who meet our standards carry the prestigious "Seal of Approval" indicating high quality large print. We are delighted that Thorndike Press is one of the publishers whose titles meet these standards. We are also pleased to recognize the significant contribution Thorndike Press is making in this important and growing field.

Lorraine H. Marchi, L.H.D.
Founder/CEO
NAVH

* Thorndike Press encompasses the following imprints: Thorndike, Wheeler, Walker and Large Print Press.

ONE

Murders are rare in Aspen.

But when one occurs, it's usually high profile, a celebrity, a billionaire, or maybe an ordinary person gilded by Aspen's fame.

Like the murder twelve years ago of Samantha Innes, the beautiful young wife of one of the country's up and coming orthopedic surgeons. Murdered by her lover, who was duly tried and convicted in the Victorian-style Pitkin County Courthouse, the events covered in breathless detail by endless talking heads.

The victim's husband, Dr. Thomas Innes, took the brunt of the attention, his anguish played out over and over in print and on the small screen. All the faces of the principle players — Samantha, Thomas, and their little daughter Olivia — became as familiar on the nightly news as did the face of the defendant.

The trial turned into a three-ring circus, only because it happened in Aspen. No tawdry back-alley murder this, but full-blown tragic theater involving people tinged by the fairy dust of celebrity.

None of that sparkling dust had fallen on Bret McSwain's head twelve years ago. He'd only been one of many assistants working in the DA's office, and he'd had nothing to do with the case. But now he was the DA. Now it was his turn.

He smiled to himself from where he sat next to Aspen Police Detective Jeb Feller, who was driving the department SUV through a spring storm. The windshield wipers swept back and forth, clearing away the heavy wet snow. The street was slushy, the sky gunmetal gray, close, laden with moisture.

They were on their way to the Aspen home of Dr. Innes, no longer the young rising star whose wife had been murdered, but *the* orthopedic surgeon in the country, the kind of doctor who fixed athletes' knees and shoulders and ankles. The kind of guy who charmed his patients as well as healed them, as likely to set up a golf game with a famous patient under his care as to fix a local ski patrolman's knee injured while on the job.

Bret enjoyed recalling the day, the moment, he'd made the decision to arrest

Thomas Innes. A couple months ago, actually, after he'd been contacted by Leann Cornish. He'd listened to the woman, and subsequently checked her background, taken a look at the original trial transcripts. Found a second witness to corroborate the nurse's statement.

Bret had weighed the pros and cons — that was his job. And he'd decided a guilty man was walking the streets, and an innocent man was imprisoned for the murder of Samantha Innes.

In the annals of the law this situation was rare. Bret had thought long and hard on the dilemma, consulted his staff, eminent law professors, the state attorney general in Denver. Ultimately, the decision was up to him. He reviewed the new evidence, found it unassailable, and went forward.

His first step, as a point of law, was to have a writ of habeas corpus granted to release the imprisoned lover, Matt Holman. Bret couldn't have it both ways: If Innes was guilty, then Holman was not.

Detective Jeb Feller sat forward, peering through the heavy snow. "Shit weather," he said.

"Spring in the Rockies," Bret replied. "Maybe it'll be better tomorrow." Small talk, which did nothing to alleviate the tension in the vehicle.

The date was April 15, the last day of the ski season. A Sunday. Bret McSwain patted the breast pocket of his jacket — the arrest warrant. He'd decided to do the dirty deed on a Sunday when Innes would most likely be home. Ten in the morning, before the doctor made plans, went skiing or something.

Gotcha, McSwain thought.

Oh, boy, was there going to be an uproar over this arrest. Every newspaper in the country, every TV station, CNN, Fox News, NBC, the works. He welcomed the attention; he knew he'd look good on camera. He was a young forty-two, slim and tall and blond. He wore trendy wire-rimmed glasses. Okay, so his hairline was receding a touch, but he still cut a decent figure. He was looking forward to the media attention. This was Aspen, the playground of the rich and famous. And he was about to arrest a celebrated local, a murderer, a particularly clever one, who'd gotten away free and clear over a decade ago.

"It's right on the next corner, isn't it?" Feller asked.

"Yeah, the yellow house."

McSwain was only minutes away from arresting Innes. His gut told him this case would make him, put his career on the fast track, and propel him into the state attorney general's office. The sky was the limit.

There was a single niggling detail: Dr. Thomas Innes's wife Julia was one of McSwain's employees. She was a deputy district attorney in the Aspen office, and she'd worked for him for seven years. She was a diligent DDA, smart, insightful, empathetic. Attractive.

He had to push aside that fact, though. He had to arrest her husband. It was his sworn duty as district attorney for the Ninth Judicial District. Justice must be served.

Hell, he'd had to keep the whole thing secret from Julia, the new evidence — a deathbed confession no less — before presenting it to the judge and having the arrest warrant issued.

Poor Julia.

Feller steered the car through a flurry of snowflakes, falling like cotton balls from the sky. A whispery silence lay over everything. You could barely see the mountain rising at the edge of town.

There'd be an instant and humongous

media reaction after the arrest. He knew the locals would be on the side of their hometown hero, the handsome, likable doctor who mended their broken body parts. They'd take his side, at first, anyway. But when the incontrovertible evidence came out, they'd have to change their minds.

Shouldn't Julia have *known* about her husband? Shouldn't she have *felt* his guilt? McSwain wasn't married, never had been, but he figured a wife would know that about a husband. Weren't women supposed to be perceptive about things like that?

Twelve years ago Bret McSwain had been a deputy district attorney, as Julia was now. Though he hadn't worked the case, he recalled it, a case for which Thomas Innes was never even indicted, much less tried and convicted. No, someone else had taken the fall.

Thank God there was no statute of limitation on murder. Twelve years, and the only murder in Aspen since then had been a drugged-up kid killing his equally drugged-up buddy.

Well, he was going to nail Innes this time.

Detective Feller pulled up to the curb,

put the car in park, and killed the motor. "Here we are," he said. Unenthusiastically.

McSwain knew Jeb Feller was reluctant to arrest Innes, reluctant even to accept the new evidence. But it was not the cop's job to make those judgments — his job was to arrest people the DA and the judge told him to arrest.

McSwain drew in a deep breath, smoothed his thinning hair in an unconscious gesture, and stepped out of the vehicle. Big flakes tapped on his head, on his shoulders, blotched his glasses. Feller came around the vehicle and followed him up the walk, through three inches of heavy spring snow, their feet sucking, leaving dark wet footprints on the cement.

McSwain's nerves twitched in excitement. He wondered if Innes would become irate, threaten, throw a punch. Try to run. He could see the headlines that would sweep the nation: *PITKIN COUNTY DISTRICT ATTORNEY BRET MCSWAIN REOPENS ASPEN MURDER CASE, ARRESTS DR. THOMAS INNES.*

He walked up the three steps of the Victorian porch with its gingerbread trim, and he stamped his feet on the doormat, stared at the shiny black door with its small stained-glass window. He reached out and lifted the brass knocker, let it drop, heard its sharp report ring out.

Who would come to the door, Julia or Thomas?

He waited, his mind calculating how long he'd wait before he knocked again. Ten seconds, fifteen? What if no one was home?

But he heard a dog bark and footsteps approaching. Not a man's heavy tread, but a woman's — Julia? He prepared himself.

She would be hurt, sure. But she'd get over Thomas in time. Maybe one day she'd thank McSwain for putting away her murdering husband. Hell, maybe he was saving her life.

It's Barb at the door, Julia thought. *She's early.*

They were going skiing, closing day on Aspen Mountain. Sometimes the last day was beautiful and warm and sunny, with corn snow and people eating lunch on the decks of the Sundeck or Bonnie's. Then there were the days like today — a total whiteout, a spring storm. But when did lousy weather ever stop an intrepid skier?

Shushing her dog Blackie, she walked to the door in her stocking feet and sweater and long underwear, not quite ready yet.

14

Barb would wait, no problem.

She pulled open the door, a smile on her lips. But Barb wasn't standing there. Bret McSwain and Jeb Feller were on the porch.

"Bret, Jeb?"

"Hello, Julia. Is Thomas home?" Bret asked.

"Thomas? Ah, no, he had an emergency surgery. He's at the hospital. What . . . ?" Thomas, what on earth did they want with Thomas?

"I need to talk to him."

"Well, he should be back in a couple hours. He was going to try to meet me for lunch at Bonnie's."

"He's at the hospital," Bret repeated. "I see."

"What's up? Maybe I can help you," she offered.

"No, Julia, I really need to speak to Thomas."

Something was wrong. Bret's voice, his manner. She knew him, and she knew his body language. "Okay, guys, what's going on?"

Her boss expelled a breath. "I'd really prefer to talk to your husband."

Her insides twisted. "You may as well tell me. I'm going to find out anyway."

15

Bret studied her for a minute, and Jeb Feller shuffled his feet, not meeting her glance.

"Bret . . . ?"

"I don't know, Julia," he said, then he seemed to decide something. He looked past her shoulder and said, "All right, I'll tell you." But still her boss remained silent, just stood there on the porch.

She waited, her heart beating, her brain gridlocked. What in God's name was this? What could he possibly want with Thomas?

"Okay," McSwain finally said, "this is the thing . . . I have a warrant for your husband's arrest."

She felt her knees turn to liquid. She put a hand out as if to ward off an unimaginable evil. "Who . . . ?" she got out. A patient suing Thomas, that must be it, but . . . no one was arrested for that, for . . .

Bret shook his head. Jeb had turned away and was staring out toward the snow-covered lawn.

"But then . . . Bret, for God's sake, the least you can do . . ." She tried to control her voice, but her throat tightened.

"Your husband is under arrest for the murder of Samantha Innes."

"*Samantha?*"

"Yes, Julia, his first wife."

16

TWO

She tried to gather her wits. "The man who killed Samantha is in jail. This is crazy, Bret."

"There's new evidence."

"New evidence?" A spurt of anger abruptly tempered her shock. "What kind of *new evidence?*"

"Julia, you know I can't tell you that."

"Well, whatever it is," she waved a hand, "it's bullshit, and you know it. The minute Thomas gets home he'll clear everything up. God, Bret, I can't believe you'd do this."

"I don't think we'll wait till Thomas gets home."

"You . . . you can't mean . . . ?"

"Jeb, let's go," Bret said, and he turned to leave.

"Bret, you *cannot* go to the hospital. He's in surgery. Bret . . ."

"Julia, you know I like you and I trust you, but Thomas is your husband, and I'm sure you'll call him and let him know we're

17

on our way." He spread his hands. "So I'd like to get this over with as quickly as possible."

"You think if you wait, I'll warn him and . . . and he'll run?" she asked incredulously.

"Let's just say I don't want to take that chance."

She stood there after they left, snow blowing in the open door, their footprints in sloppy lines on the walk, slushy tire tracks leading away on the street. She simply could not fit her mind around the reality of the situation. Thomas under arrest for killing Samantha? Too bizarre, too ridiculous, too . . . improbable.

And Bret . . . the DA coming himself to make the arrest. That was unheard of. But she knew why he'd done it — this would be a high-profile case, if it ever went that far, and he'd wanted all the glory. The bastard.

Then her mind kicked into gear. She had to warn Thomas. She couldn't let Bret blindside him with this insanity. Frantically she looked around for the cordless phone. Where had she left it when she'd spoken to Barb?

Barb. Oh, God. She'd have to let her know. . . .

She found the phone lying under the

Sunday paper, stabbed in her husband's cell phone number. It rang — once, twice, three times, and his voice mail came on. Of course, he would have left the cell phone with his clothes when he changed into scrubs. He'd never have taken it into the operating room.

Okay, okay. She punched in the number of the nurses' station, pacing, a hand on her forehead, waiting for someone to answer.

"Nurses' station. This is Megan Simonson."

"Megan! Thank God. This is Julia Innes. Can you get a message to my husband?"

"Well, he's almost done in the OR."

"No, no, this is an emergency. You'll have to tell him as soon as you can. I'm on my way up there, but . . . Megan, he has to be told right away."

"Well . . ."

"Listen, the district attorney and a detective are on the way to the hospital to . . . to arrest him."

"*What?*"

"I don't have time to explain, I'm on my way."

"But . . . Dr. Innes? Arrested?"

"Megan, just tell Thomas. I'll be there. *Just tell him.*"

She ran upstairs into her bedroom, pulled off her long johns, and stepped into a pair of jeans, grabbed her purse, her mind clicking with permutations and combinations. And disbelief.

Barb, oh, God, Barb . . . No time. She scribbled a note for her friend on the back of an envelope sitting on the hall table, grabbed her parka off a hook, and yanked open the front door, sticking the note under the antique knocker. Ran around the side of the house to the garage, pressed the garage door opener. Keys, keys, yes, in her purse. Jammed them in the ignition and backed out of the garage too fast, spun onto the street.

Aspen Valley Hospital was only a few minutes away, even in a snowstorm. She tried to collect her thoughts as she drove. Thomas would need her to be clear-headed. New evidence. What on earth did Bret mean? She knew all about the murder of his first wife, knew that he and Samantha had been having problems and were going to separate. She knew, everyone knew, that Samantha had taken a lover, a man named Matt Holman, who'd admitted to being with Samantha just before she died. Admitted to having sex with her. It had been a simple case, a crime of passion, clear-cut. Of course Holman had insisted he was innocent, but that was to be expected.

The man had no alibi; he had motive and opportunity, and he'd been convicted and given a life sentence. Thomas had started over, a young widower with a child.

She took a breath that rattled in her lungs and turned onto Main Street. Not much traffic this early on a Sunday morning, with off-season looming close. Thank goodness.

She should have demanded that Bret tell her what evidence he was basing this arrest on, but he was correct — he didn't have to tell her. He had to tell Thomas, though. Sooner or later.

She steered through the slush, took the roundabout, then Castle Creek Road toward the hospital. Had Megan told him yet? He'd be upset; he'd be angry, but he'd clear up this mess, and soon it would be a bad memory. Bret McSwain would have to eat his words. He'd have to apologize. Publicly.

What on earth had Judge Scott been thinking when he'd issued the arrest warrant? Everyone knew that Thomas had an ironclad alibi for Samantha's murder. He'd been in the OR, doing a hip replacement.

The fact had been brought out in Holman's trial when the defense had tried unsuccessfully to implicate him.

Bret McSwain had gone out of his mind. He must have. Or else he was the most hateful human being Julia had ever dealt with. And he was her boss. How could she ever go back to work for him?

The only saving grace was that he worked in the Glenwood Springs office, forty miles from Aspen, and her immediate superior was Assistant District Attorney Lawson Fine. But none of that was important now. She'd think about all that later.

She pulled into the hospital parking lot, left her car in the temporary parking zone, and ran into the building, past Admissions, down the hall to the nurses' station.

Voices, over toward the operating room. Raised in argument. Bret and a nurse, but not Thomas.

The nurses were gathered in a knot behind their station, shocked, trying to see down the hall.

"Julia, what's going on?" one of the women asked.

"Did Thomas get my message?"

"Megan went to tell him. He was in the middle of a procedure. Then those men showed up. Isn't one of them the DA, you know . . . ? And we overheard something about the doctor's first wife . . . something about the DA coming here to . . ."

"Ah, yes, yes. I don't have time to explain now. There's been a terrible mistake. Don't worry, Thomas will straighten everything out."

"I knew Samantha," the nurse whispered, obviously horrified, her hands splayed on her chest. "I *knew* her."

Samantha, this was all her fault. If she hadn't been unfaithful to Thomas, none of this would have happened. She'd still be alive, divorced but alive, and Livie would have a mother.

Julia hurried down the hall to where Megan Simonson was barring Bret McSwain from the OR. "You can't go in," she was saying sternly. "It's sterile in there. You'll endanger the patient."

"Can't you call him out?" Bret said. "For chrissakes, this is ridiculous."

"He's finishing a procedure," Megan said. "Pinning a woman's broken wrist. He'll be done soon."

Julia stepped close to peer into the OR through the small window, and Megan let her by. There was Thomas, just pulling off his surgical mask, peeling off his gloves. His face was pale, serious, but he seemed composed. Handsome in that boyish way despite his forty-five years. Broad and strong, black hair, and dark arched eyebrows.

His patient was still on the table, administered to now by the physician's assistant, an OR nurse, and the anesthesiologist. Thomas would never jeopardize a patient, never, not even in the face of imminent arrest.

Thomas took his time as he came toward the double doors, pushed them open with his shoulder, and stopped in front of Bret McSwain. His eyebrows were drawn together. "You wanted to see me, Mr. McSwain?" Then, to the nurse, "Thank you, Megan." Polite, calm, in control.

Julia stood there, biting her lip, her pulse hammering, loving her husband, so proud of his demeanor. "Thomas," she began.

But he nodded — he understood her concern; he'd handle the situation. Tears stung her eyes.

There was fraught tension in the air; every nurse and doctor in the hospital knew what was happening, and they were all waiting expectantly for the next development.

"Yes, I wanted to see you," Bret said.

"Would you prefer to go to the doctors' lounge?" Thomas asked.

"I don't think that will be necessary." Bret pulled the warrant from his breast pocket. "Dr. Thomas Leon Innes, you are under arrest for the murder of Samantha Jane Innes."

Julia was suddenly furious. Bret was enjoying this far too much. He didn't have to do it this way. He just loved the limelight. *Damn him.*

She stepped close and touched her husband's arm. "Don't worry, this is a mistake, darling. We'll take care of it."

"Of course it's a mistake. I'm not the least bit worried, Julia."

"Cuff him, Jeb," Bret said.

"Goddamn it, that's not necessary," Julia breathed. *"Bret."*

"Julia, calm down," Thomas said. "These men have their duty."

Jeb clicked the handcuffs on her husband, and she winced.

"This way, Dr. Innes," Jeb Feller was saying, a hand on Thomas's elbow.

"Julia, would you get my coat?" Thomas said mildly.

Megan Simonson said quickly, "I'll get it."

Julia followed them to the hospital entrance. The front desk personnel sat shocked and silent, embarrassed, curious.

Megan hurried up, Thomas's coat over her arm, hung it around his shoulders. She looked as if she was going to cry.

Outside into the leaden gray sky and falling snow. Jeb Feller guided Thomas toward the police SUV. Julia strode right behind.

That hypocritical kindness of ducking the prisoner's head. So awful, her own husband, a perfectly innocent man treated like this.

And then, a young man with a camera, snapping pictures. What? She positioned herself in front of him, arm out to bar his way. "What do you think you're doing?"

"Photographer for the *Aspen Times*. Hey, aren't you Julia Innes? The wife? Can I ask you a few questions?"

"No."

"Take your photo?"

"No. Stay away from us." How in hell had this guy known about the arrest? It came to her, along with another spurt of anger. Bret had called the *Aspen Times* on his way over here. That son of a bitch.

A gaggle of hospital employees stood by the doors, staring, whispering. Got their pictures taken by the photographer for their pains. This was hideous. Everyone would know. . . . Aspen was a small town.

This story would be around in a few hours, and all over the papers tomorrow, and there was nothing she could do to stop it.

She went to the open door of the police vehicle, leaned in, and put her arms around her husband. "Everything will be all right," she said fiercely.

"I know, Julia."

She kissed his cheek, while Jeb Feller stood silently by the door, waiting to close it, to close Thomas away from her.

"Don't say anything. Do you hear me? Don't talk to them. About anything. I'll call Ellen. She'll take care of this."

He bestowed a grave smile on her. "I know you'll do your best."

Jeb shut the door, and she was bereft. They were going to drive her husband away, book him, fingerprint him, take mug shots. He would go into the system then, into the cold, uncaring memory of the crime computer.

The vehicle began moving, and she felt her heart tear. She put a hand out to touch the car window where Thomas sat. He looked at her, and she mouthed, *I love you. Hang in there.*

Swallowing her horror, her sudden fear and loneliness, she strode quickly to her car. She'd sit in the police station all day if

27

she had to, until she could arrange a hearing for him.

But first Ellen. Call Ellen, one of the top criminal defense attorneys in Denver, and Julia's closest friend.

She took out her cell phone and pulled away from the curb. *Ellen first,* she thought, following the police car, and then she'd phone Livie, Thomas's daughter. And what was she going to tell the girl? "Oh, gosh, honey, your dad was just arrested for killing your mother"? *Oh, God.*

She took the roundabout toward down-town, the SUV still just ahead, her wipers swishing, Ellen's phone ringing, but cutting in and out in the storm. This would all be over in a few hours, she told herself. Of course it would. It was just a terrible, cruel mistake. But a notion kept trying to emerge from a corner of her mind — what if it *wasn't* a mistake? New evidence, Bret had said. Then she shoved the thought into the shadows. A crazy mistake.

THREE

Victor Ferris had been mired in a writer's worst nightmare for six weeks: that no-man's-land where ideas did not spark, the hook for a story did not come to mind, fresh, original plots did not materialize. His muse was silent. He had his character, Luke Diamond, a tough homicide detective. He had his location — Denver, Colorado. He'd written six very successful books with Luke Diamond as the intrepid hero. His seventh manuscript was due before next Christmas, and he hadn't had a ghost of an idea where to begin.

Until this morning.

He'd been reading the Monday morning edition of the *Denver Post*, as he always did, scanning the headlines for ideas, weird tales, murders, mutilations, kidnappings, anything that might suggest one lousy crime for Luke Diamond to solve.

He stopped flipping pages, spread the paper flat on the dining room table, and bent over to read a story.

RENOWNED ASPEN SURGEON ARRESTED FOR MURDER, read the headlines. Then, below that: DR. THOMAS INNES ARRESTED FOR 12-YEAR-OLD MURDER OF WIFE SAMANTHA.

"Holy shit," he said. His blood pressure rose. Victor actually remembered that case. He hadn't been rich and famous back then, but he'd followed the story out of intense curiosity. And here it was again, falling into his lap, when he needed inspiration so desperately.

Relief swamped him, and his brain shifted into high gear. He could see so clearly now, the whole story, the beginning, middle, and end. The title. Cover art. The inside jacket blurb. Every goddamn thing. Better still, he *knew* the detective who'd worked the Samantha Innes murder. He sure did. A grin spread across his narrow jaw.

It was early in the morning, and he was flying on adrenaline. Denver Homicide Detective Cameron Lazlo, Victor thought. Make that *former* detective, but who cared? Cam worked for Victor now. Had for years. Victor's trusted assistant, the source for all his inside dope on police procedure, source of his prose dubbed "so hard-boiled it hits you in the face" by the *New York Times*.

He figured Cam would be up despite the early hour. The man never seemed to sleep. He grabbed the phone, punched Cam's preprogrammed number.

Cam picked up after one ring. "Yeah?"

"Listen, Cam, I have it."

"That's good."

"No, seriously, I have the plot for the new one."

"Okay."

Sometimes Cam could be exasperating. "It's a great one, and you're going to shit a brick when you hear it."

"Sounds painful."

Victor ignored the remark. "You remember the Samantha Innes case? Twelve years ago?"

"You know damn well I do. You know I worked it. Guy's in jail for the murder."

"Well, think again, my man." Oh, boy, did he love shaking Cam's tree. The opportunity did not arise often.

"Okay, I give up. What's the idea? You're gloating."

"Read the story on the front page of today's *Post*. All will be clear."

"Christ, Ferris. What's with the mystery?"

"Just get the paper and read it. This one is fantastic. Over the top."

Cam groaned. "Whatever."

"You've got to get involved in this case."

"Right, I don't even know what it is yet."

"Read the paper, my man, and you'll understand everything. That's all I have to say for now."

Victor hung up, smiling to himself. He chuckled out loud. *Damn,* but he felt terrific. He was a short man, wiry, dark curly hair, and dark eyes. He worked out with weights and rode an exercise bike each day, and he wrote in enormous bursts of energy, barely eating while he was in the throes of creation.

He was also a dreadful slob, his downtown Denver loft a rat's nest of dirty dishes and laundry and books and ashtrays piled with cigarette butts. Once a week Rosa came to clean, muttered Spanish under her breath, and the apartment was tidy for a day.

Victor's office, however, was neat and organized. Rosa was not allowed in his inner sanctum. No one was, really, except for Cam, and then only to help Victor out with some inside material.

Victor worked in old sweats, and an orange Broncos T-shirt and socks. His preferred wardrobe for writing. He took a cup of coffee, his pack of cigarettes, and the *Denver Post* and practically skipped into his office.

He settled in front of his computer, a lit cigarette dangling from his lips; he flexed his fingers exactly three times, sat immobile for two minutes, looking inward, seeing the story unfold in his mind's eye like a movie.

He started typing.

Diamond in the Rough
by Victor Ferris

Chapter One

Luke Diamond drove his vintage T-Bird too fast on Interstate 70 through Denver. He always drove too fast, even if he wasn't on his way to a crime scene, even if he was in a department-issue Crown Vic — hell, if he got pulled over, he'd flip his tin. Fuck 'em if they can't take a joke.

Exits flashed by: Pecos, Federal, Sheridan. He was headed west. On a mission. After all these years, there was new evidence in the Beckett case: a deathbed confession naming Andrea Beckett's husband as her murderer.

Even though another man had been tried and convicted for Andrea's murder years ago.

Diamond's brows were drawn in a ferocious scowl, his hands on the steering wheel scarred from a forgotten number of fistfights, his heavy shoulders tensed. He was a big man, with straight blond hair, transparent blue eyes, and Nordic cheekbones. He looked a little dangerous, even when he didn't mean to, hinting at menace, which was his specialty. He was good at menace.

This was personal. This goddamn new evidence, some old broad ready to croak, wanting to set the record straight. It was crap.

The record was already straight. Mike Hanson was serving a life sentence for the murder, and Diamond had helped put him there.

He downshifted smoothly but still took the off-ramp too quickly, tires squealing hot rubber around the corner. No way was this woman going to kick the bucket before he heard her confession with his own ears. No friggin' way could he have been this wrong.

Cam Lazlo took the steps on the side of the building down to street level, where the newspaper in its bright orange wrapper lay tossed near the curb. His landlady, Mrs. Clapper — Irene — was already out sweeping the sidewalk in front of the building that housed her antique bookstore.

"Good morning, Cam," she said, stooping to pick up a crushed soda can. "You'd think folks could use the trash barrel. Golly."

"Morning, Irene." He nodded, worked up a smile, and tucked the paper under his arm.

Irene leaned on the broom handle. "Poor Fred," she lamented, referring to her husband, "his back's bothering him. It's this weather, you know. One minute it's raining, the next it's snowing, the next the sun's out."

"Um, April. Tell Fred I hope he feels better."

Cam was itching to read the paper, see what had Victor so riled up. He started back toward the stairs.

"You hear the sirens last night? About ten or so?" Irene called.

"Yep, pretty noisy."

"I always worry it's the store, a fire or something. Then I remember you're here. We're so glad you are, you know, Cam, truly."

Truth was he hadn't been in his apartment above the store at ten last night, but Irene always felt better believing he was home and watching the place twenty-four/seven, even though she and Fred lived in the neighborhood just around the corner of Broadway and Mississippi Avenue. The more elderly the couple got, the more paranoid they became. Having Cam around helped ease their fears, but not entirely.

"Gotta run," he said, still working the smile. "I'll pop in later."

She gazed at him. "What time?"

"Ah, say, one-ish?" *Geez.*

"See you then."

Cam had lived upstairs in the roomy apartment for nearly ten years. He'd still been on the force and had just gotten a promotion and raise. He'd been apartment hunting, when the Clappers' son had been accidentally shot to death in a drive-by shooting. Cam was the lead detective on the case, and one thing had led to another, and the Clappers offered him the apartment over their bookstore at a fantastic rent. Essentially the older couple paid him to be around. The arrangement had worked for everyone then. It still did. Trouble was, they had the bookstore on

36

the market, and when it sold, Cam would be out on the street apartment hunting again.

Upstairs he turned the volume down on the TV, sat on the couch, and shook the paper open, letting his eyes run down the headlines: AMERICAN SOLDIER KILLED . . . DENVER MAYOR OKS AIRPORT RUNWAY EXPANSION . . . RENOWNED ASPEN SURGEON ARRESTED FOR MURDER . . .

Whoa.

DR. THOMAS INNES ARRESTED FOR 12-YEAR-OLD MURDER OF WIFE SAMANTHA.

What?

He tried to read the article, but he couldn't concentrate. Images flooded his mind — photographs of Samantha Innes lying dead on the floor, her pale, shaking lover, her devastated husband, the poor innocent daughter. The trial . . . Memories.

The case had been cut and dried. Matt Holman was doing his time — doing it for the rest of his life. All ends neatly tied up, the wheels of justice turning efficiently for once. What in hell was this all about?

He tried again to read the article. "Thomas Innes . . . new evidence . . . statement by Pitkin County DA . . . doctor who repairs famous sports figures, list of patients long and illustrious."

New evidence?

The article went on about convicted murderer Matt Holman being released on a writ of habeas corpus. Released? "Jesus Christ," Cam whispered.

But then his shock waned and he thought, of course, if the DA was convinced he could win a murder case against Innes, he had to admit that Holman was innocent. That was the law.

So Holman was out.

The guy had been writing letters to Cam for years, ever since he'd been convicted, swearing his innocence, begging Cam to help him. The only thing Cam could figure right now was that the DA must have something pretty goddamn compelling on Innes for a judge to issue an arrest warrant for the good doctor.

No wonder Victor had been so high. No wonder he'd said Cam should get on the case. The irony was that even without Victor, Cam would have gotten involved with his case by hook or by crook. He'd been a Denver homicide detective twelve years ago, and he'd been sent to Aspen to help the local police force — Aspen hadn't even had a homicide detective back then;

they'd basically been traffic cops.

Twelve years ago . . .

Cam had been young. He'd been a good cop, working his way up to detective in record time. Had one of the best clear rates in the city. He loved his job, loved the rush of action, the power trip, the sleazy informants. Yeah, the violence, too. Loved that a little too much maybe.

And that weird rapport he'd had with the dead — the sworn internal promise he made each one that he'd find the killer, find him and put him away.

He'd admit to anyone that the communion he felt was uncanny. Some of the other murder dicks had admitted to the feeling, too. A kind of bizarre guidance that helped reverse the cosmic dissonance set off by the murder of a human being.

Well, he wasn't on the force anymore, but he couldn't quite lose the instincts that came with the badge. Like a reformed addict reaching for the pack of cigarettes that wasn't there. It never really left you.

He wasn't a cop anymore, and every day he fought the regret that came with that situation. Sometimes he even won the battle.

He certainly did have to get involved in this case. Though maybe Victor already had that problem solved, because Victor would want Cam close to the source. Yeah, Victor would take care of that end of things.

Aspen. The drama would all play out in Aspen. He'd liked the town and wondered if it had changed much. You heard stuff about the super rich taking over the place, the airport jammed with private jets. The scenery would be the same, though. Gorgeous, restful, a real Shangri-la valley set amidst tall peaks.

Scenes from his time spent there ran through his mind. There'd been a woman — hell, wasn't there always? A beautiful woman, a free spirit, cultured but still down to earth. He'd thought he loved her for a couple weeks there, but when her wealthy, older sugar daddy flew his Lear into town, she'd dumped Cam. No surprise, really.

He paused mid-thought and saw Samantha Innes's body on the slab, just before the autopsy all those years ago. She, too, had been young and beautiful. She'd had shortish auburn hair, parted on the side, a kind of retro forties look. Pale perfect skin, blue eyes, a wide mouth always curved up into a smile in her photos. Pretty, wholesome looking, like a World War II nurse in one of those old black-and-

40

white films. She'd been a potter, supposedly quite artistic. A young, married, work-at-home mother with a busy husband who perhaps hadn't paid her enough attention.

Cam had stared at her body, those eerie feelings coming over him, and he'd silently promised her: *I'll get the bastard who did this, beautiful lady.*

He thought he had.

It took till Monday morning before Julia found her nerve and finally dialed Livie's number at the exclusive Kent School in Denver. She was more upset over this chore than anything that had happened in the past twenty-four hours. Every time she thought about Thomas, her mind would swoop back to Livie and what on earth she was going to say to the girl. She made up a dozen speeches. Threw them all out. Started over again. Not only was Livie still so young, just eighteen, but she was so very needy. Pretty, smart, but forever scarred by her mother's early death.

She gripped the phone, the latest words she'd so carefully planned already gone from her head. She almost wished she didn't love Livie like a daughter — or like she *thought* she'd love a daughter of her own.

41

God, this was agony.

But she got the girl's roommate. "Oh, Mrs. Innes, oh, gee, Livie's gone. She left early this morning, before dawn even. She was really upset about something. She kept trying to call home, but the answering machine kept coming on. Finally she just split."

Oh, no. Julia hadn't gotten home from the police station till late, and then the first six calls on the answering machine had been from TV stations and newspapers, and she'd just punched Stop on the machine, hadn't listened to messages since. "Do you know where Livie's gone? Is she coming home?"

"I don't know. She ran out of here crying. She was up all night crying."

"Can you leave her a message, or if you see her . . . Listen, please just tell her to call me. But on my cell phone."

"She's probably on her way to Aspen, Mrs. Innes."

"God, I hope so," Julia said.

After making certain the girl had her cell phone number written down correctly, Julia hung up and dropped her face into her hands. Livie had heard the news. Julia should have called her last night. *Coward,* she screamed at herself.

She spent the next hours phoning Livie's number again and again to no avail. She finally gave up. One way or another, Thomas's daughter would make her way home. Where else would the distraught girl go? But then she began to fret over Livie hitchhiking or something, some faceless man coming on to her. . . .

By noon she was obsessively going to the window to see if Livie or Ellen Marshall was there yet. Blackie kept his eyes on her, head cocked, aware of her agitation. Julia had reached Ellen the day before, telling her friend of the whole story as succinctly as she could, trying to switch into lawyer mode.

After finally leaving the police department late in the evening, she'd fallen into bed in a state of utter panic — first over Thomas and then over Livie, what her father's arrest was going to do to her already fragile emotional state. Back and forth, Thomas, Livie, Thomas, tossing and turning, trying to sleep, brain churning ceaselessly. She kept seeing Thomas in the Pitkin County Jail, a country club of a jail, but still incarcerated.

Charged with murder.

The whole thing would be a comedy of errors if it weren't so deadly serious.

At five minutes to twelve Ellen's dark green Acura pulled into the driveway. Julia threw open the door and ran down the walk to greet her, then found herself falling into her friend's arms and sobbing.

Ellen was short, petite, with blue eyes and straight, very fine fair hair. Irish and proud of it. Spunky despite her stature and one of the best defense lawyers in the state, having recently won a nationally televised case.

She and Ellen went back many years, to Denver University law school, where Julia had been on scholarship and Ellen had been attending after a long hiatus from school. Ellen was forty-three now, gaining renown every year, a star in the cast of her prestigious Denver law firm.

Julia leaned her head down onto Ellen's shoulder, while her friend patted her on the back.

"I'm sorry," Julia said, gulping back tears.

"It's okay. This has been a shock. Awful. You poor thing."

Julia raised her head. "Thank you for coming."

"As if I'd miss it," Ellen snorted.

Inside, Ellen dropped her purse on the couch and flopped onto the cushions. She wore jeans, a turtleneck, and running shoes. She looked like a kid, until you saw her in court metamorphosed in a designer suit and high heels, her eyes full of fire, her body language a study in absolute self-confidence.

"Okay, so Thomas's first appearance is at one," she said, checking her wristwatch.

"Yes," Julia was saying, when the phone rang. Her whole body tensed.

"You want me to get it?"

"No, God, no, it's got to be a reporter. They've called and called. Everyone who matters will know to call my cell number."

"We've got to get you a new, unlisted number. Can you remember to do that? Sometime this afternoon?"

"Oh, sure, I don't have a thing on my calendar."

Ellen quirked a brow. "I'll call the phone company, not to worry."

"No, no, I can do it. Really. After Thomas's appearance in court, though."

"Speaking of which, will the same judge who issued the warrant be presiding today?"

"Same one. Judge Bill Scott."

Ellen nodded. "And you haven't seen the affidavit supporting the arrest warrant yet?"

45

"No. Bret refused to tell me anything. Only that there's new evidence. I've been going out of my mind."

"Um. He's got *something* interesting. Well, we'll find out at the hearing."

"Can he refuse to show us the affidavit?"

"He won't."

"How do you know?"

Ellen waved a tiny hand. "I know."

"All right, say we see the evidence, whatever it is. You can get Thomas out, can't you?"

"Probably. Most likely. I'll try for a personal recognizance bond. You know, outstanding member of the community, strong ties, a wife, a child, his clinic. Zero flight risk."

"I can get some of my own money together if you need it for bail."

"Not yet. I think we'll be fine." Ellen smiled. "Now, don't you worry. Everything will be okay."

"Right, I won't worry."

"You always were a worrywort."

Julia told her about Livie then. "I'm sure she'll show up here any minute," she said, standing at the tall Victorian window now, her arms folded across her chest.

"Of course Livie will show up here. She just panicked."

"She's probably hitchhiking. She's done it here in town, you know. But on Interstate 70? I mean, what if some molester or —"

"Livie will be okay. She's eighteen, right? Kids at her age kick butt. They're taught to kick butt."

"You're right." Julia found a weak smile. "She'll be fine. It's just that —"

"Julia."

"Right, she's perfectly fine."

"Okay, then. We need to concentrate on her father."

Julia blew out a breath. "I'll try to focus. Really."

Ellen knew her so well. Despite ten years between them, they'd been close. Ellen had listened to her fretting in law school, soothed her stress over exams and money, Julia's constant exhaustion as she'd worked and scrimped and saved to support herself in school.

Ellen was the first person she'd confided in after she met the handsome Dr. Innes when she waited on him in the Denver restaurant where she worked.

"I think I'm in love," she'd said dreamily to Ellen.

"Oh goody. Tell me all the details."

She'd told Ellen everything: how he'd ordered a chicken avocado sandwich and iced tea for lunch; how he was opening an orthopedic clinic in Aspen; how he was in Denver for a symposium on rotator cuff shoulder repair. How he'd taken her phone number and promised to call.

"Good luck," Ellen had said tartly, her track record with men not sterling.

But Thomas *had* called. That night they'd gone out, and she'd discovered he was a widower with a young daughter, and his wife had been murdered. Her heart swelled with love for the wondrously talented, dedicated, and tragic figure.

He'd phoned from Aspen every night, and they met as often as law school and his responsibilities allowed.

Positively, it had been love from the very first moment for both of them.

She'd met Livie, who was seven at the time, a darling dark-haired girl, who acted as if she'd been awaiting Julia ever since her own mother had deserted her so precipitously.

Funny, when Julia had seen Blackie in the animal shelter, one ear missing, sad brown eyes, he'd acted precisely the same way Livie had, as if he'd just been waiting for Julia all his life. Why did she attract such needy creatures?

Shortly after noon she wrote Livie a note

instructing the girl to call her cell phone the minute she got home. She signed it "Love, Julia," then P.S.ed, "Everything is okay, sweetie." She put the note under the knocker, looked up and down the street one more time for a forlorn girl walking toward the house, but the street was empty.

It was Ellen who brought up another point while they were dressing for the first appearance. "You know some of those calls on your phone are probably from your parents."

Julia knew. Combine Aspen and a celebrity doctor and murder, and every national news wire would be running with the story. Her parents always had a TV on. Always.

"So?" Ellen prompted.

"I'll call them. *I'll call.* Okay?"

"Don't bite *my* head off."

"Sorry, sorry," Julia said. "I'll take care of it, honestly I will. Dad can't do the altitude anymore, so they won't even think about coming here."

"What about Thomas's mother?"

"Maggie. Yes, she'll be calling any time now, I suppose."

"Can you handle her?"

Julia set her jaw. "Yes. Maggie and I have . . . I guess you'd call it an understanding. We respect each other."

"Sounds like an interesting relationship."

"You could call it that."

Julia wore a mid-calf length black wool skirt and dark green cashmere sweater. Ellen had changed into a pair of slacks and high-heeled boots. Ellen drove to the old redbrick courthouse in her own car, telling Julia she feared for her life if Julia drove. "You're a wreck. You'd run into something. Not a good look."

As they got out of her car by the side entrance of the building, she said sternly to Julia, "Let me do the talking. Not a word from you."

"Yes, ma'am."

"I'm not kidding."

"I know, I know."

"So, ready? Full speed ahead and man the torpedoes," little Ellen said with a fiery glint in her eye.

The hearing was held in the judge's chambers. District Attorney Bret McSwain was there, Detective Jeb Feller as the arresting officer, Judge William Scott presiding. The hearing was closed to all but the participants; nonetheless, a few reporters had gathered just outside the tall oak doors. Julia figured she would say the words "No comment" many many times before Ellen could clear up this whole mess.

Julia and Ellen waited, while the old clock on the wall ticked to ten past one, then the door opened, and two deputies ushered Thomas into the room, one at each elbow. He was handcuffed.

"This is bullshit," Ellen muttered under her breath.

Julia tried not to cry. Swallowed hard. Thomas was dressed in orange prison garb. He hadn't shaved. He looked tired. Composed, though, his nerves as steely as in the operating room. Like ice, many a nurse had said admiringly.

The hearing proceeded quickly. Ellen introduced herself as the attorney of record. She noted that the handcuffs were onerous. What she actually said was "Judge Scott, if you ever need emergency orthopedic surgery, would you want your surgeon's hands to have been in those?" She pointed imperiously.

The judge nodded, a deputy unlocked the cuffs. "Point taken, Counselor," Scott conceded.

The hearing continued. Ellen secured Thomas's release on a personal recognizance bond, as she'd promised Julia. Her arguments were clear, concise, and persuasive. "Dr. Innes won't be going anywhere. He is absolutely no flight risk. His clinic

51

and his patients and his life are here, Your Honor."

The DA did not object to the personal recognizance bond. Julia wondered if Bret had some underhanded trick up his sleeve. Or if he realized he would lose this particular point to Ellen.

A time was set for the next hearing, and the judge ordered a date in two weeks, by which discovery had to be supplied to Ms. Marshall.

Then Ellen asked a sort of legal favor. "Your Honor, I feel that a copy of the affidavit supporting Dr. Innes's arrest should be turned over to me. None of his defense team has the slightest idea why Dr. Innes was arrested."

Judge Scott looked at the DA. "Mr. McSwain, do you have any objections?"

"No, Your Honor."

"So be it."

"Before we leave here today?" Ellen pressed.

"I'll give you a copy before you leave the building," McSwain said. Smiling like a barracuda.

Julia's heart kicked at her ribs.

Thomas was released, and while he changed into street clothes that they had brought for him, Ellen was handed a copy of the affidavit. Julia held her husband's hand tightly when the three of them walked out of the courtroom that sunny April afternoon. A few reporters awaited them, and they echoed the same words: "No comment, no comment."

When they got back to the restored Victorian house that Thomas had bought when he and Julia were first married, Blackie greeted them, his stump of a tail quivering, whining and barking with exquisite adoration. Thomas gave him a perfunctory pat, and the dog turned to Julia for reassurance.

It was then that Livie appeared from the kitchen. "Daddy!" she cried. She hadn't called her father "Daddy" for years. She flung herself into his arms, a dozen incoherent questions pouring out all at once.

"It's okay, Livie, it's okay," Thomas said, letting her cling to him, catching Julia's eye over the girl's bowed head. "Shh, it's okay." Finally he extricated himself from her desperate clutch and held her at arm's length. Instead of answering her questions, he said, "And just how did you get here from Denver, young lady? Does the school even *know* where you are?"

Calming Livie was a chore. She wanted to know why her father had been arrested, and her father only wanted to know how *the* Kent School could have let her run off as she had. "As much as I pay for tuition, you'd think every cop in the state would be looking for you."

But still Livie wanted to know about his arrest. "It was on the radio, Dad," she sobbed. "They said . . . they said . . . that you . . . and my mother . . . they said you . . ."

Julia stepped in. She knew the right words to say to the girl; she always knew what to say, whereas Thomas either brushed her fears aside or got angry and frustrated with his daughter.

"Come on, Livie," Julia said, her arm around the teen's shoulders, "your dad's been through a terrible ordeal, let him sit and rest a minute. Come on, we'll go to your room and talk."

"Dad?" Livie said, uncertain.

"Go on, Julia will explain everything," he said, and he sat on the hall chair and met Ellen's gaze.

Explaining to Livie that her father had been arrested for the murder of her mother was nearly impossible. Julia resorted to using the word *mistake* so many times she felt like an idiot. "It's just a terrible mistake, honey, and that's why Ellen is here, to clear everything up. The thing is, it may take some time. In the meanwhile, we all have to go on with our lives. People will say things, awful things, to all of us. But we just have to keep remembering this is a mistake, and soon everything will be fine."

"But . . . there was even a reporter here knocking on the door when I got home. I didn't know what to say to him. He asked if he could come in, Julia."

"You knew better than to let him inside, didn't you?" *Oh, God,* she thought.

Livie nodded. "I told him he'd have to come back. He wanted my picture then. *My* picture. I . . . flipped him off."

"Good for you. Just don't make a habit of it, and for God's sake, don't let anyone photograph you flipping someone off."

"I know that," Livie said, and she actually smiled a little.

"So, just how *did* you get here?"

"I hitchhiked. I know, I know, it was stupid, but when I couldn't get you on the phone —"

"And what should we tell the school?"

"We could tell them I . . . Well, something like you needed me, and I couldn't find anyone to ask if I could leave, and . . ."

"Do you think the truth might be better?" Julia held her eyes.

55

"You mean like . . . I just took off?"

"That's exactly what I mean."

"But I'll get suspended . . . or worse."

"I don't think they'll go that far, honey. Not for this one infraction. Not if you explain how panicked you were and you didn't think, you merely reacted. Which is the truth and they'll understand. But if you were to do something foolish again —"

"I won't. I promise. My God, I graduate next month. But will you call them first, talk to them before I have to?"

Of course Julia knew she'd make the call. Even though Thomas should probably be the one to do it. Somehow it was always Julia who cleaned up after everyone.

When she got back downstairs after phoning the Kent School and getting Livie off the hook, Thomas was talking to Ellen in the living room. "You're one heck of a friend, Ellen," he was saying, and Julia saw him bestow on Ellen a look, the one that relayed so clearly his appreciation, his liking, his admiration, the belief that she was the most important person in the world. Julia knew that look.

Ellen seemed impervious, though. "You'll get my bill, don't worry."

"Oh, now, come on, don't I get the first one free?"

"You wish. Now, go on and get cleaned up, I have to read this affidavit, then we'll talk."

Julia sat across from Ellen while she read the affidavit. It was long, and Ellen frowned, absently chewed on a fingernail. She read the whole thing and started again at the beginning and read it again.

"Interesting," she said, taking off her glasses.

Julia scanned the affidavit first, searching out salient points. Then she read it again, thoroughly. She couldn't believe what was written there, not even after the second reading. *Leann Cornish?*

"I can't believe this," she started to say when Thomas came downstairs, showered, shaved, wearing corduroy pants and a red turtleneck sweater.

"So, what have they got?" he asked, sitting on the couch next to Ellen.

Ellen flicked the document with her finger. "Strong stuff. This is a condensed version of a statement given to the Aspen police by a woman named Leann Cornish. You know her?"

"Of course I know her. She was an OR nurse for years. She . . . ah, resigned last year. She has terminal breast cancer," he said in a measured tone.

"Yes, so she asserts in this. And because she's been given less than a year to live, she made this statement." Ellen peered through her reading glasses, searching the document. "She says, here it is, 'On the day of Samantha Innes's murder, I witnessed Dr. Thomas Innes's clandestinely entering Aspen Valley Hospital through a back door around the time the murder occurred.' And she says she saw a cut on your hand and you placed a Band-Aid on it prior to your next surgery."

"She's lying," Thomas said coolly.

"She also admits she lied in a statement she made to the police after Samantha's murder. She asserts it was because she was trying to protect you, and because you could have had her fired. She says she needed the job."

"That is all total bullshit," he said.

"Wait, there's more. She says, 'Most important, I am dying, and I don't want to go to the grave with Thomas Innes's guilt on my conscience, knowing the wrong man is in prison for the crime.' "

"Is that all?" Thomas said.

"Is that all?" Julia stared incredulously at her husband.

"Pretty much all," Ellen said. "That's the gist. We'll get the Cornish woman's full statement in discovery."

"She's full of it. The whole thing is a fabrication." Thomas gestured with his hand.

"Why would she go to this length to nail you?" Ellen asked, her shrewd blue eyes cutting over to him.

"Okay, okay," Thomas said, "she wasn't exactly let go last year. She was forced to resign. Some screw-ups. The hospital board just wanted to make sure she received her full benefits. Christ, the woman has cancer."

"So this" — Ellen touched the affidavit with splayed fingertips — "is revenge?"

"Yes, I suppose so."

"Hard to prove in a court of law, Thomas."

He lifted his shoulders and let them drop. "I don't understand her motivation, but I can tell you she's lying. There must be dozens of witnesses from the hospital the day Samantha died. Every one of them can testify I was there for the whole damn day."

"We'll have to rake this poor dying woman over the coals, malign her, impugn her character," Ellen went on. "He said, she said."

"I'd hate to do that."

"It's you or her, Thomas."

He glanced from Ellen to Julia and back, then sighed. "I know you're right. There's no other choice. Hell, I only wish . . ."

"We all wish this wasn't happening," Julia put in for him.

Then Ellen said, "Well, there's plenty of time to figure out a solid strategy. I need to know more, but not today."

Julia got up from the chair she was sitting in, went to Thomas, slid down beside him, and placed her head on his shoulder. "I knew you'd be able to explain it," she said.

He put his arm around her, kissed her temple. He smelled like soap and shampoo; he felt warm and comforting.

"We've got a lot of work to do," Ellen said. "Do you have a room I can use as an office, or should I rent one somewhere?"

"You will *not* rent a room," Julia said.

"She can use the dining room," Thomas suggested. "We never eat in there anyway."

Julia felt a slight flush of shame. Who had time for dinner guests and gourmet cooking?

"Okey-dokey, kids. Got a fax machine? A computer? Extra phone lines? Which reminds me, Julia, we need to call the phone company to have your main number

60

changed and definitely unlisted."

"We'll work on all that today," Thomas said.

"I want you" — she pointed to him — "to go about your daily schedule without any changes. As if nothing is amiss. Got it?"

"I had to use the jailor's cell phone to cancel today's office visits," he said.

"Okay, that's one day. Go into work tomorrow as if nothing happened. Do not discuss the case." She turned to Julia. "And you, too. Routine."

Julia paled. "How can I do that after what Bret did? I can't go back."

"We'll talk about that later."

"Ellen —"

"Just do it. For now."

"How dare he pull a stunt like this? The DA going along on an arrest?"

"I'll nail his balls to the wall for it," Ellen said.

"No," Julia replied, "that will be my pleasure. Then I'll serve them up to the press."

FOUR

"Okay, you've got your in to the Innes case," Victor said when he opened his door to Cam. Not "hello" or "oh, you're here." Nah, nothing but a bald statement of fact.

"You want to explain a bit more?" Cam looked around the big loft, which should have been a showpiece of the decorator's talent but instead was a pigpen. Place was always a pigpen, except for the evening after Rosa left.

Victor had purchased the condo just before Coors Field and the Pepsi Sports Arena were built in downtown Denver. The loft occupied over 3,000 square feet on the top story of an old factory building at the base of Larimer Street, the factory having been converted to trendy loft condominiums. Cam never had been able to decide if he liked the décor. Modern pieces of geometrical steel and glass furniture mixed in with heavy dark wood pieces, such as the carved mahogany end tables on either side of the couch — elephants, no less, their backs the flat tabletops, heads holding the lamps, tails curving up, getting in the way every time you tried to put something down on the flat surfaces.

There were multistriped cushions to go with the striped upholstery on the couch, and there were squat tables, some antique, some glass-topped. In a corner near the state-of-the-art kitchen was a huge dining room sideboard, its three doors painted with scenes of an African savanna. Slender vases filled with dried reeds and pussy willows sat on top with other scattered pieces, such as intricately carved wooden boxes, brightly painted metal trays, silver-trimmed glass brandy decanters. The fifteen-foot-high ceiling, with requisite utility pipes criss-crossing it, was gray, the walls gray, the floor made of plank wood, stained to a light bourbon color. Throw rugs representing every native tribe on earth — or so Cam figured — were everywhere, most of them lying askew when Cam was there unless, of course, Rosa had just been there.

"You want coffee before we talk?" Victor asked.

Victor made ghastly coffee. "No, thanks. Let's just hear about this in to the case."

"I found the attorney who's going to

represent Innes. I know her."

"Her?"

"A lady, a real fireball. She's good. She's a friend of Innes's wife, they went to law school together. She's from Denver, and I've used her for research in the past. Name's Ellen Marshall."

Cam knew lots of defense lawyers from his days on the force; they'd been his sworn enemies. He shook his head. "Can't say I know her."

"She's fairly new, been hot for the last few years, probably after your time on the force." Victor sat on his striped couch, pushing aside an empty pizza box and an ashtray overflowing with cigarette butts. Couple butts ended up on the floor. *Geez,* Cam thought.

"So what's my in?"

"Ellen's already in Aspen. I tried the Innes's house, but evidently they're not answering their phone. Press is probably driving them bananas. So I got Ellen's cell phone number from her office and reached her right away. She got Innes out on personal recognizance this morning. I told her you were a former homicide dick, the one who helped put Matt Holman behind bars. *That* piqued her interest. I said you'd meet with her and the Inneses to offer your investigative services. She said, 'Oh, so he's switched sides,' and I said you were in private practice, which isn't a total lie."

"What is it then, literary license?"

Victor shrugged. "Sure, whatever."

"They expect me in Aspen, I take it?"

"Ellen's there for a while. So, yes, you should get your ass up to Aspen. Ass up to Aspen, get it?"

"Victor, anybody ever tell you you've got a way with words?"

"Lotsa folks. Anyway, one thing Ellen said: It's up to the Inneses to make a final decision whether to use you or not."

"Understandable."

"Ellen was keen for the idea, especially when I told her I'm paying your expenses. So you be your usual charming self, and I'm sure they'll want you on their team."

Cam walked to the kitchen divider counter and leaned back against it. The only place he felt safe sitting down was in Victor's office. "Does this Ellen know my story?"

"She won't give a damn about your history. Not when she knows I'm paying for you."

"Give me a little rundown on Ms. Marshall."

"She's cute. Short, Irish, a bit of a hothead. They call her the pit bull with pearls. She was the lead attorney in that case they just televised. You know, the one where a city councilman was arrested for hit-and-run?"

"Yeah."

"She got the sucker off."

"Uh-huh."

"Innes you know about. Everybody knows about him. His wife" — Victor lifted his shoulders and dropped them — "I don't know. I don't know squat past her name."

"Which is?"

"Julia."

"Got it," Cam said. "Julia."

When Cam left, the Inneses' Aspen address in his pocket, Victor went back to work. He was still in the same sweats and T-shirt; he'd barely slept the night before, scribbling notes and a rough outline, writing the entire first chapter.

He was on a roll.

Larry Beckett lived in a fake Tudor House in the prosperous Cherry Creek neighborhood of Denver. Big lawns, mature trees, BMWs lined up in driveways, and lots of security.

Beckett could afford a house like this, Luke figured, because he was a plastic surgeon — a nip and tucker. The house was quite a contrast to Luke's bachelor apartment over a porn bookstore on Colfax Avenue.

Luke turned his black 1960 T-Bird into the Beckett's driveway and got out, yanked the convertible top up — hell, it might rain — and went to the door. His plan was to try to talk to Beckett himself, push a little, see if the man would let something out off the record. Any detail. Now that Luke had heard the dying woman's story himself, he needed to see Beckett in person, see his expression, gauge his body language, his tics. Luke heard someone approaching the door and allowed himself a merciless grin — might even throw in some menace if the doctor didn't feel chatty.

Spur-of-the-moment decision, that was the Diamond method. Judge the accused in person, judge the accuser in person. Judge every goddamn individual involved in the case.

The door opened. Not by a maid, not by Beckett. By a pretty lady who looked frazzled and distracted.

67

Luke was never taken aback. Well, maybe once a year. And this pretty lady took him aback. He had a stupid moment, then collected himself, flipped his badge at her. "Detective Luke Diamond. Can I see Dr. Beckett?" He realized his tone was a bit harsh, a reaction to being caught off guard.

She studied the badge, checked his picture. Careful. "Larry's trying to get some rest. He was up all night."

"I see. And you are?"

She raised a hand to her forehead. "Sorry. I'm Janet Beckett, his wife." Shit, the guy had a new wife? What was he, Blackbeard?

"Could I have a word with you, then?" He made a stab at politeness.

She met his gaze squarely. "I don't think so."

"Just a few questions."

"Not without our attorney."

"Sometimes cooperation is the best way to go," he said.

"But not this time" — a pause — "Detective Diamond."

"I understand Dr. Beckett will plead not guilty."

"He is not guilty," she said. "This whole thing is a terrible mistake."

Sure, sure. "Yes, ma'am, well, maybe I'll try him again later."

"Call our lawyer, Carole Nichols."

"Carole Nichols, got it."

Janet tilted her head to one side. "You have a lot of nerve, Detective, coming to our house like this."

"Yeah, I do, don't I? See you, ma'am."

Pretty pretty lady. Big brown eyes and short blond streaked hair, a halter top in this hot summer weather, her feet with pink painted toenails. Smart, too.

What the hell did this Beckett have going for him to get such knockouts for wives? His first one, Andrea, had been a looker, too.

Maybe it was the man's personality, a natural chick magnet. Luke wished for a moment, just a split second, that he could charm a woman like Janet Beckett off her feet, get her to marry him, and believe in his innocence despite evidence that he'd murdered his first wife.

But he was not the marrying kind. The love-'em-and-leave-'em kind, but not the stick-to-them kind. Nah, he was fucking Teflon where chicks were concerned.

That evening Cam had a date. He had lots of dates, actually, some much more casual than tonight's. Some so casual he only knew the woman half an hour before they were all over each other.

But this lady was a real friend. He'd known her for several years. She was a court stenographer whom he'd met in his days on the force. Kayla Burke was her name. She was adorable and plump, freckled, looked much younger than her forty years. They got along great, and they had good sex, but what he liked best about Kayla was her independence and smart-ass tongue.

Like, for instance, he didn't have to mention the fact that he was driving up to Aspen tomorrow. He didn't have to tell her that, didn't have to make excuses or promise to call her. None of that crap.

They were having dinner at an Italian joint, a nice bottle of Chianti between them, Kayla animated, telling him an amusing story about what had happened in court that day, and he was thinking, *Should I ask her to my place or will she want to go to hers?*

"My oldest is home on school break," she said.

"My place then?"

"Sure."

Funny, he thought, she felt it was better to be out till the wee hours than to have a man in her bedroom when her kids were home. Guess that was maternal instinct.

His apartment. He kept it neat, almost military. There were two large bedrooms, one of which he used for an office. A living room and kitchen. Not much furniture, but what he had he'd selected carefully. He didn't worry about cost; he just hated to feel cheated when a piece of furniture turned out to be shit. Not that he was a handy sort of guy, but he'd managed to build shelves for his books, VCR, and CD music collection. Country and folk music, sappy stuff.

Kayla had been around so long she even knew the Clappers. She liked Irene and Fred, always stopped to chat with them if the store was open, and they seemed to like her, Irene often asking when he was going to get married to the pretty lady.

Kayla was insatiable in his bed that night. As if she were trying to hold him, to keep him. Good thing the bookstore was closed, because she made a lot of noise, and she scratched his back. The bed must have sounded as if it were going to crash through the ceiling. Finally he fell off her, drained. He was getting old.

She ran her hand over his sweaty chest, then up his neck and through his hair.

"Umm," she purred.

Christ, not again, he thought.

Then she propped herself up on an elbow and looked at him, her heavy breasts sagging sideways. "I wonder . . ."

"You wonder what?"

"Do you ever plan on getting married?"

Jesus, first Irene and now Kayla. "Married?" He felt his heart contract.

"I mean, you're no spring chicken. Most men —"

"I'm not most men."

"Don't you want children?"

"God, no."

She laughed, but he thought he heard a tone of disappointment in her amusement. Or maybe he'd heard disapproval. Either way, she ruined the whole evening, nullified a good fuck.

After she left, he got up, naked, the sweat dried on him, and fetched a beer from the fridge. He sat in the dark, sipping it, watched the moonlight fall in a broad silver rectangle on the floor, and he thought about Kayla's questions.

Why hadn't he told her the truth? Why hadn't he admitted he thought about having a family. For about two seconds.

Then he shied away from the notion. What if he got married, say to a nice lady like Kayla, and it ended up like his parents' marriage?

The thought made him shiver. Nothing was worth a sick relationship like that.

Not even the chance of happiness.

FIVE

Julia was inundated with anxiety. Not only for Thomas, who had to be going through hell, but for Livie, too. The poor kid. What a horrible shock for her; everything was always magnified for the girl — she took life hard.

At least she was asleep. Thomas was not so lucky. Julia had awakened at two a.m. when she heard him get out of bed, heard the familiar creaks of the old staircase as he descended, saw the glow of a downstairs light.

Usually, her husband slept like a baby, even when he had a very early surgery the next morning. He'd be up, cheerful and ready to go, while Julia stumbled around the kitchen like a zombie.

Thomas had canceled yesterday's office visits, but he had a morning of appointments coming up, and probably a lot of re-scheduled ones in the afternoon.

A couple of important surgeries were scheduled soon, a famous pitcher's elbow and an Olympic skier who wanted his knee to be ready for next season. Not that every one of Thomas's patients weren't important — it was just that these professional athletes made their living with their bodies and they wanted the best of the best. Which was Dr. Thomas Innes.

What if he was distracted by worry or too upset to function? What if his loyal patients deserted him? His friends, too? She'd been around the courthouse long enough to witness human reaction to the accused. Forget that the Constitution promised innocence until proven guilty. Real life seldom worked so nobly.

She lay in bed and listened to him puttering around downstairs, the cupboard door opening and closing, a kitchen chair squeaking as he sat, and she finally got up, pulled on her fleece bathrobe to ward off the chill in the old house. She leaned over to pat Blackie — who, much to Thomas's chagrin, slept at the foot of the bed — and made her way downstairs.

"I couldn't sleep," he said when she padded groggily into the kitchen.

"Me, neither."

"You know what, Julia? I think I'm starting to get really mad." He was absently eating crackers out of a box.

He wore pajama bottoms and a white

T-shirt. He looked so defenseless, his boyish face sad, his eyes puffy, his hair standing up in tufts. He'd put on weight in the last few years, and he had a barrel chest, dark hair curling above the neck of the T-shirt.

"I don't blame you," she said.

"How dare they pull this stunt?"

She shook her head slowly.

He looked at her, his dark eyes questioning, searching. "*You* don't have any doubts about me, do you?"

"God, no, how can you ask that?"

"I knew, I just wanted . . . I don't know . . . reassurance, I guess."

She settled in a chair across from him. "I'm your wife. I love you. I know you'd never deceive me, Thomas. I trust you completely."

He tried to smile. "The worst thing . . . the very worst, is how it'll affect my work."

For a fleeting moment she thought, *What about Livie, what about me?* But then she let the notion go. Of course he was worried about them, too. "Should you take some time off?"

"Can't. I'm booked till summer. Baxter and Marcos can't take over my cases, they're busy, too."

"We'll get through this."

"I know we will. I just don't want my patients to suffer."

His patients again. "They won't, Thomas."

"I've been thinking about Livie. If I weren't in the middle of this mess, I'd be furious at her. Not only leaving school like that, and hitchhiking up here, but I . . . we don't need any distractions right now."

"She doesn't mean to make things worse. She just . . . she was undone when she heard."

"You'll take care of getting her to the airport?"

"Don't worry about it. I'll get her on the plane safe and sound."

He reached across the table and patted her hand. "You're a rock, Julia. Thank God Livie and I have you."

He was so good to her. He'd lifted a struggling law student from a morass of waitressing every spare second to make ends meet, of incessant unease about money, and asked her to marry him. He'd told her she'd never have to work, even back then when no one knew whether the Innes Clinic for Reconstructive Surgery would be a success. With a wave of his magic wand he'd relieved all of her anxieties, proposing to her, accepting her stricture that they not marry until she'd passed the state bar exam.

When she'd passed with flying colors, he'd insisted they marry right away. Eight years ago, and not one moment in that time had she stopped being grateful to her husband.

"You want to try to get some sleep?" she asked.

"I guess so."

"I'll rub your back for you."

"Deal."

In the morning there was no trace of the sleepless, troubled man of the night before. Thomas was close shaven, wearing a green shirt she loved, casual tan slacks. Was he really able to dismiss his problems with the new day? Or was his demeanor all bravado?

She wondered how they'd get through this ordeal. For God's sake, it hadn't even been three days. What about the weeks and months, maybe even years ahead?

Ellen, who'd slept in the downstairs guestroom, left the house nearly as early as Thomas to go to the courthouse to start the job of getting copies of the Holman trial transcript from twelve years ago and studying it.

Ellen asked Thomas to phone her as soon as he got home that afternoon, and they'd begin reviewing the information in the affidavit.

Julia was not nearly as brave as her husband; she called in sick, knowing every person in the office, in the whole courthouse for that matter, would know exactly why she wasn't there. Sure, Ellen had told her to go to work, to pretend nothing out of the ordinary had happened, but she couldn't. Among so many other problems, she had to take care of Livie. And there were those calls to make — her parents and Thomas's mother, Maggie.

Julia's parents were frantic when she reached them in Iowa, in the same small town where she was born. They'd heard the news on national TV and been trying to call her ever since, but the machine either came on or they'd gotten a busy signal.

"Oh, my God, Julia, oh, my God, baby," her mother cried.

She spent a half hour filling them in, telling them not to listen to the news, which got everything all wrong anyway, and that this whole thing was a ghastly mistake. She promised she'd call every day.

Thomas's mother was not so easily mollified. "It never once occurred to you to phone me? Not *once?* And you knew I was out here alone? I should be there with my son. At the very least, I should be there with Livie."

"She's going back to school today."

"What? Her father's been arrested and you're sending her away?"

"She *is* going to graduate."

There was a sudden chill silence on the line, but apparently Maggie decided to choose her battles. "I don't understand this whole thing," she said. "How could anyone, *anyone* who knows my boy, think he could harm a fly? Julia, you have to tell them this is all wrong, you tell —"

"I work for the DA."

"But . . . But isn't it the DA who arrested him?"

"Yes, it is. And I think I'm going to have to resign."

"Well, hasn't Thomas always said you should? I mean —"

"I really do have to go now, Maggie. We'll talk about your coming out here later, okay? I'll have Thomas phone you."

"See to it that he does," Maggie said sternly.

The calls made, Julia tidied up the house a bit, her heart not in it. She took Blackie for a walk around the block. There was a gray line of clouds to the west, coming from behind the peak of Mount Sopris, another spring storm, no doubt. The leafless branches of the tall, graceful cottonwood trees that lined the streets were bent to the westerly wind. She hoped the weather wouldn't close in before Livie's flight. Storms shut down the Aspen airport often enough.

Livie was finally up, sitting at the kitchen table when Julia got back. Looking sleepy. Much like Julia, Livie was never at her best in the morning.

"Okay, honey, you're on the ten-fifteen flight to Denver. It's all taken care of."

"I don't want to go back," the girl said. "Everyone'll be saying stuff, asking questions. It'll be horrible."

Julia took her jacket off and sat down. "We talked about this yesterday, remember? It's pretty awful for all of us. But Ellen wants us to act normal, as if it doesn't matter."

"Doesn't matter?"

"I know, believe me. You think I want to go back to my office? I will, though." She crossed her fingers mentally. She still wasn't so sure of that.

"What do I say?"

"You say nothing. Remember? No comment. And if you feel you have to say something, to your roommate or whoever, just tell them you can't discuss anything about the case because your father's lawyer has forbidden it."

"The old legal ploy."

"Hey, if it works . . ." Julia mustered a smile. "And you're at the end of your senior year. Like you said, only a month to go. Don't blow it. And don't even think about blowing your final exams. No matter what, you're going to the University of Michigan in the fall. And just think, not a soul in Ann Arbor will know about your dad." Again she crossed her mental fingers.

"Will you keep me up on whatever happens?"

"Of course."

"Okay, I guess. But I don't know how I'll be able to concentrate."

"You will."

"I'm so scared, Julia. Why would they do this to my dad?"

"That's what Ellen and I are going to find out."

After seeing Livie off at the airport, which was only ten minutes from downtown, Julia drove back to the house. The girl had cried and clung to her. Sending Livie back to school had been heartwrenching, but Thomas was right — neither of them needed an extra distraction. And Livie had to finish her senior year.

Poor sweet kid. First her mother and now her father. Julia's mouth tightened. No way was anything going to happen to Livie's father. Not if she and Ellen could help it.

She called Ellen's cell phone when she got home, checking in. "How's it going?" she asked.

"I'm up to my ass in papers."

"That's not exactly impressive."

"Very funny. You get Livie off?"

"She's on her way."

"Will the phone company be there this morning?"

"God, I hope so. And I swear I'm not giving the new numbers to my folks or Maggie. No way."

"Sure."

"I swear I'm not."

"Whatever you say. Oh, and don't forget that detective is coming."

"What?" Her mind was blank.

"I told you last night. His name is Cameron Lazlo. He works for Victor Ferris, the author?"

"Right, that's right."

"According to Ferris, he's tops."

"I'll make up my own mind about that."

"Well, if I'm not back when he gets there, be your sweet self and fill him in."

The telephone men arrived shortly after she hung up from Ellen. They installed two new lines, running them into the dining room, and all new telephone numbers, including the main line. All the numbers were unlisted. Julia carefully wrote them down.

Finally it was time to clean up the kitchen. But the detective arrived just as she was putting dishes in the dishwasher. She heard Blackie bark, his someone's-at-the-door bark, then the knocker.

She went to the front door, pulled it open. A man was standing there, a stranger. She got an impression of height and masculinity and cool blue eyes appraising her.

"I'm Cam Lazlo," he said.

Their eyes met. And locked. And she experienced one of those singular moments of attraction for a total stranger. Heat ran through her, a hot fist inside, clenching then releasing. Unbidden, jolting. Then it was gone, and she was saying, "Right. The detective from Victor Ferris. Well, I'm Julia Innes. Come on in. Ellen's not back yet. She's at the courthouse rounding up the old trial transcript." Even as she spoke, she was embarrassed at her reaction.

Get over it, she told herself, *flying from one emotion to the next. Get a damn grip.* Still, as she held the door open for him, she thought about the kick Ellen would get over her reaction to the detective — if she told her friend, that was.

Julia had forgotten about her initial reaction to this man by the time they were in the living room. "That would be the Holman trial," he was saying to her back.

She turned, surprised. "Yes, how did you . . . ?"

"Twelve years ago Aspen didn't have a detective, no one to handle a homicide, anyway, so when Samantha was murdered, they imported one — me."

"Oh." He'd worked the case? Did Ellen know? She must know. . . .

"So I'm familiar with what went down."

"I guess you are." She gestured to a chair. "You want something to drink? Coffee or tea or something?"

"Coffee would be good. Black."

In the kitchen Julia measured grounds into the coffeemaker. Cameron Lazlo. *Cam.* A detective. But he worked for Victor Ferris now. She hadn't even questioned that oddity until this moment.

Well, he sure must have been young

85

when he'd made detective. Twelve years ago. He must be in his forties now, she surmised. Early forties. Younger than Thomas. Tall, Nordic looking. Pale blue hooded eyes like chips of northern sky. Strong high cheekbones. Fair straight hair worn a little too long. And a quality of stillness to him, a biding sort of stillness that she guessed never left him. It was slightly unnerving; she bet Ellen would say he was sexy. *Should* she tell her friend about her reaction to him? But no, she decided, for now she'd keep that schoolgirl silliness to herself.

She returned to the living room. "Coffee will be ready in a minute." She sat on the couch, across the glass-topped coffee table from him.

"Ellen Marshall didn't tell you much about me, did she?" he asked.

"Not really. It's been hectic around here."

"I bet."

He got to the point, didn't he? No messing around.

"You want to know why I'm here."

"Ellen said you're a detective. I assume she wants you to help with the investigation."

"I *was* a detective. I resigned five years ago."

"Oh."

"Ellen may have told you I work for Victor Ferris now. The author? I do research for him. Police stuff."

"I've read Ferris," she said. "I love his books."

"So do a lot of people," he said dryly.

"That hero of his . . . Luke Diamond?" She rolled her eyes. "He's great, but I'm glad he's not a real person. He's so violent."

Luke Diamond, she thought. A lone wolf, always in trouble with his superiors, even though he solved every case. He was a sap for kids and dogs but had a terrible time with commitment. Something set up in one of the earlier books about Luke Diamond's childhood, some sort of childhood abuse. Still, Luke was a real cool customer, though Julia suspected the hero was drawn that way on purpose, strong yet internally wounded. And all the women in the stories fell for the character. *Right,* she mused.

"Where's your husband now?"

She had to shake off her thoughts. "At the clinic. He has patients to see today."

"Okay, so it's business as usual."

She nodded. "Ellen wants it that way."

"Right," he said.

She looked down. "Thomas is one thing,

87

but I'm not sure I can oblige her. The thing is, I'm a deputy district attorney. The DA is my boss."

"And he'll be prosecuting the case against your husband."

The main phone rang then, and her heart jumped. She let it ring.

Cam looked at her.

"We're screening calls. The media's been bothering us." Then she looked up. "Oh, God, I've already forgotten. . . . The phone company was here not an hour ago, and we have a new number and it's unlisted." She started to get up to answer it, but then she sat down. No one knew the number yet. Most likely the phone company was testing the line. My God, she was a mess.

"So," she said, looking down at her clenched fists, forcing them to relax, "I just don't know if I can go back to work."

He stared at her as if finally really noticing her.

"You should go back."

"I know, I know, Ellen and I went over all the reasons, but —"

"Here's another reason — you'll be on the inside, maybe pick up some good inside dope on what the prosecutor plans."

Easy for him to say. *She* was the one that had to work for Bret McSwain.

"Bret won't let anything about the case get near me," she said.

"Bret?"

"The DA. Bret McSwain. Do you know what he did, Mr. Lazlo?"

"Cam."

"Cam. Okay. He came here to our house, and he arrested Thomas."

"Really."

"That is low."

"You're being polite."

"Yes, I am, because I don't know you very well. You should hear what I called him to Ellen."

A ghost of a smile touched his lips.

She got coffee for both of them. Away from him, a lot of questions popped into her mind.

"So you're more than a little familiar with the Holman trial," she said, setting the mugs on the coffee table.

"As you know, I investigated the murder. Also testified for the prosecution."

"So you must believe Holman is guilty. Did you know he's been released from prison?"

"Yeah." A storm gathered in those hooded eyes. "Guy's guilty as sin. Believe me."

"So Thomas can't be guilty."

"Unless they were in it together."

"Unlikely," she said coolly.

"Damn unlikely." He turned his ice blue gaze on her. "Do you know what the DA has for evidence?"

"Yes. He has the deathbed confession of an OR nurse named Leann Cornish, who worked with Thomas for years, long before I even met my husband, in fact. She says she lied to the police twelve years ago, and now she wants to set the record straight because she has terminal cancer."

"Heavy duty."

"Well, Thomas had to ask her to resign last year because she was making too many mistakes."

"Revenge," Cam said.

"Absolutely."

"The DA and the judge who issued the warrant bought her story." His brow wrinkled, then he said, "I wonder . . ."

"What?"

"Oh, nothing, just something to check on, but I might have been the one who took this nurse's statement."

"You don't remember?"

"Huh," he said, not exactly laughing. "I've taken thousands of statements. Doubt if I'd recall a dozen of them. Anyway, the DA, your boss?"

Julia frowned and waved her hand dismissively. "Bret McSwain thinks he's going to get famous from this case. He's a glutton for attention. I bet he sees himself in the state attorney general's office. Hell, I bet he sees himself as the *next* attorney general."

"Nice."

"Well, he's going to lose this one," she said with determination. Then, curious, she asked, "Why did you quit the police force? I thought you guys were all lifers."

He didn't say anything for a minute, and she got the distinct feeling she shouldn't have brought up the subject.

"You'll hear about it sooner or later," he finally said.

"Listen, you don't have to —"

"You have a right to know."

"Maybe I don't."

"I didn't exactly quit. I was forced to resign."

She stared at him, at his expressionless face with its carved features, at his pale heavy-lidded eyes, at his big hands, and the expensive slacks he wore that fit his narrow hips to perfection, and the nubby blue silk of his shirt. She saw for the first time the small white scar that bisected his left eyebrow. When Ellen noticed the scar, she'd never shut up about it.

"A couple other cops and I were accused. For roughing up a suspect."

"Did you do it?"

His glance switched away, and she felt again that incredible stillness, as if everything alive in him was being held at bay. "Not exactly. I was there. I should've stopped them."

"So you watched."

"I watched and I was glad they did it. I kept my mouth shut."

"I see." She wondered who the suspect was, what exactly he'd done to deserve a beating. She wondered how Cam really felt about leaving the force. Not that he'd ever tell her. Then she wondered if Ellen knew why he wasn't a policeman anymore.

He shrugged. "It's over and done with. I work for Victor now. We get along."

She sipped her coffee, eyeing him over the rim of the mug. "Is Victor Ferris planning to put my husband's story in a book?"

That wisp of a smile again, as if Cam were surprised she'd thought that far ahead. "The way Victor works is like this — he gets an idea, say from a headline. The hook, he calls it. Then he goes with the idea, gets his creative juices flowing, but by the time he's done nothing's recognizable, not the characters or the plot. He gives it, you know, his own spin."

"Is that how he got the idea for *Diamond Bright*?"

"Which one's *Diamond Bright*?"

"Don't you read his books?"

"I try not to."

She stared at him. He gave Victor Ferris inside information on police procedure, all that great, low-down grit in the Diamond books, the pithy dialogue, and you really believed that's the way cops talked and thought, but he didn't even read the finished product.

"Aren't you curious?" she asked.

"I read one once."

"*Diamond Bright* is about a big sports figure who rapes a girl in a small Colorado ski town. The media destroy the girl's reputation, and Luke has to prove she was really raped. And she falls for him."

"Naturally."

He was drinking coffee, the mug diminished in his large hand. His knuckles were scarred, and she wondered about that. He put the mug down and looked at her. "Victor said you and your husband have the final say in whether you want me to help with the investigation."

"Ellen must have told him that. Do you know Ellen personally?"

He shook his head. "Not really. Only what Victor told me about her. He said she's good."

"She is. She's also an old friend of mine. We went to law school together."

"Um," he said, as if filing the information for future use.

"I kind of think Thomas will leave it up to us."

"What about you?"

"If you can help my husband, that's all I care about."

Ellen arrived then, pushing the door open with her back, a box in her arms. "Damn, but this is heavy."

Cam got up and took it from her. She stood there, little Ellen, gazing up at him.

"You're Cam Lazlo," she said.

"And you're Ellen Marshall."

"Welcome to Aspen," she said, and she held her hand out.

He took it, engulfing her hand in his.

"So you're Cam Lazlo," she said again, still looking up at him.

"Guilty as charged."

Ellen seemed to shake herself mentally. "Okay, so, we'll talk. Meanwhile, my car's full of boxes. Do you think . . . ?"

"No prob," he said.

When he was gone, Ellen looked at Julia, raised an eyebrow.

Julia held her hand out, as if warding off any comment. "Yes, I know, he's very good-looking."

"A hunk," Ellen said.

"A *hunk?* What are we, high school kids?"

"And did you see that scar on his eyebrow?"

She sighed. "Yes, I saw it."

Ellen sank down on the couch. "Did you know he was forced to resign from the police a few years ago?"

"He told me."

"He told you?"

"He said I'd hear about it, so he might as well tell me."

"Did he tell you why?"

"Yes."

"Hmm. Give him points for honesty."

"Do you trust him?" Julia asked.

"You mean because he was booted off the police force?"

"Yes."

"Oh, sure, I trust him. If he's good enough for Victor Ferris, he's sure as hell good enough for me. Look, he was a top detective in Denver. And he worked the Holman case. Basically, his investigation put Matt Holman behind bars. So we've got a head start on what went down back then."

"Okay, sounds fine to me."

"Thomas still needs to meet him," Ellen said.

"Trust me, Thomas won't give it a second thought."

Cam returned, carrying a couple more boxes filled with papers and files. "Where do you want these?"

"On the dining room table." Ellen gestured. "That's my new office." She watched him walk away, caught Julia's eye. "Nice —"

"Don't say it," Julia hissed.

"I was going to say 'nice pants.' "

"Damn it, Ellen."

Julia had to duck her head when Cam came back into the living room and spoke to Ellen. She really would have to tell her friend to be professional.

"I guess I need a place to stay tonight," Cam was saying.

"Definitely," Ellen replied.

"Oh, that shouldn't be a problem. It's off-season now. All the lodges will be practically empty. I'll call around and find you a room," Julia offered.

"I'd appreciate it."

She went into the kitchen, and pulled

open the drawer where she kept the phone book. She could hear Ellen and Cam talking, and she wondered if her friend was interested in him. She'd forgotten to ask Ellen whether she was still with Mason Schultz, her latest boyfriend. But even if Ellen and Mason were an item, Ellen was a notorious flirt. Julia had always envied Ellen her ability to do that.

As she leafed through the phone book under "Lodging," she thought about Thomas. Maybe the routine of office visits was taking his mind off his arrest. She hoped so. Wasn't it bad enough that his wife had been murdered? No man should have to endure that. But now, making everything so much worse — oh, God, there was no word for how awful this was — the whole ugliness had been raked up again, only this time with him as the center of it all.

She phoned the Bavarian Lodge, which was located on Main Street, only a few short blocks away. Yes, they had a room, a nice quiet one facing Aspen Mountain. The off-season rate was slightly over a hundred per night, but they offered monthly rates.

"The Bavarian," Cam said. "Didn't I pass it on my way here?"

"You might have. It's not far. Maybe you

should look at the room first."

"I'm not fussy."

"Well, you might be there a while. Tell you what, I'll go with you, you can check it out, see if the rates work for you, then I'll walk home."

"I can give you a ride."

"I like to walk. It clears my head."

"You two go on," Ellen said. "I'm going to try to put some of this stuff in order."

He drove an older model Ford Bronco, black, with big tires. Julia had to practically climb up to the passenger seat, and Cam tossed a few things in the back that were in her way: a couple roadmaps, a pair of driving gloves, a well-worn baseball cap. And something else . . . Her mind took a second to fit itself around the reality of what she was seeing — a shiny leather shoulder holster and gun.

"Good Lord," she whispered. "You don't think . . . ? I mean, there's no reason you'll need that thing here, is there?"

"You never know. I only locked it in the car because I figured you might object to it inside."

"I see. You always carry it?"

"Yep," he said.

He didn't say another word during the short drive. She got the impression that he

98

was uncomfortable with small talk, maybe even uncomfortable with her. He hadn't been standoffish with Ellen, though.

She wondered if he was married, snuck a sideways glance at his left hand on the steering wheel. No ring. But that didn't necessarily mean a thing. Or he might have a live-in lady friend. A man as attractive as Cam . . .

"Cute" was all he said when she directed him into the parking lot of the white stuccoed, half-timbered lodge.

The weekly and monthly rates suited him, so she waited in the reception area while he went with the desk clerk to check the room out. Wondering again how Thomas fared. Maybe he was on his way home by now. Maybe by the time she walked home he and Ellen would be hard at work, heads together at the dining room table.

Cam returned, obviously satisfied with the room. "It's fine," he told her, handing his credit card to the young man behind the desk.

When he was through checking in, he turned to her. "I'm in Room 201, but it's probably easier to get hold of me on my cell." He reached into a back pocket, pulled out his wallet, and extracted a business card, handed it to her, fingers brushing hers.

"Do you have any plans for this evening?" she asked.

"Plans?"

"I mean, I think you should meet Thomas. Why don't you come over for dinner?"

"That sounds like a plan."

"Okay. Seven or so."

"You sure you don't want a ride home?"

"No, honestly, I need a walk."

"All right, see you at seven."

It was gray and chilly out; the front had come in. Spring in the Rockies was a risky proposition, warm and sunny one moment, cold and stormy the next. Mud season, the locals called it. That's why so many of them left — closed their shops or restaurants or hotels and went to Mexico or the Caribbean.

She walked briskly, liking the cold tang of the air on her face. In the west the sun was low, sinking behind Shadow Mountain, bathing Aspen's West End in pre-twilight.

Cam carried a gun with him — always carried it. Well, she thought, crossing Bleeker and heading down Second Street toward Francis, he sure didn't strike her as paranoid. So the habit must have been formed when he was with the police; a habit he had yet to break. She'd have to tell Ellen about the gun. Ellen was going to indulge herself in fantasies.

She cleared her mind and started to think about cooking dinner for everyone. What to make? They'd have to eat in the kitchen, because the dining table was now stacked with boxes of old case files. Something simple, baked potatoes . . . maybe a pork roast. A big green salad. She needed to go to the market.

She realized, as she strode past the restored Victorian houses that flanked the streets of the West End, that she was hoping Thomas would have no objections to letting Cam Lazlo work his case. There was something about the man that gave her confidence. Despite his coolness, his predatory quiescence, even the loss of his detective job — there was something self-assured about him. A competence. A knowledge, as if nothing could get past him, no subterfuge or lie or deceit. Because he knew all those tricks only too well.

Maybe he was as good as Ellen thought. She hoped so. Thomas needed every advantage, no matter who or what or how.

Maybe Cam could get straight to the

heart of this ridiculous, tragic situation. Maybe he could interview Leann Cornish, get her to admit she lied. Maybe he was an expert at sweet-talking women into confessing.

Oh, hell, she thought, she didn't give a damn what methods the man used to clear her husband — anything to end this surreal nightmare.

SIX

The Bavarian Lodge was only a short distance from the core of Aspen, and Cam
checked his watch — he had hours before
dinner — then walked into downtown along
Main Street. He recalled from his time spent
here before that you could have shot a rifle
down the street and not hit anyone during
off-season. Not so anymore. There were
workers' pickup trucks hurrying up and
down the street, a cement truck chugging
along, a few dump trucks hauling dirt and
giant boulders; a flatbed passed him with a
load of spruce trees ready for spring
planting.

Then there were the idle rich who hadn't
left town yet. They all drove new SUVs,
and they were all on cell phones while
driving. Everyone was on a cell phone, it
seemed, whether in a vehicle or walking.
Busy folks, he guessed.

But for all the traffic, the town retained
its charm. The elegant cottonwoods along
both sides of Main Street had grown, and

the city had installed 1800s-style street lamps, painted a quiet green. The older Swiss-type lodges still mingled nicely with the hodgepodge of Western buildings and modern stone-and-glass structures. And no building rose above three stories. Cam recalled that ironclad city ordinance, put in place a half a century ago, to preserve everyone's view of the ski mountains and 14,000 footers that jutted skyward in the distance.

Another thing he'd always liked was how the town was laid out in square city blocks. Had been laid out this way since its inception during the boom days of silver mining, when stagecoaches and the narrow gauge railroad had been the only transportation into the Rockies.

He strode past the Hotel Jerome, thought how great it would be to share a room in the wonderful old Victorian landmark with Kayla, but then he felt a spurt of unease — God, he wished she hadn't brought up the subject of marriage.

He strolled another block and waited for a traffic light at the intersection of Galena and Main Street to cross into the hub of town. The courthouse was right there; the exterior hadn't changed a bit — peach-blow stone at its base, red brick up to the old tin roof, the crab apple trees in front of the short iron fence still weeks away from bloom, that crazy statue of Justice holding up her scales, only this lady had never worn a blindfold. He'd been one of the few people to ever make that observation.

He was idly looking for a liquor store to buy a bottle of wine for Julia's dinner, but he was in no big rush. A block up Galena Street, he eyed City Hall, which still and always would resemble an old hay barn to him, and the new café across the street, all the upscale shops, none of which he recalled. Yet Aspen was Aspen, and the buildings housing new stores were the same as they had been for well over a century. Awnings were changed, flower boxes added, but that was it. Had to be more of those strict city ordinances.

Cam knew that ski bums and hippies had flocked to the town in the sixties, families in the seventies, and the rich had discovered Aspen en masse in the eighties, but the mountains were never going to change. Before him, rising like a wave ready to break over town, was Aspen Mountain — Ajax to the locals. Behind him, across the valley floor, was Smuggler Mountain, equally massive but farther from the heart of town. No skiing there, as the exposure was southern and the mountain did not hold snow. Nor did Red Mountain to the west of Smuggler, where the mega-wealthy had built bezillion-square-foot homes, and just beyond that was Starwood, where the even richer built their enclaves. Everyone knew Starwood from the John Denver song. And everyone wanted to drive up to see the magnificent houses, but no one got past the security.

Next to City Market, where the locals did their grocery shopping, he finally found the Grog Shop. Now *that* hadn't changed. Shops and art galleries came and went, but liquor stores seemed to hold their own. Aspen, Denver, Vail, New York, didn't matter. Booze stores hung around.

He browsed the aisles, finally bought an expensive bottle of Cabernet. He hoped it was a good choice — he was more a shot and beer kind of guy.

It was dusk by the time he walked back up Main Street toward the Bavarian Lodge. The Victorian lamps on the broad street had come on, and snow was spitting out of the gray sky. Hell, 3,000 feet below in Denver, they'd been playing golf for a couple months now.

He shaved, showered, and drove his Bronco over to the Innes house. He parked on the street behind Ellen's green Acura. Dinner at the Inneses. Might be interesting. If nothing else, he was keen to see the good doctor again.

He'd met Thomas Innes during the Holman trial over a decade ago. Interviewed the man at length at least a couple times. He recalled a big man, dark, very youthful looking, even though he'd been thirty-three at the time. Cam had been unable to tell if Innes was genuinely undone by his almost ex-wife's murder or if he'd been putting on a seamless act. After all, Innes had known full well that Samantha and Matt Holman had been doing the dirty deed.

How had Innes aged in the last decade? He was extraordinarily successful now, a big name in sports medicine. Held up as a paragon all over the country — and beyond. Hobnobbed with the top athletes, the wealthy, movie stars, you name them.

When Cam pictured the new wife, Julia, he had a hard time putting them together. On the surface the woman seemed absolutely unpretentious, a deputy district attorney in the small satellite office in Aspen, when her husband was pulling in millions. Why did she even bother to work?

Julia Innes . . . a pretty lady, a certain

unnerving resemblance to Samantha, the first wife. Auburn hair, wide-set blue eyes, medium height, a good figure. But then, weren't people always attracted by the same type?

And she was quite a bit younger than her husband, younger than Cam, too. But not a trophy wife, none of that aspect at all.

She was taking her husband's arrest hard, he could see that. She'd been stretched thin that afternoon, although her brain worked fine. Fiercely protective of Thomas. She must love him a lot.

The doctor let him in, saying, "Jesus, Cam Lazlo, I thought you might be a reporter. The jerks have been coming right up to the house, knocking on the door."

"Okay," Cam said, "I'll see if I can't get the cops to keep an eye out, and you might want to have a sign put up on the fence, no trespassing. That usually makes them stop and think. If not, we'll go to Plan B, real security."

Yeah, Cam thought, Innes was the same man, not changed much except for a distinct heaviness about the jowls and gut, a kind of sleek patina successful men possessed, like the well-groomed gleam of a top racehorse.

"Glad you could make it," Innes finally

said. "I remember you from the Holman trial. You did a super job there."

"Looks like I have to do it all over again," Cam replied.

"Yes, I suppose so. What a mess, what a horrible mess."

The doctor was clearly stressed out, and Cam didn't blame him. He hoped that there would be no need to handhold — that was not Cam's strong suit. He could investigate, make sure the house was secure, lean hard on witnesses if necessary, separate truth from fiction — that stuff was easy. And he could stop and be quiet for a while, turn inward, listen to the story the dead victim had to tell. He could do all that, but he sure as hell couldn't play nicey-nice with a rattled defendant.

"Well, come on in," the doctor said, "we're almost ready to eat."

Cam handed the bottle of wine to the man. "Brought a little something."

"Thanks. It wasn't necessary, you know. It seems you're going to be here quite a bit, so let's not stand on ceremony, Detective."

"Cam . . . just Cam."

They sat around the kitchen table. The room was large, an old-fashioned country kitchen, remodeled, naturally, with glass and chrome, pale oak cabinets and polished granite countertops. The walls were painted a muted soft yellow; floor was hardwood, new and shiny. The house must've been renovated, because almost everything was stylish and spiffy and absolutely up-to-date.

A welcoming house, homey and comfortable. Whoever had decorated had retained the Victorian feel. Wainscoting painted white, wood floors with Persian carpets, couch and chairs in jewel tones of red and green and blue. Tassled throw pillows. Heavy off-white drapes pulled back by swags. He wondered if Julia had chosen the décor.

There were twice-baked potatoes, string beans and roast pork, a fresh salad. After she'd left him at the Bavarian Lodge, Julia must have cooked all afternoon.

A pie for dessert. She'd given in and bought a frozen one — he knew the exact brand — he bought one for himself from time to time.

He didn't talk much, wanted the opportunity to assess the situation and the players.

You had fiery Irish Ellen Marshall, not one to pull punches. Buzz around Denver had it she was a savvy defense counsel. Unrelenting, got away with a touch of drama because of her diminutive size. Manipulative, it was said, which was excellent for her client.

"So I told the dope that if I couldn't have the state's evidence soon, I was going straight to Judge Scott," Ellen was saying.

"The dope?" Innes asked.

"The assistant DA, Lawson Fine, McSwain's hatchet man."

"You might want to cool it a little, Ellen," Julia said. "Bret McSwain can go for the throat."

"Let him." Ellen waved a hand. "You know Detective Feller?"

"Sure," Julia said.

"Well, did you know he was forced to sign the arrest warrant?"

Julia stopped, a fork halfway to her mouth. "How did you find that out?"

Ellen wagged a finger. "I've got my ways."

Cam sliced a piece of roast, studied and judged, trying to get a feel for what he'd be dealing with.

You had Julia Innes, looking tired at the moment, trying to be a good hostess, but obviously wishing she could get her husband alone and talk to him. Just talk.

Funny, she seemed so down to earth, not a match for the celebrity doctor. He wondered how their relationship worked. Not that Cam was any judge of relationships — Mr. Noncommittal, one of his women had called him. Then slammed her door in his face.

"Anyone for coffee?" Julia asked. "I have decaf." Probably wishing she was anywhere but here, doing anything but hosting a dinner.

"Got any high-test?" Ellen asked. "I've still got work to do."

"Sure. Anyone else?"

"I'd like some, please," Cam said.

"None for me," Innes put in.

Then you had the kingpin, Thomas. Everything going for the man: money, renown, good looks, a loving wife, a great house. He was obviously really tops at what he did. But involved in a murder, years ago, even if he didn't do it. And now — the same crime returning to bite him in his ass. Nasty business.

Cam listened carefully, sipping his coffee, as they discussed initial strategy.

"Okay, here's how it works. Cam, I think we're all pretty much decided you're part of the team, am I right, Thomas?" Ellen asked.

"Yes, ma'am," Innes said, a little too jocular for the occasion.

"Ellen and I will both be working the case," Julia explained. "Obviously, I won't appear in an official capacity, but I'll do a lot of the background work — motions, research, evidence searches, things like that."

"We'll make a great team," Ellen said. "Partners after all these years."

But Julia appeared to be concentrating on business. "This is the way I see it. Ellen, tell me if you're on the same wavelength. I work behind the scenes; you're the star in court."

"The star." Ellen rolled her eyes.

"And Cam, a lot of the investigation will be your responsibility. As they say, most cases are won in the field, not in the courtroom. Ellen's going to bring one of her paralegals from the firm up here. To handle the paperwork, computer searches, faxes, all that."

"There's a kid named Dennis, young, unattached, so he won't mind spending time in Aspen. I'll call him tomorrow," Ellen put in.

"If you don't mind my asking, how are you going to find time for all this, Julia?" Cam asked.

"I'll finish my case load and quit my job."

"You will not," Ellen said.

"I've thought about it a lot, Ellen. It would be ethically and morally wrong for me to continue to work for Bret McSwain."

Ethical. Moral. Cam hadn't heard anyone talk like that in a long time. Maybe never.

"I told you, Julia —"

"I can't." Julia shook her head. "And, believe me, I wouldn't learn enough about the case to make the job worthwhile. You know I'd stay on if I thought it would help Thomas." She paused. "But I will definitely finish up my cases. I have a responsibility not to dump them."

"How long?" Ellen asked.

"I don't know. I'll figure it out when I go back to work."

"Well, I don't necessarily agree, but it's your decision," Ellen said.

"I always told you to quit," Thomas added.

There was a moment of silence at his statement. Ellen pursed her mouth, turned her coffee cup in the saucer, then said, "Now, I'm assuming a worst-case scenario, that we go to trial. Meanwhile, we'll try our damnedest to squelch the whole thing. We'll fight every bit of discovery, we'll file motions until everyone is sick of the sight of us, at the preliminary hearing I'll fight the finding of probable cause. Okay, a lot of what we're planning may not be necessary, but we have to be prepared.

"So . . . assuming, as I said, we have to prepare for trial, we dig through the old evidence files and the Holman trial transcript until we're totally familiar with every bit of information. Now, you all realize we can't use Holman's conviction in our defense? Because his conviction was nullified, all that is forbidden territory. In other words, the jury won't know anything about his previous trial. Well, theoretically. Of course, everyone who lived in Aspen will remember, but *we* can't mention it. We have to re-interview all the witnesses and anyone who gave a statement to the police twelve years ago, all the nurses, doctors, neighbors, the works. We talk to acquaintances of Matt Holman, even his cellmates. Make that *former* cellmates," Ellen said flippantly. "Not that we can use anything we come up with in court, but we gather all the info we can. We also question Holman — Cam, all this is your area. Have the murder weapon and body fluids, if there were any, the semen from Samantha's body, sorry, I have to say it, you guys, but have the body fluids, if viable, retested. DNA tests on everything, the tests that weren't available back then."

"Holman always admitted he was with Samantha," Cam said, glancing at Innes for a moment before continuing. "Admitted having intercourse with her. DNA will only prove that."

"Yes, of course, but our job is to create reasonable doubt of Thomas's guilt. Without referring to the previous trial, we'll prove that Matt Holman's DNA was at the murder scene but Thomas's wasn't. Who knows, maybe we'll even find Holman's DNA on the weapon."

"Do they still have all that old evidence?" Thomas asked, looking decidedly ill-at-ease with the subject.

"You bet. I checked. It's been stored in a cool dry basement at the courthouse — everything is stored there. The temperature and dry air will help. As I said, the DNA may not be viable any longer. But we'll give it a go."

Cam was impressed. Ellen had been here one day, and already she and Julia had mapped out a strategy.

"Don't forget Leann Cornish," Julia said.

"Ah, yes, Leann. Someone has to interview her. Someone who can handle her with kid gloves. Obviously, Julia can't do it. And I can be abrasive sometimes — now, I'm not bragging, just realistic — so, Cam, that task falls to you."

He nodded.

"We need her motivation, her reactions, every nuance."

Cam listened closely, but he found his focus shifting to Julia. She had put her hand on her husband's. She looked determined. She also looked so much like Samantha Innes the skin on his neck prickled. He'd seen many photographs of Samantha, and he'd seen her pale, nude body on the autopsy table. Seeing Julia's face superimposed on a corpse was going to be tough. Real tough.

He spoke little, but he did have one question. "Just how near death is Leann Cornish? Does anyone know?"

"Good point," Ellen said. "Cam, that's something you can do. Find out who her doctor is."

"I'll write up a subpoena for her medical records," Julia put in.

"Okay, good." Ellen drank some of her coffee. "When we get that information, we better get an interview lined up. Before she croaks."

"Christ," Innes said, flinching.

"Hey, if there's a trial, it may not be for months. And as terrible as this sounds, we can't count on Leann being around. I only meant that she might —"

"All right, just don't say it again," Innes said. "You sound so . . . heartless."

"I'll accept that compliment, Doctor."

Innes twisted his mouth. Cam could see Julia's fingers tighten on his. "It's okay," she said. "This is what we have to do."

"God, it's ugly."

"Yes, it is," Ellen said. "But what you're charged with is even uglier. Murder, Thomas. Second-degree murder."

The man blanched and seemed to shrink.

"I'm pushing for discovery, but it's too soon to expect it at this point."

"I'm sure Leann will tell the truth now," Julia said. "She just wanted to pay Thomas back for getting her fired. I know she'll recant when she realizes how serious this is."

"It's possible," Ellen said without conviction.

Cam knew better. Julia was engaged in wishful thinking. In his experience, people who went to the length of making a deathbed confession did not recant. They were in a state of mind other people could not begin to understand, and their motiva-

118

tion was pure. Either way — the absolute truth or a lie to extract some sort of punishment after they died — their motivation was thought out and unchangeable.

So why *was* Leann Cornish incriminating the doctor? Revenge was certainly one possible motive. The dying woman was living in a skewed reality, and who could blame her? Unless, of course, Innes had really done the crime.

Cam halted the notion, thought, *Nah, no way. Holman did it.*

Innes said he was beat and was going to bed, early as it was. Julia appeared to be out on her feet. The dishes were still on the table, the food still on platters and in bowls. Did she have to clean the mess up herself or did they have a cleaning lady?

"Uh, you want some help with the dishes?" Cam asked, feeling foolish.

"Oh, God, yes," Ellen said. "My mind's on the case. I'm useless, Julia."

"That would be nice," Julia said, trying a smile. "I'd do it in the morning, but I have to go to work."

The three of them cleared the table. Julia rinsed dishes and put them in the dishwasher; Cam sponged off the table. Victor should see him now, he thought. He'd laugh his ass off, maybe put it in a book.

Have Luke Diamond wearing a frilly apron.

The dishes done, Julia said she was going to take Blackie out for a walk.

"Thanks for coming," she said to Cam. "I mean it." She tried to smile again. "Maybe the trial won't happen, and you'll have come up here for nothing."

"Could be," he said.

"I hope that's what happens, but I bet Victor Ferris doesn't."

"Victor. He's not exactly my primary concern right now."

"That's good to hear," she said softly, then, "well, good night."

Ellen was bent over some papers on the dining table, looked like old evidence files from the Holman trial. She flicked one file with her finger. "Crap," she said. "Shoddy investigation."

"Glad to hear it." As an ex-cop he still got pissed at lawyers who thought they knew how to run an investigation better than the cops.

"You leaving now?"

"Yeah."

"I'll talk to you tomorrow." She followed him to the front door. She was so short she had to tilt her head up to talk to him. "You know, and I wouldn't say this to Thomas and Julia, but I'm a little worried. The evidence that convicted Holman in the first place was all circumstantial."

"Nothing wrong with solid circumstantial evidence."

"No. But the motive —"

"Holman went into a rage because Samantha told him she was never going to divorce Thomas. Happens."

"Yes, I know. I read it today in the transcript. Holman denied there was an argument with Samantha over divorcing her husband, and later in the trial Thomas's testimony on the subject was questionable."

He shrugged.

"I want you to concentrate on two people — Leann Cornish and Matt Holman. I want you to play nice with the dying woman but hardball with him."

"Can do."

"I know you can. I've heard."

He stayed silent.

"And I want that sample from Holman for DNA testing. Most likely, I'll have to get a court order for that. At the least to establish his presence at the murder scene. Maybe, if we get really lucky, we'll even find it on the murder weapon. But what I'd really like from Holman, hell, I'll leave that up to you, but I'd like a confession."

"Could be a bit harder than the DNA sample."

She flourished a hand. "That's your thing."

"I'm on it." Then he hesitated. "I didn't want to say this in front of them . . ."

She cocked her head, narrowed her eyes. "What?"

"Holman wrote me for years. Kept begging me to reopen the case. He doesn't know I'm not on the force anymore. Anyway, he swore he's innocent."

"Yeah, aren't they all?" Ellen said.

SEVEN

Julia liked to take Blackie out at night. No matter the weather, she found the close darkness comforting, the sky at this altitude endlessly fascinating — either black velvet sprinkled with diamonds, storm clouds scudding across the moon, sometimes a full moon so intensely bright it cast distinct shadows. Tonight was cool and very dark; she could barely see Blackie on the end of the leash.

She was tired, really done in. Ellen was so damn full of energy, and Cam didn't seem to grow weary, either, though it was hard to tell with him because of his aloofness. But then, they weren't personally involved in the emotions of this miscarriage of justice.

She felt a little better, though. At least she wasn't alone anymore; she had two people who were committed to proving Thomas not guilty. Ellen, of course, and Cam Lazlo, who'd already helped put a man in prison for the crime.

She walked Blackie down the block, feeling the sidewalk beneath her feet, because she couldn't see clearly. Finally she returned to the house, hung her jacket up, and went into the living room to find Ellen brandishing a stack of papers from where she sat, Indian style, on the floor.

"He *cried* on the witness stand," Ellen said, peering over her glasses at Julia.

"Who cried?"

"Matt Holman. He's one damn good actor."

"Maybe he was sincerely sorry Samantha was dead."

"Sure, right. He was sincerely sorry he'd *killed* her."

Julia sank down onto the couch, rubbed her eyes. Blackie nestled at her feet.

"Go to bed," Ellen said.

"Let's have a glass of wine. To relax."

"How about opening that bottle Cam brought?"

"He doesn't look like a fine-wine sort of guy," Julia reflected.

"No, but I bet he picked an expensive one. That's what someone like him would do. Hey, it all goes on Victor Ferris's tab."

Julia dragged herself up and went to the kitchen, opened the bottle, poured two glasses, and carried them into the living room. Blackie half opened an eye, saw she was back, and groaned contentedly before dozing off again.

"Um, tasty," Ellen said from her position on the floor. "I told you."

"So, are you and Mason still a couple?" Julia asked.

"Oh, sure."

"You think he's the one?"

"I don't know yet. We seem to get along, but, really, either I'm in the office late or he's out of town. Still, so far it's working." Mason was a lobbyist in Washington for the Colorado Cattlemen's Association. "Or maybe it's working *because* we're not together much."

"That's one way to look at it."

"I know you don't think much of Mason, but he's really a great guy. Sometimes . . . I don't know . . . sometimes we get along so well, and I just adore him."

"No one ever said relationships were easy."

"God, isn't that the truth? If only I could go about a relationship the same way I prepare for a trial. It would be so simple." Ellen laughed. "I'm a hell of a lot more successful as a lawyer than a lover."

True enough, Julia knew. Ellen had made bad choices in men for as long as

Julia had known her. There'd been a bipolar law student at DU, a married dentist a few years ago. A couple very forgettable flings. And now Mason Schultz.

"So, how are you and Thomas?"

"Oh, other than this little snafu" — she rolled her eyes — "we're fine. The truth is he's so busy, sometimes I don't see him for days at a time. He's been traveling out to Sun Valley a lot, you know, for that new orthopedic clinic he's opening up there? And there's his surgery here. Oh, and he's been lecturing at some medical schools.

"You know Thomas, he's so ambitious, and he doesn't delegate very well. He cares so much, Ellen, for his patients. And not just the rich ones. He agonized over a young ski patrolman's ankle last month, worried about it. And I can't fault him for that."

"You're busy, too, though."

"Yes, but my job, well, it's easier to leave my problems at work when I walk out of the office."

"Um. How do Thomas and Livie get along? When I've been up here visiting, I rarely see them together. You seem to take up most of the slack in that area."

"I suppose I do. But I think Livie understands how tied up with work her dad is.

She *is* emotional, though. Understandably, of course, after losing her mother so tragically."

"Did she ever have help, professional help, that is?"

"I don't think so. Thomas's mother came out to stay with them for a couple months after Samantha died. I know Livie loves Maggie a lot, and she goes out to San Diego to visit her for a couple weeks every summer. Maybe that was enough support. Maybe I've been enough. I try. Or maybe Livie will get help later in life, you know." Julia shrugged.

"Whatever happened to Samantha's parents?"

"Oh, gosh. Apparently they went into a shell after her death. I understand they were here for the trial, but then they dropped out of sight."

"You mean they never see Livie, their grandchild?"

"Well, for one thing, Samantha's mother died a few years ago, and I believe her father is ill or something. Livie used to get birthday cards and checks, you know, when they were both alive, but it's been a while."

"If this case goes to trial, do you think there's chance of Livie's grandfather showing up for it?"

127

"Now, there's a question. If I had to bet on it, I'd say no, he won't show. God, for all I know, he passed away, too."

"Well, you're here. And you're great with her, that much I know."

"Like I said, I try. And I've grown to love her as if she were my own."

Ellen was leaning back against the couch, the wineglass resting on her chest. She watched Julia over her reading glasses.

"What?" Julia said.

"Now, don't get mad."

"Ellen."

"Okay, here goes. Is there any chance, any chance at *all*, that Thomas could have been involved in Samantha's murder? An accident, of course, a quarrel over Matt Holman?"

Julia had been expecting the question, as if everyone she saw, everyone who read the papers or watched the news on TV, wanted to make that same query. She drew in a deep breath — the answer was so clear to her, so unquestionably obvious if you knew her husband as she did. "Thomas is not capable of striking anyone or murdering anyone, much less covering it up. Ellen, he heals people — that's his vocation. He couldn't hurt anyone."

Ellen pursed her lips. "Okay, I believe

128

you. But the district attorney, the people's representative, believes otherwise. It's going to be tricky getting past that nurse's statement."

"She'll recant," Julia said.

"We'll see. Of course, her being forced to quit will certainly bolster our case. Then again, her being terminally ill" — Ellen clucked her tongue — "that's a point for the prosecution. Sympathy. I'll try to get as few women on the jury as I can."

"If it goes that far."

"Correct. *If.*"

Julia yawned. The wine was a smooth red; she could feel the effect of the alcohol already.

"What do you think of Cam?" Ellen asked then.

Julia had her eyes closed. "Hard. Something bad happened to him."

"Interesting. Why do you say that?"

"Oh, I don't know. He guards himself too carefully."

"As an opponent, he'd scare me to death. But that's not why he's here. I'd have had to use an investigator from the firm and bill you for his hours. Cam is free."

"I asked him if Victor Ferris would use this as a story. I mean, after all, Ferris must have a good motive for offering his right-hand man plus paying for his expenses. Anyway, Cam said Ferris starts with the idea, but makes it very different. Puts his own spin on it. I believed him. You ever read any of the books?"

"A couple."

"What do you think?"

"Great entertainment. Pretty damn accurate legal-wise and investigation-wise. The man does his research. That's how I know him. He called me a couple times for info. I think he's kind of living on a different plane of existence, but he does write good books."

"So Cam does all the cop stuff for him?"

"So I gather."

"That Luke Diamond," Julia reflected, "he's a great character. He just doesn't care, you know? But he *does* care, and somehow you get the feeling he's soft-hearted and scared to death to show anyone."

"Exactly how I read him, too, how Victor *wants* us to read him. But back to reality. You're going to work tomorrow, okay?"

Julia sighed. "I mean it, Ellen, I'm only going back for as long as it takes to finish my cases."

"Okay, okay. But get what you can in the office."

"Bret isn't even in my office. He's all the way down in Glenwood Springs. And he hates, I mean *hates* to make the trip up to Aspen."

"Really?"

"It's the traffic."

"Nevertheless. Keep your ears open." Ellen sipped some wine, licked her lips. "Cam will be a lot of help. We'll have him locate and interview all the witnesses from Holman's trial. He'll remember most of them, I bet. And like I suggested earlier, he should be the one talk to Leann Cornish. Oh, and Matt Holman. Can't forget him. Now that he's out and can't be sent back, he may have a new slant on the murder. And you should know that Cam said Holman's been writing him all these years and protesting his innocence."

Julia absorbed the information and then nodded.

"We might get some DNA evidence. And if we do, it'll be up to the judge how much we can admit into the record. The idea is not to retry Holman . . ."

"Which would be double jeopardy."

"Exactly. But we'll get into the court record the findings of the DNA testing, get into testimony from a forensics expert that Thomas's DNA was *not* found on the

131

bedsheets or in body fluids taken from Samantha at her autopsy. And it wasn't found on the murder weapon, either. The jury will hear that Holman's DNA was all over the goddamn place, and that has to create reasonable doubt as to Thomas's guilt."

"It's crazy, you know? Matt Holman."

"That he was released on a writ of habeas corpus?" Ellen said.

"Everyone knows he did it. And the legal system is going to come away from this whole fiasco with a huge black eye."

"Thanks to your DA Bret McSwain."

"Yes, thanks to my boss." Julia yawned again.

"Go to bed."

"I will." She emptied her wineglass, stood, and stretched. But as weary as she was, she couldn't help asking, "What happened to Cam, exactly, you know, about being kicked off the police force?"

"Hmm. As I recall, it was Cam and two other cops. They arrested a child molester, a *repeat* molester."

"Oh, my God," Julia whispered.

"Anyway, the perp tried to escape, and two other cops beat the man half to death. Cam watched, didn't stop them, wouldn't rat them out to IA. There was a public outcry, like with the Rodney King beating, and somebody had to pay. Cam was in the wrong place at the wrong time."

"I bet he was a good detective."

"Apparently. And now he works for Ferris and probably makes twice the salary with a lot less aggravation."

"I get the impression he misses being a detective," Julia mused.

"I guess that's a hard habit to kick."

Julia finally climbed the stairs, undressed, brushed her teeth. Quietly, so as not to awaken Thomas. She slid into bed, lay still for a moment, and heard his deep rhythmic breathing. Thank heavens he was asleep. She knew he had surgery all day tomorrow. Shoulders and knees and ankles and hips. Frightened, hurting people that her husband healed.

She snuggled up against him, feeling better than she had in three days. Everything would work out all right. Of course it would. There was no way on earth that a jury could find him guilty. Ellen would work like a demon for him. So would Cam. And she herself would do whatever she could. Like write a letter of resignation tomorrow.

She heard his breathing, felt the warmth of his body, drew in his familiar scent, and she couldn't help thinking about the question Ellen had posed: Could he have been involved in any way with Samantha's murder?

She almost laughed, lying there in bed with her husband. Thomas? No, never. Impossible. She'd know. How could she not?

EIGHT

DA Bret McSwain saw his job like this: He dealt with the worst kind of people. Murderers, rapists, child abusers, robbers, dope dealers. His own witnesses and sometimes the victims themselves were as unsavory as the accused. And he dealt with these lowlifes every day of the week, every week of the year.

Even his triumphs were often tainted — the victim's family dissatisfied with the perpetrator's sentence, the victim of domestic violence recanting and turning against the DA.

But — and this was a big *but* — inside and, yes, outside the courtroom, he exercised extraordinary authority and the ability to affect lives in the most profound way.

He'd been duly elected by the people to keep their lives safe. Okay, so his district wasn't exactly South Philly or South Central LA, but he had his responsibilities nevertheless.

And this Innes case was the biggest one thus far during his tenure. Murder, a famous doctor, glitzy Aspen. The works.

Innes had retained Ellen Marshall to defend him. Little Ellen, the prosecutors in Denver called her, but little only in stature. In talent she was big.

She'd do her damnedest for Innes; she'd put on a goddamn tough defense, and Bret knew he had a job of work ahead of him. But he had a few tricks up his sleeve, and he wasn't hesitant to use them.

He was relatively certain he knew what direction the defense would take. They'd present Innes as an upstanding citizen, husband, and father, a great doctor, blah, blah, blah. She'd try to impugn every one of Bret's witnesses, most notably Leann Cornish and Matt Holman.

That was okay. That was the way the system worked. He was prepared.

Then there was Julia Innes. Actually, he'd been surprised she hadn't already quit her job. Maybe she still would, though. Too bad; he hated losing a competent DDA.

He sat behind his desk in his office, and he thought suddenly of a phone call he needed to make.

He buzzed his secretary. "Clara, can you get me Judge Scott in Aspen? If he's not

136

available, please leave him a message to call me."

"Sure thing, Mr. McSwain."

Then he went back to work on a case he had to try next week — a woman who'd been beaten up by her boyfriend so badly she'd lost the sight in one eye.

He really wanted to nail the son of a bitch.

Cam went for a run every morning before going to the Innes house. He wasn't much of a runner anymore, two bad knees, but he tried to do a couple miles, maybe three, twice a week no matter where he was. His stab at healthy living. But here in Aspen the altitude got to him, made him suck air, slowed his stride to practically a crawl. Still he made the effort, and figured at the very least the exercise helped keep his head straight.

This late April morning he took the Rio Grande Trail, which followed the old railroad bed. The train that had run between Aspen and Glenwood Springs, forty-some miles down the valley, was long since gone, the right-of-way turned into a bike path. There were some young joggers — all passing him as if he were standing still — quite a few walkers with their dogs, and a couple bikes whipped by him. The trail was pleasant, following the many twists and turns of the Roaring Fork River, which flowed from the top of Independence Pass at the Continental Divide east of Aspen, down the valley to Glenwood Springs, where it joined the Colorado River.

He ran a mile down the trail, then veered to a footbridge across the river and climbed a steep dirt track up to the back side of the Aspen Meadows complex. The Meadows had been one of the first resorts in town. It still offered all the amenities: rooms, conference center, health club, tennis courts, restaurant. The acreage was beautiful, abutting the Aspen Institute — a think tank that drew ex-presidents and world leaders — the big music tent, and the Physics Institute. But the resort was over fifty years old, and nothing much had been modernized. Many visitors preferred the less pretentious aura here, including a lot of the physicists who came for the Physics Institute, the musicians who played at the Aspen Music Festival, a few of the world leaders who were not invited to stay at private residences.

Cam reached the top of the path leading up from the river, and he jogged through the complex, then he swung through Aspen's West End streets, near the Inneses', and back to his lodge. Hands on his knees, catching his breath, he figured he'd done close to three miles. And he'd only slowed to a walk once when climbing the hill from the footbridge. Not bad. Then again, his lifestyle up here had been a whole lot cleaner than in Denver, when he too often hooked up with some of his old cop buddies after a Bronco or Avalanche game, and stayed out till the wee hours. He liked to blame Victor, telling himself he was merely keeping up-to-date with police procedures and the endless bar gossip — but that, of course, was bullshit. What Cam liked was the familiar camaraderie.

The past couple weeks had been drudgery for him. Every day seemed a repeat of the previous one, the days molding into a monotony of stultifying work, sitting on his ass, going over reams of transcript testimony from the Holman trial. He remembered a lot of testimony clearly, despite the twelve years that had gone by. The fact of which only served to make him all the more bored. What he wanted to do, what he craved, was action. But Ellen and Julia were still planning their initial strategy, still deciding the order in which they wanted witnesses interviewed, when they wanted the interviews conducted, the questions Cam would ask — a minutia of details and more details. He could never have been a lawyer. He needed to be on the hunt; needed to be moving.

Showered, shaved, and dressed, he headed to the Innes house, ran into Julia at the front door. She looked good to him, especially in the morning, when she was fresh. Before she went to the office, insisting on seeing through her last few cases. Moral, ethical. That was Julia. Today she wore boot-cut black slacks, a reddish camisole top beneath a short, lightweight black sweater. Her auburn-colored hair was still damp, full and shiny and curling a little around her face. She had on lipstick, just enough to set off the deep rich color of her hair against the smooth creaminess of her skin. She was a beautiful woman.

"Morning," he said, holding the front door for her.

"Good morning, Cam," she replied, and she smiled. "Got to run . . . crazy day in court."

Thomas was already gone — early surgery at Aspen Valley Hospital. Ellen was in the kitchen, yawning, brewing a second pot of coffee in her bathrobe. "Hi, Cam, I suppose you've been up for hours."

"Yeah. Went for a run. Got enough coffee for me?"

"All you want. Oh, I put a portion of Holman's trial transcript out for you last night. I'd like you to go over it, make some notes, check them against mine, if you would."

"No prob." Same old same old. It was funny, though. On weekends — he'd been here two weekends now — when Julia was home, he didn't mind the forced enclosure of the dining room-office nearly as much. He guessed it was her optimism, that and those occasional smiles she bestowed on him. Nothing like a pretty lady's smile to smooth the edges on the day.

He took a mug of coffee and settled in the dining room while Ellen went to get dressed. Focused on the stack of papers she had left out for him. *Okay, concentrate,* he told himself. He picked up the pile, began to read, remembering, as he had so often, the long hours he'd spent in the Pitkin County Courthouse all those years ago. The distinctive Victorian courtroom with its oak benches and the graceful, curved balustrade that separated the judge and jury from the audience. The tall windows covered by Venetian blinds and the moss green carpet on the floor.

He recalled the taut atmosphere and the judge, Jerry Fiske, and the district attorney who'd prosecuted Holman, Glenn Willis, and he recalled Holman's defense lawyer from Denver, a sharp man who did his best, but his best couldn't save his client from the guilty verdict. And, as he began reading through the transcript, he remembered the testimony of the young, upcoming surgeon whose wife had been murdered.

"I knew she had a . . . a boyfriend," Thomas said in answer to the prosecuting attorney's question. Cam remembered that the widower had been pale and morose, his voice quavering. *"I . . . I hated it, but our marriage was . . . It wasn't very good, and I knew she was going to move out soon."*

"What about custody of your daughter, Olivia?"

"Livie? Samantha and I would have agreed on that. Samantha was a good mother. And she knew how much I loved my daughter. That wouldn't have been an issue."

"Did you personally know Matt Holman, Dr. Innes?"

"No."

"You never met him?"

"No."

"Never saw him from a distance?"

"No, I'm sure I didn't."

"Did he visit Samantha in your house?"

"I . . . I don't know. I didn't think so, until . . . until the . . ."

"Do you want a break, Dr. Innes?"

"No, no. I'm all right."

Cam scanned more of the doctor's testimony, made a couple notes — such as was Thomas Innes lying when he testified he'd never even laid eyes on Matt Holman before Samantha's death? — then flipped the transcript pages to a section from the prosecutor's cross-examination of Matt Holman:

"Mr. Holman, is it true you were having an affair with Samantha Innes?"

"Yes, but I didn't —"

"Mr. Holman, simply answer the question." The judge.

"Yes."

"And you knew she was married and had a daughter?"

"Yes, but she told me —"

"Answer the question, Mr. Holman."

"Yes, I knew."

"How long had the affair been going on?"

"Ah, since the previous November, I think."

"Where did you meet Samantha Innes?"

"I'm a bartender . . . I was, anyway. . . . I met her the weekend after Thanksgiving, I think."

"You think?"

"I'm pretty sure. The mountain had just opened for the ski season, and I think it was that weekend."

"Samantha came into the bar? Had cocktails?"

"Ah, yes. With a friend, I think."

"A friend?"

"A lady friend."

Cam scanned a couple pages, then read the more pertinent questions from the prosecutor.

"You were present in the Innes home that morning of May eighth?"

"Yes."

"And you left around noon?"

"If that's what I told police."

"You don't recall the time now?"

"I, yes, it was around noon. If that's what I told the cops . . . the police, then that was it. It was six months ago, and I just —"

"Mr. Holman," the judge admonished again. "You will answer only the question posed to you."

"Yes, sir. Your Honor, I mean."

The judge. "You may continue your cross, Counselor."

DA Glenn Willis: "When you left Samantha, she was still alive?"

"Yes. Yes!"

Cam sat back against the hard wood of the dining room chair and saw Holman as clearly as if the man were sitting across from him. He'd damn near burst into tears when he'd cried, "Yes. *Yes!*" his body language convincing unless, of course, you hadn't investigated the case and known he was guilty from the get-go. There simply had not been another suspect once Thomas Innes's alibi had been checked out and found to be ironclad. Truth was and always had been, a family member or a jealous lover committed most murders. When Cam had been a cop, the statistic was something like ninety-eight percent of all murders — and he'd bet that figure hadn't changed.

Holman murdered the woman. Cam knew that twelve years ago — knew it today. And the goddamn politically motivated DA should have revisited all the evidence before buying into this Leann Cornish's bullshit story and taking his so-called new evidence to the judge. Well, he'd started a ball rolling, all right, and there was nothing left to do but stop that ball and prove the DA wrong.

He was placing the folder back in a box when he saw a corner of a black-and-white photo sticking out of a file. He took the file out, opened it. Drew in a breath. Copies of original police photos of Samantha — sprawled in death on her living room rug, a circle of blood beneath her head.

The photos took him back a dozen years, transported him instantaneously to the morgue, to Samantha's body on the coroner's slab. To his solemn promise to her.

Well, pretty lady, I'm still working on it.

After a time he put the photos back in the file. The originals would be presented as evidence in this trial, too. Passed among the jurors, and sure as hell the media would get its hands on copies and publish them.

Ellen's assistant Dennis arrived a short while later and took a look at the pile of notes Ellen had left him, a mountain of paper. "How does Ms. Marshall come up with all this?" the young man said in awe. "She must be up working all night."

Cam found a smile. "She's an A-type, that's for sure. You get settled into your room okay?"

Julia had found Dennis a room at a neighbor's house for the summer months — a free room in exchange for watching the house, watering plants, all that, while the family was in Europe. They hadn't even minded that Dennis planned on spending a lot of his weekends at home in Denver. A good deal for the family; a great deal for Dennis and Ellen and ultimately Julia and Thomas, who'd be billed out for his expenses in the end.

He was a nice-looking kid, fresh out of college and planning on going to law school. He was tall, over six feet, skinny with dark curling hair and a thin face, reminded Cam a little of pictures of Victor Ferris from thirty years ago. Except Dennis was much taller. His job here was to answer all phone calls, send and receive faxes, reply to e-mails, send e-mail attachments, enter everything into computer files

147

— every note and letter and motion and brief Ellen and Julia dashed off, which was plenty. He would also spend many long hours in the law library at the courthouse.

When Ellen had told him that, how he'd be looking up legal precedents for her, he'd barely hidden a frown. But Cam had piped up with "Hey, you know the serial killer Ted Bundy used that library every day? It was that very window that he jumped from, made his escape."

"No shit?" Dennis had beamed. Then, "Oh, sorry Ms. Marshall."

Ellen had made a face. "Like I don't know what *shit* means? Just keep it to a manageable level, kid, and we'll do okay. And by the way, call me Ellen. Ms. Marshall makes me feel old. Really, *really* ancient, and we don't want to do that, now do we, Dennis?"

"No, ma'am." But Dennis still slipped and often called her Ms. Marshall.

Late that afternoon, after Julia returned from court, Ellen pushed her chair back from the table, peered over her glasses at them, and said, "You're wondering why I haven't mentioned changing the venue for the trial," she said.

"Okay, why?" Julia said.

Ellen steepled her fingers. "It's like this

148

— there is no corner of the country that hasn't heard about this case, and trying to get an impartial jury is pretty damn impossible. And here, in Thomas's hometown, where he's done so much good, there will be a lot of sympathy for him."

"I agree," Julia said.

Dennis was in the process of locating witnesses from the Holman trial. He'd done fairly well. A lot were still in the area, so interviewing them wouldn't be difficult.

"I've talked to Bret McSwain, and he'll be getting the discovery to us in less than a week. It should be an interesting document, guys."

"Think there'll be any surprises?" Cam asked.

"I think their whole case is based on Leann," Julia put in.

"Never, never trust the prosecution," Ellen said. "They'll keep whatever they can from us. It might be an insignificant detail; it might be vital. But, sure as hell, there'll be some surprise they'll spring on us."

"We have to talk to Leann," Julia said. "As soon as possible."

"I've been trying to get hold of her. Left messages," Cam said. "She lives in Glenwood Springs, but I understand she's been in and out of the hospital. I'll keep working on her."

"And Holman?" Julia asked.

"Yeah, I found out he's living with his mother in Mesa, Arizona," Cam replied.

"Will he talk to you?" Julia raised a brow.

"I haven't called him yet. But I'm betting he will. He was sure eager for me to believe him all these years. The thing is, we still need to get a court order for him to provide DNA for testing."

"I'm working on it," Ellen said.

"Maybe I can talk to Judge Scott," Julia began.

"We'll see. Don't want to push that angle yet. Just keep your ears open at work. And speaking of which, have you heard any gossip?"

Julia shook her head. "It's as if the DA instructed everyone not to talk about the case anywhere around me. I warned you."

"Well, don't give up."

Cam grinned. "Hey, not to worry, someone will slip. They always do."

Julia looked at him. "Spoken like a cop."

"An ex-cop."

"Once a cop, always a cop. . . ."

Ellen shook her head. "Okay, guys, back to work. Cam, I'm thinking it won't hurt to give Holman a call, at least touch base with him, let him know you'll be asking to interview him in the near future. And find out who his best friends were in jail. Line them up for interviews."

"Yeah, fine. But I think I'll leave the subject of DNA testing for later. Holman's going to be pissed when he gets a court order."

"So what? He can't get around it."

Julia sat straighter in her seat. "What if he takes off, runs away?"

Cam shook his head. "I don't think he's a flight risk. No reason to be. He can never be retried for the crime."

"Pathetic," Julia muttered. "When this is all over, our illustrious district attorney should be recalled from office."

"If I was a voter in this district, you bet your ass I'd sign the petition," Ellen said.

Sometimes Julia cooked dinner for everyone. Though usually they ordered in. Thomas often worked late, came home tired, and avoided conversation about the case. He was much more interested in talking on the phone upstairs to his architect for his new Sun Valley clinic, scheduled — if all went well — to open sometime next winter. Cam figured the doctor was in a state of denial. Curiously,

151

the publicity hadn't hurt his practice; he seemed busier than any one man should be. In Cam's experience, whether guilty or not, the accused became a pariah. But not this dude. Too much of a local hero. Everyone adored him, wanted to rub elbows with the man who'd patched up the Broncos' star quarterback and God knows how many other celebs. None of that bothered Cam — none of his business — but watching Julia cater to him, fuss over him, when Innes barely noticed, made Cam's gut clench. Even if Innes wasn't constantly belittling his wife, the man still had an avuncular manner that grated on him. If someone were to ask his opinion, Cam would probably say the guy was an asshole. Which didn't make him a murderer, of course.

Julia . . . She was still working hard in the office, then came home to more work. She was looking thinner and more harried, and sometimes Cam wanted to tell her to take it easy. Wanted to catch her eye, elicit a smile, maybe lay a hand on her shoulder and tell her he and Ellen and Dennis had it all under control, and she should take some time off. Not that she would.

Ellen stood up and walked around the dining table, stepping over stacks of files.

"Once we get discovery," she was saying, "we go into high gear. Cam will reinterview every witness, okay. He will also arrange for the old evidence in the local cop shop to be sent to the CBI lab in Denver for testing. We can thank our lucky stars they kept this stuff.

"Along with the body fluids and bedsheets, there's the murder weapon, a fourteen-inch-tall jade Buddha that was covered in Samantha's type O positive blood and brain tissue. Samantha's finger-prints were on the Buddha, naturally. And there were all sorts of unidentified smudges. Even if Holman's prints are on the Buddha, it only proves he touched it, not that he killed Samantha. The cost of all that high-tech testing is prohibitive, so what we've decided is to go for DNA testing on the Buddha.

"If Holman cut himself, if his blood or body fluid is on the murder weapon, maybe the lab can match it. Then we have proof."

"Let's hope," Julia said.

Ellen glanced at her paralegal. "Dennis, you taking notes on all this?"

"Yes, Ms. Marshall . . . *Ellen*."

"Then there's the psychologist who in-terviewed Holman before the trial. We need his report, and Cam, you need to talk to him," Julia said.

Cam scribbled in his notebook. "Too bad the psychologist's testimony will never be allowed in this new trial."

"There might be a way to slip some of it in," Julia said. "Ellen? Any thoughts on that?"

Ellen smiled. "There's always a possibility, let me think on it. Dennis, make a note of that. Also, we're putting together a list of character witnesses for Thomas who are eager to give him references. They'll all have to be prepped for testimony, but that's in the future."

"What about Holman's former defense attorney?" Julia asked.

"Yes, Gary Ludlow. I know him. Good man. Cam, when you get back to Denver, you can talk to him. I'll call him and set it up."

Another note in his book.

He survived working with Ellen and Dennis during the day, but when Julia arrived home — no matter how early or late — despite her weariness, it was as if a dim room had suddenly been bathed in a soft glow of light. He tried not to dwell on that aspect of her, but it was hard. Some days just too damn hard. Then evening came, and with it the stress. Whatever tension there was in the house seemed to notch up the minute the good doctor came through the front door. Everyone made it a habit to tiptoe around him, because whenever the case was mentioned — which was constantly — Thomas Innes got real testy.

Yeah, an asshole.

Over Chinese take-out in the kitchen that night, Julia talked about her day at the office. "There was a young kid who stole nine bottles of water from the local community college. He was caught and returned the bottles. So there was no restitution issue," she said. "But McSwain wanted to go ahead with a theft charge anyway. I mean, nine bottles of water? We're busy enough as it is."

"McSwain's on a roll." Ellen stabbed at a chunk of twice-cooked pork as if stabbing her fork at McSwain.

"It's really difficult in the office," Julia went on. "Especially since I gave Bret my letter of resignation."

"You shouldn't set foot in that lousy place one more day," Thomas said in a pedantic manner.

Cam felt a spurt of anger. In one sentence Thomas destroyed his wife's calling, her self-worth, her pride. He tried to pic-

155

ture them in the bedroom together. Julia gentle and loving, doing her best to give Innes the support he needed during this trying time. But the man seemed too busy to give a shit.

Then Cam remembered just last night, when Innes had been going up to bed, and he'd grumbled loud enough to Julia for everyone to hear about how his house wasn't his own anymore, and he was sick and tired of coming home to all the long faces, and he could hardly wait till the whole thing was over. After her husband had climbed the stairs, Julia had come into the dining room to apologize to everyone. Ellen had put her friend's mind to rest and made light of it. Dennis had looked embarrassed, and said nothing, and Cam had stayed very still. Julia had gone to bed. Gone upstairs to share the bed with the asshole. And the same question that was beginning to haunt Cam flew into his head: Did they make love these days? Or were they both too tense and distracted?

The more he was around Julia, the harder it was to imagine why she stayed with the jerk.

"I'm not going to drop my cases, Thomas," Julia was saying over the Chinese take-out, her voice low, her tone that of a person who's repeated something too many times. "I have a responsibility to these people."

"What I mean," Thomas said, "is that you shouldn't have to put up with that garbage from McSwain. You don't have to."

Julia didn't reply. She kept her eyes downcast, her hands hidden in her lap like an averted glance. Cam had the urge to grab Innes by the shirt, jack him up against the wall, and tell him to fucking respect his wife.

Ellen went on as if nothing had transpired, but Cam was sure she'd noted Julia's reaction. "The next big thing is the motion for dismissal," Ellen said matter-of-factly. "I'm working on it, and I'll present it to the judge in a couple days."

"What's your basis?" Cam shifted his gaze from Julia to Ellen.

"The obvious, that another man was tried and convicted for the crime. And that the confession of Leann Cornish is tainted by her enmity against Dr. Innes."

"Amen," Thomas said.

"Now, don't get too excited. It's unlikely the judge will dismiss. Then we have another shot at the preliminary hearing. The state has to show probable cause for the case to come to trial. We have to show it doesn't exist. The preliminary hearing is scheduled for August first. So there's plenty of time."

"Do I have to attend this hearing?" Thomas asked.

"Absolutely."

He looked disgruntled, Cam thought. It was his life, for God's sake.

"And," Ellen went on, ignoring Thomas, "we've got word of a couple of defense witnesses from Holman's trial who testified to a fight between Samantha and Thomas. Public fights." She leveled her stare on Thomas. "Sorry, but they have to be interviewed again. McSwain will have spoken to them already, or he will soon, no doubt about it. Cam needs to talk to them. They're both locals. Dennis can give you their names, Cam."

Cam jotted down another note in his book.

"I know who you mean," Thomas said. "A couple of nobodies. One was a waitress or something."

"Will they be credible witnesses for the prosecution?" Ellen asked.

Thomas shrugged. "I don't know. The jury didn't pay them any mind in the last trial."

"But this time *you're* on trial, so what they say goes directly to your character.

Last time the defense was trying to suggest someone other then Matt Holman could have a motive. Apples and oranges, Thomas."

"Well, who doesn't have a fight with his wife?" Thomas asked.

"Which I will point out, naturally."

"I'm going upstairs. I have to call Sun Valley," Thomas said, his chair scraping on the wood floor.

Ellen looked put upon; Julia didn't eat another bite. Only Dennis, the skinny young kid, took seconds, even thirds.

Cam glanced from Innes to his wife and back, mentally shook his head — what the hell did she see in that guy? Had to be money and position. Had to be.

The phone rang, and Victor Ferris answered it, reaching across the plate of Pad Thai he'd ordered in for dinner.

"It's me."

"What's up?" He shoved the food aside, lit a cigarette.

Cam gave him an abbreviated version of the day's activities. "Nothing too interesting," he said at the end of the recital. "Except Innes is a jerk."

"Ah, but is he a murderer? Therein lies the rub, Sweet Prince."

"I think you got that line wrong," Cam said.

"So what? Poetic license."

"And I'm not sweet."

"Don't quibble. I'm really interested in this Leann Cornish. You'll tape the interview with her?"

"Yeah. When I do the interview."

"Surely you're going to interview her?"

"She's in, then out of the hospital right now. But, yes, eventually I'll get my interview."

"And Matt Holman. I can't wait to hear what he has to say. I want his every move, every expression."

"I haven't set it up yet. But trust me, I do know how to do an interview, Victor."

"You mean an interrogation," Victor said cheerfully.

"I'll have to fly to Phoenix," Cam said.

"So you will. You'll make it. Course, there's those air currents over the desert —"

"Stop right there."

"Found your Achilles' heel, did I?"

"First it's Shakespeare, now it's Homer."

"Don't avoid the subject. Face it like a man, my boy. You're scared to fly."

"Geez, Victor, you got me. I hate to fly 'cause I have control issues. You know, that macho thing. You satisfied?"

Jesus, there was a lot of paper to go through, Luke moaned inwardly. *Endless reams. The whole Beckett trial transcript.*

Then he had to make a list of witnesses from twelve years ago to re-interview. If he could find them. If they were still alive. If they'd talk to him.

Sitting at his desk in his cubbyhole at the department, he idly flipped through pages of the transcript, got to his own testimony, read it. *Not half bad,* he thought. *Pretty damn convincing.*

Yeah, he was good at what he did. He couldn't do a whole lot to make the world a better place, but he could catch the assholes.

This case . . . He'd found the murderer, put him away, and now he was supposed to prove that it wasn't the guy after all, but somebody else?

That somebody else being Dr. Beckett. A saint according to all reports. Friend, husband, doctor to the best of the best. And with a lovely wife — second wife, that was — who was also no slouch.

"I'm outta here," he finally told Davie, who was in the cubbyhole next to his. "Going to Alice's." A favorite cops' hangout. Run by an aging madam. Courtesan, she liked to call herself. Luke loved to flirt with her. Then again, so did all the cops. "You coming along?"

"Nah, wife'll kill me, man."

Wife, Luke thought, that was a problem. Not that Luke had that particular problem.

He pushed his chair back and stretched his arms over his head, heard his spine crack. Mrs. Beckett, what was her first name? Pretty lady, kind of old-fashioned looking. Smooth skin. He caught himself. She was someone's wife, for chrissakes.

"Don't go getting a DUI," Davie called to Luke.

"Hey," Luke called back, "there isn't a black-and-white in Denver that can catch my T-Bird."

"Huh," Davie said.

The bar was on Colorado Boulevard. Sat right in front of a big Target store, plenty of traffic out front. Plenty of women and kids. Luke figured the neighbors would love to see the place gone, but it had been here since the sixties and was nowhere near ready to shut down.

Some of the guys were already at Alice's. Wonderland, they called the place. Other than cigarette smoke, it had no atmosphere, only cheap drinks, couple pool tables, an electronic dartboard, a knockout female bartender, and waitresses with big tits.

Luke bought a pitcher of beer and sat down at a table with the usual suspects.

"Here he is, Mr. America," Dean from Vice said.

"Fuck off," Luke replied good-naturedly.

"What's with the Mike Hanson case? Did they really let Hanson out of jail? After all these years?" another cop asked.

Luke sighed. "Yeah, he's out on a writ of habeas corpus. Once they arrested Beckett, they had to let him go."

Another homicide dick. "I can't fuckin' believe it."

"I know." Luke shook his head.

"Beckett, isn't he the one who did that movie star?" Jack asked. "And that lady who keeps playing teen-agers even though she's forty if she's a day?"

"He did the mayor's wife, right?"

"I think he fucking did the mayor, too."

"He's supposed to be a good guy. Gives to charity, all that stuff," Dean said.

"What've they got on him?"

Luke took a long drink of beer. "What we got is a confession by a nurse who used to work with him. Says she saw him coming back into the hospital when he should've been getting ready for surgery. The nurse has terminal ovarian cancer, and she's gonna croak soon."

They threw ideas back and forth, got onto old stories, told some bad jokes, went through another couple of pitchers and several shots of whiskey.

Luke loved his job. He loved the male bonding, no matter how much the pundits ran the concept into the ground. He didn't love the endless

164

meetings in the department or its brutal politics, he detested the paperwork, but he loved the hunt — and the violence.

"I can't believe the DA would let a convicted murderer out of jail," Jack mused.

"Yeah, it's fucked up." Luke absently rubbed the scar over his eyebrow with a fist. "Hanson's been writing me ever since he got convicted, keeps insisting he didn't do it. You know, the two-dude defense."

"Yeah," Dean said, "some other dude did it."

"This nurse, she a good witness?"

Luke shrugged. "Guess the DA thinks so."

"Well, it'll be interesting," said the fat cop from Arson.

"It always is," Luke said.

"Why in hell would a guy like Beckett, a rich doctor, kill his wife?"

"Who knows? Maybe she was a real bitch."

"Still . . ." The fat cop laughed. "My wife's a real bitch, and I haven't killed her . . . yet."

Against his better judgment, Luke poured himself another glass of beer, leaned back, and thought about Mrs. Beckett. Her eyes were blue and wide-set, her hair that color of dark honey. Wavy, shiny. Her husband had been arrested and charged with a twelve-year-old murder. She must be out of her mind about that.

He wondered then if she had any doubts about the man she'd married. If there was any crack in her loyalty. She certainly knew about his first wife being murdered. Another thought ran through Luke's head — would the present Mrs. Beckett worry she might be the next victim? She had to at least consider the possibility no matter how remote.

Well, heck, he mused, maybe he'd just take a ride on over to the house, let the pretty lady know all she had to do was call him — Luke Diamond to the rescue.

He sat forward, grinning.

"What's so funny, Diamond?" one of the guys asked.

"Ah, just this fantasy I keep having."

"About a lady?"

"No way, man. I'm off women," Luke said, the grin spreading across his handsome features.

NINE

The Innes defense team had given the media nothing since Thomas's arrest back in April. Still, there were hangers-on, mostly rag-sheet reporters, who wouldn't take no for an answer and at the least opportunity ambushed anyone connected to the case.

Julia blamed her boss, Bret McSwain, who was delighted to be on camera or have his statements quoted nationally. He constantly posed for cameras, giving cheerful, optimistic waves of his hand even when just getting out of his car at his Glenwood Springs office. And he always had some tidbit, utterly irrelevant, for the press.

"He is such an ass," Julia said to Thomas one morning while they dressed for work. "If he would quit with the interviews, maybe the media would back off. Are you still getting hounded as much at the hospital?"

"Not quite as much," he said, standing at the bathroom mirror, shaving.

"Well, the pace will pick up the nearer we get to August."

"Oh? Why?"

She stopped buttoning her blouse, stared at him through the open bathroom door. "The preliminary hearing? You remember that."

"Right, right." Distracted as always.

"Thomas, sometimes I wonder, I really do."

"Wonder what?" He turned on the faucet in the sink.

"I wonder," she said, forced to raise her voice over the running water, "if you're really aware of how serious this is."

"Of course I am."

"You just seem so . . . so bored by it most of the time."

"What do you want me to do? Tear my hair out?"

"You could *show* some interest. I mean, everyone is working so hard, honey."

"And I'm not?"

"No. Not on the case. *Your* case."

"I don't think I like your tone," he said.

"Well, I'm sorry, but you give off an . . . unattractive, careless air about it."

He turned to face her. "That's just too damn bad, Julia. But I have to wonder why it is I get along so well with everyone at the clinic and hospital. Why it is I feel like a goddamn stranger, a *criminal,* for chrissakes, every time I walk through my own front door." He threw the towel on the bathroom floor, grabbed his jacket off the back of a chair, and brushed by her, practically slamming the bedroom door. She heard him bound down the steps and then his pleasant greeting to Ellen. "Hi, sleep well? . . . Good, got to run, busy day at the clinic." Then he was gone.

Julia just stood alone in their bedroom breathing deeply while counting slowly to ten.

Thomas's day was full. Often patients were scheduled ten minutes apart and shuffled from X ray to an exam room, where a physician's assistant talked to them and took notes before the doctor actually popped in to discuss their aches and pains while going over X rays and the PA's notes.

Thomas saw a dozen patients before noon that morning. Most were returns, three were new. One of the new patients was a woman who'd had a serious mountain bike accident, in Vail, her ankle crushed. She'd driven to Aspen to get a second opinion and discuss surgery.

Another new patient had torn an ACL, anterior cruciate ligament, while skiing that winter and was finally facing the reality his knee wasn't going to get better by itself. Trouble was, the older man had a deathly fear of clinics and hospitals. Thomas had to handle him carefully.

The last was a young man complaining of tenderness in his elbow. He said he was from out of town and golfed a lot and had heard Dr. Thomas Innes was *the* man to see. The PA examined him, X rays were taken, and then Thomas examined him. And couldn't find anything particularly wrong with the guy that a massage therapist couldn't fix, so Thomas figured he was a hypochondriac. They got plenty of those. All doctors did.

At dinner that evening Cam listened to Innes as he recounted the story of this particular patient. "The guy was . . . different, not the usual golf nut I get in the office. He even dressed differently, more like someone from the city," Thomas was saying. "Anyway, about halfway through my examination, he started asking all these questions. It took me a minute to catch on. It turned out the son of a bitch was from the *National Observer.*"

"Oh no," Julia said.

Cam had shifted his gaze to Julia. He noticed she was studying her husband with a serious expression that he had never seen on her face before. He couldn't quite read it. Disappointment? Repressed anger?

Ellen was shaking her head. "What did you do, Thomas?"

"I told him to leave. He wouldn't. So the assistant and I escorted him out."

"No violence?" Ellen asked.

"No, but I'll tell you, I wanted to kick his butt."

"Oh, Thomas," Julia said.

"Did he get enough for a story?" Ellen pressed.

"I doubt it. I told him he had tendonitis. Use ice and lay off golf for a week. Anti-inflammatories. He can put *that* in his rag sheet."

"Did you call the police?" Julia wanted to know.

"Yes, I called. They said if it happened again, they'd send someone over."

Cam cleared his throat. "Do you want me to check out a private security outfit? I believe there are several here in the valley."

"No, no," Thomas said. "I can handle it. The guy just caught me off-guard is all."

"Fine," Cam said.

The next morning Cam took his usual

run. It was a warm spring day for a change. The trees were starting to bud, robins clucked, the snow was receding on the mountainsides each day, and the grass was green. Spring green, that tender, succulent color of new growth. He had always liked spring; rebirth, new chances.

When he'd showered and dressed, driven to the Inneses' house, Dennis greeted him with a slip of paper.

"Hey, that lady called back. The one you've been trying to get hold of?"

"You mean Leann Cornish?"

"Yes, that's her. She wants you to call her."

"Okay. That's good." *Well, well, Leann. Finally.*

She wanted to see him the following morning, on a Saturday. Cam had been planning to return to Denver, spend time with Victor, take care of his own mail, and check in with his landlords, who were probably panicked he was not around right now. But this appointment with the Cornish woman was far too important, so the trip to Denver would have to wait.

That evening, when he told the group about the appointment, Julia said, "Oh, great, maybe I could ride down to Glenwood Springs with you and catch up on my errands while you see her. I have to get to Wal-Mart."

Cam didn't know what to say. Why didn't she ride down with her husband, take a short break from Aspen? Plus Cam worked alone, always alone. He muttered something, tried not to be rude.

Evidently whatever he said had not been enough to put Julia off. "Oh, I won't be in the way, like I said, you can drop me at Wal-Mart while you conduct the interview."

Cam glanced across the table at Thomas, who looked as if he couldn't care less what Julia's plans were. Cam said, "Sure, you can ride along. No problem."

Nevertheless, the following morning, while he waited out front in his Bronco, he was uncomfortable at the thought of all this time he was going to spend alone with Julia. Hell, he was good with women — loved 'em, liked their shapes and their smooth skin, their hair. Ankles — he liked trim ankles and satiny calves. He truly gloried in the differences between the sexes, and women could tell that about him, despite his bouts of long silence — or maybe because of them — regardless, he had no shortage of dalliances.

But Julia — a married woman. Not that

he hadn't had affairs with married women in the past. Married, but usually separated, that was. And Julia was most definitely not separated.

Aside from that, she was very different. She was totally committed to her husband. No hanky-panky. She didn't even look at Cam as if he were a male human being; he was merely a tool to help her husband. And it made Cam uneasy that while she barely registered his existence, he sure as hell noticed hers.

She appeared in blue jeans and a beige turtleneck sweater. A far cry from the tailored clothes she wore to work. She looked terrific, he couldn't help thinking, then he caught himself. *She's married, you sap, really married.*

Then he saw the dog, Blackie, tagging along behind her.

She opened the car door. "I hope it's okay, but can Blackie come along? Ellen is thinking of running into Denver for the night, and Dennis already left. Thomas is meeting with this local engineer, something about a structural problem with the Sun Valley clinic, and he wants a local opinion, and, well, there's no one to let the dog out." She smiled expectantly.

"Tell me he doesn't vomit in cars."

"Oh, my God, Cam, I'd never ask —"

"I'm kidding. Just kidding, Julia."

"Oh." She smiled again. "I guess I've lost my sense of humor lately."

"Happens," Cam allowed.

The drive to Glenwood Springs followed the Roaring Fork River for forty miles downstream, to where it emptied into the Colorado River. The road was a winding four-lane highway, built along the narrow valley floor, squeezed between mountains and the river.

The sun was shining, and as they descended, from the 8,000 feet of Aspen to the 5,000 feet of Glenwood Springs, the trees were more fully leafed out, the underbrush darker green, the grass taller, the air warmer.

Blackie fell asleep as they passed the Pitkin County Airport a few minutes outside of town, and Julia attempted to make conversation, trying not to be as reticent as Cam was. She asked him a few questions, seeming not to care that his replies were curt.

"So, how long have you lived in Denver?" she asked.

"Since I got out of school."

"Where did you go to school?"

"Colorado State."

"Oh, Fort Collins."

"I was raised there."

"Were your family ranchers?"

The question was logical, because Fort Collins used to be surrounded by ranch land. Not so much anymore, many of the ranchers having sold their acreage for subdivisions. "No, my parents weren't ranchers."

"Oh." She paused, then valiantly went on. "You still have family there?"

"My mother died years ago. My father died when I was a kid."

"I'm sorry."

He didn't answer. Only shrugged.

"So there's nobody? No brothers or sisters?"

"No. I have a stepfather."

"Is he in Fort Collins?"

He hesitated. "He moved to south Texas." That was all he said. He sure wasn't about to tell Julia that he hadn't talked to his stepfather in a decade. Had no intention of talking to him again, if Cam had his way.

Something in his voice must have cautioned her not to go further, because she was silent for a time. He drove past fields dotted with cattle and horses, then the valley narrowed, the four-lane on split levels, one perched on the hillside above the other.

"Amazing highway, isn't it?" she said. "It's brand-new, cost a fortune. I'm sure it wasn't here when you were in Aspen before."

"No, it wasn't."

"Well, they certainly did a nice job."

"Yes."

"Actually, they were just beginning the highway when I first moved to Aspen, eight years ago."

"Uh-huh."

"When I was in law school, I used to come and visit Thomas as often as I could. We didn't get married until after I'd passed the bar."

"You met Thomas in Denver?"

"Yes, would you believe I waited on him when he had lunch at the restaurant where I worked?" She gave a little laugh.

He never should have asked about Thomas; the subject was like picking at a scab.

"We just hit it off, you know?"

No, he'd never be able to see what there was in the man that attracted her. He made a noncommittal reply, then said, "Where are you from, originally? Denver?" He'd talk about anything but Innes at this point.

"Would you believe Iowa?"

"That so."

"My family owned a farm there. Corn, you know. But business got really terrible, so many small farms being squeezed out by the big guys, and my folks lost the place to the bank. I was young, but I remember. It was pretty traumatic. So we moved into town, a little place you've never heard of, and my dad worked in the local John Deere dealership. My mom did books for some businesses. We were really poor."

He steered around the long curve that led out of the narrow canyon, stopped at a red light at the Old Snowmass intersection. Poor, she'd been poor. He never would have guessed that.

"But you went to law school, Denver University." He was curious now.

"I got a scholarship." She hesitated for a moment, and he thought she might be a little embarrassed. "I was valedictorian of my high school class. Well, it wasn't a very big school. But I was, you know, one of those classic overachievers."

He shot her a sidelong glance, and he could have sworn she blushed. She smiled at him, a little ruefully maybe, a little abashed. A charming, innocent smile that made something inside him shift.

"The light's green," she said.

He was beginning to get it now — her

178

devotion to the asshole she'd married. It was all about money. What else could it be? Yeah, money and position, that's what he'd failed to see. Okay, he felt a little better now.

"Do you follow any particular procedure when you conduct an interview, or do you just wing it?" she was asking.

He had to think for a second. Yeah, Julia was referring to his upcoming appointment with Leann Cornish. "I did a lot of interrogations as a cop. Interviews, interrogations, call them what you want. All the same."

"Ellen prepped you."

"Some. But I know my job."

"I didn't mean —"

"It's okay. I get it. You're wondering if I'll know when Leann's being straight and when she's lying."

"Yes," she said in a careful voice.

He shot her another glance, then put his focus back on the road. "I'll know," he said.

She gave him directions to the street where the Cornish woman lived, then got out at Wal-Mart. Blackie stayed with him.

"Do you think you could, ah, park in the shade?" she asked.

"Don't worry, Julia, I'll find some shade for Blackie."

179

"I'll bring him a bottle of water from inside when you get back. Just call me on my cell and I'll be out front."

"See you."

"See you in a while," she said, shutting the door, glancing in the back at Blackie, then waving goodbye to Cam.

Christ, he felt like an old married man.

Glenwood Springs was a tidy resort town founded in the 1880s when the railroad was completed and people flocked in droves to the West, this particular town attracting them because of its world-famous hot springs and world-class hotel. Leann lived on the near side of the Colorado River, across from the Hot Springs, close to the downtown shopping area. Her place was a small, neat clapboard house with a deep front porch, in a line of similar houses on Second Street, one block off Grand Avenue. Parked on the street out front beneath a huge willow — Blackie took a look, seemed satisfied, shifted positions, and went back to his nap — Cam took a minute to check his handheld tape recorder, made sure he had two spare cassettes with him. He didn't think the interview would take that long, but he always went in prepared. Besides, she'd said her lawyer would be present, and Cam had no intention of slipping up in front of a goddamn attorney.

He'd searched his memory, trying to recall Leann from his notes twelve years ago, a brief statement he'd taken, one of several that had established Thomas Innes's alibi. But he hadn't been able to put a face to the police file.

Leann came to the door, and he knew he wouldn't have recognized her in any case. He'd been prepared for an ill woman, but even so, her condition set him back. Gaunt, a grayish cast to her skin, pale fuzz for hair, just growing in from chemotherapy. She wore baggy black pants and a white turtleneck under a green fleece jacket. He was sure all her clothes were baggy, and she probably felt cold a lot of the time, thin as she was.

"Mr. Lazlo?" she said.

He nodded. "Ms. Cornish."

"Please, come in. This is my attorney, Steve Larkin."

"Mr. Larkin." Cam nodded again, held out his hand to a solid, bald man with a short gray beard.

"Call me Steve."

"And I'm Cam."

"I assume you read Leann's statement?" the lawyer said.

"I have."

"I'm basically here for moral support," Steve said. "Leann can speak for herself."

She could only have been in her mid-forties, Cam thought, not much older than he. She must've been an attractive woman once. Very fine features, big dark eyes. Emaciated, but good bones under paper-thin olive skin. Poor soul.

They settled in her living room, Cam in a comfortable chair across from Leann and her attorney, who were seated on the couch. Cam asked permission to tape the interview, then set up his recorder on the coffee table, aware that Leann was staring at him intently.

"I *knew* your name sounded familiar," she finally said. "You were a policeman, right? You interviewed me when Matt Holman was arrested?"

"Good memory."

"I'm not likely to forget that," she said solemnly. "I lied to you. To everyone."

Not yet ready to begin taping, Cam checked the first cassette while idly commenting on a few photographs on a bookshelf behind the couch.

"Those are my children," Leann told him. "Marcy and Brian."

"Nice-looking kids. They live around here?"

"Not far. Marcy's in Rifle and Brian lives in Denver."

"You don't seem old enough to have kids that age."

"I look like a hag. I look a hundred years old," she said, straightforward.

For lack of anything else to say, he said, "You look fine."

"Mr. Lazlo, Cam, you don't have to sweet-talk me. All I'm trying to do is right a terrible wrong that was committed years ago."

He thought he detected a bitter edge in her voice, wished he'd had the recorder going so he could listen to it later. He said, "Do you mind if I switch this on now, Ms. Cornish?"

"Sure, go on."

Cam started the tape, spoke the date, the time, the place, and the parties participating in the interview into the little machine, and he asked, for the record, if everyone was aware that the interview was being recorded. They were.

Cam went straight to the pertinent questions. "Leann, I'd like to know why you waited so long to come forward with your statement concerning Dr. Thomas Innes."

"Mr. Lazlo, *Cam*, I'm dying. They gave me a year at the most. The cancer has metastasized; it's all over me. I have nothing to lose now, so I want the truth to be told."

"Can you tell me what happened that morning of May eighth twelve years ago at the Aspen Valley Hospital?"

She bowed her head, stared at her hands, which were clasped tightly in her lap. "It was a sunny day," she reflected, then seemed to collect herself and got down to the facts. "Thomas, Dr. Innes, that is, had a full day of surgeries. I was the senior OR nurse at the time, so I knew his schedule. Normally I didn't keep track of what he did between surgeries, you know, while we prepped the patient. But that afternoon, around one, I think, I needed to ask him something, and I couldn't find him. I searched all over the hospital. I figured he must've gone to the bathroom, but finally I saw him through one of the windows at the rear of the hospital."

"And the windows face in what direction?"

"Oh, I don't know exactly. The west?"

"That's all right. And then what happened?"

"Anyway, I saw him walking back from the Meadowood subdivision, where he was living at the time."

"So, Dr. Innes lived within walking distance of the hospital?"

"Yes. Well, if you were in a car and driving to the hospital from his house, it's not that close. But there's a footpath behind the hospital that leads over a small hill and right into the subdivision."

"And do you know approximately how long it would take to walk from the hospital to the doctor's former house?"

"Oh, my, five minutes, eight minutes? It's not very far."

"You saw him walking from the direction of the Meadowood subdivision toward the hospital, and then?"

"At the time I didn't think much of it. As I said, it was a nice day. I assumed he'd gone home for a few minutes, oh, I don't know, to see his wife or grab some lunch. Anyway, I went out back when I saw him and got the information I needed. It was about a drug allergy his next patient had forgotten to mention earlier. Anyway, while we were talking, I noticed a cut on the doctor's hand. He saw me looking at it, and he said he'd just been outside getting some fresh air, and he stumbled and cut himself on a sharp rock. He said he'd put a Band-Aid on it.

"Of course, at the time, I didn't think

185

much about it. But then a few minutes later in surgery, I noticed he was preoccupied. Not at all himself. He's usually so cool under pressure. But that day he was, I don't know, nervous and even short with the nurses. He was also sweating a lot, too. I remember that, because at one point I mopped his brow for him."

"Let's back up a minute. You're positive you saw the doctor coming along the foot trail from the Meadowood subdivision to the hospital?"

"Obviously I didn't see him the whole time he was on the trail, but he was definitely coming down this little slope from the direction of his house on the foot trail."

"Okay. I'd like to talk more about what went on in surgery after the doctor allegedly left the hospital and returned. You stated the doctor was nervous. Did he make any mistakes during this surgery?"

"No, not that I noticed."

"Did anyone else in the operating room comment at any point about the doctor's agitation?"

"I can't remember after all this time, but I'm sure everyone in the OR was aware of Dr. Innes not being himself."

"Let's move on. When did you first hear that Samantha had been murdered?"

186

"Oh, my gosh, it was that afternoon. The entire staff was in shock. Evidently one of Samantha's girlfriends who'd picked up Livie and her own daughter at school that afternoon discovered her body."

"When the news circulated around the hospital, was Dr. Innes still there?"

"Yes, I believe he was in the doctor's lounge when a policeman found him."

"Okay. When you first heard about Samantha, did you immediately recall that you had been unable to locate the doctor that morning in the hospital?"

"I didn't think of it immediately."

"When did you first think about it?"

"That evening. I'll never forget it. I suddenly remembered seeing the doctor coming down the foot trail, and I remembered the cut on his hand. It had gotten out that Samantha had been killed by a blow to the head with a Buddha statue, and I knew . . . I just knew." She shook her head sadly. "I didn't know what to do at the time, and the police, well, even you, Mr. Lazlo, never even looked at Thomas, Dr. Innes that is, because everyone in the hospital including me had stated the doctor was there all day in surgery. And it was the very next morning when we all heard, everyone in town heard, that

Samantha had a lover and he'd been with her and the police arrested him. Matt Holman. Of course Holman kept saying he was innocent, but in my heart I simply couldn't believe the doctor would have harmed his wife. For a long time I *wanted* to believe Matt Holman was guilty. Now I know I was in denial."

"So just when, exactly, did you come to the decision that Dr. Thomas Innes killed his wife?"

"I guess I finally admitted it to myself during Matt Holman's trial. Dr. Innes testified he'd been at the hospital all day, and he never came forward with the information that he had been at his house. I think I expected him to tell the truth under oath. But he didn't. He flat out lied. There was only one explanation for that — it was Dr. Innes who killed his wife, not Matt Holman."

"So, you lied to the police right along with the doctor. Even though, in your opinion, Dr. Innes was guilty of the crime, you stayed silent as to what you saw?"

"God forgive me, yes," she whispered. "I was in awe of him, of the doctor, you understand? We all were. He was doing procedures we'd never seen before. He was practically a miracle worker in our eyes. He had a beautiful wife and a darling little daughter. I didn't know his marriage was on the rocks. None of us at the hospital did. He never brought his problems to work."

"So you lived with your beliefs for twelve years."

"I've lived with the knowledge of what Dr. Innes did, yes, and there hasn't been a day or an hour or a minute that I haven't suffered."

"All right, I'd like to ask about the circumstances of you leaving your job last year."

"Mr. Lazlo, Cam, I know what you're thinking, that I went to the district attorney and made this statement as some sort of revenge against Thomas Innes. But that just isn't so. I should have taken a leave of absence from the hospital, because I was screwing up. It was no one's fault but my own. I blame myself, not Dr. Innes, not the board of directors or the hospital administrator or my co-workers, just myself."

"So you're telling me, you harbor no ill will toward Dr. Innes or anyone else at the hospital?"

"That's what I'm telling you."

"You realize that may be hard for a jury to swallow?" Cam asked.

Steve Larkin leaned forward. "Leann, you don't have to answer that."

"Sorry, rhetorical question," Cam said.

"Mr. Lazlo, I want you to understand, I'm doing this to set the record straight. It's what I have to do."

"Leann," Larkin said then, "do you need to rest?"

"No, Steve, honestly. I'd like to get this over with."

"All right," Cam said, "according to your statement, according to your beliefs, the doctor has been aware all these years that you witnessed him returning from his home the morning his wife was killed, you saw the cut on his hand, you were aware that he lied to the police then, and later he'd lied on the witness stand at Matt Holman's trial. You've been of the opinion that for twelve years Dr. Innes has known about your beliefs —"

"Oh, yes, he's known. You bet he has. And I won't lie, not anymore, I think when I started messing up at work last year, he was damn glad to see me go."

"This, of course, is your opinion. The doctor never said as much to you, did he?"

"God, no. For twelve years he's avoided me like the plague."

"I see. And was anyone else aware of this at the hospital?"

"I really can't say. I never talked to a soul about it. And all I'm saying is that in my opinion he was relieved to see me go. Can't blame him for that," she said, the edge back in her voice.

"And you hold no grudge against him?"

"No grudge? I've lived with this terrible secret all these years because of him. For that, Mr. Lazlo, I detest him, that and the fact that he murdered Samantha and allowed another man to go to jail for his crime. If you want to call that a grudge, then, yes, it is."

"Okay," Cam said.

He wound the interview up shortly after that, shook hands with Leann and Larkin, thanked them for their time, and said he'd have a typed transcript of the interview mailed to both of them.

Out front he checked on Blackie, who was snoozing away, and called Julia on her cell phone. "I'll be there to pick you up in, say, five minutes? You ready?"

"Yes, but how did the interview — ?"

"I'll tell you when I get there. Hey, you want me to stop at this little park down the street, let the dog out for a minute?"

"Oh, you don't mind?"

"Not a bit."

"He went this morning, so you won't

need a plastic bag or anything."

"Thanks for the info," Cam said, "but it's more than I needed to know. See you in around ten minutes, then."

"I'll be waiting," she said and they both clicked off.

At the park Cam walked the dog and thought about Leann. Ellen, everyone on the defense team, for that matter, was going to want a blow-by-blow of how the woman came off. They'd listen to the recording, of course, over and over, but they hadn't seen her body language, her facial expressions. He needed to think about that, think hard on exactly what he was going to tell them.

Julia was waiting outside the door of Wal-Mart. She had two large bags that she put into the backseat of the Bronco. After giving Blackie a big hug and scratching his tattered ears, she got into the passenger seat and closed the door.

"Thank you so much for watching Blackie," she said. "Well? How *did* it go?"

"Interesting woman. Very sick. Sicker than I expected."

"I mean, how did you find her, bitter, angry?"

"I wouldn't call her bitter, but she's hurting. Of course, she could be close to

192

death, but, and you might not like this, I found her pretty convincing."

He was instantly sorry he'd told Julia that, because her expression altered from expectant to troubled. "Convincing? But I —"

"Look, you can listen to the tape and decide for yourself."

"But if your impression . . . if you . . ."

"Hey, I'm a wuss when it comes to sickness, stuff like that. If I saw Hitler in as bad shape as Leann Cornish, I'd feel sorry for him."

"I'm not sure how to read what you're telling me."

"Like I said, listen to the tape."

Neither of them talked much on the way home. Julia sat very quietly, her brow furrowed. It was late afternoon; commuter traffic leaving Aspen was heavy, as usual, but they were traveling against it, so he made good time.

And as he drove he went over the interview with Leann in his mind. Over and over it. Her thin, pale face with the big dark eyes that held all the energy of the woman's dying body. She was hurting, and she admitted holding a grudge against Thomas Innes, but her words rang of the truth.

Could he have been wrong about everything? About Holman and Innes? Could the doctor be a murderer? He felt the facts morphing, moving, realigning themselves in his brain. Like muscles contracting in your body. Rearranging themselves to shoot a basket, say, instead of tackle an opponent.

Mental muscles. Focused now on Innes, not Holman. He knew at that moment, as he drove past the turnoff to Carbondale, Mount Sopris rising like a behemoth on the right, that he had to search out the truth, no matter who the hell got hurt. His job, even now that he was no longer part of the brotherhood of the badge, was to be the advocate of the dead.

They must have been twenty miles up the valley, when Julia finally turned to him. "Tell me, honestly, did you really believe Leann?" she asked, her voice halting.

"Hey, lots of people are really great liars," he said.

Like me, he thought, wondering at his reluctance to truly level with her.

TEN

"I can't do it, Barb," Julia said.

"What?"

"I can't do that getaway this year."

"But, God, Julia, you need it more than you ever have."

They were discussing the annual girls' getaway, a weekend at a Santa Fe spa, put together by her ski buddy Barb through the travel agency where she worked.

"I know, but I can't. There's just too much going on."

It was mid-May, a gray cold day, the kind that descended on Aspen's high alpine valley in the spring, claustrophobic and depressing after a spate of warm sunny weather. Julia and Barb were having lunch at the Wienerstube, practically an Aspen institution, good food, Swiss Alpine décor, with a giant skylight set high in the middle of the ceiling, a jumble of overgrown plants beneath it. The Wienerstube boasted the "joiners table," where anyone who came in alone could sit, usually along with a half-dozen of their old friends.

"Look, I feel guilty even having lunch with you. I have so much to finish up at work, and then I get home and Ellen has more for me to do."

Barb, a small, curvaceous dark-haired lady, cocked her head and studied her friend for a minute. "Is it the money?"

Julia almost laughed. All her friends knew she insisted on paying half the bills at home and was frugal to the point of obsession. The whole town knew she drove Thomas crazy with her penny-pinching, but she couldn't help it. She'd never outgrow the fear of being poor.

"No, it isn't finances, not this time," she said.

"You sure?"

"For once, honest to God, it has nothing to do with money. I can't leave Thomas now, and even if I could, I'd never be able to relax at the spa anyway. I'd be on the phone every two seconds. I wouldn't be any fun."

"But think of the massages, the facials, the time to relax."

"Ha, relax. Today's the first social outing I've had since his arrest. My personal life is nonexistent."

Barb reached out and patted Julia's

hand. "I wish you'd come. So do the other girls."

Julia felt tears sting behind her eyelids. She so badly wanted to join them, had been looking forward to the three-day holiday at the Bishop's Lodge all winter — until the last day of the ski season, that was. She had a weak moment then and darn near said what the hell, of course she'd go. Ellen could handle the case for a few days. Then she thought about her husband, thought about the torment he had to be suffering even though he hid his innermost fears so well from everyone — including her, especially her. Now, more than ever, she couldn't abandon him even for a brief respite.

"The trip would be so good for you," Barb was saying.

Julia looked up, focused on her friend's face. "I know, Barb. But I can't," she said.

She walked the three blocks back to work after lunch. Thinking about her cases. There was the woman who'd broken into her ex-boyfriend's house and was punched out by him. Who exactly should face punishment here? Who was the aggressor?

There were the "domestics," any crimes related to assaults in the home or between cohabitants. Third-degree assault being the most common.

Drunk driving, public fighting, smoking dope in public, shoplifting, the mundane plethora of petty offenses one person could commit against another. With Julia as the facilitator, negotiator, sometimes the unofficial judge and jury.

And one case in particular, which she was very concerned about. A lady named Dana Stern had been arrested for DUI. The arresting officer had noticed her car weaving, had flashed her over, given her a sobriety test, which she'd flunked, and arrested her.

The blood test came up negative for alcohol, but positive for several prescription medications, among them Percocet, Ativan, and Celexa.

Dana needed counseling, not jail time. Julia was going to recommend a suspended sentence for the woman, random drug testing if the judge insisted. Community service, possibly, but not incarceration.

It was sometimes ironic that Julia, who represented the people — in other words the prosecution — would attempt to alleviate the punishment of people brought before the county court judge. Often these defendants had no legal representation, so she dealt with them directly, as in Dana's case.

A public defender, from the District Court in Glenwood Springs, came to Aspen once a week, but he usually did not even bother with Julia's cases, instead concentrating on the higher-profile ones.

So it fell to Julia to play both prosecutor and defender, consider both sides of her cases, to make value judgments about what was right and what was wrong. What punishment was fair and reasonable. Basically, what she did was dispense justice. Which was the one reason she wished she could keep working. The system needed people like her, the small cogs that kept the machinery running. But she had to quit, and she only had a short time to go.

Very few people arrested in Aspen, a tiny percentage, ever came to trial. Most cases were plea-bargained or settled out of court or just plain dismissed. But Dana Stern was scheduled to come before Judge Ralston this afternoon, and Julia was worried.

Dana was already waiting for her when she got back from lunch. The woman was a nervous wreck, but she'd remembered to dress as Julia had suggested, in a skirt and a blouse and a blazer, not much makeup, her short hair brushed back from her face.

She was fifty-five, a divorcée, and she'd been trying to pull her life together. She'd said more than once that her arrest might have been the best thing that ever happened to her. That remained to be seen, of course.

The county court sat on the third floor of the Pitkin County Courthouse, on the opposite end of the long hall from the elegant district courtroom where the big cases were tried. All of Julia's cases were heard in the smaller courtroom, a simple no-nonsense room with hard wooden chairs and plain long wooden tables sitting in front of the judge's bench. All small claims were heard in this room; protests against traffic violations, most DUI cases, a lot of the domestic violence cases. People spoke for themselves before the judge, and seldom were lawyers involved at this level. Except for Julia as the DDA, who acted in all legal capacities for the accused.

When her case number was called by the judge, which turned out to be the last case of the day, she presented the charges and evidence against Dana Stern, the blood test results, the arrest for DUI. The judge then spoke directly to Dana, asked her a few questions, not the least of which was her opinion of her own guilt or innocence.

Dana admitted her guilt. A good move under the circumstances, one that Julia had advised. The judge then gave Dana a serious lecture over the gravity of her actions.

When Julia saw that he was done, she rose and asked to speak a few words in behalf of the accused. "Your Honor, I would like to ask for leniency in the case of Ms. Stern, as she has been attending group therapy for drug addiction and has been drug-free for six months now. I believe some combination of community service and drug testing would be most appropriate."

"I'll take your recommendation under advisement, Mrs. Innes," Judge Ralston said. He pinioned Dana with a glare, his bushy white brows drawn. "Ms. Stern, do I have your solemn promise that you will prove Mrs. Innes justified in placing her faith in you?"

"Yes, Your Honor," Dana said, her voice halting.

"At the very least, you'll be required to do community service."

"I'll be glad to, Your Honor."

"All right, you'll have my ruling on this case" — he looked down at his calendar — "CC 409, by three p.m. tomorrow. Court dismissed."

Bang went his gavel.

Dana looked stunned, afraid to hope, unsure. "What does that mean?" she whispered to Julia while the judge gathered his files and disappeared into chambers.

"I think he'll go along with my recommendation."

"You do?"

"I think so."

"Oh, oh, I hope . . ." Dana's voice caught on a sob. "Thank you so much, Julia. I know you could have thrown the book at me. Thank you."

"Just make sure you don't get yourself mixed up with drugs again, Dana. That's all I ask of you."

"I won't, I swear. You know I won't." Then she put her arms around Julia right there in the courtroom and hugged her.

Phew. Dana gone, Julia leaned over the table and started gathering file folders. The hearing hadn't taken long; she could go home now. Go home and face a list of phone calls or motions to be drawn up or . . .

"Julia?"

She whirled around. She thought she'd been alone.

"Oh," she said. It was Cam, sitting at the very back of the room. "What are you doing here?"

"Sorry if I startled you."

"Oh, that's okay."

"I was looking something up in the county clerk's office, thought I'd stop by."

She stuffed the files in her briefcase. "Curious?" she asked.

"Maybe." He stood up, stretched his neck, and strode toward her.

"Well, that wasn't much of a case, but then, most of mine aren't. The assistant DA and Bret hog all the felonies."

"No, it was good."

"The case?"

"I mean the way you handled it."

"Oh . . . Dana. I thought it was silly for her to go to jail, cost the taxpayers money when she's just a screwed-up divorcée."

"But you could have come down a lot harder on her."

"I could have. Which would have been counterproductive."

He was standing next to her now, quite close, and she caught the slightest whiff of some sort of aftershave. Nice, masculine. And she suddenly recalled the moment when she'd first seen him at her door, her instant physical reaction.

"Are all your cases like this?" he was asking.

"No. They're all different. I get DUIs,

drug possession, but only pot and then only less than an ounce. I get domestics, and disorderly conduct, petty theft. You know." She picked up her briefcase, held it to her chest.

"Yeah, I know."

"You didn't have anything to do with these kinds of cases when you were a detective, did you?"

"No."

"Well" — she smiled and headed out of the courtroom — "I guess somebody has to do it."

"Yeah, I guess." He followed her down the broad staircase to the first floor, where her office was located near the front door to the courthouse.

"How often are you in court?" he asked.

"Only once a week. The rest of the time I'm preparing, calling defendants and witnesses, looking up case law, the usual. But Dana, well, she was my last case. I'm retired as of Friday."

He nodded. "Need a ride home?"

She usually walked. Maybe a ride would be wise, though. The day was still gray and threatening rain now. A ride in his black Bronco. She hesitated a minute, and she looked at him standing there, tall and slim in a pale blue polo shirt and khakis, his hair very gold in the dimly lit hall, hitting his shirt collar in back and curling up a little, the ice-blue eyes that were paradoxically both keen and cryptic.

He'd come to see her in court.

Then she smiled again, a pleasant, generic, social smile, and she said, "Thanks, but actually I'd rather walk."

"Okay."

"You going back right now?" she asked.

"Uh-huh."

"Tell Ellen I'll be there in about an hour."

"Sure."

His lip curled up into the semblance of a smile, then he gave her a casual goodbye salute with two fingers to his forehead and disappeared into the gray, blustery day.

She plumped into the rickety swivel chair behind her desk. So much still to do before Friday. All these case files to be sorted and refiled, a few to go to a fellow DDA for follow-up. Would she ever be in this office again?

Maybe Thomas's case wouldn't even get beyond the preliminary hearing. Then would Bret hire her back on? Would she even *want* to work for him?

Cameron Lazlo had come to see her in court. Her skin was still tingly. Soon she'd be at home working all day with Ellen. *He* was there so much. In and out of the house. There more than her own husband.

She tapped a pen against her teeth, wondering if her girlish infatuation would diminish in time. Probably. Definitely.

Her gaze came to rest on a corner of a note sticking out from a page on her desk calendar.

She sat forward, took the note out, and read: Former dietitian AVH Rick Krystal.

Her brow furrowed. What on earth . . . ? A dietitian from Aspen Valley Hospital. Rick Krystal. She couldn't begin to fathom the cryptic note, much less who would have stuck it in her calendar. The writing was vaguely familiar, but more important, what did it mean?

Aspen Valley Hospital. Did this have something to do with Thomas's case?

She thought about it for another minute, then put the note in her purse. And then, instead of sorting files, she sat and listened to the sleet begin to spatter on the windowpanes and shamefully daydreamed about Cam.

Ellen tried very hard to make room for Mason in her life. But with him in Washington half the time and her in Aspen the other half, it wasn't easy.

They finally both had a day when they were home in Denver at the same time. A Saturday. So they made plans — dinner at the Buckhorn Exchange, then home to bed. Ellen's bed, because her house on Race Street was much nicer than his condo.

She dressed carefully in black silk pants — she hardly ever wore skirts except in court, they made her look too short — a pale blue short-sleeved blouse with a V-neck, and a raw-silk tweed blazer.

Mason picked her up, a proper gentleman, in his Mercedes.

"Hi, honey," she said, leaning over to kiss him. "How was your flight?"

"The usual, you know. Mostly I work."

"When do you go back?"

"Tuesday."

"What a crazy life," she said, shaking her head.

They had a wonderful dinner, the popular Denver restaurant a fantasy in dark old Wild West décor, bison, elk, antelope, and deer heads cluttering the walls. Cozy. A wonderful Cabernet Sauvignon that Mason ordered without even consulting the wine steward.

"How's the case going?" he asked over dessert. There was only one *case*.

"Oh, it's early times still. Nothing really firm yet. I'm still feeling out the DA's strategy."

"He any good?"

"McSwain? Time will tell. He's got some promising witnesses."

"Could you lose this one?"

"No way. Thomas didn't kill anybody."

"Which doesn't rule out a guilty verdict."

"Of course not. But he has me. When Julia called, I knew I could do the job. Believe me, if I thought anyone else at the firm could do better, I would have told her. But Thomas needs me. Partly, I must admit, because I'm a woman. Invalid logic, sure, but the fact that a woman is defending him makes people believe he couldn't have hurt another female, or no lady lawyer would take him on."

"Always an angle, that's my Little Ellen."

"You know I hate that name."

"But you *are* little."

"Mason."

"I love you the way you are."

"Let's go home," she purred.

"Hey, I haven't finished my coffee. And I want another cognac. Take it easy."

"Mason, come on, I have to get up early tomorrow and drive back to Aspen."

She knew the minute the words were out of her mouth she shouldn't have said them. He got tense in his shoulders and his head. His dark eyes narrowed in that too-familiar way.

He leaned forward. "Give me a goddamn minute to relax, will you?" he hissed.

She almost cried. Things had been going so well, and now, because of her big mouth, he was uptight. The mood was spoiled. She'd done it again.

"I'm sorry," she said softly. "Take your time."

But he would not be mollified. He drove her home without a word and dropped her off in her driveway. Didn't even kiss her that night.

In Denver for a few hurried days, Cam had a mountain of catch-up work. First and foremost was his employer. He spent most of Saturday morning with Victor, expanding on the notes he'd taken in Aspen. Then Victor popped up off the couch and disappeared into his office without so much as a "see you later" or "good job." Presumably, he was already composing a new scene in his head.

Cam took off for home, where he caught up on bills and spent time with his landlords. They were used to his frequent absences when he was on assignment for Victor. But usually he was only gone for a couple days tops. This assignment was unique. He was in Aspen a lot more than Denver, and would be for months. Half a year if Innes was held over for trial after the preliminary hearing — which wasn't even scheduled till August.

"We'll just have to get along," Fred said. "Your work comes first."

Irene, who was dusting in the bookstore, wasn't as comfortable with the situation. "Oh, gosh, Cam, I feel so much better when I know you're here."

So he arranged to have one of his cop buddies put the bookstore on regular nightly drive-by. The arrangement was going to cost Cam a bundle — Monday night pitchers of beer for a year at McSorell's Pub. Monday night being boys' night out. The get-together had begun for football and now went year-round.

"Even if you're not at the pub, Lazlo," homicide detective Morris said on the phone, "you owe. First two pitchers. For a year."

"You drive a hard bargain," Cam said.

"Yeah, well, I'm the one who's gotta schedule drive-bys for your landlords, and it's gonna take some finagling."

"Okay, okay," Cam said.

"Beginning this Monday at McSorell's. You going to be around?"

"Oh, absolutely."

That night he got together with Kayla and explained the situation. "I don't know how long I'm going to be in Aspen. Months, anyway."

"But you'll be in Denver on weekends, won't you?"

"I just don't know," he said, not entirely lying.

They made love at his place. The sex was good, and he was able to sleep a little. But Kayla awakened early and over coffee began asking him about the Inneses and Aspen and would the case really go to trial and did Cam think the doctor was guilty?

He didn't want to discuss the case. Hell, he'd rather make love again. But Kayla persisted with the interrogation until he finally showered and dressed and drove her home with the excuse that he had an interview to conduct that morning.

"On Sunday?" Kayla asked.

"Only time I could get with the guy," Cam said — the interview was actually twenty-four hours away.

Monday looked to be hectic. The day

was scheduled to begin with an appointment with Gary Ludlow, Matt Holman's defense attorney from twelve years ago. Then Cam was planning to drive down to Canon City, talk to a couple of inmates at the state prison, Holman's former roomies. Julia was still trying to locate the psychologist who'd interviewed Holman for his trial, but apparently the man had retired and moved out of state.

"Well," Julia had said, "he's not crucial. He might even be detrimental to our case. I'll keep looking, though. Got to cover all bases."

That was Julia, killing herself working, covering every detail. She never forgot anything, a name, a date, an address. She was a superb foil to Ellen, who was a criminal defense expert and knew her way around a courtroom the way Cam knew his way around a crime scene. But Ellen wasn't great on details or the day-by-day tedious labor the way Julia was.

And here *he* was, busting his balls to get Innes off when he wasn't even sure the guy deserved getting off. Christ, Innes deserved to go to jail for the way he treated Julia, if nothing else.

Well, he'd signed on for the long haul, and he'd go the distance. Besides, Victor would crucify him if he quit.

He had planned one last stop on his way back to Denver from the prison — the Broadmoor resort hotel in Colorado Springs. With the help of Julia, who'd gotten the former hospital dietitian's Social Security number, Cam had located the man named on the cryptic note left on her desk. Apparently he worked at the resort, had worked there for years. Thing was, no one recalled this Rick Krystal, not even Thomas, and what this dietitian had to do with the case remained a puzzle.

But he'd worry about Krystal later — first stop was Gary Ludlow, the defense attorney.

Cam dressed in a white linen shirt, gray flannel slacks, and tweed sport coat. Drove into downtown Denver and found a parking place, no easy task.

Gary Ludlow's office was located in a high-rise, the so-called "electric razor" building because of its shape. Ludlow was tall and a little stooped, sixtyish. Cam remembered him from Holman's trial, remembered being cross-examined by the attorney.

His office was cushy, as was his firm. Ludlow had done well for himself. "Sure, I remember you," Ludlow said, shaking

Cam's hand. "So you're in private practice now."

They chatted, then got down to business.

"You know, I always believed Matt was innocent. I was really pleased when I heard he'd been released."

All defense attorneys said that. "But the evidence . . ."

"Purely circumstantial."

"Solid, though," Cam had to point out.

"It was a bad call," Ludlow said, shaking his head. "I wish I'd never taken the case. It kind of tarnished the legal system in my eyes."

"The legal system has never been perfect."

"Far from it. But I'll tell you, when you know a client is innocent, that's the worst burden, the hardest thing. It's devastating when you lose."

Cam filtered the man's words through a veil of skepticism, cop against defense lawyer. Adversaries. *They always say that.* But why bother to keep it up all these years?

"I bet," Cam said insincerely.

"So, what do you think about Innes as the murderer?" Ludlow asked.

"I think he's innocent," Cam said. Toeing the party line.

Ludlow looked at him. "Seems to me you've been on the wrong side twice now."

Whoa. Strong words for a member of the notoriously slick legal profession. "Just my luck," Cam said, mock ruefully.

Still, on the drive south to the prison complex in Canon City later that morning, he couldn't get Ludlow's words and body language out of his head: Holman was innocent.

Only one of Holman's former cellmates agreed to talk to Cam. They sat across from each other, each with a black phone receiver in hand, Plexiglas separating them, and the dude said, "That asshole never shut up about being innocent."

To which Cam said, "Hey, don't take this personal, but isn't everyone in here innocent?"

"Not *that* innocent, pal," the guy said.

He was halfway back to Denver, in Colorado Springs, by three. The Broadmoor was quiet this time of year; its season wouldn't begin for a couple more weeks. Rick Krystal worked in the main dining room kitchen as a *sous* chef, had been at the resort for nearly a decade. When Cam had found him and set up the meet, he'd said only that he was on the Thomas Innes murder case and needed just a minute of Krystal's time. Winging it.

Krystal was a hefty man in his late thirties. He wore a black beret on a shaved head and a heavily starched, white, double-breasted chef's jacket. His face was florid. Cam figured him for a drinker. They settled in the deserted dining room overlooking the golf course and had coffee. Cam had simply flipped an ID as if he were official and said he had only a couple questions, then Krystal could get back to the kitchen.

Now came the touchy part. "So how long were you employed as the dietitian at the hospital?" Cam asked, wondering just who exactly this guy thought Cam was — a cop? A court official?

"Only about eighteen months. It was a gap job. I was just out of cook school, wanted to ski-bum for a couple years before getting too serious."

"Sure," Cam allowed. Then he took a shot in the dark. "And you met Dr. Innes . . . ?"

"Oh, I don't know, when I first started at the hospital, I guess. Everyone knew him, knew who he was."

"Right. So, tell me exactly what went down." Jesus, Cam thought, he was really groping here.

"I already told . . . ah, the DA, McSwain?

216

Anyway, I already made a statement. Must've been four, five weeks ago. Yeah, he came down himself and took it, very legal and official."

"Oh, sure," Cam said, his pulse quickening. Jesus, McSwain had already been here. Yet Rick Krystal's name wasn't on any witness list. Bret McSwain sure was one sneaky bastard. "But I'd like you to repeat it for me. You know, follow-up and all that stuff."

"All I can say is what I said before. The day his wife was killed I saw him out back," Krystal said.

"Uh-huh." *Holy shit.*

"Yep, outside the back door of the hospital cafeteria. There's a row of windows over the sink area." Krystal shrugged thick round shoulders. "I must've mentioned it back then to this nurse, Leann somebody, and I guess she told the DA about it just a couple months ago. The DA found me here in the Springs. You know the rest."

"Sure."

"Do I still have to testify?"

Cam swallowed the last of his coffee and stood up. "McSwain will let you know."

He drove down the long driveway a few minutes later and whistled out loud —

217

Julia and Ellen were going to shit when they heard this one.

That night, at McSorell's Pub, he bought the guys two pitchers of beer and God only knows how many shots. There was a Rockies game on the wide screen TV. The Rockies actually won.

"Early in the season," Morris pointed out. "Fuckers always win early. Then it's down the drain till September. I hate 'em."

Four of them — three homicide cops and Cam — were shooting darts at an electronic board next to the pool tables in the back of the pub. Cam arched a dart at the board, scored badly. The guys laughed. "Real funny," he said, tossing a second dart. Another lousy shot.

"You're for shit as a partner tonight," Morris said. "You pissed or something about buying all the beer?"

"Nah," Cam said, "just a little preoccupied."

"Well, get *un*-preoccupied, buddy, we're losing our asses here."

Cam concentrated, threw a bull's-eye. "That better?"

Morris grinned. "Ever so much."

But Cam couldn't concentrate. He didn't give a damn that McSwain had himself a corroborating witness to Innes returning to the hospital the day Samantha was murdered. That McSwain was keeping this witness under wraps till the last possible minute — one lawyer screwing another. Nothing new there. But he did care that he'd been smacked in the face three times in this space of a day with the possibility of Matt Holman's innocence.

And Cam just couldn't have been this goddamn wrong.

ELEVEN

When Cam dumped the news about Rick Krystal in their laps, Ellen displayed her Irish temper. "That bastard McSwain! I knew he was holding back. I *knew* it! And I'm going to bust his ass on this, too."

But Julia remained calm. "Yes, but we wait. We'll wait till we need a ruling in our favor. Then we drop Krystal in the judge's lap, use him as leverage. And Bret won't make a peep. He won't dare."

In the meantime, the task of trying to find something with which to discredit Rick Krystal was left to Cam. "I'm already on it," he said. "I spoke to Thomas, though, and he has absolutely no memory of the man. So this could take some time."

May crawled by. Julia barely noted the trees and bushes leafing out, the red and yellow tulips in front of her house. The weather was irrelevant; a snow squall meant no more to her then a glorious summerlike day. She was completely consumed with Thomas's case.

Ellen returned to Denver a couple times. Thomas Innes wasn't her only case, after all, and she had her house to attend to, and personal bills — not to mention Mason. And Dennis usually went back to the city on weekends, too. On his motorcycle.

The dining table was stacked with file folders and loose papers and Post-it notes. The fax machine clicked on often, papers peeling from it. The office phone rang constantly, Dennis as always taking all messages. Their home phone rang seldom — neither Julia nor Thomas had given out the new unlisted number to many people. Thomas had changed his cell phone number and used that almost exclusively. Julia, too, used her cell phone a lot, but she always checked the caller ID number on the tiny screen before answering. Most of the calls came from family — Thomas's mother Maggie from San Diego, threatening to come to Aspen any day now for the duration, and Julia's parents, needing updates and a whole lot of reassurance.

At the end of May, Memorial Day weekend, Livie graduated from the Kent School. Thomas and Julia drove to Denver for the occasion, did the obligatory proud-parent thing. Whenever Livie introduced a classmate or a friend's parents, Julia wondered if they'd heard about Dr. Thomas Innes's arrest. She figured most of them had heard, because for weeks and weeks the TV news broadcasters had been covering the story, and the newspapers still carried updates, and the tabloids made up just about anything they could to attract readers and sell those rag sheets. Julia stood in the warm May sun on a grassy lawn sipping a Coke, and she smiled and tried to be gracious, but her skin crawled with tension, waiting for the inevitable query or raised eyebrow or horrified whisper.

She sat next to Thomas at the graduation ceremony with all the other parents; she held her husband's hand in a show of solidarity, and she smiled until her face ached. And she cried when the graduating class filed in to the music of *Pomp and Circumstance*.

Livie was salutatorian of her class. She looked beautiful and happy in a gown, her dark eyes glowing. So young, Julia thought. So very young and hopeful, with everything ahead of her.

Livie's speech was short and eloquent. She thanked her teachers. She quoted Emily Dickinson and John Donne. Julia knew the speech by heart — she'd helped Livie with it all spring.

"So, as we leave our sheltered lives and go into the world to meet our fates, we must appreciate what we are leaving at the same time as we yearn for new experiences."

Yes, Julia thought, that came out well. And Livie didn't even seem jittery. She was far more sophisticated than Julia had been at eighteen.

"And most of all, I want to thank," Livie was saying, "my father and my stepmother, who is my very best friend. Thank you, Julia."

Surprised, Julia cried again. She couldn't stop the tears. Her mascara ran, and she thankfully took the handkerchief Thomas gave her. She blew her nose discreetly.

That evening they took Livie to dinner at the Brown Palace Hotel, along with two other school friends and their families.

For the younger set, a festive affair, the girls sneaking sips of wine and giggling. Julia was ever so glad to return to their room, though. She was exhausted, her stress level ratcheted up, wanting, needing so desperately, to make Livie's time happy.

The following day they drove back to Aspen, all of Livie's paraphernalia piled to the roof in the back of Thomas's Sub-urban.

"I have to find a job," Livie said from the backseat.

"It shouldn't be hard," her father said. "You know Aspen in the summer. What about that store you worked at last year?"

"Maybe."

"Or you could baby-sit, teach swimming. Or how about seeing if the Music Festival has any paying positions, temporary, you know," Julia suggested.

"I was wondering, Dad," Livie said, "if you need anyone at the front desk at the clinic."

He turned and gave her a surprised glance.

"Watch the road, Thomas," Julia said.

"Oh, sweetie, you don't want to do that. It's tedious work, and you have to know all about insurance, and deal with the people who're upset and hurting."

"I wouldn't mind. I'd sort of like to see how the clinic works. And, besides, it's *your* clinic."

"We'll talk about it," he said dubiously.

Life went on.

The house was very full, Julia often thought. Especially with Livie home for the summer. She found it hard to keep up with housework and shopping for food, all the motions and briefs and tactics, all the decisions to make.

Thomas came home early one afternoon to find Julia vacuuming.

"For God's sake," he said when she shut the vacuum off. "Will you get a cleaning lady?"

"Thomas, please."

"Yes, I know, I know. It would be too expensive, and you can do it better. I've heard it all before."

"I'll think about it," she said. But she knew she wouldn't.

As she clicked on the vacuum again, Thomas stalked upstairs. Cam came into the room, saw her husband's retreating back, and asked, "Do you want me to pick up all the stuff off the floor so you can do the office?"

Her dining room — the office now. "That would be great," she said.

"Give me about five minutes."

She pushed her hair back with a wrist. "Okay, thanks." As she worked the vacuum back and forth across the living room rug, she couldn't help wondering if he'd heard Thomas berating her. Or was he just being considerate? Then she couldn't stop her mind from leaping to comparisons —

Thomas and Cam, Thomas and Cam.

In early June, Ellen sought permission from the DA for Thomas to travel to Sun Valley, Idaho, to check on the progress of his new clinic, which was still in the construction phase. The DA approved the petition and promptly gave a press conference, though no one connected to the case had a clue why the general public would be interested in a business trip Thomas was to make. Still, the media covered his departure from Aspen — such as his getting out of Julia's car and entering the Pitkin County Airport. They even took photos of her behind the steering wheel.

That afternoon Ellen gave in to the media requests and agreed to a formal interview.

"Are you sure this is wise?" Julia asked as Ellen dressed for the occasion. "I know all they do is speculate right now, that old police-blotter-mania, but isn't it too early to give them anything?"

"I'm not going to give them a damn thing, but it's time we drop the hint the prosecution might be playing dirty pool and holding out on us. I also want to leave them with the impression we have a few things up our sleeves, too. Let McSwain stew about it for a while."

"I guess as long as you come off as confident . . ."

"Oh, I will. How do I look, anyway? It's going to be held in front of the courthouse. The crab apple trees are in bloom, and I'm wondering . . . the rose camisole or beige? Maybe rose is too icky."

"You're wearing a blazer, so go with the rose. It's a softer look."

"Rose it is."

The interview, which was aired for days on end, came off without a hitch. Rumor had it McSwain was scrambling to find out what Ellen was holding back.

Aside from the flurry over Thomas's departure and Ellen's interview, the house seemed calmer without him, more restful. Then for several days Ellen was in Denver finishing up another case, Cam was in Durango interviewing a witness, and only Dennis was underfoot. And Livie, of course.

Julia felt as if she could relax for a few days.

Livie was still looking for a job, had some promising possibilities — one at a cashmere boutique, another as a salesperson for Riff-Raft, a white-water rafting outfit. Before leaving for Sun Valley, Thomas had put his foot down about her working in his office. It had happened over dinner one night. There was no one in the house for a change but the three of them, and Livie had broached the subject again.

"Look, sweetie, you have to do all the insurance filing. It's a nightmare," he had said.

"I could learn."

"I don't think it's a good idea."

Julia watched as the girl's face fell. "Dad, I could try, couldn't I?"

"No, and that's the end of it," he'd said curtly.

He had no idea how he hurt his daughter. To him the idea of working for her father was a teenager's foolish whim. To Livie there was only rejection, pure and simple.

Julia had comforted the girl and told her the rafting job sounded like a lot of fun. "All those cute young boys who steer the rafts," Julia said. "And I bet you could go on trips on your days off. What a ball."

"Maybe," Livie had said, still pouting.

Shortly after that, she noticed her stepdaughter had started hanging around the dining room office. She'd chat with Dennis, especially now, when Ellen wasn't around to shoo her away. Livie and Dennis even went out for lunch together on his

228

motorcycle, and when they came back, Julia could hear them laughing together as they walked up the porch steps. Their laughter was so innocent, so carefree, and for the first time in weeks Julia felt her spirits lift.

By the beginning of June, off-season was officially over, and tourists were trickling back into town. Aspen wouldn't really fill up until the end of the month, but the series of summer events began with a bang. There was the Aspen Jazz Festival, the Food and Wine Festival, Physics Institute seminars, Given Institute lectures on medical advances, the Music Festival, the International Design Conference. The schedule of internationally renowned events went on until Labor Day.

Julia got home from running errands Friday afternoon just as a black cloud loomed over Aspen Mountain, kicking up wind gusts, tree limbs lashing, flowers bent. It was June 10, but you wouldn't know summer had arrived from the weather. She could see a veil of snow across the valley hanging on the mountainside. But then snow in June wasn't that rare at 8,000 feet.

Dennis was in his usual place at the table, Livie idly reading a magazine in the living room. "Mr. Lazlo called and left a message," Dennis said.

"What did he say?"

"He'll be back from Durango tomorrow, and he found that anesthesiologist and interviewed him."

"Oh, good," she said. The anesthesiologist, a Dr. Romano, had been in the OR with Thomas that day twelve years ago. He'd told the police that Dr. Innes had been in the operating room all morning, had completed all the scheduled procedures, and that he had no recollection of the doctor being late for any of his surgeries.

And Cam had tracked him down. What would they do without Cam? Or rather, what would *Thomas* do without him? Not that he acknowledged Cam or anyone else who was working tirelessly to save his life.

To Julia it seemed her husband had forgotten that he had a preliminary hearing in two months and very possibly a trial after that. She didn't know if he was in denial or merely supremely confidant that his legal team would take care of everything.

But she worried. Oh, God, did she worry. About everything. The preliminary hearing, the very real possibility of a trial, Thomas's careless attitude, the way he failed to see the hurt on his daughter's face or the anxiety that constantly gnawed at his wife. He cared about his clinic in Aspen and the new clinic in Sun Valley. Oh, yes, he certainly cared about his professional life and his public image. But did he care or even want to know that when Cam had interviewed Leann Cornish he'd come away thinking that the dying woman was too convincing? Ellen cared. Julia certainly cared. But not Thomas, not so anyone would notice. And Julia began to wonder if his avoidance of reality wasn't going to take a toll on his health. Would the phone ring one day and she'd learn he'd suffered a breakdown?

Cam arrived back that next afternoon. Julia was unsettled by how glad she was to see him. She had to admit that he was very good-looking. Like a modern-day Viking. She could imagine him on the prow of one of those dragon ships, staring out across the sea through eyes that saw to the horizon, all the way to where the earth curved down and away, and there was nothing more to be seen.

He knocked, and she let him in, aware that she had on a pair of wrinkled cropped pants and a plaid shirt tied at the waist.

"You don't have to knock," she said. "You practically live here."

"Not really. It's still your house, yours and your husband's."

Dennis had gone home to Denver for a long weekend, and Livie was at an interview with the owner of the rafting company. No one else was in the house.

"Thought I'd drop by, give you Romano's statement," Cam said, and she saw his quick assessment of her attire.

"Ellen isn't back from Denver yet," she said, wondering if her face wasn't smudged with dirt or something. "Tomorrow, I think."

"Well, you might want to read it."

"Would he make a good witness?" she asked.

"Absolutely. An older man, very with-it. Going to retire soon, but his memory's sharp. He convinced me."

"*Will* he testify?"

"He said so."

"Good," she said, then again, "good."

"My reports on Ludlow and Holman's cellmate are in here, too," he said, gesturing with the folder he held.

"Anything we can use?"

"Not really. Ludlow stuck to his guns on Holman, and the inmate just said Holman kept repeating he was innocent."

She made a face. "Well, at least neither

side can use Holman in court. By the way," she said, "any news on Rick Krystal yet?"

"You mean have I found any dirt on him?"

She nodded.

"Not yet, but I'll get something. Everyone has a skeleton or two in his closet."

They were still standing in the hallway when he handed her the folder, and she noticed his hand, long fingers, sensitive looking, with those scars on the knuckles. Scars undoubtedly from hitting something or someone. Like the scar that bisected his eyebrow. And she had to wonder, were there scars elsewhere on his body? From fights or gunshot wounds or . . .

"Would you like something to drink?" she asked. "It's a long drive from Durango."

"I'd like that."

"Iced tea?"

"Sure."

It was warm enough to sit outside that day, so they had their iced tea on the back patio, looking out on the green grass of the lawn that was surrounded by big old lilac bushes, that in June had just started to bloom.

"Don't you love the smell of lilacs?" she said.

"Want the truth?"

"Always."

"Lilacs make me queasy. They're sickly sweet."

She tilted her head back and laughed. "My goodness, do you have some childhood trauma connected to the smell of lilacs?" She'd asked the question lightly enough, but when she glanced at him, the lines in his face were taut and his eyes had turned a wintry blue.

"That must be it," he said caustically. Moments later he put his glass down, stood, and said, "Thanks for the drink," and was gone.

TWELVE

Ellen returned on Sunday, Dennis on Monday morning. That Monday afternoon Ellen called a strategy session.

"Okay," Ellen said, "Cam has some . . . well, some unfortunate news for us. You want to tell them, Cam?" Ellen folded her hands on the dining table and looked at him.

He was standing by the door to the kitchen, a shoulder against the wood trim. He rubbed his jaw. "The CBI lab in Denver was unable to get viable DNA from the body fluids on the sheets." He glanced from Ellen to Dennis and then Julia. "And the blood on the jade Buddha is also degraded."

"Is that a dead end then?" Julia asked, discouraged.

"Not exactly," Cam said. "I've got a friend in a forensics lab in Denver who'll send the evidence to the FBI lab in Virginia. They're cutting edge. Their techniques are top-notch."

"You think the FBI can get results where the CBI couldn't?" she asked.

"Possibly."

"It's certainly worth a try," Ellen put in. "All they could do twelve years ago was type the blood and semen, *if* the perp was a secretor. Now, hell, the sky's the limit. They can find DNA, match it to an individual, tell you what the person had for breakfast, for God's sake."

"There's another hitch." He frowned. "Not a big one yet, but it could become significant. Ellen?"

"It still your turn, Cam," Ellen said.

"Okay, then," he said. "Say the FBI can extract DNA from the old evidence, we still need Matt Holman's DNA for a match."

"We know," Julia said. "We've been over and over this."

"Well, here's the glitch . . . Holman's lawyered-up, and the guy's been stonewalling us," Cam explained.

"Why would Holman object?" Julia asked.

Ellen rolled her eyes. "I guess he wants us to sweat it."

"Well, Judge Scott can order him to give a sample."

"He could. But will he?" Ellen said.

"Of course he will."

"I could try petitioning him," Ellen said. "But I already know he won't like the possibility that if we go to trial, we're going to try to point the finger at Holman all over again."

"We're not going to try Holman again, and Judge Scott knows it," Julia said.

"Well" — Ellen looked at her fingernails — "the truth is, if we go to trial, we *are* going to retry Holman to a certain extent. Actually, to whatever extent the good judge will allow. Because if we try Holman, and he looks guilty to the jury, then they have to find Thomas not guilty."

Julia waved her hand. "Regardless of that, the judge will want DNA evidence if it's at all possible to get it. He's not going to risk a mistrial or an appeal based on the fact that he refused to admit DNA into the court record."

Ellen sighed. "The situation is still touchy, and there's not a lot of precedent in the law here. What we need is Holman's cooperation, unless we can talk the judge into issuing a court order directing him to submit to the test."

"Huh," Cam said, "fat chance."

Julia thought a minute, leaning her cheek on her hand. Finally she looked up and said, "Okay, we can assume Holman and his new lawyer will not cooperate, so I'll talk to the judge myself."

"You think that's advisable?" Cam arched a brow.

"Advisable, so what? My husband's life is at stake."

"By the way," Cam said, "I've got it set up to be at Leann's formal videotaping."

"Okay," Ellen said. "When is it?"

"Next week."

"We'll need a full report," Julia said.

"You'll get it."

Thomas came back from Sun Valley the next day, and the house was again full. Livie had accepted the job with Riff-Raft and spent her days at a kiosk on the downtown pedestrian mall signing people up for rafting adventures. Julia noted that when the girl was home, she took a long time with her grooming. Eye makeup, hair done just so, and those low-rider pants and cropped tops that showed off her firm young midriff were in abundance.

Hmm, Julia thought again.

Even Thomas noticed. "What's going on with Livie?" he asked one night, as they got ready for bed.

"Nothing much."

"I mean, she's hanging around like somebody's pet dog."

"We have a pet dog."

"You know what I mean. And today, I swear she was half naked. I wanted to drape her with a sterile sheet, for chrissakes."

"I think she's interested in a guy. She's eighteen, Thomas."

"Is it Lazlo? I'll kill the son of a —"

"Cam?" Julia said. She wanted to laugh, but nothing came. *Cam?* That Thomas even considered Livie could be interested in him . . . Then she thought, well, why not? He was an extremely attractive man. And there was that latent air of danger to him, heightened by his aloofness and those long silent spells. Oh, yes, he was quite the mysterious man. And she'd bet he could have lots of young girls if he wanted them.

She shook off her musing and glanced at Thomas. "No, not Cam," she said. "It's Dennis."

"That *kid?*"

"He's twenty-two."

"That's not a kid?"

She smiled. "*I* think that's a kid."

"Well, at least Dennis has a good job," he muttered, and he got into bed.

There was no off-season at all for

Thomas. The minute the ski lifts closed, and ski injuries became scarce, other sports mishaps filled the vacuum. Hikers fell, mountain bikers skidded off dirt roads, softball players, over-the-hill but still itching with competitive spirit, injured themselves in all sorts of fascinating ways. As did golfers, skateboarders, four-wheelers, dirt bikers, and horseback riders.

The emergency room at the hospital was busy, as were the three doctors at Thomas's clinic. Then he had to get permission from the DA to fly to North Carolina to speak at Duke University's medical school on cutting edge techniques for ceramic joint replacement.

The following week, Julia asked Cam if there'd been any progress getting Holman to submit to DNA testing. Cam said, "I can't even get his lawyer to return my calls right now."

So she made up her mind to talk to Judge Scott herself about ordering Holman to give that sample. All it took was a mouth swab, after all. It wasn't as if the procedure was painful.

She took Blackie out for an early walk, mentally rehearsing her spiel to the judge: "Say the DNA can be extracted from the old evidence, say it matches Holman's DNA, it should be no skin off his teeth. It can't hurt Holman, he can't be retried, but it can help Thomas."

The question was: Did she have the guts to talk to Judge Scott?

She knew the judge was in court that day, too, but he presided over district court, while she had tried cases in the lowly county court. She also knew that, as the defendant's wife, she should recuse herself from the case and appear to have absolutely nothing to do with it. For her to write up a motion or interview a witness or ask for a court order regarding the case was pushing the ethics envelope. In law school she'd learned that representing anyone close to you was called the "stupidity prohibition." Because a jury, naturally, would not believe a word you said.

But, hey, Aspen was a small town, the courthouse was a close-knit community, and the judge knew her. To ask him for a favor might piss him off, but she decided that the request was worth the risk.

After lunch she walked the few blocks to the courthouse and made her way down the hall to Judge Scott's chambers. She knocked on the solid oak door and heard him call, "Come in."

"Well, Julia, good afternoon. How're things going?" he said.

The judge was seated comfortably behind his large antique desk, a slim man with prematurely white hair. He'd been reading a brief — she recognized the form.

"Uh, fine, but I have a favor to ask," she said.

"Okay, first of all, sit down. Relax."

Relax, sure.

"How are you doing?" he asked then, and she knew exactly what he meant.

She smiled ruefully. "It's been hard."

"I can't even imagine," Scott said. "Now, it's very possible I'll get your husband's case, so let's make sure nothing we say here is prejudicial."

"Can we speak off the record?" She held her breath.

He regarded her for an endless time, and then said, "Whatever we say in these chambers will all be between us."

"Yes, of course."

"I assume you've come to find out about that petition Ms. Marshall made. . . ."

"Which one?" Julia asked dryly.

The judge snorted and gave a low chuckle. "Yes, she's a busy lady, isn't she? A damn good defense counsel, too, I might add."

"We went to law school together," Julia said.

"Really?"

"Yes, we're old friends. But I'm actually not here about any motion she placed before you."

"Well, at any rate, as long as you're here, you can inform Ms. Marshall that I've ruled on her motion objecting to Mr. Holman's release. I'm afraid I've had to deny it. I'll send my decision to her today."

"She thought it was worth a try." She smiled and shrugged.

"And so it was." He shifted in his chair and eyed her. "But obviously that's not what you're here about."

"No. I'm here because we need a DNA sample from Matt Holman, and his lawyer is being obstructive."

Judge Scott leaned back in his chair and studied her over steepled fingers. "I'm aware of the situation."

Julia looked puzzled. How could the judge . . . ?

"Oh, yes, Holman's lawyer phoned me last week with very strong objections. And, frankly, I'm troubled by the request. I know where Ms. Marshall is headed."

"Your Honor," she said, "Holman is in no danger from Thomas's defense. You know that. And so does his lawyer. Double jeopardy — he can't be tried again."

"Okay, Julia, let's assume the case goes to trial. For the purpose of this conversation. Now, we both know Mr. Holman can't be tried again in court, but Ms. Marshall is going to try him in the press."

"Ellen, *Ms. Marshall,* won't give anything to the press, Your Honor."

"Things do have a way of leaking out."

"We'd never do that. But regardless, we can't ignore DNA evidence that might prove Thomas was not at the crime scene. To do that, we need Holman's DNA for comparison or elimination. All Ellen needs is a sample from him."

"I've already decided I'll allow the statement from Holman's previous trial to be read into the record — that he was at the crime scene," Scott said.

She had to convince him. It was now or never. She took a breath. "It would be better if we have DNA. It's the only certain way to eliminate Thomas from the scene. Look, all there is from twelve years ago is blood typing from the bedclothes and the murder weapon, the Buddha. Type O positive blood, Your Honor, which doesn't say much, because eighty percent of the population is O positive."

She sat up straighter. "Your Honor, Matt Holman, Samantha, and Thomas all are blood type O positive. For that matter, so am I. We cannot eliminate anyone, least of all Thomas, from the scene without the DNA. Judge, it's worth a try, isn't it?" She felt her heart pounding. She swallowed. This was as bad as pleading a case in court. No, worse. Much much worse.

Scott continued to stare at her over steepled fingers. He said nothing for a long time. Then, "Julia, have you considered that your tactics might backfire?"

"Backfire?"

"Yes. Any test results you acquire will by law be presented in discovery to DA McSwain. What if your husband's DNA is found on the old evidence?"

Her mouth went dry, and blood surged to her head. She . . . hadn't considered that. Never in a thousand years would she believe Thomas capable of such an act. No. *No.* She licked her lips, prayed the judge had not seen her confusion, and managed to say, "That won't happen, Your Honor, so we're prepared to submit Thomas's DNA to the FBI lab right along with Matt Holman's."

There was another swollen pause in time while the judge fixed his gaze on her. "All right," he finally said, "I'll issue an order for Mr. Holman to comply. But I'm warning you, and Ms. Marshall, don't exploit this angle. Should we go to trial, keep your findings short and sweet and purely factual. No rehashing Holman as an adulterer, any of that. Got it?"

She had to wet her lips again. "I got it."

"I admire your loyalty to your husband. And between you and me and these walls, I think he does wonderful things for people."

"Thank you, Your Honor."

"And tell Ms. Marshall to come talk to me herself next time. I won't bite."

"I'll tell her." She stood up, her knees watery, hands shaking, mouth still so dry she wondered if she could get another word past her lips.

"Keep up the good work, Julia."

"I'll try."

When she got home, no one but Cam was there. He was on the phone, pacing, for what seemed like hours. He kept turning to her, holding up a finger as if to say, *I'll be with you in just a sec.*

"I did it," Julia said breathlessly when he was finally free.

"What?" he asked.

"I talked to Judge Scott." She practically collapsed onto one of the chairs that seemed perpetually set at odd angles around the table.

"Huh."

Then she looked up and couldn't help smiling. "He said he'd do it."

"Goddamn," Cam said. He grinned and gave her a thumbs-up.

Ellen came in a few minutes later, saw their faces, and said, "What? *What?*"

"Julia got Scott to agree to order Holman to provide DNA," Cam told her.

"Oh, baby, I knew you could do it," she said to Julia, then she hugged her. "Hot dog, we got him!"

It was nice to be the center of attention, nice to have succeeded at something significant, nice to be appreciated. Julia felt the tension recede and a warm glow spread inside. She hadn't felt this elated for a long time.

"He said to tell you to go see him next time," Julia said to Ellen. "Said he wouldn't bite."

"I'll try to remember that," Ellen commented.

"Oh" — Julia felt the lightness dissipate — "your motion objecting to Holman's release?"

"No go, huh?" Ellen said.

"No."

"Ah, well, I figured it wouldn't work. But nothing ventured, you know."

"Well, I might be getting a leg up on Rick Krystal," Cam said then.

"Oh, yes," Ellen said, "the phantom witness. McSwain, that asshole."

"Anyway," Cam said, "I made a . . . friend, shall we say, up at the hospital, and she thinks Krystal got his butt chewed out royally by Thomas. She's looking into it for me."

"That's great," Ellen said. "Isn't it, Julia?" She rubbed her hands together. "God, I'd *love* to have the goods on this Krystal when McSwain finally puts him on the witness list."

"Yes," Julia said, "it would be a nice coup." But she was wondering who Cam's friend was at the hospital. He'd said *she*.

Then Ellen said, "Do whatever you have to do, Cam, but get the specifics from your new best friend."

"No prob," he said.

After that the three of them sat around the table talking about the next step.

"It's time for you to go visit our friend Holman," Ellen told Cam. "Now that he can't dodge the DNA sample."

"He's not going to be a happy camper," Julia put in. "Do you think he'll even agree to see you at this point?"

Cam looked unconcerned. "Oh, I think he will. He's gonna want to brag about being released from prison. Really stick it to me. And, hey, it won't be the first time I've interviewed a hostile witness. Won't be the last."

"So you'll make plans to fly down to Arizona to see him?" Ellen asked.

"Yeah, fly." He made a face, a kind of grimace.

"As soon as possible," Ellen said.

"I can't drive?"

"Are you kidding? What would that take? A couple days there, a couple days back? Besides, it's a bezillion degrees in Arizona right now."

"My Bronco has air-conditioning."

Ellen regarded him, and then realization dawned on her face. "Jesus, Lazlo, you're afraid to fly."

"Hey . . ."

"Well, you are. You're afraid to fly."

"Ellen, Christ —"

"Ha! I got you on this one. A tough guy, all macho and cool. You're a wienie. You're afraid to fly."

"Okay, Superwoman, you got me. I'll do it. I've flown before, you know."

"Julia, can you believe it? He's afraid of airplanes."

Julia tried not to smile at Ellen's crowing. "Ellen, you're such a bitch."

"Oh, I am, aren't I? And I love it. Okay, okay, Cameron Lazlo, you get the . . . what is it? The four feathers. Yes, that's it. The four feathers!"

He was taking her glee in stride, laughing a little at himself. He looked entirely different when he laughed, boyish and without a care, a separate person from the man who'd said lilacs made him queasy and had stalked out of her house.

He was vulnerable then, had some weak spots, some fears. Perhaps other ones besides flying. Up to then he'd seemed ironclad, without failings. She looked at him and she saw him with new eyes; perhaps she could penetrate his surface now. Not much, but enough to guess what was underneath.

Ellen finally pushed herself back from the table. "Well, that was our moment of Zen for today. Back to work."

"You don't give a guy a break, do you?" Cam asked.

"Depends on the guy. You? Nah, no breaks."

Julia heard the sound of a motorcycle outside. Dennis. And there was someone with him — a girl's voice. Of course, Livie.

"Hi, everybody," she said. She looked happy, her gleaming dark hair mussed by the ride.

Dennis was behind her. "Sorry, am I late?" he asked.

"No problem," Ellen said, looking from Dennis to Livie and back.

"Livie, listen," Julia said. "It's fine if you ride on Dennis's motorcycle, but you have to wear a helmet."

"We just came from downtown. A few blocks."

"Your father would want you to use a helmet."

"Yes, Livie, you should," Dennis put in. "I'm really sorry, Mrs. Innes, I should never have let her get on my bike without one."

"God, I can't do anything," Livie moaned and she fled upstairs.

"I'll get her a helmet," Dennis said. "I promise."

"Don't worry, I'll see she buys one for herself."

When Thomas arrived home, they were still at work, discussing exactly what information Cam was to extract from Holman.

"Any possibility of dinner around here?" Thomas asked.

"Guess what your lovely wife did today?" Ellen said.

"What did she do?"

"She got Judge Scott to agree to issue a court order for Holman to provide DNA."

"I guess that's good."

"It's great."

"I don't know exactly what it's going to prove, though."

"The results will demonstrate that there is no evidence linking you to the crime scene."

"That's kind of a negative thing, isn't it?"

"Yes. But a *good* negative thing."

Thomas lifted his shoulders, dropped them. "Whatever."

"How about we order in pizza?" Ellen said.

"Oh, God, not pizza again," Thomas said.

"I'll make a salad," Julia offered.

"Fine. I've got some calls to make, I'll be upstairs."

He came down to eat with them at the kitchen table. He seemed in a better mood, recapturing some of the boyish charm that had so endeared him to Julia.

"This" — he gestured at them — "reminds me of when I was in med school. Living on pizza and bad dorm food, staying up studying till all hours."

"Medical school?" Ellen said. "Reminds *me* of law school."

"I guess they aren't so different," he said, taking another slice of pizza.

"Any interesting cases lately?" Ellen asked off-handedly.

"Oh, yes." He ducked his head and swallowed. "A biker hit by a car, a broken pelvis and femur. Is he one sore puppy."

"But you fixed him up," Ellen said.

"Sure. Spit and baling wire. He'll be fine."

"Tell them about the old cowboy," Julia said, taking an olive and popping it in her mouth.

"Great old guy," he said. "He had this bad leg from a million years ago when he broke it falling off a horse. The leg was bothering him more and more. So he came in, and I told him I'd have to rebreak it, put in a plate, screws, the works."

"Ouch." Ellen made a face and shivered.

"Not as bad as you might expect. We've gotten quite handy at putting bones together. Anyway, I did the procedure for him, and he's just off crutches, doing well. He brought me a lucky horseshoe."

Julia was glad to see him at ease and enjoying the company for a change.

"And then there was this woman, she was . . . let's say difficult. Insisted on having her ACL repair done without an epidural or a general, only a femoral block and local anesthesia. Tough as nails. Didn't make a peep when I drilled on her bone. My anesthesiologist was a saint."

Julia couldn't help noticing that Cam didn't say a word. He was a laconic guy, but he usually had something to say. Apparently not tonight.

Thomas retired early — he had surgery in the morning. Ellen yawned and said she had to call Mason, who'd gotten back from Washington today.

Cam helped Julia with the dishes, not that there were many. He was good that way, always offering to help when everyone else conveniently vanished.

"Your husband loves what he does," he said as she rinsed out the salad bowl. He was sitting at the table now.

"Yes, he does. It's his passion."

"That's good."

"It's wonderful."

"He's a lucky man."

She turned from the sink to face him. "Not so lucky right now."

"Aside from that."

"There is no 'aside from that.'"

"No, I guess not."

"Want some decaf?"

"Sure. Unless you have the real stuff."

"I do. But I wouldn't sleep."

"Me neither."

"Then why would you want it?"

"I never sleep anyway."

She frowned. "That's terrible."

"I'm used to it."

"Why don't you sleep?" She wondered why she was pressing the issue. His sleeping habits were none of her business.

"I think at night."

"What do you think about?" She busied herself trying to separate the coffee filters.

"Little bit of this, little bit of that."

"Do you think about the past or the future?" She sat down at the table with him.

"I try to think about the present, live in the moment, as they say. Doesn't always work."

She cocked her head and unabashedly studied him. He had on a light blue work shirt, sleeves haphazardly rolled up; the color was precisely a shade darker than his eyes. He wore blue a lot, and she wondered if a woman had once told him he looked terrific in that color.

"You've never been married?"

"No."

"Why not?"

"Haven't met the right woman. Or

maybe I've met too damn many of them."

The coffeemaker burbled and dripped. The house was very quiet.

"You shouldn't be so sarcastic about relationships."

"It's sarcasm or slitting my wrists."

She smiled. "Women aren't that hard to understand. We want emotional security, then, after that, some kind of home, a nest, I guess you'd call it."

"Sounds simple."

"It is."

She poured the coffee. "How is Victor doing on his book?"

"He doesn't tell me. I report to him, he digests the info, and it comes out on a page."

"So you really don't know how the story's going?"

"Nope."

"Will you see any of it when he's done?"

"He gives me parts of it to fix the dialogue, you know, the cop jargon."

"Do you like working for him?"

"Sure. We get along. I have a lot of freedom. Suits the both of us."

"Do you miss being a policeman?"

He took a drink of coffee, met her eyes her over the rim. "You are full of questions, aren't you?"

"Sorry." But he never answered her.

June turned warm. Cam and Ellen continued to shuttle back and forth to Denver. Livie bought a motorcycle helmet with Julia's credit card, and saw more and more of Dennis, who went home to Denver less and less. Julia wondered if Dennis ever discussed the case with Livie, but she didn't think so, because Livie was so lighthearted; she had her man. Julia was amused by the girl's subterfuges, her attempts to be around Dennis whenever she could.

Eighteen. What had Julia been like at eighteen? Working hard at the grocery store in the Iowa town where she lived, busing tables at the local café at night, trying to save money for college. Focused on that. She couldn't recall having a date that whole summer before college.

That Friday Thomas had a morning off. Ellen was in Denver, but Cam had come over early to copy a few papers he needed for the Arizona trip.

Livie was grabbing a piece of toast, on her way to work.

"Dennis and I are going rafting tomorrow. I get to take him for free," she announced.

"Sounds like fun," Julia remarked.

"I can't wait. See you." And she was out the door.

"Kids," Thomas said.

"It's wonderful to see her so happy," Julia said.

"You mean, despite what's going on around her?"

"Well, yes. Of course."

"You'd like all of us to be walking around in a state of depression," he said, somewhat surly.

"Oh, Thomas, that's not true. I just worry. I worry about you and what you have to go through."

"Worry, worry. That's all I hear. Lighten up."

She felt the blood rise to her face. And she was embarrassed in front of Cam. She went to the sink, just so she could turn her back to them both.

"I'm golfing this morning," Thomas was saying. "First game I've been able to play this season. You golf, Lazlo?"

"No, I'm more of a hockey sort of guy."

"Hm," Thomas said. "I'd have figured you for a wide-receiver type."

"Not me."

Then Thomas left to get his clubs out of the garage, and she turned around, and she saw the set expression on Cam's face. As if a darkness had brushed him, like the shadow of a bird's wing.

"He's under a lot of pressure," she said.

"Uh-huh."

"He's not really like this. It's just —"

"You don't owe me any explanations."

But she felt, somehow, that she did. She wanted him to know, to understand, to forgive her husband. She liked Cam Lazlo. She liked him more and more. And she knew he liked her. She could tell by the way he was polite, helped her out when he could, listened to her when she talked to him, watched her face intently. A woman just knew those things.

And despite her attempt to shut down her thoughts, she wondered what it would be like to be married to him instead of Thomas. They were so different. Cam would be difficult — unforthcoming, repressed, tough. Too damn many women, he'd said. So he'd probably be unfaithful.

She worked at writing a motion that morning, still musing over the differences between the men. But then she had to concentrate on what she was doing, trying to counteract one of Bret's moves, his attempt to keep from evidence Leann's statement made just after Samantha's murder. Bret held that all such statements were irrelevant.

Well, Julia was going to convince the court that the statement *was* relevant. In clear, concise legalese, an oxymoron, if there ever was one.

And it amused her, in a wry sort of way, that Ellen would get credit for this motion, along with all the others Julia worked on.

That night, in bed next to Thomas, she thought about what Cam had said: He never slept. He spent his nights thinking.

She herself was sleeping better these days than she had at first. Amazing what a person can get used to — a husband charged with murder.

She couldn't fall asleep that night, though. She lay there and she thought about her marriage. Eight years of marriage, and the two years they'd been together before that when she was in law school. She knew him so well and had loved him so much.

But why? *Why* had she really been attracted to him in the first place? Had it been immediate, as she'd always told everyone? Or had she assessed who and what he was and then been drawn to the doctor? It was true; he'd come with lots of baggage, a ready-made daughter, a murdered wife who'd cheated on him, and a vocation that obsessed him. But she'd told herself she was head over heels for the man.

She recalled the early days of their marriage as she lay there, the window open, the cool mountain air drifting in, the sound of crickets from outside, an occasional car going by. The fragrance of lilacs.

She *had* fallen in love. And she'd been secure for the first time in her life; secure in his love and, true, secure financially. Over the years she'd thought about that — the money angle. But she'd never considered or, she realized, allowed herself to consider until now that she might have been a little in love with the doctor's financial position from the very start.

THIRTEEN

Cam headed out of Aspen, east over Independence Pass, thinking about tomorrow's flight to Arizona — dreading it. But Ellen was right; a roundtrip by car would waste four days. Days they couldn't afford to waste with the summer tearing by.

He'd phoned Holman a half-dozen times before reaching him, and then it'd taken a whole lot of Cam's persuasive talents to talk the man into an interview. Cam was halfway to Denver, just taking the on-ramp to Interstate 70, hitting a bunch of summer tourist traffic, when it came to him — his persuasive talent wasn't the reason Holman agreed to see him. Holman wanted to rub Cam's face in the fact that he'd gotten away with murder. And do it up close and personal. Which might possibly work to Cam's advantage. Like Ellen had once said, hell, get Holman to confess. The guy had nothing to lose now.

Unfortunately, in order to do that, Cam

had to get to Phoenix — in a goddamn airplane.

He parked the Bronco in the alleyway behind his apartment and climbed the stairs, let himself in. The place was neat as a pin, though hot and stale and musty. He turned on the window air-conditioner and called Frankie Meredith at the police forensics lab while he waited for the apartment to cool down.

"Got your message," Frankie said. "I can send the stuff to the FBI. It'll take fucking forever. They have a backlog I wouldn't wish on my worst enemy."

Cam frowned. "What are we talking, months, years?"

"Months for sure."

"Okay."

"Can you get someone to deliver the items to me? To keep the chain of evidence clean."

"I'll work on it."

"You must still have contacts in the department."

"Sure, no problem."

"By the way, how many items are we talking?"

"Couple bedsheets, some clothes, a jade statue, which was the murder weapon."

"How long did you say?"

"Twelve years."

"Good luck, Lazlo. Hope somebody's life doesn't hang on these results."

"It may, Frankie, it just may."

Then, while he sat as still as he could so as not to sweat too much in the heat, he phoned Kayla.

"Just roll into town and expect me to jump through hoops?" she said. Smart-ass, the way he liked them.

"Well, yeah, I was actually."

"Okay." She laughed, and he liked the sound of the woman's laughter, free and uncluttered by emotional hang-ups. Although she had asked him about marriage, then the Innes case. Oh, well, he was in a forgiving mood.

He and Kayla went to a Rockies baseball game that evening. The Rockies played the Atlanta Braves and lost, bigtime, but Coors Field was such a great venue, the creaming almost didn't matter. They ate hot dogs with sauerkraut and drank beer and sweated streams until the sun finally fell below the mountains and bathed them in blissful shade. Then they went to a local brewpub and had more beer, until he was relaxed and Kayla was giggling a lot.

"How's Aspen?" she asked. "All those poor little rich kids."

"It's a helluva lot cooler than here," he replied.

"Meet any women up there?"

"Oh, sure, hundreds, in all my spare time."

"Cut the shit, Cam. I bet you did. I know you, a girl in every port."

"Aspen happens to be thoroughly land-locked."

She grinned and shook a finger at him. "Don't quibble."

"No women, Kayla, honest."

"So, you're lonely up there in the mountains?"

"No time to be lonely."

"Did he do it?" she asked, leaning forward so that her breasts pressed against the rim of the table.

"What?"

"*Did* the doctor do it?"

He looked at her. A gust of irritation shook him. "We've covered this ground before. How the hell should I know?"

"Well, you're investigating the case."

"It doesn't work like that, Kayla, where I know right off who's guilty and who's not. First of all, anyone who *is* guilty says they're not."

"Can't you tell if they're lying?"

"Sometimes."

"Not this time."

"No, not this time."

"Everyone here, in Denver, you know, thinks he's innocent."

"Oh, yeah? What about you."

"Honestly?"

"Yes, honestly."

"I think he's a hunk. I think all the ladies think he's a hunk, not to mention talented, oh, and rich."

"Yeah, sure. Whatever. But does that make him innocent?"

"I guess it must." She smiled coyly.

"Maybe Ellen Marshall should get an all-female jury."

"If I lived in the county, I'd volunteer."

He felt annoyance ripple along his limbs.

"So, you must have an opinion, Cam."

"I'm hired to investigate, not form opinions. Period."

"Sorry," she said, the corners of her mouth turning down.

He made a disgruntled noise, then muttered, "It's just me, been busy and got another long day tomorrow."

Kayla was silent for a time, then she said, "I met someone."

He cut his eyes to her. "You did."

"At work. He's a great guy."

"Is it serious?"

She leaned back from the table. "I'm not sure."

"Well . . ."

"He's the marrying kind."

"How can you tell?"

"Oh, women can tell that sort of thing. I admit he's not as much fun as you are, exciting, you know. But still . . ."

Exasperation and a guilty relief swept him. "So, congratulations, I guess."

"Please, it hasn't gone that far."

"But it will?"

Kayla smiled shyly, an expression he'd never seen on her face, and he relented.

"Hey, I'm happy for you if it works out, Kayla."

"Thanks," she said.

He begged off when she invited him in to her place. Said he had work to do that night, said he had a real early flight. He lied on both counts.

When he got home to his cooled-down apartment, and he realized he would be sleeping alone, he was slightly amazed at himself. When was the last time he'd turned down an offer of sex? And with a woman he liked.

He sat there for a while, and then he

switched on the tube, got a beer from the fridge, and settled on his couch. He thought about what he'd just done, turning down Kayla, and he made up myriad mental excuses, but deep inside he knew he'd turned Kayla down because he was afraid he would have seen Julia's face in the darkness.

He would have imagined his fingers sliding through her soft shiny auburn hair, her wide blue eyes closed, the smooth skin and curves of her body. He would have imagined that special scent of hers, always very faint, always there, though, lingering even when she was gone. In the night, his body over Kayla's, he would have conjured up the sound of Julia's voice, her whispers and moans, even though he'd never heard anything but ordinary speech from her.

How the hell had he let this happen? All these years of studiously avoiding en- tanglements, and he was lusting after the forbidden fruit: a married woman who loved her husband.

He slept very little that night, which was not unusual, but his nocturnal musings were very specific. They alternated be- tween Julia and the fact that in a few short hours he would be in a thin-walled metal contraption 30,000 feet up in the air.

In the morning, after checking in with the Clappers downstairs in the bookstore, he headed over to Victor's loft. Dropped off a pile of notes, his impressions of the people involved, a few anecdotes, his talk with the forensic specialist Frankie Meredith.

"Fucking forever," Victor said, scanning some of notes. "I like that."

"You mean when I asked Frankie how long results would take?"

"Yes. Good line. This I can use."

"Hey, don't use any of that stuff word for word, I mean that stuff from Aspen."

"Do I ever? Jesus, give me a break, my man. The plot is so far from what's happening, even you won't recognize it. I'm not positive yet, but I think the husband is going to be guilty. Of course, I have to write as if he could be innocent. So it could go either way. You think my job's easy?"

Victor wore gray sweatpants and a Denver Nuggets T-shirt today. Bare feet. He wore socks six months of the year, went barefoot the other six. Otherwise, his dress varied only in which team his T-shirt represented. However, he could dress. He had a closet full of tuxedos, summer and winter formal, for his late-night TV appearances and high-priced dinners with agents and sales reps and publishers.

"I'm on my way to the airport," Cam said.

"Off to see Matt Holman?"

"Yeah."

"And you're actually flying?"

"Got to."

"Good man. Keep a tight asshole, as James Jones used to say."

"Thanks for the tip, Victor."

"Oh, wait, I need to pay you for the last two weeks. I'll give you a check."

"Why don't you wait till I get back?"

"Okay, good idea. That way, if you die horribly, like get mangled in a plane crash, I won't have to pay you at all."

Victor's laughter trailed Cam all the way out into the hall, even while he waited for the elevator. The doors slid shut and finally cut the sound off.

Fucking writers.

Diamond in the Rough

The phone rang in the middle of the night, and Luke jerked awake, grabbed for the receiver, dropped it on the floor, and finally answered it. His voice was sleep-clogged. "Yeah?"

"Randall here, duty officer. I got a call telling me to get you up and at 'em."

"What the hell?" Luke pried his eyelids open, glanced at his digital clock — 3:15.

"Your partner told me to call you, blame him. I rousted him first."

"What's up?"

"Homicide, over on Cherry Creek Drive, 3044 it says here. Young white female. The crime scene people are on their way."

Luke cleared his throat. "Okay, I'll be there. Damn you, Randall."

He rolled onto his back and rubbed his eyes, felt the warm satiny skin of Kristin against his flank.

"Who was that?" came her muffled voice.

"Cop stuff. I have to leave."

"Luke."

"I know. But it's what they pay me for." He reached across and put his arm around her, kissed the side of her neck, right at the corner of her jaw. She smelled of sleep and flowers. "Go back to sleep."

"Um."

"If I'm not back by the time you

271

have to leave, just make sure you lock the doors."

"Luke."

"See you, sweetheart."

He tugged on pants and the wrinkled shirt Kristin had ripped off him the night before. Good, all the buttons were still intact. Sometimes . . .

He strapped on his shoulder holster, patted his pocket for keys, badge, and wallet, let himself out of the apartment in the dark, descended the rickety stairs on the side of the building. There was plenty of light to see by, because the porn bookstore that occupied the bottom floor of the building was still open, its door ajar, bilious yellow light spilling out onto the pavement. Luke couldn't see the front door, but he figured there were the usual insomniacs inside, trying to, well, stimulate *themselves.*

The T-Bird started, as always, like a dream, settled to a throaty purr. The top was still down from when he'd driven home earlier. Probably a foolhardy habit in this neighborhood, leaving the top down, but all his neighbors knew and respected the fact that he was a homicide dick.

They weren't about to screw with him.

He drove quickly through the hot summer night to the address Randall had given him. Homicide in upscale Cherry Creek. Interesting. He squealed around the corner onto Speer Boulevard, downshifted, and streaked along the almost empty street.

The house, of course, was lit up like a Roman candle. A crime scene van was there, a coroner's wagon, several black-and-whites, an ambulance, its flashing bar pulsing technicolor strobe light on everything. Yellow crime-scene tape draped all over. Neighbors in bathrobes huddled, watching. The universal human wonderment at death and destruction.

He flipped his tin and pushed through the phalanx of uniforms stationed around the perimeter of the scene. Inside, in the kitchen at the rear of the house, the techs were bent over the body, doing their thing. The place was lit up so brightly, he had to blink. Davie Lachine stood aside, latex gloves on, looking tousled and drowsy.

"What we got?" Luke asked him.

"Female, twenty-nine years old, lives here with her boyfriend, according to the neighbors. Killed by a knife to the throat. That" — he pointed — "is the murder weapon."

A bloody kitchen knife lay on the floor. A tech was photographing it, along with the body. Then they'd package it carefully in an evidence bag and deliver it to the forensics lab.

"Not an accomplished killer," Davie said. "Saw what he did, probably panicked and threw it away."

"The boyfriend?"

"In Las Vegas on business. One of the uniforms found a note by the phone with his hotel."

"Good alibi."

"So it seems."

"Next of kin?"

"Don't know yet."

Luke snapped on a pair of gloves and went to stand over the body. The kitchen was white and black, the floor tiles white with a few black diamond shaped tiles scattered throughout. He looked down at the sprawled figure, the deep gash in her throat, the pool of almost black blood under her head. Staining her long blond hair. Drying on the shiny white tiles. If it weren't for the blood and the slashed throat, she could be asleep, except that her skin was beginning to take on the gray pallor of death.

How long had her heart kept pumping that blood out before it had stopped?

"Time of death?" he asked the ME, who was kneeling and bagging the girl's hands.

"Rough estimate, between twelve and one this morning. But the house is air-conditioned, so maybe a little longer."

"Defense wounds?"

"Not that I can see. Just the neck."

"Huh."

Luke stood there, and he stared at the young woman's body, like he always did with murder victims, and he got those weird vibes that he invariably felt. He saw her alive and happy, saw her sit and stand and move around this nice house. Saw her walking across the gleaming floor. He felt a communion with his victims, a lot of cops did. And if he stood there long enough, studied her long enough, she might tell him something that would help catch her killer. Not DNA or fingerprints or the skin under her nails, not semen or anything like that. What he got was communion with her, with the living part of her that had escaped this dead husk.

"I'll catch him," he muttered to her. "He's an idiot, slit your throat and left the knife. He'll be easy."

Then, without a bridging thought, his mind turned to Andrea Beckett's dead body, that night twelve years before, when he'd stood over her and promised he'd catch her killer. And he had — he'd piled up evidence — okay, so it was circumstantial, but solid circumstantial — and he'd seen her killer tried, convicted, and put behind bars.

And now, someone was saying he'd been wrong. Someone was saying her husband had killed her. The successful plastic surgeon with the pretty new wife, the second Mrs. Beckett.

Had he let Andrea down?

He'd been working on the Beckett case, hadn't come up with much so far. Interviewed the terminally ill nurse who swore she saw Beckett come into the OR late, swore he was *agitated, swore he had a cut on his hand.*

And now — now it was time to talk to Mike Hanson, the guy Luke had put in prison for the crime.

Jesus, could he really have been that wrong?

Cam's flight to Phoenix was a nightmare. Heat rising from the Rockies on strong summer thermals shook the plane, then, descending into Phoenix, you got the desert thermals tossing the crate around so bad your brains shook. Why did they fly in such weather?

Cam sat erect, eyes closed, hands on the arms of his seat, knuckles white, ready to grab the oxygen mask when it dropped, pull it to start the air flow, curl his body into a protective ball when the flight attendant told him to. Not that it would help.

He said his goodbyes to the world, as he always did, hoped the crash would be fast. Wondered how long you stayed conscious as the plane spun nose-first toward the ground at a thousand feet a second.

People always told him to down a stiff drink on a flight, the booze would calm him. But he was sure alcohol would only make him vomit. For the same reason, he never ate a bite when he flew.

He set foot on the jetway in Phoenix surprised, once again, that the plane had made it. Then he had to switch mental gears, from facing certain death to getting to Matt Holman's address.

He rented a car, a full-size nondescript sedan that was sure to have a good air conditioner, consulted the map the rental agency supplied, and began driving toward Sunrise Lane, Mesa, Arizona.

He took Route 60, a multi-lane freeway where everyone drove erratically, too fast, and then slowing up too quickly. He simply stayed in the far left lane, going way over the speed limit — and spotted the traffic camera on the bridge ahead too late. No damn wonder everyone had been slowing down. But he'd been had, caught on film, and he'd been doing twenty-miles-per-hour over the limit. *Shit.* They'd mail him a whopping ticket soon as they got his name and address from the rental car agency. The only saving grace was that a camera had gotten him and not a cop. He'd brought along a jacket — like he needed a jacket in this inferno — but it held his tape recorder and notepad and his handgun, which he'd properly checked through airport security as he always did.

Thing was, he wasn't licensed to carry in Arizona. Oh, yeah, being nabbed for speeding on film was far preferable to having the local cops pull him over, give the car a look-see.

Thinking about that, he slowed down a bit and took the time to gaze around. A huge, hot city, broken by arid, cactus-dotted mountains spread before him, behind him, on either side of him. This was no pretty desert, this was ugly, too built up, too many roads, with the same searing landscape that killed illegal immigrants when they tried to walk across the border into the United States.

Even with air-conditioning, the sun burned his arm through the window. The car's thermometer read 112 degrees. Christ.

Sunrise Lane was one of a labyrinth of similar streets, an adult community, with cookie-cutter stucco houses, each with a red tile roof, Xeriscaping, a neat concrete driveway that would fry eggs today, and a large square swamp cooler on the roof.

The Matt Holman that Cam remembered wouldn't have been caught dead in a place like this. He'd been handsome and young, younger than Samantha, a Tom Cruise type but taller. A bartender, an athlete, and in Cam's opinion, despite the guy's protestations of loving Samantha, Holman was your all-around healthy, gold-digging boy-toy.

By the time Cam knocked on Mrs. Lee Holman's door, his shirt was dark with sweat, and he still felt sick to his stomach from the flight. And there was the damn ticket he was going to get in the mail, compliments of your friendly Grand Canyon state.

Lee Holman was a tall, attractive woman in her mid-sixties. Cam could see where Matt's good looks came from. All things considered, she welcomed him graciously. She even offered him an iced tea, for which he was pitifully thankful. Then she called to Matt, who was apparently upstairs, although doubtless he knew someone was there, and he had to know exactly who it was.

Holman finally came down, a different man than the one who'd been convicted twelve years ago. He was thinner and still had jailhouse pallor, even though he was living in sunny Arizona. And he looked older than his forty years. Drawn, hardened.

"Well, well," he said, intentionally not holding out his hand, "Cameron Lazlo, Sherlock Holmes incarnate."

"Matthew," his mother said. "Let's be

civil." She walked into the kitchen area, took up her purse, searching for sunglasses and car keys.

Matt never took his eyes off Cam. "By all means," he said, "civility will get you everywhere."

"I'll leave you two to talk. I have a bridge game," Mrs. Holman said.

Matt still kept his gaze fixed on Cam. "Okay, Mom. See you later." When she was gone, he pulled out a chair from the dining table, turned it around, and straddled it, his arms folded on the back. "I hope you haven't come all this way expecting me to help you."

Cam had carried the jacket inside with him, and he reached in a pocket, took out his tape recorder. "Mind if I tape this interview?" he asked.

"No way."

"It can't be used against you, no matter what you say."

"So what? I don't want to be recorded."

"Okay." Cam shrugged, put the tape recorder away, took out his notepad, flipped it open. "So, Matt," he said, looking up, "what's it like being a free man?"

"Like you give a damn."

"Hey, remember what your mom said, be civil." Cam grinned.

"I don't know why you think I'd help you. I mean, *help you get Innes off?* That sucks."

"Look, I'm just working for the defense team. Let's not be adversarial here."

"You should have been working for the defense the last time," he snarled.

"I was a cop. I followed orders. The Pitkin County DA prosecuted you, not me."

"No, but your investigation put me in jail." Matt's dark blue eyes bored into Cam's. "Twelve years of my life. You know how long twelve years is, man?"

"Sorry about that."

"The hell you are. You're sitting there so smug, and you still think I'm guilty, don't you?"

"No reason for me to go on the record one way or the other. Obviously, my job is to help Dr. Innes."

"That prick. That pumped-up jerk. Samantha didn't decide to leave him because of me. She found out what a self-centered bastard he was. She only stayed as long she did because of their kid."

Cam actually agreed with Holman's assessment of Innes. Not that he'd ever let on. "Hey, the doctor's personality isn't the issue. His guilt or innocence is."

"Well, I know *I* didn't kill Samantha, so I guess he did. Got any other suspects?" His voice dripped sarcasm.

Cam thought, *yeah, right.* He said, "By the way, you already know the old evidence is going to be run for DNA. I'm just curious, how're you going to feel when it comes back covered in yours?"

"It should come back covered with my DNA, for chrissakes, I always admitted I was with Samantha just before her fucking husband murdered her."

"Yeah, well, I'm not talking the bedsheets or her clothes, I'm talking DNA on the murder weapon, the Buddha."

"You make me laugh, Lazlo, how many times I got to tell you I didn't kill the lady? There's no way in hell my DNA is going to be found on the weapon."

Cam was sitting on the edge of the couch, leaning over the coffee table, making occasional notes on the notepad. He looked up, studied Holman for a second, looked back down and began to jot notes. He was not often confused, or at a loss for words, but he had not expected this. He'd expected to rattle Holman's cage, get him to slip up, brag how he was a free man now, stick that fact in Cam's face, and maybe, just maybe, let it out that he'd gotten away with the crime. But the interview was not going down like that.

Cam looked up again, tried to judge Holman's body language, the direction of Holman's gaze — was he staring up and to the right, up and to the left? — judge all those little things that clued a cop or investigator that a person was lying or telling the honest truth and just nervous. Holman was sitting there in an open position, his stare locked to Cam's, and if pressed, Cam would have had to say Holman was telling the truth. But that wasn't right. Couldn't be. Most likely, Holman had learned to lie and hold his own in prison. He wouldn't be the first inmate to acquire those skills.

Cam decided to try a new tack. "So, where did you really go that afternoon Samantha was murdered? I know what you said, what the court records say, you went home, showered, went to work, but was that it? I always kind of figured you showered, then ditched your clothes, you know, get rid of that telltale blood splatter, but we never found them."

"Come off it, Lazlo. You know as well as I do that I didn't ditch any clothing. Because what I had on when I was with Samantha was right there on my bathroom floor when the cops came and arrested me."

"I know that's what you said."

"Well, it's the truth."

"Hey, it's just you and me now, Holman. What'd you do? Toss the clothes in some alley Dumpster on your way to work?"

"Go to hell, Lazlo. I told you the truth then, and I'm telling you the truth now. And come to think of it, I must have told you the same damn thing in about a hundred letters I wrote you over the years. But you couldn't even give me the time of day. You never even answered one of them."

"What was the point? There was nothing I could do to help you."

"Oh, that's right, you were kicked off the police force. I forgot about that."

"Sure you did." Cam smiled.

After a time Cam rose, asked if he could get more iced tea, and headed into the kitchen. He had to admit he was quite surprised by how fiercely Holman was sticking to his original story. Didn't make much sense, now that he was free, now that he could never be retried for the murder. If their roles were reversed, Cam would take this opportunity to stick it to Holman, do a little bragging, engage in some payback. So what was going on here?

He sat back down on the couch and tried yet another tack, tried talking about

Holman's real relationship to Samantha. "Let me ask you one thing, strictly off the record."

"You can ask."

"You were never going to marry the woman, were you? I mean, you were in it for the alimony. Let's face it, Samantha would have been set for the rest of her life."

Holman finally stood up, put his hands on his hips. "You didn't get it then, you don't get it now. . . . I really loved the lady. I really wanted her to get a divorce, I really wanted to marry her, and I would have made a better father to Livie than that asshole of a father she has. And I'll tell you another thing, Lazlo, I really don't give a shit what you think anymore."

"Okay, I'll accept that." Cam drained the iced tea. He was parched, and he had a headache, partly from the heat, partly from a severe anticlimax attack. He tried for a few more minutes to get Holman to say something, anything, that deviated from his original story. Holman was sticking to his tale; if it was a tale. Or maybe Cam was misreading everything, conducting a poor interview — it happened. Everyone had bad days. And in this heat, after that hair-raising flight down through the thermals, who knew? One thing was for sure, Ellen was not going to like the outcome of this interview.

"So, Holman, what're you going to do now?" he finally asked.

"I'm trying to get back to Colorado. I need a job, some money. But it's hard here in the summer, real hard. And with my record . . . forget I was released on new evidence . . . Anyway, I want to write. Got a lot of practice in jail, writing to you, to lawyers, writing and writing, because it was the only goddamn thing there was to do."

"You mean write fiction?"

Holman shook his head. "Journalism. Then maybe a book about being innocent and incarcerated. I've put out feelers. Even got an agent."

Cam raised an eyebrow. "Good for you."

"Don't patronize me, Lazlo."

"Sorry, didn't mean to."

Holman made a grunting sound. "So, did you get what you wanted?"

Cam gave him a guileless look.

"Coming down here, questioning me all over again. Learn anything new?"

"Frankly, no."

"That surprises you, doesn't it?"

"Right," Cam said, not about to admit he was absolutely correct.

"So when does the world-famous doctor go to trial?"

Cam flipped his notebook shut. Stood up. "Hasn't been decided yet. But if and when he does go to trial, I'll be sure to let you know. Fact is, you'll be one of the first persons to know, because you'll be called to testify."

"I figured as much. So did my lawyer. And you know something, Lazlo? The more I think about it, the more I'm looking forward to it."

"How's that?"

"I just want to see the look on Innes's face when the jury finds him guilty."

"If they find him guilty."

"Oh, they will, they will. And I'm going to write all about it in my book, make a bundle off his suffering, maybe even visit him in prison, see how he likes it."

"Whatever."

Driving back to the airport, Cam couldn't push Holman out of his mind. If he was still on the police force, and he interviewed Holman as a suspect, he'd have believed the man. What he said, and how he said it, but more important, his body language would have been convincing.

Oddly enough, Leann Cornish had been convincing, too. The two of them, separately, without shared motive . . . It was damn hard to figure.

He was going to see Leann again in a couple of days for the videotaping of her statement. He'd listen really hard, watch her carefully. Her motivation was the thing that bothered him — a dying woman just wanting to set the record straight? Maybe she was telling the truth, maybe not. Maybe the truth was tainted by some other motive.

He drove too fast again, not really caring, cold air blasting his face, and he felt shaken. Headachy from the heat, still surprised at being alive from the flight, his faith in his own righteousness undermined.

What if he had been wrong about Holman all those years ago? What if he had put an innocent man behind bars? But all the evidence had pointed straight to Matt Holman, every goddamn piece of evidence. The motive, too. Samantha Innes had told him she was never going to leave her husband, there'd been a quarrel, and he'd picked up the Buddha and swung at her.

Still, what if he had been wrong?

Or maybe right this moment he was engaging in wishful thinking. Kind of hoping

Thomas Innes was really the guilty party. Maybe he just didn't like the guy, and maybe he liked his wife a little too much.

He remembered standing over Samantha's body in the morgue, remembered the fetid air swollen with death and chemicals, saw her blood-matted hair and broken skull. She'd been young and so pretty, and he'd stared at her corpse, telling himself he was going to find her murderer and put the fucker away.

He switched on the radio; scanned for a decent station, found nothing much but rap and heavy metal. The air conditioner was roaring, a few dusty palms slipped by the car window. But he thought he could hear Samantha's voice over all the interference: *You promised . . . and you failed me.*

FOURTEEN

The preliminary hearing was scheduled for
August 1, and Ellen ratcheted up the level of
activity during the preceding week.

"I figure the chances of the judge *not*
finding probable cause for this case to go
to trial is about zero," Ellen said just the
day before the hearing.

"I know," Julia said.

"We'll pull out all the stops. We've got
the hospital administrator lined up to
counteract Leann Cornish's statement."

"Right. Patrick Askew. How many witnesses did we figure?" Julia stood up and
paced the dining room.

"Let's see. The DA will put Leann on
the stand for sure. McSwain asked the
judge if he can use the videotape of her
statement if she's too sick, but as of yesterday, she's planning to be there." Ellen
ticked names off on her fingers.

"I thought preliminary hearings were pretty
much routine and quick," Julia reflected. "In
my court, they take about ten minutes."

"How long we'll be in session depends on how much of the case McSwain wants to try before the judge. We'll see."

"The whole thing makes me nervous."

"I know. Showtime."

The following day all of them arrived at the courthouse for the nine a.m. hearing — Ellen, Thomas, Julia, and Cam. A gaggle of reporters awaited their arrival, thrusting microphones at all of them, snapping pictures and rolling tape on video cameras. There were three satellite vans parked on the side street next to the courthouse, plenty of cops around to make certain order was kept. Thankfully, along with Cam's assistance and four Aspen police officers, the media was held at bay when the crush almost got out of hand, and the defense team made it inside the building without incident.

"Jesus," Cam, said, straightening his tie, "can't wait till the trial. Every goddamn news agency in the country is going to show."

Thomas stopped at the base of the interior steps, turned to Cam. "Who says there's going to be a trial?" His voice was edgy.

Cam smiled, but his eyes remained glacial. "Hey, I'm only preparing for the worst. It's what I get paid to do."

God, Julia thought, didn't they have enough trouble without those two circling each other? She exchanged a glance with Ellen, who shook her head.

Once inside the courtroom, which already had a full gallery, including more than enough reporters and sketch artists — the judge had disallowed cameras of any sort — Julia thanked heaven she didn't have to get up in front of Judge Scott. She couldn't believe everything that had happened that morning — such as Livie crying when they told her she couldn't go with them, Thomas changing ties three times, Blackie having one of his stomach bouts, and Julia running around with paper towels and spot remover, not to mention her husband might be bound over for trial today on a murder charge. She was fairly certain this hearing was only a formality, that the case would go to trial, but through all her tension and doubts, she still harbored a forlorn hope the whole mess would end right then and there.

The main courtroom, where Judge Scott held sway in felony court, was a stately oak-paneled room, the spectators' benches, the curved rail setting off the spectators, the tables for the defense and the prosecution, all were gleaming oak. Sitting on one of the oak benches directly behind the prosecution table was Leann Cornish. Also present was her lawyer and a young woman who resembled her so much, she had to be her daughter. Julia tried not to stare; she'd known Leann slightly, and the woman looked dreadful. This had to be an unbearable ordeal for her. And Julia had to ask herself once again why Leann was putting herself through this hell — didn't she have anything better to do with the precious time she had left than try to pay Thomas back? Leann was sick, all right, in more ways than one.

Ellen took her seat at the right-hand table with Thomas, DA Bret McSwain at the left. With him was Aspen Police Detective Joe Feller, looking stiff and uncomfortable in a suit.

Cam sat with Julia across the aisle from Leann in the first row of the benches. Julia looked around, taking in the scene, and, in an unconscious gesture, she almost reached over and took Cam's hand. But she caught herself. What on earth was she thinking?

The door opened to the right of the judge's bench, a lady with a long black ponytail entered, the court clerk, and asked, "Are we all ready?" Then she disappeared to return in a minute with Judge Scott in his black robe. The clerk said, "All rise," the judge said, "Please be seated," and the hearing commenced.

At that point Judge Scott read from a page: "This is case O3R35, matter is set for preliminary hearing in this case."

McSwain stood up, consulted an open file on the table before him, then straightened. He called Leann to the witness stand. The court clerk gave her the oath. She told her story, the same one Julia and Ellen had read in her formal statement and then heard on the tape from Cam's interview. Cam was right — Leann was convincing, far too convincing, and Julia felt the skin tighten on her face.

McSwain asked Leann a few questions when she finished her story. "Can you tell us, Ms. Cornish, why you waited so long to come forward?"

"Look at me," Leann said. "I'm dying. I wanted the truth to come out. I want to set things right."

Oh, God. Julia quailed inside. The woman would have the jury eating out of her hand in a trial. They'd be crying like children.

"Ms. Cornish, please tell the court how you perceived Dr. Innes in the years you worked with him," McSwain said.

Leann found Thomas, then looked back at the DA. "He's a marvelous surgeon. He cares about his patients. But" — she slid her glance to Thomas again — "he can be difficult to work with. He's very exacting, he finds fault, sometimes where there is none. He can be . . . arrogant."

"But that's not why you've come forward in this case, is it?"

"Absolutely not. I'm here today to see justice done."

McSwain nodded and smiled at her. "Thank you, Ms. Cornish."

"Cross, Ms. Marshall?" the judge asked, peering at Ellen.

"Yes, Your Honor." Ellen rose, came around to the front of the table and approached Leann. Ellen stood in a non-threatening stance, looking professional in navy high-heeled wedges, a summer-weight dark blue skirt and off white blouse buttoned at the collar. "Please tell the court about your termination last year, Ms. Cornish," she said, her tone even.

Haltingly, Leann told the story, careful not to blame the loss of her job on Thomas. *Clever*, Julia thought. But the former nurse admitted that in her opinion Thomas was relieved she was fired, because he was afraid she'd eventually tell people about him not being in the hospital the morning of Samantha's death.

Ellen said, "That is pure conjecture, isn't it, Ms. Cornish? You have no proof of Dr. Innes's so-called relief."

Leann met her gaze squarely. "No proof that I can show you. I just know it."

"She just *knows* it. Your Honor, this is not evidence, this is speculation."

"I didn't mean . . ." Leann began.

"You need to answer questions, Ms. Cornish, not make commentary," Judge Scott said. Gently.

Julia thought, *Leann is hurting her own testimony. Good.* She noted Bret McSwain and Detective Feller with heads bent to each other, whispering together. She could hear cars driving by the courthouse on Main Street, and she wished with all her heart she was out there on the street, running errands, with nothing more to think about than the summer rush of tourists.

"Redirect?" Scott asked McSwain.

McSwain half stood. "No, Your Honor."

"Witnesses?" he asked Ellen.

"Yes, Your Honor, I call Patrick Askew to the stand."

The hospital administrator stepped up, took the oath, was asked to give his name and address for the record. He was a tall man, heavy around the middle, receding fair hair, and a graying sandy mustache. He looked ill at ease.

Ellen plunged right in. "Tell the court, please, Mr. Askew, about your termination of Nurse Leann Cornish."

He told his story, how there'd been complaints about Leann from the staff, how ill she was, then Dr. Innes and another surgeon had come to him with real concerns about their patients if Leann remained in the OR. "My job is to see that the patients at Aspen Valley Hospital get the best care possible. Their safety is my number-one concern. If a doctor complains, especially if more than one complains, I have to respond."

Ellen: "So you asked Nurse Cornish to resign?"

"Yes, after a board meeting, I did."

"When was this?"

"It was on June the third, last year."

"Do you feel that Dr. Innes had any ulterior motives for complaining about Nurse Cornish?"

"No, not at all. As I said, I'd received a complaint from another doctor and a couple members of the staff."

"Thank you, Mr. Askew, that's all I have."

"Mr. McSwain?" the judge asked.

"I call Cameron Lazlo to the stand."

What? Julia turned quickly to him, and he gave her an imperceptible shrug, rose, and walked to the witness stand. Took the requisite oath, sat, gave his name and address for the court record.

"I want to inform the court that Mr. Lazlo was a Denver police detective at the time of Samantha Innes's death," McSwain said. "He was on loan to the Aspen police to investigate the case. And, if I may say so, he did an exemplary job."

You weasel, Julia thought.

"Your point, Mr. McSwain?" Scott asked.

"I have one question for Mr. Lazlo. Did Matt Holman contact you at any time during the last twelve years? Matt Holman being the man incarcerated for Samantha Innes's murder."

"Objection," Ellen said. "Mr. Holman's previous history cannot be brought up, Your Honor. If this holds true for the defense, it should hold true for Mr. McSwain."

"Mr. McSwain, Ms. Marshall, approach the bench," the judge said.

Lowered voices, nods. *What now?* Julia thought.

The lawyers returned to their places, Ellen scowling.

"I'll allow this one reference," Judge Scott said. "Continue, Mr. McSwain."

"All right, Mr. Lazlo, I repeat: Did Mr. Holman contact you?"

"Yes, he did," Cam said.

"About what?"

"He wanted me to help him prove he was innocent."

"And these pleas were in the form of letters?"

"Yes."

"What did you do when you got these letters?"

"I ignored them. I couldn't do anything to help."

"Do you usually receive letters from inmates asking you to help them prove their innocence?"

"No."

"No more questions, Your Honor."

Scott swung his gaze to Ellen. "Ms. Marshall?"

"Yes, Your Honor." Ellen got up and went to stand in front of Cam. "How many defendants have you helped convict, Mr. Lazlo?"

"An estimate, okay?"

"Sure."

"Say, about two hundred, maybe more."

"And, tell me, Mr. Lazlo, how many of them told you they were innocent?"

"About a hundred ninety-nine."

"That's all I have, Your Honor."

"If there are no more witnesses, I'll take this testimony under advisement," Judge Scott said. "You'll have my ruling tomorrow. Court's dismissed." He banged his gavel.

Ellen gathered up her papers and files and put them in her briefcase. Bret McSwain did the same. He turned and saw Julia and nodded casually. *Nothing personal,* she took the gesture to mean. *Right.*

"Well, what do you think?" she asked Ellen as they left the courtroom.

"I think Scott will find probable cause."

"So there'll be a trial," Thomas said.

"Yup. And now we prepare for it."

"When will it be?" he asked. "I've got the Sun Valley Clinic opening, and —"

Ellen shot him a look. "Thomas, the judge will inform us of the date, and you'll be here, your Sun Valley Clinic notwithstanding."

"Yes, ma'am," he said meekly.

After dodging the mass of reporters with the help of Cam and the local police, they all drove home in Cam's Bronco. On the

301

way Ellen said, "That was a bit of a surprise, Cam."

"Yeah."

"How did he know about the letters?"

Cam turned off Main Street onto Third. "You want to bet Holman contacted him?"

"Bets are not my strong suit."

"He's going to be a problem," Cam warned.

"Holman?"

"Yeah."

"This is news?" Ellen said.

The judge's decision came down two days after the hearing, not the next day as he'd said. Julia tried to do some research for Ellen, but her mind was totally obsessed with the agony of waiting. When the fax came, the news was almost anticlimactic.

"The trial's on," Ellen said.

"Yes," Julia breathed.

"No surprise here."

"I know, but this makes it, I don't know . . . official."

"Oh, yes, it *is* official."

Ellen left for Denver that afternoon. Cam was already gone. Dennis would leave for the weekend, and there would only be Julia and Thomas and Livie, who was hardly ever home between the busy rafting season and casual dates with Dennis — at least Livie called them casual. But Julia wondered. As for Thomas, he didn't seem to mind Livie going out with Dennis, who was older than his daughter. Thomas was too preoccupied at the clinic and hospital and then fretting over the progress of the Sun Valley project.

She cooked Thomas's favorite dinner that Friday night. Nothing gourmet or nouvelle, but plain old meat loaf and gravy, mashed potatoes, and peas. Chocolate cake for dessert.

"It's only us," she said as they sat down to eat.

"Hallelujah," he said.

"It's been hard."

"You know, Julia, I'm trying my best not to think about my situation, but you keep reminding me. You're like a dog worrying a bone."

She felt her face heat up, and a sharp retort came to her lips, but she held the words back. She had to forgive him. He was going on trial for murder. He could be excused for his temper.

"Sorry," Thomas said then. "I've got a lot on my mind. At the hospital, and now the new clinic. I should be flying out there once a week, for God's sake, but every time

I wipe myself, that asshole DA wants me to get permission."

"It's not quite that bad," she said.

"Easy for you to say." He left the table without touching his dessert.

By the following Monday, she was near tears all day long. She needed a break. God, how she needed a break. She phoned Ellen at her law office in Denver.

"Can I come stay with you for a few days?" she asked.

"Wow. You sound uptight. Sure, you can stay. Anytime. You know that. What about Thomas and Livie?"

"They'll have to fend. I need some time off."

"Are you bringing Blackie?"

"No, he'll be fine here. He sleeps all day, anyway, and they can let him out when he needs to go. He doesn't have to be walked for a couple days."

"By the way, Mason's in town," Ellen said, obviously a hint that she wouldn't have much time for Julia.

"That's okay. I'll hang around. Shop. Maybe go to some movies. Eat junk. Veg-out, as Livie would say."

"Sounds like a plan."

By that evening, she'd made the three-hour drive to Denver and was ensconced in the guest room of Ellen's house on Race Street near the Denver Country Club. A quiet street lined with big willowy trees and manicured green lawns and gracious older homes. Ellen's house was near the dead end, and it had a beautiful lawn and even a gazebo, which cost Ellen a fortune for upkeep.

The interior of the house was totally unstylish, verging on cuteness. Ellen had indulged her feminine wiles when decorating the place. Chintz and ruffles and muslin curtains and a beautifully polished pine floor covered in girlish pastel braided rugs. The kitchen was state-of-the-art, not that she cooked. Not even for Mason. But Ellen's theory was to spend the big bucks on kitchens and baths — good for resale.

In shorts and a T-shirt, Julia sprawled on the couch in the media room, remote in hand, watching *Star Trek* reruns. Ellen was out with Mason. She felt more relaxed than she had in a long time. Yes, this short vacation had been a great idea. She kept thinking about calling Thomas or checking on Livie, but she didn't. Besides, Livie would be out with Dennis. The truth was, she worried more about Blackie, that someone would be home to feed him and let him out the back door when he needed to go, than she did her husband and step-daughter. There was just something so innocent and vulnerable about animals. And some men, too, she mused. The kind she always went for.

She watched Captain Kirk demolish an alien and kiss another alien, who looked suspiciously human, considering she was from a planet on a far quadrant of the galaxy. She watched the doctor, known as Bones, cure half the crew of the *Enterprise* of a virulent otherworld virus. Mr. Spock said, "Fascinating," at least ten times a show.

She clicked the remote, and there was Audrey Hepburn cajoling Cary Grant. Another click and there was Hoss on *Gunsmoke*. More clicks. The weather, diamond bracelets for sale, a real-life cop show, a handsome patrolman forcefully arresting a man.

A cop show . . . Cam. She knew he was in Denver. Working the forensics angle of her husband's case.

Where did he live? She had no idea. She tried to conjure up a vision of what kind of place he'd inhabit, but she couldn't. In so many ways, he was a cipher.

There were some hints at his inner being, though. The fear of flying, his self-deprecation about it. His careful noting when Julia needed something, always offering his assistance. Praising her cooking. Running errands for her if he was going into town anyway.

He liked her, she knew that. A woman *knew*. He had a half-adversarial, half-joking relationship with Ellen. To Livie he was polite but distant, a little uncertain how to treat the young woman. Dennis obviously idolized him, had even begun to emulate the tough ex-cop by talking less and answering questions in clipped sentences.

Around Thomas, Cam was rigid and absolutely neutral. He did not like her husband. Which didn't really bother her, because she knew Cam would never let personal feelings compromise his work.

She clicked the remote, unseeing, and allowed herself the luxury of idle musing. She thought about nothing in particular for a time, but always her thoughts settled back on Cam Lazlo. What lay behind his hard façade? Some kind of psychic wound, she was sure. And she admitted that drew her, the same way the widower status of Thomas had drawn her. She was a sucker for men who needed nurturing.

The next day she indulged in an orgy of shopping at Target and Mervyns and

T.J. Maxx. Underwear, socks, linens, a new coffeemaker. The kind of everyday things that Aspen boutiques disdained. She made a stop at Petsmart, went up and down the long wide aisles, amazed, and bought a giant bag of kibble chow and a toy for Blackie. She'd never been in a Home Depot, and she stopped there, too. Guilt stabbed at her a few times as she thrust her credit card at a salesclerk, but she ignored her reticence. Think how much money she was saving. Not that Thomas cared. Her frugal ways either made him laugh or irritated him.

At the new factory outlet stores, she found an adorable stretch top for Livie, a beautiful silk shirt for Thomas at half price, a silk tweed blazer for herself on a summer clearance rack in front of a shop.

Ambling along, window shopping as if she hadn't a care in the world, she spotted a pale blue linen shirt, and it struck her that Cam would look very handsome in it. The shirt had a small stain on the collar and was reduced to $19.99, "as is" on the tag. She held the shirt up into the light and thought, *I could get that stain out in a minute*. She studied the shirt, vacillating, and then she hung it back on the rack. Stupid idea, buying a shirt for Cam.

Dumb. And then she wondered how she could be thinking about him, and at a time when Thomas needed her so badly. She finally convinced herself she was wasting effort feeling guilty — it was okay to find someone attractive, it was the most natural thing on earth. As long as she didn't take it further, that was. Which she'd never do.

That evening she had Chinese take-out. She'd only seen Ellen for a few minutes when she got home from work, showered, dressed, and raced out for a tryst with Mason.

"We may go to a movie," Ellen said, "and if I don't come home" — she smiled coyly — "not to worry. I'm in good hands. So to speak."

Julia stuffed herself with Sechuan Beef and Hunan Chicken, and then obeyed the dictates of her guilt and called home.

Livie answered. "We're fine. Ellen called today and got some stuff from Dennis faxed down to Denver. I sold ten raft trips today, which is pretty good for August, because the river is so far down now, you know, the snowmelt is gone." Livie, the white-water rafting expert now.

"That's great, honey. Tell them to give you a raise. Is your father home?"

"Sure, here he is."

"Thomas, are you okay? Is there enough food in the house?"

"Don't worry. I thawed the lasagna. We're all set."

"If you have time, heat it in the oven with some fresh sauce, it's in that glass jar on the right side of the fridge, it's better that way. Nuking it is easier, but it can get rubbery, you know."

"Hey, Livie and I are doing just fine. Stop micromanaging."

He seemed almost relieved that she wasn't there. That stung. "I'll be home the day after tomorrow. Any messages for me? Did Lawson call?"

"Not a thing."

"How's Blackie?"

"He's conked out in the dining room. Livie gave him too many scraps from dinner last night and he threw up."

"Oh . . ."

"We cleaned up, all's well."

"Well, thank you. Maybe I shouldn't have —"

"Jesus, lighten up. Stay as long as you like," he said.

And that stung, too. Not so long ago, Thomas would have said he missed her. When had that aspect of their marriage changed? Since his arrest? But she didn't think that was right. It seemed he'd begun to show disinterest before that — long before. Why hadn't she noticed? How could she become so complacent about her marriage?

"Well," she said, "I'll let you go."

"Oh, I forgot," he said. "Guess who's arriving next weekend?"

She looked heavenward. "Maggie?"

"You got it. I tried to tell her not to bother until the trial, but you know my mother."

"She'll be here until the trial? For *months?*"

"She'll be in the garage apartment. I don't think she'll be in the way."

Julia said nothing.

"It's okay, isn't it? Livie's looking forward to seeing her."

"It's fine," she said. But when she was off the phone, she thought about the clutter in the apartment, the dust and cobwebs she hadn't gotten to.

Well, there wasn't anything she could do tonight. Tomorrow, she thought. She'd pull a Scarlett O'Hara and worry about Maggie tomorrow.

She read a book she'd found on Ellen's bookshelf, a murder mystery. The radio on a twenty-four-hour classical station, broadcasting an evening of Dvořák.

Trying to relax, putting aside anxiety about Blackie's stomach, Thomas's state of mind, Livie's relationship with Dennis, and Maggie's imminent arrival. The trial.

Tomorrow she'd run by one of the lighting stores she'd passed on Colorado Boulevard; they needed a new reading lamp in the living room. And there was a movie she wanted to see at one of the theaters downtown. A matinee, popcorn for lunch. Maybe even candy. Then should she buy new sheets and towels for Maggie's visit? *Three-month visit?*

At ten she heard Ellen's car, heard the garage door go up. Hm, no overnight for Ellen? Then she heard the back door into the kitchen open and close, and she called out, "Ellen?"

"It's me."

"I thought you were going to —"

"I'm really tired. I'm going to bed. See you in the morning."

Something in her friend's voice was off. She'd had a fight with Mason, or maybe he didn't want her to spend the night. Something. As if she'd been crying.

She hesitated for a moment, then went upstairs to Ellen's bedroom — the door was closed. She knocked lightly, then

312

didn't wait, but turned the knob and pushed the door ajar. The first thing she heard was a sob. Ellen sobbing. She pushed the door open the rest of the way and went in. Ellen was sitting on the edge of her bed, her face in her hands, strangled sobs wrenching her.

"What?" Julia said, going to her friend. "Oh, Ellen, what happened?" They *had* fought.

"Leave me alone," Ellen whispered.

Then Julia saw the marks on her neck, red welts, scratches, running down her neckline, angry contusions.

"Oh, my God," she breathed.

Ellen cried harder.

"What happened?"

"Nothing."

"Ellen, damnit . . ."

"Nothing."

"He . . . he . . . did that. Mason. *He did that?*"

Ellen didn't answer, only moved her head from side to side as if in misery.

"Do you want to go to the emergency room?"

"No! I'm okay. I just . . ." She wiped at her nose with the back of her wrist.

"You should call the police," Julia tried.

"No! Goddamnit, don't you . . . don't you dare!"

"All right. Okay. But you should at least —"

"This is none of your business."

"Ellen, come on, I just want to help."

"I don't need help."

How many times had Julia had the same conversation with battered wives and girl-friends? Sometimes you just couldn't convince them to do anything at all to extricate themselves from an abusive relationship. But she couldn't believe that Ellen, smart, sharp, with-it Ellen, would let this happen. Not Ellen.

"Let me get a washcloth."

"I'm okay."

Julia eased down next to her friend on the bed, carefully put an arm around her. Ellen leaned against her and cried harder. "Has he ever done this before?" Julia asked in a soothing voice.

"No . . . never. He just . . . we had an argument. . . ."

"You know that's not an excuse."

"But . . . but, Julia, I love him. And . . . and I know he loves me. It's just . . ."

Next thing you knew, Ellen would say it was all her fault. Oh, God, Ellen. She hugged her friend more tightly.

Then the phone rang. It rang twice, the cordless set on the nightstand, and they both froze.

"It's him," Ellen whispered. "I can't —"

"Maybe it's Thomas. I'd better . . ." But she didn't believe it was her husband.

"You get it."

Julia picked up the receiver; it wasn't Mason and it wasn't Thomas.

"Ellen?" came a male voice.

"No . . . um, it's Julia, I'm staying at Ellen's. . . . Cam? Is that you?"

"Julia, oh. Didn't think it sounded like Ellen. I didn't know you were in Denver."

She turned away from Ellen, who was sobbing again. "Ah . . . listen, is it important? Can Ellen get back to you?"

There was a silent moment on the line, then, "Is anything wrong?"

"No." Damn, he'd heard the crying. "What makes you —"

"Something happened." His voice was flat and uncompromising.

"No, really, I . . . She isn't feeling well and —"

"Cut the crap. I'm not deaf. I'm coming over."

"Oh, no, Cam, really —"

But he hung up.

Ellen sniffed and raised her head. "What?"

"It was Cam. He must have heard you, and he's coming over."

"I don't want to see him," Ellen said faintly.

"I'll . . . I'll talk to him. Tell him . . . you're really sick. Something."

Twenty minutes later, when Cam knocked at the door, Julia was prepared. She planned to get rid of him fast and then go back to Ellen. But that wasn't the way it worked out.

"What happened?" he asked the moment he stepped inside the house.

She'd never seen him like this, cold and still, his eyes like prisms of blue ice, his stillness scarier than motion, more threatening. "Nothing, honestly. Ellen got sick . . . a stomach thing . . ."

"Yeah, I've heard that before."

"What do you mean?"

He made a gesture with his hand, a slice through the air. "I mean, she's not sick, and I want to see her."

"She doesn't want to —"

"Where's she?"

"In her room, but she . . ." There was no dissuading him. He was full of menace. She was almost afraid, but she knew instinctively that he was not angry with her. Or Ellen.

"It's all right, Julia." Ellen's voice from behind them.

Cam turned and glared at her. Nothing moved but his eyes, their focus shifting, glinting. "Did your boyfriend do that?"

"I'm okay, Cam. You didn't have to come over."

"Hell I didn't."

"You can go home now," Ellen said.

"It was that Mason character, wasn't it? That guy you told me about, Mason something."

"Please, Cam, it's not your concern."

"Yeah? Then who the hell's concern is it?" He thrust his head forward. "You call the cops?"

"No. No, I don't want them involved," Ellen said, her voice breaking. "Please . . ." Tears filled her eyes. "Will you just go."

"Christ," he said, and he began pacing the living room, head bowed, hand at the back of his neck. "You're crazy to let this happen. You're smarter than this."

"Cam," Julia said. "She's upset enough."

He pivoted toward her. "Yeah, well, she should be. Just where is this Mason right now?"

"Leave him out of this," Ellen said.

"Right. It was all your fault, I know." What was going on here? His reaction was too strong, too . . . knowledgeable.

"Please," Ellen said, and she sank down onto the couch, her face back in her hands. "Oh, God, this is worse than . . . this is . . ."

Cam came over to her, rested a hand on her back. "Hell, I'm sorry. Ellen, you hear me? Christ, I'm such a hothead. I just hate to see . . ."

"I'm so . . . embarrassed," Ellen got out.

"That's crap," he said.

"We were just having an argument."

"About what?"

Ellen had a tissue balled in her hand. She'd dabbed at her eyes with it. "About him being in Washington so much. And then he got mad, because when he's home I work all the time. And I've been up in Aspen so much."

"Nice guy," he muttered.

"He *is* a nice guy. He's good to me, and he loves me."

"Tough love," he said.

"Please, this is hard enough."

"Okay, okay." He drew in a breath, seemed to be calming down. "Where does this Mason live?"

"It doesn't matter," Ellen said.

"I'd like to talk to him. Someone's got to talk to him."

"Cam, for God's sake," Ellen said.

"I've had some experience with this."

But he was a homicide detective, Julia thought, wasn't he? What experience was he referring to?

"No, I don't want —"

"Believe me, it's helpful. Someone objective."

Ellen sat with her head hanging, elbows on her knees. "I don't know. It seems . . ."

"An advocate," Cam ventured. "An objective advocate."

"Let me think."

"It's better to do it right away. So there's no time to make mental excuses."

"It was my fault," Ellen said in a low voice.

"No, it wasn't," Cam said. Final, certain.

In the end Ellen agreed to let him pay Mason a visit. That night. Before her boyfriend could build up mental layers of denial.

"He lives just off Wadsworth Boulevard, in the Mountain Vistas condos on Jacquard Street. Number 4B."

"Got it."

"You'll tell him," Ellen said, her voice quivering with misery, "you'll tell him I'm sorry, that I didn't mean it? That I love him?"

"Yeah, sure." Cam shook his head, and Julia stared in disbelief at her friend.

"You won't, I mean, you won't . . . hurt him?"

"I won't lay a finger on him."

When he was gone, Julia sank down next to Ellen and placed her hands over her friend's.

"Do you think I should have let Cam go?" Ellen asked, blowing her nose again. Tough little Ellen, so deflated, so wounded.

"Oh, yes," Julia replied, but she had misgivings. Cam seemed too emotionally involved. And his experience with battered women — what exactly had he meant by that?

Well, she had never liked Mason very much, as Ellen knew, and this only cemented her opinion. If Cam visited the man and put the fear of God in him, then so much the better.

"What's the matter with me?" Ellen asked. "How did I get myself into this? What the hell is *wrong* with me?"

"There's nothing wrong with you, sweetie," Julia said. "It's not you."

"Every man I've ever gone out with, something happens, something's wrong. It's me, I know it's me."

"Shh, it's not your fault," Julia said, but even as she spoke she wondered about — not Ellen — but herself. She was equally as flawed as her friend. She'd just spent this whole trip, day and night, fantasizing about Cam when her own husband's life was at stake. And she was questioning *Ellen's* behavior?

Cam sucked in a lungful of warm night air before he knocked on Mason Schultz's door. He let the air out. Sucked in another breath. There, he was in control. Okay.

He knocked, waited, shifted from foot to foot. Finally heard footsteps, the door cracked on a security chain.

"Ellen, I . . ." came the guy's voice.

"It's not Ellen."

"Okay, well, who . . . ?"

"Friend of Ellen's. Cam Lazlo. I've been working with her."

"Oh, yeah?"

"Yeah. You going to open the door or what?"

"Look, she mentioned you, but it's late, and —"

"Just open up." Then he added, "Please." He almost choked.

Finally Schultz undid the safety chain and opened the door. He was of medium height, big-barreled chest, with dark brown eyes and dark blond hair. He'd be called handsome, Cam guessed, if you were a chick.

"Okay, Mr. Lazlo, what exactly can I do for you?"

"It's about what you did to Ellen tonight." He stood there in the entry hall of Schultz's condominium, facing the man, feeling familiar fury spread in his gut. He stared at Schultz, trying to hold the rage at bay.

"She was okay when she left here."

"Yeah, right. Okay. Look, pal, a man never lays a hand on a woman."

"Hey, I was a jerk. I admit it. She pissed me off, her and her big mouth. Like she's so damned perfect." Schultz shook his head.

"So you tried to choke her," Cam said, his voice hoarse.

Schultz smirked. "You know women. I didn't hurt her, I just made my point." As if Cam was his buddy, as if they were comparing their latest conquest. "She thinks she can run my life."

"That is no fucking reason to lay a hand on her."

"What's it to you? You interested in her?"

"I'm her friend."

322

"Some friend, coming over here at night and hassling me. Okay, you can leave now." Schultz held the door open.

Cam lost it. He slammed the door shut with one hand and seized Schultz's shirt with the other. "You'll apologize to her."

Schultz grabbed his hand and tried to yank it away. They wrestled for a moment — the man was stronger than he appeared. He broke Cam's hold, and they stood facing each other, panting.

"Get the hell out of here," Schultz whispered harshly, "or I'll call the cops."

Cam decked him. A quick right to the jaw, so fast he hadn't even known he'd swung until he felt the jolt up his arm all the way to the shoulder. Schultz went down to his knees.

Cam stood over him, shaking with fury, swelled up with a twisted kind of triumph. Glad he'd punched the guy, knowing he'd regret it. Pushing that shit thought away.

"Touch her again and next time I'll really hurt you, pal," he ground out.

He left Schultz on his knees, shoved the door open, and walked out into the warm night. He was breathing hard, as if he'd run a race. Still pumped, the blood chasing itself through his veins. Good, it felt good.

Then, in his Bronco, driving away, the

violence ebbed and logic slipped back into his brain.

Shit. He was as bad as Schultz. Out of control. Just like his asshole stepfather. Just like everything he despised.

What was he going to tell Ellen? And . . . Julia? Jesus, *Julia.* He'd sworn there'd be no violence. Goddamn it, he'd sworn.

FIFTEEN

Bret McSwain's office chair was pushed back, his legs stretched out, and his fingers laced together behind his head, elbows akimbo. He was on the speakerphone in his Glenwood Springs office, because Lawson Fine, the assistant DA from Aspen, was present, listening in.

"Dr. Winagle, would you mind telling your story again? I've got my ADA here," Bret said, an unctuous tone in his voice.

"I guess," Craig Winagle said.

"You were a resident at University Hospital in Denver with Thomas Innes back in 1990?" Bret prompted.

"Yes, we were doing our residencies in orthopedic surgery." The disembodied voice filled the office. "Thomas and I met our first year there. We were friends, both from out of town. He was a brilliant surgeon, and I really respected him."

"Until?" Bret said.

"Yes, well . . . until one particular surgery, a lumbar spine fusion, on an elderly patient. Something went wrong, and the man became a paraplegic. No one ever knew exactly what caused the paralysis. It could have been one of several things, most likely a mistake on the surgeon's part."

"And Thomas was the surgeon."

"Yes. I was assisting on the surgery, along with the head of residents, who, I should tell you, insisted nothing had been done incorrectly. On the part of the primary surgeon, that is. The paralysis was blamed on the anesthesiologist. Well, it could have been her fault. But nothing was certain. In the end, she was let go, and that was that."

"But you discussed the surgery with Dr. Innes?" McSwain pulled a face for Lawson's benefit, unclasped his hands, made a whirling motion with an index finger, as if to say, *Go on, Winagle, get to the point.*

"I ended our friendship."

"Why?"

"I felt that Thomas's attitude was very bad, very negligent. He really didn't give a damn about that old man. Or, for that matter, about the anesthesiologist. I was quite upset, especially for the distraught family, but Thomas seemed to brush the incident off like a piece of fluff on your lapel or something."

"Would you say he showed an abnormal attitude?"

"To my mind, yes. He didn't care about the patient and he didn't care about his colleague, who, for all practical purposes, was fired."

"Was it possible his attitude stemmed from something else? He was in residency, perhaps he was exhausted, overwhelmed, and he couldn't allow himself to get emotionally involved."

"I wish that were the case. Unfortunately, that was simply Thomas. In a nutshell, he was arrogant and egotistical and cared more about the starch in his shirts than he did his patients."

McSwain grinned at Lawson. "And you're willing to testify to this at the trial?"

"Yes, I am."

"Could you repeat, for my ADA's benefit, how you happened to contact me, Dr. Winagle?"

"I read about the case in the *New York Times*."

Bret mouthed to Lawson, *He lives in New York*.

"I never heard about his first wife being murdered. I remember her, Samantha. I met her once or twice. So when I read about him being arrested, I was shocked.

But then I remembered our residency and that incident in particular, and I thought someone should know about his dark side."

"Okay, Dr. Winagle, we'll be staying in touch with you. The trial is scheduled for October 26, unless the defense attorney asks for a continuance. I'll keep you posted."

When the New York doctor hung up, Bret leaned forward and planted his elbows on the desk. "A character witness from heaven. Dr. Craig Winagle, respected orthopedic surgeon at Mount Sinai Hospital."

"Sounds good."

"Ellen will try to have his testimony repressed or thrown out entirely."

"Well . . ."

Bret waved a hand. "I know, he's not mentioned in discovery, he's not on the witness list. Hey, he just called me last week. I'll delay, then I'll forget."

Lawson looked uncomfortable.

"Even if Ellen gets the judge to disallow his testimony, the jury will have heard it."

"Dirty trick, Bret."

"Small-time dirty, not big time."

"But you have another dirty little secret, the dietitian . . ."

"Rick Krystal."

"Right. Isn't the case solid enough without a second undisclosed witness?"

"You never have an airtight case, Lawson, even with a goddamn confession. Something always pops up to bite you in the ass."

"What if Ellen finds out about these two before the trial?"

"How?"

"I don't know. Julia?"

"Julia's resigned, or did you forget?"

"Of course not."

Bret held his hands out, palms up. "I rest my case."

"Well, there're always leaks," Lawson said, still looking uncomfortable.

When Lawson left for the drive back to Aspen, Bret went over his notes on the three phone conversations he'd had with Dr. Craig Winagle. Then, before he went home, he handed them to Clara Pratt, his indispensable secretary.

"Type these up and put them in the Innes file, will you, Clara?"

"Sure. Tomorrow okay?" She glanced at the wall clock.

"Tomorrow's fine. No rush." He hesitated. "Oh, Clara? Don't leave these lying around before they're typed up. For your eyes only." And he winked at her.

★ ★ ★

"I've got an idea," Julia said.

"Okay." Ellen looked up.

"I've been thinking. I need to talk to Clara Pratt."

Ellen cocked her head.

"Bret McSwain's secretary."

"Ah-ha."

"She's a friend. She's older, no-nonsense, probably smarter than the attorneys she works for. We've always gotten along."

"And?"

"And she might have something on Rick Krystal, for instance."

"You think she'd tell you anything?"

"She might."

"Go for it," Ellen said.

Julia phoned Clara at home and left a message: "Clara, we haven't talked in ages. Let's get together for lunch or something. Call me."

The next day Clara returned her call. "Oh, Julia, I was so sorry to hear you resigned. We need more people like you."

"You know I had to."

"Sure, I know."

"How about lunch? Will Bret let you out of jail?"

"Lunch would be great."

"I'll come down to Glenwood. I've got

330

to get my car serviced."

"We can gossip," Clara said, too carefully, Julia thought.

"I *love* gossip," Julia replied.

They settled on a day and a time. Clara was going to pick her up at the Jeep dealership, and they'd go to Los Desperados, a Mexican eatery.

Julia drove the forty miles to Glenwood Springs on a Thursday, left her Grand Cherokee for its scheduled service, and waited in front of the dealership for Clara. It was hot in Glenwood, 3,000 feet lower in altitude than Aspen. She waited, and she plotted — how to get Clara talking.

As it turned out, she didn't have to resort to any ploys.

"It was fate, you calling me," Clara said.

"Really?"

"I've been agonizing over this." She was jittery, playing with a fork. Turning it around and around in her fingers. Not meeting Julia's eyes.

"What is it, Clara?" Julia leaned forward over the table.

A waitress appeared and handed them menus. "Can I get you something to drink, ladies?"

Damn, Julia thought.

"Iced tea," Clara said.

"Same," Julia said, then, "What's up, Clara? Are you okay?"

"Yes. No. I'm upset." Clara closed her eyes for a second. "Bret has a character witness that's not in discovery."

"What?" *Rick Krystal?* Julia thought. But he was not a character witness.

"I shouldn't be here. I shouldn't be telling you this, but . . . but I didn't sleep a wink last night thinking about it, and then you called. . . . I just know it's the right thing to do."

"Okay, Clara. About this . . . character witness?"

"A doctor named Craig Winagle, that's W-I-N-A-G-L-E, from New York, who was a resident in Denver with your husband." Clara drew in a breath. "He's spoken to Bret three times now, and from what I gather from the notes, he's volunteered to testify at the trial that your husband was . . . let me think . . . the words were *negligent* and *arrogant* in his treatment of his patients. There was a particular incident involving an elderly man . . ."

When Clara was finished, Julia leaned back, glad for the cool of the air-conditioning. *Craig Winagle.* Thomas had never mentioned him. And the man's story . . . regardless of whether there was an ounce of truth to it, the jury could be impacted. That made two witnesses Bret was not disclosing. How many more rotten tricks was he going to pull on them?

"Thanks, Clara," she said.

"I'm glad I told you. Oh, God, Julia, please don't tell anyone where you heard this."

"You know I won't."

"Bret will figure it out, though. Who else could it be?" Clara was so anxious, she was almost in tears.

"He won't get it from me or anyone on the defense team, I swear it."

"Okay, okay, thank you, Julia. I *do* trust you" — she drew in a shaky breath — "but then, Bret trusted me, didn't he?"

Julia straightened and put her hand on Clara's. "You did the right thing. I appreciate what it took for you to tell me this. Thank you."

The waitress returned. "Ready to order?"

Clara looked up at her, said, "We need a couple minutes, okay?"

The waitress flounced away.

"I don't want to lose my job over this," Clara said when they were alone again.

"You won't. I promise you won't."

They finally ordered lunch, although neither had much appetite. Julia's mind

333

whirled with questions. *Craig Winagle.* *Negligent and arrogant. An elderly patient.*

Clara dropped her off at the Jeep dealership, and she paid the lady at the service counter, got her keys, found her car — all in a daze. Then she had to go to the grocery store: fruit and meat and salad and also Livie's newest health-food fad. Ice cream for Dennis. And Maggie was due to arrive on Saturday. What crazy Hollywood diet was she on now?

But the whole way up Highway 82 to Aspen, Julia thought only about Clara's story. An ugly tale. If it was true. *Damn Bret, damn him.* But Clara had said this Winagle had called Bret. Out of the blue, because he'd read about Thomas's arrest. Still, it was unethical for Bret to keep two witnesses secret from the defense. For an instant she thought about going to Judge Scott — wouldn't that just cook McSwain's goose — but if she ratted McSwain out, he'd know about Clara. And Julia suspected Lawson Fine had left her the note about Krystal. So no running to the judge.

She was furious at Bret one minute, scared for Thomas the next. What Ellen said all those weeks ago? That the prosecution always kept something secret

— something big or small, but that was the name of the game. How right Ellen had been.

Of course Ellen had to know. And Cam. Oh, God, *Cam,* hearing such a terrible thing about Thomas. She thought and thought about her reaction to his hearing this New York doctor's story, and she couldn't comprehend why she felt so much worse about Cam hearing it than she did Ellen.

But she did know why. In a corner of her overworked mind, she knew.

Well, one thing was a certainty, she wasn't going to tell anyone until she'd spoken to Thomas and heard his side.

Groceries in the rear of the car, she drove into Aspen, straight down Main Street to her husband's clinic, parked in front, and marched in. Thomas hated to be disturbed at work, hated it. But this couldn't be put off.

She waited while the receptionist checked a patient in, then she stepped up to the desk, and said, "I need to see Dr. Innes. It's very important."

The girl looked up at her, startled. "Mrs. Innes?"

"Please, it's important."

"Can you wait a second? He's with a patient."

"Yes, but tell him it's important."

He appeared from one of the exam rooms in a couple minutes and met Julia in the central area where the nurses held sway. "Julia?" He looked surprised. "Is Livie okay? Is it . . . ?"

"It's not Livie. She's fine. Thomas, we have to talk. Privately."

He studied her for a moment, then nodded. "My office."

She told him the story. Not mentioning Clara. Only that someone she trusted from the Glenwood Springs office had relayed the information to her. He sat quietly behind his desk, listened, did not interrupt, did not change his expression, made no exasperated or defensive gestures. He was a good listener; *he must sit here and listen to his patients like this,* she thought.

"That's it?" he said when she finished, and somehow his tone gave her comfort.

"Thomas, if this Winagle tells his story on the witness stand, it will look bad for you."

"Julia, Julia. The man is telling a story that has nothing to do with what really happened. Craig Winagle, God, I haven't thought of him in years."

"Well, he thought of you."

"Of course he did. Christ, I've been in

336

every newspaper in the country. You know, I love you for being so protective, but honestly, Julia . . ."

"We're just lucky I found out, because if Bret sprang this other new witness on us, and we weren't prepared —"

"Look, you're making too much of this. I'll tell you what really happened. You can tell Ellen, I guess. As far as I'm concerned, there's no problem."

Julia kept her eyes on him, trying to be the prosecutor now, trying to judge, to analyze.

"Winagle was an acquaintance, a kind of . . . well, call him a nerdy guy, a mediocre surgeon. Someone should have guided him to another specialty, but that's not relevant, is it? He was a hanger-on, you know the type. He tried too hard to be one of the boys. He tried too hard to make it with women. I don't want to say he was a loser, but . . ." He shrugged.

"Anyway, this patient he's alluding to. An older man with the worst sort of stenosis. His prognosis wasn't good to begin with. We warned him and his relatives. He signed a release because he was desperate, in so much pain. So we went ahead with the surgery, and it didn't work out. His pain was gone, but he had significant paralysis, just as Winagle says.

"But — and this is the crux — we traced the problem to the anesthesiologist's epidural. No question, it was a bad block. There was a hospital investigation, I'm sure there's paperwork somewhere that you can look up, but anyway, I was absolved of all blame. The anesthesiologist was let go — fired. Rightfully. What was her name? Wait, I'll remember in a sec. Hold on. Yes, Rosalyn Dangelo. Can't believe I remembered."

Julia felt as if she were drawing her first real breath in hours. "That's it?" she asked.

"That's my story and I'm sticking to it." Thomas smiled.

"It's not funny."

"Sorry. The whole thing's just so ridiculous, Craig Winagle bringing that up after so many years. He's looking for some attention, that's all. Still trying to be somebody."

"Thomas . . ."

"Do you know how many incidents like that there are in big hospitals in the space of a year? Hell, in a *month?*"

"What happened to the poor man who was paralyzed?" she asked.

"Who knows? As residents we had dozens of patients a day. So many sur-

338

geries, we lost count. Usually we never saw them again."

"And the anesthesiologist?"

"I think she left Denver. I don't really know. I'm sure she found a job somewhere."

"And paralyzed some other patient?"

"Oh, she'd never make that particular mistake again, believe me."

Julia thought about that and tried to believe him. Otherwise . . . "I'll have to tell Ellen about this Winagle."

"Tell her. He's a nobody. Honestly."

She drove the few blocks home, relieved. Yet a bit uneasy. She was sure Thomas was telling the truth, but his seeming disregard for the people who got hurt by the incident — the patient and . . . Rosalyn. Yes, it had been years ago, and Thomas had been an overworked, underpaid resident with a wife and child, but still . . .

Then the question that had been hovering in the back of her mind for weeks materialized, and she couldn't dismiss it as easily as Thomas had dismissed Craig Winagle's story.

Why did so many people have it in for her husband?

At home Ellen and Cam were reviewing a witness list. Julia could hear Ellen saying,

"So this former hospital employee is right here in the valley. Okay? And you've talked to her?" Cam's deeper tones, only a word or two. "Saw her just yesterday."

Julia put the groceries away; the ice cream was soup despite the dry ice she'd asked for, and the top came off as she lifted the carton from the grocery bag. Stupid, stupid. She almost broke into tears as she sponged up the sticky mess. Then she crept upstairs without saying a word to either of them. She was aware of Cam pivoting toward her. She could feel his eyes bore through her, and she ran up the steps to escape his scrutiny.

She pulled off her damp blouse and kicked off her shoes, got a cool wet washrag and sprawled on the bedspread, sweating, feeling sick from the heat, the rag on her forehead.

First there was Bret McSwain out to get Thomas. Then Leann Cornish. Then the hospital dietician. Now this Craig Winagle. Thomas had called him nerdy. There was also Matt Holman, who, no doubt, was giddy with glee at the prospect of getting on a witness stand and testifying about Thomas and his relationship with Samantha. Holman could say anything he wanted, too, because Samantha wasn't there to back him up or defend Thomas. And how many more were out there, lurking, just biding their time until they, too, could vomit up a horrible lie about her husband?

She calmed down finally, and stopped sweating and feeling nauseated. From downstairs she could hear the office phone ring, the muted voices of Ellen and Cam. She heard Livie come in and leave almost immediately. Going somewhere — Dennis wasn't here. Maybe Livie was finally spending some time with her girlfriends.

A few minutes after Livie had come and gone, Julia got up, found a very lightweight short-sleeved blouse, buttoned it up, pushed her damp hair back, and descended the staircase.

"You all right?" Cam asked in a low voice when he saw her.

She nodded. He noticed entirely too much. "Just hot, that's all."

"Huh."

"I need to tell you guys something," she began.

Ellen looked at her quizzically, Cam without expression.

"I had lunch with my friend," she said. "She told me about a character witness Bret has lined up. Another one who isn't on the list."

Ellen snorted. "Am I surprised?"

"It's a doctor who lives in New York now, but he did his residency in Denver with Thomas. Craig Winagle."

"Go on," Ellen said when Julia hesitated.

"Okay, I'll give you this Winagle's version, then Thomas's." But she didn't make Clara's version as bad as she should have; and she related Thomas's story with more optimism than she'd felt when he'd told her. Regardless, no matter how she told the two tales, there remained the paralyzed old man, the anesthesiologist who'd lost her job, and, of course, Craig Winagle's opinion of Thomas.

She finished by telling them, "And he's agreed to testify at the trial."

Ellen whistled, pushed her chair back, and started pacing the room, one hand on a hip, the other gesturing.

Cam stared silently at Julia.

"I told you he'd pull this stuff," Ellen finally said. "That prick."

She stopped pacing, put a hand up to her mouth, and thought for a minute. "Okay, Cam?"

"Yes, ma'am."

"See if University Hospital has any personnel records from 1990. Rosalyn Dangelo, right?"

"Yes," Julia said. Then, "Should we tell Bret we know about these witnesses? Or will you tell Judge Scott?"

"Neither, not right away. Let me think about it. I can't say who told you?"

"No. I promised."

"But that would lend more credence, if I —"

"I *promised*, Ellen."

"Okay. As long as we know about the witness. Good work, Julia baby."

Cam turned to Ellen. "You want to tell her the good news now?"

"Oh, God, please, I'd love some good news," Julia breathed.

"You tell her," Ellen said.

Cam leaned back in his chair. "First off, my hospital contact put me on to a former food worker who witnessed Thomas reaming Krystal over a dinner tray."

"A . . . dinner tray? That hardly seems like —"

"Thing is," Cam interrupted, "the patient was supposed to be on a strict liquid diet, and Krystal sent her solid food."

Julia whistled. "Thomas was right to chew him out."

"See?" Ellen said. "If McSwain puts Krystal on to testify, I tear him to pieces."

"There's more," Cam said. "The preliminary results came in from the FBI lab on the bedsheets. Far as the DNA goes, everyone else on earth has been excluded but Holman. Oh, and there's DNA from an unknown female."

"Unknown?"

"We don't have a sample from Samantha to compare. But, of course, it's hers," Ellen put in. "Unless Holman was screwing another woman on Samantha's bed."

"You're a laugh a minute, Ellen, but that is good news," Julia said. "What about the Buddha?"

"Nothing yet. Usual preliminary tests failed, but there are other ways to extract DNA now. Lab's still working on it," Cam said. "They're really backed up. We're lucky we got any results at all."

Julia sat there for a moment longer. She was tired out, the emotional ups and downs of the day taking their toll. She'd love to retreat to her room again and fall into bed and go to sleep. She'd like to sleep until November, when the trial would be over. She craved oblivion.

But that wasn't possible. She had dinner to fix, a stepdaughter to care for, a mother-in-law arriving, and she had to help her husband beat the murder charge. Just thinking about that — a murder

344

charge — still made her brain reel.

She put her hands on the dining table and pushed herself up. "Okay, I've got to start dinner. Ellen, will you be here?"

"Yes, if you don't mind."

"Cam?"

"Thanks, but I've got plans tonight. And I'm driving back to Denver tomorrow. I'll look into the University Hospital records on Monday. See what I can find on this Rosalyn Dangelo. Got a few other things to do."

I've got plans, was all Julia really heard. A date? Someone he met in Aspen? His hospital contact? She couldn't ask him, but Ellen could. Not that Ellen cared. Julia pictured Cam out to dinner at the Crystal Palace or the Hotel Jerome or Montagna at the Little Nell. With a gorgeous woman. Single, unattached, not bowed under the burden of home and work and husband and stepdaughter. Someone with whom he could have fun. Someone he could make love to.

She went into the kitchen, buffeted by an ineffable sadness, and she began dinner. Mixing ground beef with bread soaked in milk and an egg and seasonings for meatballs. A big jar of ready-made spaghetti sauce, her one concession to efficiency. A

345

salad. Garlic bread. The refrozen ice cream for dessert. If they noticed the icy crust on top, tough.

She thought about the new tests the FBI lab would run on the Buddha, assuming any organic material remained viable after twelve years. Tests done back then had only been able to show blood type — type O positive, as she'd told Judge Scott. Samantha had type O positive. So did Thomas and Matt Holman. Which rendered those old results inconclusive. The blood on the Buddha could have come from all three, or just two of them or only one. But which one?

Now, however, with DNA testing, the lab could — maybe, possibly — determine exactly whose blood was on the statue. Samantha's, of course. But was there another person's DNA on the Buddha? Matt Holman's, for instance? Had Holman scraped or cut his hand while crushing Samantha's skull? Julia didn't remember any testimony alluding to a wound on his hand from the trial transcripts.

She looked into the middle distance and couldn't help remembering that Leann Cornish had said Thomas had a cut on his hand. He'd cut it on a rock, he'd told her. A rock.

She stood in the kitchen, over the bowl of meatball mixture that awaited her ministrations, her head lowered, dread seeping into her. She desperately wanted to tell Ellen to call off the DNA testing of the Buddha; she wanted them to stop right now, because she was so terribly afraid of what the tests might show.

She took a deep breath, then another, lifted a fork to begin mixing the concoction. She heard the front door open, then close. Footsteps. Not Livie. Thomas was home.

Then she was aware of someone in the doorway. She glanced up. Cam, his eyes on her vigorously.

"Oh," she said.

"Are you all right?" he asked again.

"Sure, I'm fine. Tired, you know."

"You had a rough day."

"That I did."

"The person who told you about Winagle. That was lucky."

"Yes."

He stood in the doorway, with that aura of stillness peculiar to him, then leaned a shoulder against the frame. Folded his arms across his chest. He grew still again, said nothing for a time, while she mixed the ground beef.

Finally he said, "You work too hard."

She stopped and looked down, afraid to meet his gaze, afraid his sympathy, his caring, his noticing, would shatter her.

But what she really wanted at that moment was to go to him, to lean against his chest, to feel his arms around her, to stay there and let his strength flow into her, his comfort bolster her. The fantasy was so powerful that, for a moment, she felt his arms around her, smelled his scent, heard his voice rumble in his chest where her head rested. But then the notion fled. And Thomas strode into the kitchen.

"Hi," he said, giving her a peck on the cheek.

For Cam's benefit, no doubt.

"What's for dinner?" Thomas asked. "Oh, good, spaghetti and meatballs again."

She glanced at Cam, and she saw how intently he watched Thomas. She recognized the look in his eyes, the cool appraisal, the slight contempt, and she knew in a single beat of her heart that he had doubts about her husband's innocence.

SIXTEEN

September in Aspen is utterly gorgeous. The days are still warm and dry, the air fresh, the sky so cobalt blue it seems impossible. On some days there are clouds, puffy, alabaster, piling in downy billows over the mountains. In the mornings frost glazes the grass until the sun melts it, and the aspen trees turn color, slim trunks whose branches hold a largesse of golden coins.

Most of the tourists leave, the starter castles of second homeowners stand vacant, and the locals reclaim their town. Children go back to school, the football and hockey and soccer seasons get underway. Traffic lessens, restaurants close for a time.

Of course, there's nasty weather in the valley, too. Days of chill rain or even snow, so that when the clouds dissipate, you can see the glistening white on the mountaintops. The snow will stay up there, even if it melts on the valley floor, and on Aspen Mountain, it provides the base for skiing. There's endless rejoicing in the ski town — snow.

Livie had pulled a real shocker at the end of August. She'd sat with Julia and Thomas at dinner one evening and announced, "I've decided not to start college till the second semester."

"*What?*" Thomas had said.

And Julia: "Livie, honey, you can't be serious?"

Then Maggie, who always played devil's advocate: "It wouldn't be the end of the world. College will always be there."

Well, Livie had been quite serious. She and Thomas had waged battle for days, Maggie smack in the middle, but there was no changing Livie's mind on the subject, and, she'd decided, she might even go to school in Denver instead of the University of Michigan. Her arguments were many and fierce, but, as Thomas said, the kid was only making this decision for one reason: Dennis. Livie wanted to be near Dennis, even if it meant blowing off college.

"Dennis is a fine young man," Maggie kept interjecting.

Somehow they got through those awful days with Livie and Thomas barely speaking and Dennis avoiding Thomas at all costs. Ellen and Cam stayed out of it entirely. Ellen only saying, "Well, it's her life, after all, and Denver University is a great school."

To which Julia had replied: "*If* she goes to DU, that is. This remains to be seen."

And Maggie: "It's Livie's life, as Ellen pointed out."

Thomas's trial was to be held in six weeks. *Six weeks.* The spring and summer that had dragged by suddenly seemed to have flown. Ellen wasn't planning on asking for a continuance unless something new came up. Most of the witnesses had been located and interviewed. Strategy was set.

One last thing: Cam was going to fly to New York to interview Dr. Winagle.

"You hate to fly," Julia said to him the day before, as he was getting ready to leave for Denver.

They were standing by the table; the tall windows of the Victorian dining room were bright with late-afternoon sun, and a swath of gold bathed him, shining on his head, gilding every hair on his forearms.

She hadn't really needed to talk to him, but she'd been drawn into the office without volition.

"Yeah, I hate to fly," he said in that way he had, flat and half-joking at the same time, as if he didn't want anyone to recognize what he said as personal. Hiding behind a caustic levity.

"But you get on the planes anyway."

He shrugged. "No way around it some-times."

She watched while he gathered files and papers, checked one carefully, frowned.

"How's Victor Ferris's book coming?"

"Fine."

"Does he always know how the book will end?"

"Don't know. I never asked."

"Maybe he'll give you an advance copy, you know, if he gets some, and you could let me read it."

"Sure."

The phone rang and Dennis answered, handed it to her. "Ellen," he said.

She listened, said, "Uh-oh," listened some more, then hung up. "Cat's out of the bag. Bret's found out we know about Krystal and Winagle. He's going to put them on a *revised* witness list."

Cam grinned. "About time."

"Um," she said.

"You think McSwain knows who leaked the info to you?"

"God, I hope not. I kind of doubt it. I'm not bragging or anything, but I've got a lot more friends around the courthouse than our illustrious DA."

"You've been a real trooper."

"What choice do I have?"

"You could cut and run, leave it behind."

"That's not my style."

"Exactly my point."

"Would *you* cut and run if someone you loved was in trouble?"

He gazed at her from under hooded eyelids. "Probably."

"You're full of it," she said.

"Maybe. Maybe not."

She started toward the staircase. The phone rang again. Dennis answered. She stopped and turned, tried to smile. "Hey, good luck on your flight tomorrow."

"Aren't you supposed to say 'break a leg'?"

"God, no, that's for actors."

"Well, then, I'll try to *act* as though I'm not afraid that damn thing's gonna fall out of the sky."

"It won't."

"If you say so, Julia."

She climbed up the stairs, musing about the sound of her name when Cam said it. Julia. A jewel, something old-fashioned and precious. Her name had never sounded that way before. *Julia.*

Her relationship with Thomas had become almost intolerable. They barely spoke except for the mundane. "Did you get the oil changed in the car?" "Can you pick my shirts up from the cleaners?" "Don't forget I'll be working late today, hospital rounds till eight or nine tonight."

He hadn't touched her since before the preliminary hearing. The last time they'd made love had been July 25. She remembered the date because it was her father's birthday, and she'd called him just before bed. Talked to both her parents for almost an hour, and Thomas had complained she was always on the phone.

They'd argued. Then made up. He'd slipped the straps of her nightgown off her shoulders and been so tender with her. She'd been surprised and happy, thought that was exactly what they'd both needed. Love and relief from all the weeks of stress. But somehow the foreplay had stopped too soon, and he'd found release too fast, then rolled away and gone to sleep.

After that she hadn't encouraged him. And she was ashamed at how little she cared. They were growing apart, each surrounded by a private cocoon, carefully, diligently spun to keep them separate. And inside each sac a change was occurring, like the metamorphosis of caterpillar to butterfly. When the cocoon was finally opened, who knew what new creature would appear?

She thought a lot about the man she'd married, about his character, about why she'd married him. And whenever she did, guilt assailed her, because she didn't think she loved him anymore. Oh, it wasn't any one thing he'd done, or even the legal charges against him. It was the accumulation of a multitude of small sins: his emotional carelessness, his lack of empathy, his disinterest.

Had he always been like that, or had the crisis brought out his true nature? Why had she never seen these failings before?

She held the feelings at bay — she simply would not, could not abandon him now. It wasn't her style, as she'd told Cam. If she couldn't give Thomas her love, she at least owed him her loyalty. He'd taken very good care of her for eight years. He'd taken very good *financial* care of her.

Whenever she thought about that, the ache filled her chest, as if a giant sob awaited release. The failure of their marriage was her fault — she'd married Thomas for the wrong reasons. And to think, she might have languished in the marriage for years if this crisis hadn't occurred.

Cam landed at Newark International Airport and caught a cab into Manhattan.

The day was warm and a touch muggy but bearable. Last time he'd been to New York had been in early August years ago, when he'd still been a cop and had been sent to a nationwide seminar on new forensic techniques and how to handle evidence. He'd been in the city for a week, and suffered from record-breaking heat and humidity. He'd vowed never to fly east again in the summer.

Today was okay. And he wasn't staying the night, anyway. Soon as he interviewed the doctor, he was out of here, on a red-eye back to Denver.

Founded in 1852, Mount Sinai Hospital was old and venerable and one of the finest facilities in the country. There was also the Mount Sinai School of Medicine and the Mount Sinai Medical Center, but Dr. Craig Winagle worked as head of orthopedic residents in the main hospital. Cam arrived an hour early for his scheduled appointment with Winagle, located the man's office, then took a walk to shake off the after effects of the flight. Of course, he still had to get back on a plane this evening, and the east to west flight took longer, what with bucking the jet stream. . . .

Winagle was a few minutes late for their

appointment, and he apologized for keeping Cam waiting. He showed Cam into his office, offered him something to drink, then sat down for the interview.

The first thing Cam noticed was the man's stature. He was a big-boned guy, tall, probably six one or two, with thinning sandy brown hair and large features. Good features. He had keen blue eyes and an easy manner, a soft-spoken voice. Controlled. Thomas Innes had said Winagle was a hanger-on, a nerdy type — pretty hard to imagine from Cam's initial impression, and he was often right on the mark in his assessment of people.

"Long way to come for an interview," Winagle pointed out as he handed Cam a Diet Coke. "Sorry, I know, bad for you," he nodded at the Coke, "but I'm addicted."

"It's fine," Cam said. "And yes, it was a long trip. Can't say I enjoy flying."

Winagle laughed. "Yeah, I feel the same way. I try to stick to cars and trains."

Cam put the Coke on the man's desk, took out his tape recorder. "Mind if I record this?"

"Be my guest."

Cam switched the tape on, set it on the desk between them. He spoke the time and date and location into the machine, their names. "Okay, Dr. Winagle, I'd like to begin by asking why you'd go to such lengths to assassinate Thomas Innes's character."

"That's direct."

"Obviously you're a busy man. Might as well get to the crux of the matter."

"Fair enough," Winagle said. "For starters, Thomas, in my humble opinion, is the worst sort of doctor. He's brilliant and callous. Bad combination. And in my experience with him, he's willing to step over as many bodies as needed in order to achieve his goals."

Winagle stuck to his story as it had been related to Julia: that Innes, or possibly anesthesiologist Dangelo, messed up during a particular surgery, rendering an elderly patient paralyzed. Dangelo took the fall. Thomas Innes didn't give a shit, brushed off the incident as if it meant nothing to him. Winagle never forgot the patient or the man's family, and especially Dangelo, whose career was most likely ruined.

"I read about Thomas being arrested last spring, and I thought, Jesus, he probably did murder Samantha and didn't give a damn, either."

"What makes you think he's capable of

murder? Screwing up in surgery is one thing, but murder?"

"Samantha probably got in his way." Winagle shrugged. "The story I read said there was another man involved; I guess he went to prison for the murder but was let out?"

"That's right."

"Anyway, my knee-jerk reaction was that Thomas saw huge alimony payments coming his way and took care of the problem."

"That's a real leap in thinking. Murder?"

"You asked, and I'm just telling it like I see it."

"If you come out to Aspen to testify as a character witness, you realize that sort of opinion will be disallowed in court."

"I'm sure it will. But I still feel someone should let a jury know what Thomas is really like. Brutally ambitious and smart as hell."

Cam talked with the doctor for another half hour but couldn't shake him from his story or opinions — not that Cam really disagreed. But he'd been fairly certain Winagle had a personal motive for trying to destroy Innes. Now, as he switched off the recorder and stood to leave, he wasn't so sure.

He got on the plane at eight that evening and before he went into his fear mode, he thought about Leann Cornish — he was pursuing his own angle there. But then there was Holman and Rick Krystal and now this New York doctor. Ellen might be able to rip their testimonies apart on the stand. Maybe Ellen was that good. But so was Cam. And he hadn't been able to shake them one lousy bit.

Thursday night Julia and Ellen decided to take a break. A night off, just the two of them. And Blackie, of course.

Thomas had left for Sun Valley the previous morning, a sudden trip reluctantly approved by the DA. Livie was at the movies with Maggie and Dennis; Cam had flown to New York. They watched a tearjerker on TV, *The English Patient*. They cried and ate Starbucks ice cream, Ellen sitting in her favorite position on the floor. And they talked.

"What do you really think, Ellen? Can Thomas get off?"

"Well, you know what I always say, taking any case to a jury is a crapshoot, but I think we have a very good chance."

"Oh, God, I pray you're right."

The truth was she hoped, secretly, that

he would be found not guilty for reasons unrelated to justice. Because if he were found guilty, then she'd have to stick by him, no matter what. Through years of imprisonment and appeals. There'd be no out for her. However, if he was found not guilty, there might be a life for her. Then she could . . . But she wouldn't think about that.

"How are things with you and Mason?" she asked during a commercial break.

"Pretty good. He's in Washington. You know, that night . . ." Ellen studied her fingernails. "That was not like him, or me, for that matter. It was as if aliens took over our bodies."

"I just hope it never happens again."

"I don't think it will. He seems, I don't know, different. More careful around me. I'm not sure I like it very much."

"Did he ever tell you what Cam said to him that night?"

"Nope." Ellen pulled her knees in, Indian-style. "But Cam must have said the right thing, that's for sure. I guess it was a good idea to let him talk to Mason."

"Aren't you curious, I mean, about what he said?"

"A little. But I asked once, and Mason evaded the question, so for once I let well enough alone." During commercials, they went on to talk about other things, but Julia felt as if she were lying the whole time. Lying by omission. She wanted so badly to talk to Ellen about her relationship with Thomas. But she couldn't risk verbalizing her innermost feelings; if she brought up the subject, the whole carefully constructed house of cards that was their marriage and the defense team's effort would tumble down. The house was fragile, constructed of hypocrisy and forced negotiation and emotional dishonesty. But she couldn't let it collapse.

Cam drove back from Denver and his trip to New York the next evening. He stopped by to drop off the report on Dr. Winagle. Julia was alone in the house, wearing sweatpants and a gray sweatshirt that read *Never Forget 9/11*.

She was always amazed at how pleased she was to see Cam. As if when he stood on the threshold, everything in the world clicked into a better, happier mode. He always looked so handsome. In an aqua shirt this evening, made of an expensive cloth that slid and draped over his torso and arms like heavy liquid.

"How did your flights go?" she asked.

"I made it. What else can I say?"

She smiled. "I think it's kind of . . . cute, a big strong man like you scared of something like that."

"Not strong enough to hold up a whole goddamn plane."

"Well, come on in. I'll make coffee. How was Craig Winagle?"

Cam followed her into the kitchen. "Seemed like a good man."

She turned and looked at him. "Not *that* good."

"Yeah, well, he must have his reasons to go after Thomas, I guess."

"Everybody has reasons to do things, not always good reasons, though." She measured coffee into the filter and wondered at Cam's evasiveness. "So, what do you think his motivation is?"

"You can read my report."

"I'd rather you tell me."

"Hey," he said, "my report says it all." Then, before she could question him more, he asked, "Where's Ellen?"

"On the phone to Mason."

"So, she's still seeing him." He settled on a kitchen chair, leaned on his elbows.

"Oh, yes."

"He's been behaving himself?"

"I think so." She hesitated. "You know, I never liked him much. Ellen knows that."

"You have good instincts."

The coffee machine burbled, and she got out mugs, set them on the counter.

"I hope you don't think I'm too nosy, but what happened between you and Mason that night?"

"Ellen didn't tell you?"

"Ellen doesn't know. She said Mason wouldn't talk about it."

"Huh."

She poured the coffee. Waiting for his response. He sat there, both hands cupped around the mug, staring down. She was afraid she'd overstepped a boundary. "Sorry, it's none of my business. I shouldn't have asked."

He glanced up, his expression set in stone. She felt a frisson of unease.

The silence stretched out, then he seemed to decide something. He made a noise in this throat and said, "Look, what happened at Mason's . . . I'm not proud of it. Let's just say the guy pissed me off." He moved his shoulders, a release of tension. "He wasn't sorry he'd hurt Ellen. Didn't even think he done anything wrong. I lost it. I punched him out."

"Oh," she said weakly. "Oh."

"Like I said, I'm not proud I did it. No excuse. He just reminded me —"

But Julia interrupted. "No *wonder* he didn't tell Ellen."

"Look, I didn't hurt him. And, let's face it, he deserved it. But I was wrong."

"It must have been . . . ugly."

He grimaced. "Not my finest hour." Then he looked down again. "Goddamn good thing I never got married," he muttered.

She wondered if she'd heard him right, but she didn't know exactly how to ask. What to ask. He was obviously suffering regret over his fight with Mason. Over something in his past that made him resort to violence.

A hardcore ex-cop, a bachelor, terrified of marriage and commitment because of an abusive father or stepfather? Something clicked in the back of her mind. *Something.* Someone else she knew who reacted exactly the same, with violence, because he'd come from an abusive childhood, and he was deathly afraid if he ever got in a long-term relationship, he'd be as abusive as his father. . . .

"My God," she said, staring at him, really seeing him for the first time. "*You're* Luke Diamond."

"Ah, Jesus." He ran a hand through his hair.

"You are! I can't imagine why I didn't

see it before. Victor Ferris based his hero on you."

"That's horseshit."

"No, it's true. Don't you see? Oh, but you don't read his books, do you?"

Cam didn't meet her eyes. He seemed abashed and angry at the same time. It was true, and he knew she was right.

Then the front door opened and slammed shut and Livie burst into the kitchen.

"Hi, guys."

"Have you eaten yet?" Julia asked, a little impatient. She wanted to continue the conversation with Cam.

"I grabbed something at Johnny Maguire's, had to work late." But she took an apple from a bowl of fruit, a can of pop from the fridge, and a bag of natural corn chips from the cupboard. "Where is everybody?"

"Your father is still in Sun Valley. I think your grandmother is up in the apartment."

"Oh. And everybody else?"

"I guess you mean Dennis."

"He went to Denver this morning. I know that." She gathered her snacks and headed out, then stopped at the door. "Hey, did I interrupt something? Sorry."

"We were just having a cup of coffee," Julia lied.

Cam lifted his mug toward Livie, managed a wry grin. When she was gone, he mumbled something.

"What?" Julia asked.

"I said, women always know."

"Know what?"

"Whatever. Anything. Everything."

"So you admit you're Luke Diamond."

"I admit nothing. Okay, Victor takes liberties. Sometimes. He asks me things. My job is to tell him."

"Does he ask you about your feelings?"

"Hell, no."

"But Luke has feelings, and if you ask me —"

"Didn't ask you."

"You're pissed."

"No." He held his mug in both hands and studied it. "Yes."

"But it's so obvious, now that I think about it."

"Hey, how would you like a few million people reading what goes on in your head?"

"Or your heart," she said softly.

"Yeah, well, that, too. It's spooky."

"Does Victor know how you feel about this?"

"Oh, yeah. But he's making a bundle, what does he care?"

"Now, wait a minute. If Victor Ferris is

such a greedy, awful guy, why do you work for him?"

"He's not that bad. I guess."

"I see."

"You don't see. And you don't know me because you read a few books."

She nodded. "You're not easy to know."

"Sure I am."

"On the surface maybe."

"Something wrong with that?"

"Only that you can't have a meaningful relationship if you only show your surface."

"Meaningful relationships seem to be a lot more trouble than they're worth."

"Oh, no, that's not —"

"Take you and Thomas."

She froze, looked at him.

"What I mean is, you're stuck in this situation with him, and you didn't do anything to deserve it."

"Neither did he."

She was cleaning the coffeepot when she remembered something Cam had said about his family. Nobody left but the stepfather, who moved to . . . South Texas. Right. Good God, she thought, that was why . . . His stepfather was abusive, and he'd seen his mother hurt, and that was why he'd reacted so strongly to Mason Schultz.

And a scene from *Diamond Bright* flew into her head, the scene where Luke beat a rotten drug dealer half to death, then agonized over his lack of control, took his punishment — time off without pay, as just medicine. That was Cam exactly.

"No wonder Luke is such a popular hero," she said.

"I don't get it myself." Cam shook his head. "He's kind of a jerk, over the top, mean, then he melts at some dog run over in the street."

She smiled. "I knew when Blackie liked you . . ."

"Please."

"Come on, you know it's true, Cam."

"What? That I'm like Luke Diamond?"

"No, the other way around. Luke's like you."

"Jesus."

"Oh, don't worry, nobody knows but us. And Victor." Then she leaned her back against the counter, folded her arms. "You know what I'm really curious about?"

"Here it comes."

"The women. All those women Luke makes love to. Are they based on women you've been with?"

He met her gaze squarely, his eyes shadowed, the overhead light glinting on his fair hair. "Every last one."

"Does Victor ask you . . . details?"

He grinned. "Hell, no. Those are all his fantasies."

"Really."

"And I'll never budge on that one."

Just the two of them in her kitchen, coffee long gone, the dark closing in around them. Blackie lying contentedly at her feet. As if . . . as if they belonged together like this. And yet they'd never touched, never kissed, never seen each other undressed. And she was married to another man. But that didn't stop her, not for this short time, this enchanted interlude when they could talk like old friends.

"Tell me about your mother," she said. "Was she a lot like you?"

"Swedish. A big woman, a little like Ingrid Bergman. She was okay until my real father died, then she couldn't handle anything."

"But she remarried."

"Oh, yeah, to a real son of a bitch."

"Did you ever . . . I mean, get into fights with him?"

"You bet. Soon as I was big enough to take the bastard on." She noticed he was flexing a fist.

"That must've been horrible."

"I left as soon as I got out of high school. Went to Colorado State. Took me five years, what with working all the time."

Julia twisted her mouth. "You don't have to tell *me* about working and going to school. My folks helped as much as they could, but it wasn't much. I did have a full-tuition scholarship to law school, but it costs more than just tuition to go to school."

They talked into the night, about college and friends and Aspen. About her job and his.

And then she asked him why he'd gone into law enforcement.

"Oh, boy," he said. "Hard one."

"Tell me."

"I always wanted to be a cop. I don't know, some kind of power trip, maybe? A need to control things. But also," he closed one eye and thought, "I wanted to make things right. The bad things people do to each other."

"And you miss it," she said, remembering last time she'd raised the subject, he'd avoided answering.

He looked into the middle distance — that faraway Nordic gaze — and he said nothing for a time.

"You don't have to —"

He held up a hand. "No, it's okay. Yes, I

371

miss being a cop. I was a good one, too. But I deserved to lose the job. And sooner or later, I'm pretty damn sure I would have done something I regretted forever."

"You think you're capable of — ?"

"I don't know. Best not to test it, though."

"But I see" — she wanted so much to touch his face or his hand — "I see someone who's hiding from how good he is."

"You're confusing me and Luke," he said dryly. He moved his shoulders again, that way he had. Letting off tension, but also avoiding something, a defensive gesture.

"Well, it's late," she said.

"Yeah." But he made no move to go.

"I have to take Blackie out."

"I'll go with you."

They put on jackets; it was chilly out. Julia snapped on Blackie's leash. "Come on, boy," she said. He wagged his stump of a tail, so excited, as if he were being given a treat. One ear stood up, and the tattered one lay flat.

They went outside, down the sidewalk, Blackie pulling, as he always did. She had expected Cam to get in his Bronco and leave for the night, but instead he walked along with her. She tried not to question that, or even think about it. Darkness hid the world, yet it revealed, too. Julia almost put her free hand out to take Cam's. The gesture would have been so easy, so natural.

"It's getting cold," she said.

"Amazing how early fall comes up here."

She was aware of his shadow, a black darker than the night. She could hear him breathe, sense the heat from his body. The faint scent of his aftershave wafted to her nostrils, and a fist clenched inside her belly. Hot and hard and needful.

The dark gave her courage. She moved along the sidewalk while Blackie sniffed and tugged.

"Cam . . ."

"Uh-huh?"

"Do you believe Thomas is innocent?" She was amazed that she'd finally mustered the courage to voice the question. Her whole body tensed.

"Whoa," he said, then nothing.

"You can tell me." Her heart began to pound. Why was she torturing him, torturing herself, for God's sake?

"Look, I'm an investigator. I investigated Samantha's murder twelve years ago. I made a promise to her . . . like I do, *did*, to all the murder victims I was handed. I promised her I'd find out who her killer was and make him pay. It was a solid investigation. I did my job. The evidence was presented to a jury. Holman was found guilty. I thought I'd kept my promise to Samantha."

"But now you're not so sure?" It seemed as if her whole life had come to this point, to this man, here in the chill autumn night, saying what he believed.

"Julia . . ."

"Tell me."

But his silence was all too telling.

She sucked in her breath sharply. Tears sprang to her eyes. She dropped Blackie's leash and put her face in her hands. "Oh, God."

"Julia, hold on."

"I can't stand this!" she cried brokenly. "Thomas . . ."

"Hey, I didn't mean . . ."

"And you, *you* don't even believe . . ." She felt so stupid, so utterly deluded. She tried to muffle a sob.

He stepped close then, and she sensed his hand on her arm. The spot burned, right through her jacket, the heat spread. Then his other hand was on her, tugging. She tried to resist, tried to step back, but her body did not obey, and the gentle pressure of his hands drew her in. She gave up any idea of resistance, and she let him, felt his chest hard against her, his arms around her, her head bowed. Her arms moved, sliding sinuously around his back.

"Don't cry," he said tenderly.

She did cry though. She stood there under the big old cottonwood trees in the cool night, and she held on to him for dear life, and she cried as she had not been able to for all these long months. He said nothing, only gently stroked her back.

She quieted, finally, and found her cheek against his chest, the fabric damp, her fists grasping the back of his jacket. She knew she should push herself away, apologize, find Blackie, and retreat into the house. But she couldn't move: the illicit moment, the forbidden man, the concealing darkness.

"I'm so sorry," she said into his chest.

"Don't be. Here." He reached into his back pocket and pulled out a handkerchief, pressed it into her hand. She wiped her eyes and blew her nose.

"Better?"

She turned her face up to tell him — what? — and his face was close, his hooded eyes and shadowed features so close.

"Julia," he said into the darkness.

Their lips touched, warm and tentative, and her arms were clasping him; he held her face cupped in his hand, and looked at her in the night, and kissed her again. He was warm and cool and soft and hard, and he smelled of man and the tang of after-shave.

She drew back. "Oh, God," she whispered.

"No," he said, putting a finger on her lips.

"I . . . I have to go. Cam I . . . Oh, God, where's the dog?"

He let her go and studied her face for an endless moment. "So, what the hell would your hero Luke Diamond do now?" he asked, and a sad sarcasm roughed his voice.

She knew exactly what Luke would do, *exactly*. He'd take the woman inside and make exquisite love to her.

She found Blackie a half block down, trotting home. Cam walked beside her silently, then got in his car. She stood beneath the porch light and watched his Bronco disappear around the corner. Oh, God, she thought, how could she ever face him again? How could she face herself?

SEVENTEEN

Ellen dropped Mason off at the main terminal of Denver International Airport on a chilly October morning, accepted his perfunctory kiss, said, "See you next weekend, honey," and she drove away.

He was off to Washington for two weeks, and she was on her way up to Aspen right now. There was less than a month to go before the trial. The strategy was fairly well set, the character witnesses lined up and prepped, the flurry of motions still settling on desks at the courthouse.

She drove back toward Denver, hit Interstate 70, and stepped on the gas. Ahead of her, beyond the foothills that rose to the west of the sprawling city, clouds massed on the peaks, gathering over the Continental Divide. While it was partly cloudy and cool in Denver, it could very well be snowing up in the high country. She'd have to have her snow tires put on soon, especially with all these trips to Aspen. Hell, she'd need more than snow tires — she'd need a new car, maybe one of those snazzy new SUVs. A Lincoln. A Lexus would be even better.

Thomas was going to owe her tens of thousands by the time this was over, but she knew she was worth it. She was going to save his ass.

She drove the familiar route and thought about the past six months. Thought about poor Julia. She really shouldn't think about her best friend like that, but she couldn't help it. A husband like Thomas Innes, a nice enough guy at first glance, quite good looking, but puffed up and superior. He stuck it to Julia far too often with his thoughtless remarks.

But Julia stood by her man, no matter what. That was her, through and through, dogged, loyal, loving, worked her butt off. Then cooked for the crew. Strong enough to do all the grunt work for a trial, keep the house, feed everybody, take care of Livie, entertain Maggie, for God's sake, and she never complained. That good old Midwestern upbringing.

Then Ellen thought, whoa . . . Who in hell was *she* to put down someone else's relationship? She and Mason, well, that was fizzling out, she guessed. And before that she and Ben and before that she and Shamus.

She was beginning to catch on — the trouble wasn't bad luck in men, the trouble was her. That incident with Mason. He'd been an angel since then. . . . But an angel who'd lost his passion.

The interstate ascended from the high prairie of Denver at 5,000 feet to the Eisenhower Tunnel at over 11,000 feet, where cars were whisked directly beneath the Continental Divide. If it wasn't snowing, she could take the shorter route on up to Aspen, over Independence Pass — save herself an hour's drive — but if the roads were bad, no way was she going to drive that snaking highway stuck to the side of cliffs like an afterthought.

She knew there was a very good chance of Thomas getting off. A respected doctor, a husband and father — oh, yes, she'd play on his character, his talent, the good he'd done. So many people had phoned Dennis to offer themselves as character witnesses, she'd had to put a lid on it.

Yes, she believed she could win the case for the defense. But there were several hurdles to jump in order to do so. One was Rick Krystal, another Craig Winagle. The major one was Leann Cornish. Too bad she was so sick, but her condition could work in Thomas's favor — if she were too ill to testify in court, McSwain would have to resort to the videotaped statement, which would be nowhere as effective as a live performance.

Ellen, Cam, and Julia had discussed that at length — how they'd get the circumstances of her having been fired from the hospital admitted into evidence in the event Ellen couldn't cross-examine her in person. The question continued to nag Ellen, though: Which would be better for their case, Leann in person or Leann on tape? Either way, the terminally ill woman was a formidable witness.

Then there was Matt Holman. Ellen drove past Georgetown and Silver Plume, and snow began to tap her windshield. Up ahead, she could see the blurred outlines of the mountains. Definitely a snowstorm. So she'd go the long way around, through Vail and Glenwood Springs.

Holman. Cam had been quite disturbed by the man's commitment to the same story he'd been telling for over a decade. He hadn't budged on a thing. And for Cameron Lazlo, man of steel, to be so impressed by a witness, a convicted murderer, no less, bothered Ellen. She'd sent him to Arizona to taunt Holman into confessing to Samantha's murder or, at the very least, to gain perhaps one tiny tidbit she could use to cement her defense of Thomas. Cam had returned with nothing but the belief that maybe, just *maybe* Holman had not murdered Samantha. That Cam had been wrong twelve years ago. And of course that meant Ellen's client might be the killer — not that his innocence or guilt could matter to her. He deserved the very best defense his money could buy. The only thing bothering her was Julia — her best friend might well be married to a murderer. And Ellen had a moral obligation to talk to Julia seriously, but not until the trial was over.

Once she'd gotten over Vail Pass the roads were completely dry and she made good time on into Glenwood Springs and up the Roaring Fork Valley to Aspen. She arrived just before one in the afternoon, parked, and took her briefcase out of the backseat. Cam's Bronco was parked there, too, in front of the Innes house along with Dennis's motorcycle. The crew was at work.

"Hello, hello," she said, striding into the office — another thing Julia had never complained about — the loss of her dining room. "What's up, guys?"

Cam gave her one of his long, slow, assessing looks.

"What?" she said, sitting and giving him her full attention.

"I've been keeping tabs on Leann," he said. "I've got an in with a paralegal in Steve Larkin's office."

"Leann's lawyer," Ellen said.

"It seems she's been doing better lately, and she's determined to testify in person."

"Damn it all," Ellen said, then hastily, "not that I wish the woman ill, but for our purposes —"

"Yeah, I know."

"Well, we'll deal with her."

"You'll be able to cross-examine," Cam said.

"That's a plus."

They worked all afternoon, until Julia arrived home from a trip to the store, then everyone took a break. In the kitchen Ellen told her about Leann, hating to trouble her with the news, but there was no evading the issue.

"Oh," Julia said. She looked tired and drawn. Her nose was red, and she coughed from time to time.

"It's just a cold," she said when Ellen frowned at her.

"Want me to make you some chicken soup?" Ellen said.

"Oh, sure, and just when did you learn to cook?"

"Well . . ." Ellen began.

But it was Cam who put on water for a pot of tea. Ellen watched him make his way around the kitchen, obviously concerned about Julia, and she wondered. Not for the first time, either.

Back to work, sipping on a cup of tea along with Julia, Ellen said, "All right, folks, we have to consider the fact that Leann might very well be in court. Looking like hell, but there, and the jury will feel sorry for her. How do we counteract that?"

"Get her to admit why she left the hospital," Dennis said. "That she blamed Thomas."

"Definitely," Ellen replied. "Anything else?"

"I'm working a couple angles that don't quite fit," Cam said. "For instance, why did Leann pick Thomas out to crucify? Why not all of the doctors who wanted to get rid of her?"

"Why indeed," Julia said.

"Anyway, we'll see what I can dig up."

That evening they ordered in from Little Annie's, chicken fried steak and ribs and coleslaw. Julia joked that they had menus from every restaurant in town. She blew her nose a lot, and had a box of tissues sitting on the table in front of her. Cam kept giving her concerned glances. *Oh, boy.*

Thomas, who'd had late rounds at the hospital, arrived home at eight and got the news over dinner.

"Leann may be well enough to testify," Ellen told him. "Apparently she's been feeling better lately, and she's determined to be at the trial."

"That can happen with cancer, a lot of ups and downs. Unfortunately, the ups don't last very long." Thomas shook his head. "Poor woman, misguided. But no one will believe her when they find out she was forced to retire. Hell, she was fired. They'll know she's lying."

"Damn right she's lying," Maggie put in. "She's got an ax to grind is all."

"Hopefully the jury will see right through her," Ellen said, amazed at Thomas's ability to brush off adversity. As if the upcoming ordeal was nothing more than a pesky irritation. And his mother only reinforced his cavalier attitude.

"The trial begins on October 26?" Thomas said. As if the date had little importance. Then, "I need to get up to Sun Valley again. I was just wondering —"

"Thomas," Julia said, "you know you

have to be in court. Don't even *think* about scheduling anything in Sun Valley. I mean . . ."

Ellen fixed Thomas with a stare. "You know that, don't you?"

"Of course, of course, I was just pointing out that I have other obligations." Testily.

The king of denial, Ellen thought. Some defendants just never got it.

After dinner Livie helped Julia clean up. Cam helped, too. If the trial didn't come and go soon, Ellen thought, Cam was going to turn into a little old lady. Maggie always had her TV shows to watch, and, as for Thomas, he routinely disappeared upstairs to either make telephone calls or hit the sack early, especially if he had surgery in the morning.

The following morning Ellen made sure she got up in time to catch Julia before anyone else showed up.

"We need to talk," Ellen said.

Julia coughed, hand to her mouth. "Okay."

"Why don't you go back to bed?"

"I can't. I've got to work on that motion. . . ."

"Do it some other time."

"Really, Ellen, I'm fine." Julia paused, then asked, "What do you want to talk about?"

"The case. A few things."

"Sure."

"Look, I'm driving back to Denver tomorrow for a couple days. Come with me. You look like hell, and you sound like hell. Come stay with me. You won't have to do anything."

"Oh, Ellen, I have to —"

"Bullshit. You're stressed out. You're sick. Come to Denver."

"Maybe . . ."

"You'll give everyone here your cold. You're a Typhoid Mary, for God's sake."

Julia gave a little laugh. That was good. She was such a worrywart. "Okay, I'll consider your offer. Then you can get my cold."

"I never get sick," Ellen said.

Julia left for the post office just as Cam arrived. Ellen was aware of the two of them halted just inside the front door; she could hear their voices, low and . . . intimate. She couldn't make out the words, but she sure as hell recognized the tone.

After a couple minutes Cam strode in, looking angry. "She shouldn't go out," he said.

"She said she's fine."

"Right."

"Cam, Jesus, she's a big girl."

He swiped at the air with a hand. "Sure, I know. Christ, Ellen."

Thomas came downstairs and left, saying not a word to them. What a guy.

The following day was warm and sunny, a truly peerless fall day in the mountains. Julia threw her overnight bag in the backseat of Ellen's car, got in, and they drove out of town just after lunch. This time Ellen took the shorter Independence Pass route. The colors were reaching their peak, brilliant gold shading to chartreuse and to summer green. The brush was deep red and maroon. The sun bathed everything in brilliant light, the sky was sapphire, the mountains as clear-cut as paper silhouettes.

Twenty miles out of Aspen, at the top of the pass, there was snow on the ground from two days before. The road was clear, though, and Ellen hurtled around the curves, making good time.

"So what is this trip really about?" Julia asked.

"You need a break. Look at your nose, it's red as a cherry."

"That's it?"

"That and I'm sick of watching you slave over that crew. I need you in tip-top shape for the trial."

Ellen braked the car around a sharp switchback, and the mountains fell off on the other side of the road. Julia had her hand braced on the door.

"Too fast for you?" Ellen asked. She was grinning.

"No, I sort of like it. But my ears don't want to pop."

"That's your cold."

"It really is getting better."

They drove through the mountain hamlet of Twin Lakes, where there was a cop car parked at the far end of town — it was always parked there — with a rubber blow-up cop sitting behind the steering wheel. Everyone who lived within fifty miles of Twin Lakes knew about the spoof, but tourists invariably freaked out and jammed on their brakes before they realized the cop was fake.

"That damn thing gets me every time," Ellen said.

"It's *supposed* to make you slow down."

"I know that." Ellen sped up. After a minute she said, "You know what, Julia? Sometimes I think I'm sort of obsessed with work. And I think" — she hesitated — "I think men sense that in me and feel they'll always come second in my life, and that's why —"

"You mean Mason."

388

"Maybe. I'm beginning to see a pattern, Julia. I'm forty-four years old, and my job is my life. Yes, I'm good at it, but is that enough?"

Julia was quiet for a time, and Ellen steered the car onto the highway toward Leadville. "Ellen," she finally said, "maybe some people aren't suited for marriage. Maybe . . . you don't need a long-term relationship." She paused again. "Apparently I do."

"Has your marriage made you happy?"

Julia looked out the side window, her face averted. "I thought so."

"You're rethinking things?"

"I don't know. These last few months have been so awful. You know, you've seen it all. Thomas doesn't show it, but he's terribly upset about the whole thing. And I . . . I don't know how I get through every day. I'm trying, but . . . I guess I'll have to wait till the trial is over and then . . . then maybe I can figure things out."

Ellen was driving through Leadville before she spoke again. It was tough, but she had to ask. "What's going on between you and Cam?"

Julia visibly stiffened. She kept her face turned away for so long Ellen didn't think she'd ever answer.

Then, finally, she sighed. "Is it that obvious?"

"It is to me."

"We haven't done anything, I swear. Oh, God, I sound like a high school kid. We haven't and we won't."

"You like him."

"Yes."

"He likes you."

Julia looked down at her lap. "Yes."

"I told you he was a hunk the first time I saw him."

"It's not how he looks, Ellen."

"That doesn't hurt, though."

"He's . . . he's just so . . . I don't know. Wounded. Strong. Moral. Caring. Boy, do I sound like an idiot."

"Nope. You sound like a girl in love."

"I won't do anything to hurt the case, Ellen. You know that. I realize if there was a hint of anything between Cam and me, any gossip, the media would compare me to Samantha."

"Poor Samantha."

"I always thought she was self-absorbed, spoiled, but now . . . I think I understand. Thomas can be —"

"Don't say a word. I've seen him in action."

"I thought I loved him, Ellen. I *did* love

390

him. Or I loved the man I *thought* he was. But he isn't. Did he change or did I?"

"Who knows? Relationships are the hardest thing in life." They drove up over Fremont Pass outside of Leadville, then descended down to Interstate 70, which would lead them to the Eisenhower Tunnel and then down into Denver. "What's going to happen if, *when,* Thomas is acquitted? What then, Julia?" Ellen finally asked.

"I don't know. God, I don't know." She drew in a breath. "I care about Cam, I really do. But even if I were free, well, you can see it, Ellen, he's got a problem with commitment. He's, what, your age? And no wife. Women, sure, plenty of them, but I don't want to be just another female to him."

"He tell you about his other women?"

"No. I know because . . . well, he doesn't just work for Victor Ferris. I finally figured it out, he's the hero in Ferris's books. Cam is Luke Diamond."

"Oh, come on."

"No, really, he is. He admitted it to me. Think about it, he's just like the character. Except Cam's an ex-cop, but that's minor. The way he talks, the way he handles people, even the way he looks."

Ellen shot her an amazed glance. "You've got to be kidding."

"It's true. Just don't let on that I told you."

"Never. What a kick. Luke Diamond?"

"Sure, Cam even had a rotten family life. An abusive stepfather. That's why he . . ."

But Ellen's mind switched off at the word *abusive*. No matter what she said, no matter how often she blamed herself for the argument, she would never forget Mason's hands around her neck. "Well, that's quite a story, Julia, but more important," she said, "where are we going to eat tonight?" And the subject of abuse was closed.

Julia lay in bed in Ellen's frilly guest room and thought about Cam. She knew he was in Denver; he'd left earlier than she and Ellen had that day. She still had no idea where he lived. Somehow the subject never came up when they were in Aspen. In Victor's books Luke Diamond lived over a porn bookstore on East Colfax. Was that where Cam lived?

He was in Denver, maybe not even very far away. She could call him — she knew his cell phone number by heart. Not that she ever used it.

No Thomas, no Livie, no Maggie, no acquaintances or neighbors. A big city, her

392

and Cam lost in it, two drops of water in a sea. Who would know?

But she couldn't.

Maybe he was with another woman, someone young and sleek and adoring. Someone not married. He once mentioned that he'd been seeing someone on and off for years. Was he with her?

Of course, whomever he was with probably didn't have a red, runny nose and a nagging cough. A beautiful young thing on Cam's arm wouldn't be sick.

Did he have friends in Denver that he hung around with, old police buddies? But the Cam she knew probably didn't have any really close friends. Like Luke Diamond, he was a loner. Except for a woman in every book that Luke fell for, and for 300 pages you could really believe that he'd found the love of his life, the one woman he'd stick with. Which, of course, would ruin all the rest of the books to come.

So something always happened to mess up the relationship. And that was probably the way Cam was.

She wondered how he'd make love. Slowly and sensuously? So that women melted at his touch? Yes, he would. He'd be an artist at sex, finding fulfillment in physical contact when he couldn't find it in emotional closeness.

She couldn't stop thinking about him. In Aspen, in Denver. It wouldn't matter where she was or if she never saw him again. The ceaseless wanting. To be with him, to talk to him, to touch him, to hear his voice, see the way he walked or gestured or smiled.

Did he feel the same? Did he crave her presence? Did he suspect she was falling in love with him?

Marriage was a revered and holy sacrament, Julia told herself when she got back to Aspen. A promise, a social contract, a troth of love. All those things. It required negotiation, patience, forbearance, forgiveness. Love. It required the married partners to have sexual relations, to bear children.

Well, Thomas didn't want any more children. There was Livie, after all. Julia had practically raised Livie.

Julia was back at work. Her nose was still a little stuffy, but she felt okay. Blackie and Livie had been glad to see her, Thomas less so. Nothing had changed.

She decided she had to do something to save her marriage and her soul. Not to mention her sanity. So she decided to seduce her own husband.

A nice quiet dinner for the two of them — Livie was taking a computer course at the local community college, Maggie was ensconced in the apartment — a glass of wine, her sexiest nightgown.

"You mind getting dinner on your own tonight?" Julia asked Ellen that afternoon.

Ellen looked at her over her glasses. "Sure, no problem. Special occasion?"

"We'll see. I'm going to try, let's put it that way."

"I'm out of here in five," she said.

"Thanks."

She started dinner, a shrimp curry that Thomas particularly liked, got out a good Chardonnay, tore up greens for salad and put them in the fridge with a damp paper towel over the top so the lettuce wouldn't wilt.

Then she took a bath. A bath . . . she hadn't had a bath in a year. With bubble bath. She washed her hair, rinsed it squeaky clean. Shaved her legs and under her arms.

She blow-dried her hair, dabbed perfume between her breasts and on the inside of each wrist. Pulled on tights instead of baggy sweats and a peach-colored, scoop-neck top. No bra.

Downstairs she put the rice on to cook, turned on the CD player with some of her favorite Mozart piano concertos. Soothing, lilting, exquisitely melodic. Maggie came into the kitchen, took a look at Julia, then said, "huh," and thankfully disappeared.

Thomas came home after eight o'clock. "I'm beat," he said. "Long day." He seemed distracted, as usual.

"It's just the two of us for dinner," she said.

"Great. I'm starved."

"We can eat in a few minutes. You want a glass of wine?"

"Oh, boy, what's up? Did you smash your car?" he asked too jocularly.

"Thomas."

"Sorry, I didn't mean that. You know I didn't."

They ate, the two of them, at the kitchen table. She tried to be pleasant and entertaining over the meal. But it was hard to interest him. She did her best, though. He'd always liked her anecdotes from the DA's office.

"Remember that case, not my court, but the district court, the one where the ex-husband tried to kill the boyfriend?"

"Sure, the one in the papers."

"Well, I heard that after the preliminary

hearing, where the boyfriend was the main witness, and I guess the defense attorney gave him a rough time, anyway the boyfriend went home and trashed his girlfriend's house. So now he's not only the victim of a crime, but the defendant in a new crime."

"What a jerk."

"It's quite a threesome, the ex-husband tried to kill the wife's new boyfriend, the wife, the boyfriend, all living together in the same house."

"Amazing," Thomas said, drinking the last of his wine.

After dinner she left the dishes. She'd do them in the morning. Thomas turned on the TV set in the living room and was watching the news. She sat down next to him, close, and leaned against his arm. She sat there like that for a minute, then another minute, with no response from him, getting more uptight by the second. She knew she was trying too hard, but she didn't know what else to do.

Finally he spoke. "I know, Julia . . . I know I've been . . . not so nice sometimes. I'm sorry. I'm working so much, and this trial . . . it's pretty hard to take when you're charged with . . . a crime you didn't do. And all these people. I know you're all doing your best, but . . ."

"I know," Julia said.

"It'll be over soon," he said. "Then we can get back to normal."

Normal, she thought. What was that?

They went upstairs together, early, and she brushed her teeth and put on the black nightgown with spaghetti straps, one that clung to her body, one that Thomas admired.

He turned on the TV in the bedroom, settled himself under the comforter, pillows propped under his head. He was watching one of his favorite programs, a cop show.

A cop show.

She got into bed next to him, shivered in her thin gown, and pulled the covers up to her chin. She watched the program for a few minutes, two partners, one a tough veteran on the force, the other a younger idealist. She lay there in her marriage bed next to her husband, and she tried with all her might not to think of Cam.

She finally turned to Thomas, ready to kiss him, to touch him so that he responded, ready to sacrifice whatever was needed to save her marriage. She took a deep mental breath, and she rolled on her side, put her hand on her husband's chest, and she saw with hurt anger and an equal measure of relief that he was fast asleep.

She woke too early after a restless night filled with disturbing dreams. Thomas was already up, shaving in the bathroom. She decided she'd confront him now, this morning, and tell him how much she needed him, how abandoned she felt. She'd even decided to voice her terrible doubts. They desperately needed this honesty between them; he had to know how she felt. And he'd reassure her.

She got out of bed, padded to the closet, and pulled her old fleece bathrobe on over the sexy black negligee. She was about to say something to Thomas when there was a light knock on the bedroom door.

Ellen's voice in a stage whisper: "Julia, are you awake?"

What on earth was Ellen doing up at this hour? She went to the door and opened it.

"Sorry, sorry, did I wake you?"

"No, we're up."

"Listen, I just got a call . . . Julia, Leann Cornish had to go into the hospital here, after a meeting she had yesterday with Judge Scott, I guess she had a relapse, and . . . Julia, she died in her sleep last night."

"Oh, God," Julia breathed.

"What's going on?" she heard Thomas

say from the bathroom. He came to the door, face half shaved. "Ellen?"

"Thomas, Leann died last night," Julia said.

A stricken look gathered on his face, and he shook his head, let out a ragged breath. "Jesus, *Leann* . . . I never wanted this. I know what she did, I know she just wanted to get back at me, but . . . she was a good woman. Oh, Jesus."

EIGHTEEN

The jury was seated. Seven men and five women. During jury selection, Ellen had won a couple points; Bret McSwain had won a couple. Par for the course. The only juror who concerned Ellen was a middle-aged guy, a local stockbroker, who'd objected to the time he'd have to take off work. Neither DA McSwain nor Judge Scott had paid the least bit of attention to the man's protests. Sometimes, in Ellen's experience, an unwilling juror could cause problems for the defense, just because he was so pissed off.

Ellen sat next to Thomas at the defense table. She was aware of Julia in the first row of oak benches, and Cam was there, too. Maggie between them, wringing her hands. Behind them were Dennis and Livie — Livie who'd fought tooth and nail for her father's permission to be there for him. No cameras were allowed in the courtroom, but as in the preliminary hearing there were sketch artists and reporters aplenty.

Bret McSwain was making his opening statement. For pity's sakes, Ellen could have written it herself. No surprises, every point clearly made, nothing Ellen hadn't prepared for.

"I will show," McSwain was saying, "that Thomas Innes had motive and opportunity to murder his wife Samantha. I will prove he was the last person to see her alive. There is a witness to his whereabouts at the time of the murder, a woman who unfortunately died a few weeks ago. However, I have her videotaped testimony. There is also a corroborating witness to this woman's testimony. I will seat witnesses who saw Thomas and Samantha fighting in public. I will present witnesses who will attest to Dr. Innes's character flaws."

The DA went up to the jury box and inclined his body toward the men and women sitting inside. "I will also call to the stand a man who loved Samantha Innes and who can testify to her relationship with her husband and her state of mind that last day of her life. So, members of the jury, all I ask from you is your attention, your innate sense of right and wrong, and your good judgment. Given that, I will prove beyond a reasonable doubt that Thomas Innes is guilty of the murder of his wife Samantha. He has escaped punishment for twelve long years. What I ask of you is justice, finally, for Samantha Innes."

Yadda, yadda, yadda, Ellen thought as she rose from behind the defense table. She wore a dark gray pant suit and her highest heels. Had her glasses on, even if she didn't need them. She was pumped, prepared, righteous as the sword of Gideon. But she kept her voice low and nonconfrontational. The old rule still held: If you want people to really listen, talk quietly.

"Ladies and gentlemen of the jury, you've heard your esteemed district attorney, and now will hear me. I am defending Dr. Innes, not only because every defendant in this country is promised an adequate defense, not even because every defendant is assumed to be innocent until proven guilty, but because Dr. Innes is innocent of the crime of murder.

"I won't address every point Mr. McSwain made in his opening statement — that's for later in the trial — but I will assure you that there is a logical and simple defense for each and every witness he will put on the stand, each and every event, each and every ugly insinuation. So I, too, ask you to listen and watch and use

403

your common sense, and if you do, the outcome of this trial can only be a judgment of not guilty for my client.

"I won't even go into the enormous benefits this community has reaped from Dr. Innes's clinic. And there's his family and his respected standing in the community. You know all that if you're an Aspenite. You probably personally know him or his wife or his daughter, for that matter.

"When this trial is over, there can be no other outcome than not guilty. And there should, also, be an apology. Thank you."

There, she thought, *short and sweet. Take that, McSwain.* She turned to walk back to the defense table, shot Julia a secret smile, then stopped in her tracks. My God, there was Mason, sitting in the spectators' section directly behind Cam. Mason, here?

Confusion swept her. Shit, she didn't need this kind of surprise. But there was also the warm thrill. He'd never, ever come to see her at work before. Not once. She met his gaze, gave him only a brief nod. If she smiled, someone would notice. Someone would see, and her private life would be broadcast coast to coast.

The first witness McSwain called to the stand was Matt Holman. He was dressed properly in a suit, and, figuring from

Cam's account of how broke Holman was, the good citizens of Pitkin County probably bought the clothes for him. Holman looked a little older than his forty years, Ellen thought, but she could see what a good-looking guy he'd been. Real attractive to a bored housewife whose husband worked long hours. Oh, Samantha, what did you do?

McSwain took Holman through his background, how and where he'd met Samantha Innes, the precise nature of his relationship with her.

"Now, Mr. Holman, please tell us about that day, May eighth, the day Samantha was murdered," McSwain said.

Holman looked directly at the jurors — sure, Ellen thought, McSwain had coached him. "It was a snowy day, I remember, one of those days we get in spring, sun, then snow, all morning. Samantha called me and asked me to come over. She wanted to talk. I asked her where her daughter was. A friend's mother was picking her daughter up after school, she said. I asked her where her husband was. He was in surgery all day. Okay, fine, I went over."

Ellen stole a glance at Livie. She shouldn't be here. The memory of her mother's body was too much to take. And the police and autopsy photos were going to be placed into evidence. Too late now, though. But at least Dennis was with her, probably squeezing the girl's hand tightly. And directly behind them was Mason. . . .

The DA was asking: "Did you make it a general practice to visit Samantha at home?"

Holman shook his head. "Hardly ever. She didn't think it was smart. Neither did I."

"Where did you normally meet?"

"My place."

"And that was" — McSwain consulted a paper on his table — "104 First Street."

"A dump," Holman said.

There was a rustle of appreciation among the spectators. Damn, Ellen thought, certain the DA had asked that particular question in order to glean sympathy for the witness. Point for McSwain.

"Tell us what happened when you went to the Innes's house that morning, Mr. Holman."

"I got there around ten or so. She'd had another fight with Thomas that morning. She'd told him she was leaving him."

"That was the first time she'd told him that?"

Ellen came to her feet. "Hearsay, Your Honor."

406

"Objection is sustained," Judge Scott said.

"All right, I'll rephrase. Was this the first time you heard that she'd told him she was going to leave him?"

"Yes."

"What happened next?"

"I tried to comfort her. I wished I could have asked her to come live with me, her and Olivia."

"Olivia being?"

"Her daughter. But there was no way. I lived in a one-bedroom dump, I was a bartender and part-time ski instructor. I had no money, no way to support her. She was used to a big beautiful house. She didn't have to work."

"Go on, what happened next?"

"Well, I just told her to do what she had to do. I'd be there for her, you know, however I could. She knew I had no money, no real prospects. But she didn't care." Holman leaned forward, eyes on the jury. "We loved each other. Anyway, then we made love, and I left. I left her there in bed. I never saw her alive again."

"What time was that, Mr. Holman?"

"You mean, when I left?"

"Yes."

"Early afternoon. Around one or so. I

had to go to work later."

"What did you do when you left?"

"I drove around for a while, thinking. I was upset. I was mad. Then I went home, took a shower, and went to work."

"Thank you, Mr. Holman."

"Cross-examine, Ms. Marshall?"

"Yes, Your Honor."

Ellen got up slowly and walked to the witness stand. She stood for a moment, as if thinking, then she began to question Holman, going through his whole story step-by-step. She remembered every word he'd said and as she went over detail after detail, he began to grow impatient, then irritated. He started shifting around on the chair, frowning, cracking his knuckles. A few times he said: "I already told you that."

Her timing was superb. She stopped just short of boring the jury, but left the jurors with the impression of Holman as twitchy and angry.

Then she shifted to new territory. "Mr. Holman, I was just wondering, and I'm sure a lot of other people are, also — but why would Samantha Innes, a woman with a little girl, even consider leaving an up-and-coming surgeon for a bartender?"

Holman bristled, exactly as Ellen had planned.

"Your Honor . . ." McSwain said, half rising. "Move to strike."

"I'll allow you to continue, Ms. Marshall, but let's not get contentious."

"Mr. Holman, can you tell us why Samantha Innes would give up her position and financial security for you?"

Holman's mouth tightened. "How many times do I got to say it, we were in love."

"Were you and Samantha planning to get married?"

"We hadn't planned that far."

"Were you going to raise Olivia Innes as your child?"

"We hadn't discussed that. It was too soon. We were in a bad position, and she worried about her kid and all."

"But you're sure she wanted to leave her husband?"

"Yes."

"For you or just leave him?"

"She wanted to leave him. I don't know if it would have worked out between us." His tone was testy. She was really getting to him.

"To your knowledge," Ellen went on, "did Samantha tell anyone else of her plans to leave her husband?"

"I don't know."

"Had you and Samantha discussed her financial situation if she divorced Thomas Innes?"

Holman was quiet for a heartbeat too long. "Not really."

"You never discussed alimony?"

"I don't understand the question."

"Simply stated, did you ever discuss with Samantha how much alimony she'd receive if she divorced her husband?"

"No."

"Hmm," Ellen said. "So, is it possible Samantha told you that morning she wasn't going to leave her husband?"

"No, that isn't the way it was."

"You didn't have an argument?"

"No, I told you, Samantha had argued with Thomas, not me."

"You didn't get furious when she told you she couldn't leave Dr. Innes?"

"Goddamn it, no! I —"

"Your Honor," McSwain rose quickly, "Ms. Marshall is badgering the witness. He's already answered that. . . ."

Ellen put up a hand. "I'll withdraw the question," she said pleasantly. She'd already scored her point. She gave Holman another look, then said, "Thank you, Mr. Holman, that's all I have." The tone of her voice was meant to convey to the jury that she didn't believe a word of his testimony, so why continue.

Judge Scott called for a lunch break then. He warned the jury not to discuss the trial between themselves, certainly not to discuss it with anyone else, including the hoard of media out front, and he dismissed them.

Ellen had lunch with Mason, a hurried affair, a sandwich from the Butcher's Block. He was admiring, but her mind was on the trial.

"You were great," he said. "Pissed that guy off royally. He's the one who was in jail, right?"

"Yes, he's the one. Did you believe him?" she asked.

"Yeah, I sort of did. Until you got hold of him. And the way you dismissed him from the witness stand . . . That was something."

"Good, that's the point."

"You seem nervous," Mason said.

"Trial nerves. Normal. It's like going on stage and remembering your lines." She smiled. "Are you going to stick around?"

"I'll stay a couple days. That okay?"

"That's wonderful. But I have to warn you, I'll be really distracted."

His expression fell. "So what else is new?" he asked.

Shit, she thought.

Cameron Lazlo was on the prosecution's witness list. Ellen wondered whether Bret McSwain was going to call him to the stand after lunch, to testify to the letters he'd received from Holman declaring his innocence. But after the way Cam had demolished McSwain at the preliminary hearing, she doubted he would be called. Of course, McSwain would try to keep her guessing. That was fair. That was the game.

McSwain did not call Cam. He did have several witnesses lined up to testify to arguments they'd witnessed between Samantha and Thomas, witnesses who'd testified twelve years ago at Holman's trial — Cam had interviewed them months ago, and Ellen was prepared for cross-examination.

What she wondered, what concerned her night and day and in her dreams, was when McSwain was going to show the videotape of Leann. Last, probably. If it were she, if this were her strategy, she'd wait until the very end of the prosecution case to drop that ticking bomb.

Immediately after the lunch recess, McSwain placed into evidence State Exhibits A through M — the police and medical examiner's photos of Samantha's corpse.

The audience did not view the exhibits, but the discomfort in the courtroom was palpable. Thomas sat motionless, a single bead of sweat running down his temple. He didn't even wipe it away. Ellen donned her solemn face. She was aware of Maggie shifting uneasily behind her, and she heard several people leave the room. Once the jurors had viewed the exhibits, which seemed to take an eternity, she half turned and noted that Maggie, Dennis, and Livie were gone. Thank God, she thought. And how was Thomas holding up?

None of that mattered. Ellen had a job to do. That was her only concern.

The ghastly exhibits placed aside, McSwain called a middle-aged woman named Mary Lambreau to the stand. Too much makeup, Ellen thought, like she was going on stage. That would turn off the jury, the women anyway. Ellen stood up, her hands on the table in front of her. "I object to this witness, Your Honor. Hearsay." She knew her objection was not valid, that this woman had testified all those years ago, and no doubt would be testifying in a few minutes, but Ellen was trying to break McSwain's concentration — whenever she could.

"Your Honor," McSwain said, "this goes

to the motivation of the defendant. It is not hearsay. It is eyewitness testimony."

"I'll allow it, Ms. Marshall."

McSwain tossed her a look. She smiled sweetly. He turned his back, approached the witness stand, and began to ask his questions.

The woman described being out to dinner with a friend at the Steak Pit. They'd been sitting next to an attractive young couple — her friend recognized the man as Dr. Innes. The couple had argued, their heads close together, but Mary Lambreau had nonetheless overheard them. The fight was about their daughter, something about the man never being home. Eventually the wife had gotten up and left him there alone.

Ellen cross-examined. Mary Lambreau didn't remember much, only the rough outline of the argument.

"Could you tell who was more angry, the doctor or Mrs. Innes?"

"Oh, she was."

"Did you hear any threats? For instance, Samantha Innes threatening to leave or Dr. Innes threatening her in some way?"

"Oh, I can't remember exactly what they said. It was, you know, a husband and wife quarreling. I don't recall any real threats."

"And you're sure the couple you saw twelve years ago in a restaurant were Samantha and Thomas Innes?"

"Oh, well, yes, sure. My friend . . ."

McSwain rose. "Your Honor, the witness already identified the defendant as the man she saw that night."

"Sustained."

Ellen had one more arrow in her quiver. "Have you read about this case before the court right now, Mrs. Lambreau?"

"Well, sure I have."

"And seen it on TV?"

"Yes."

"You read about Samantha Innes's murder twelve years ago and testified then, too?"

"Yes."

"And how is it that you're a witness in this trial today?"

"My friend Sally told me to call the DA, remind him about what I saw that night and how I'd testified at the other trial."

"So, Mrs. Lambreau, you called DA Glenn Willis twelve years ago and offered your services, and you called DA Bret McSwain last spring to offer your services again?"

"Yes, I did."

"That's very civic minded, Mrs.

415

Lambreau. Most people detest getting up on the stand to testify. But evidently —"

McSwain leaped up. "Your Honor, I strongly object —"

"Yes," the judge said, cutting him off, peering at Ellen, "objection sustained."

That was fine by Ellen, she'd trashed the witness's credibility. She said, "Thank you, Mrs. Lambreau. That's all I have."

Julia watched the proceedings with equal measures of fear and anticipation. She trusted Ellen, but she was still scared to death. A jury could surprise even the best legal expert. She couldn't wait for the trial to be over, for Thomas to be out from under this terrible burden. She refused to consider a guilty verdict.

So far McSwain had made several points. But then, Ellen had effectively brought the score back to even, and Ellen hadn't even presented her defense yet.

Odd that Mason was there. Julia hoped his presence wasn't going to distract Ellen. But then she thought, no, of course not, nothing could distract her friend when she was in court defending a client.

It had been only too obvious that Cam and Mason hadn't been thrilled to see each other. At the lunch break everyone had studiously ignored their refusal to speak to each other outside the courtroom. And this was certainly not the time for Ellen to find out what lay between the men. Cam would never say anything, and Julia was fairly sure Mason wouldn't. Still, Ellen wasn't blind.

Regardless, Ellen had handled Matt Holman perfectly, had pretty much destroyed Mary Lambreau's testimony. All according to carefully laid plans. The only bad moments had been the police photos passed among the jurors, and Livie rushing from the courtroom. At least that was over. Still, poor poor Livie, the horrible memories brought so vividly back to life. For once Julia was glad Maggie and Dennis were with her.

There was another witness who'd testified previously to having overheard an argument between Thomas and Samantha. A waitress at the time, the woman was now the owner of a bicycle shop in town.

McSwain called her to the stand; she gave her name and address — Sandy Sampson, 798 Laurel Drive.

Julia knew her. Not well, but she'd been in her bicycle shop, bought things there. Livie's road bike, for instance, when the girl had been in her biking phase.

Julia listened attentively as Bret asked Sandy what she'd seen when she'd waited on the Inneses that night twelve years ago. She listened, but part of her was always aware of Cam sitting next her, his trouser leg occasionally brushing her skirt. She wanted desperately to turn and look into his eyes, feel the comfort of his touch. Her throat closed at the memory of their kisses, the scent of his skin, his breath, his warmth.

But the whole thing was so impossible.

And how could she think about Cam when Thomas sat before the court, next to Ellen, at the defense table? He was on trial for murder, for God's sake. How could she spend even a fraction of a second thinking about Cam?

She set her gaze on Thomas. He wore a beautiful suit, a dark olive color, silky sleek and perfectly tailored. A beige shirt, a patterned silk tie. He looked prosperous and self-confident. He did not look like a killer.

She could only see his profile from her vantage point, but she studied her husband — his expression, his bearing, his hands, folded in front of him on the table, manicured and cosseted, the tools of his trade. How did he feel? Afraid? Nervous? He appeared, to her, as if he were in a classroom, listening to a subject in which he was mildly interested.

Bret was asking Sandy what she'd overheard that night at the Cantina.

"I was giving them the check," she said, "but they didn't even notice me. Usually people give you a look or a smile or a thank you. Or they put a hand on the check. You know, to say to their group, hey, I'm picking this one up. But these two were having an argument. It wasn't loud, and I tried not to listen in, but I couldn't help hearing a few things."

"What things, Ms. Sampson?"

"She was saying things like 'I can't stand it anymore. You have to change,' and he was swearing at her. He said, 'How the hell do you think the bills get paid?' "

"Did you know who the couple was at the time?"

"Sure. He'd done my boyfriend's knee."

"Your witness, Ms. Marshall," McSwain said.

"Okay, Sandy . . . do you mind if I call you Sandy?"

"No, Ellen."

Oh, my, Ellen was going to have her hands full with *this* one, Julia thought.

"You're sure the couple you saw was the Inneses?"

"Yes. I knew who he was. I'd taken my boyfriend to a post-op appointment and sat in the exam room with him."

"And you still recall what the doctor and his wife said twelve years later?"

"Yes. It struck me at the time."

"Did you ever hear a couple have a fight in public before?"

"You mean, when I was waitressing?"

"I mean ever."

"Probably."

"Have you ever had a public argument with someone?"

"No, I have not."

"You're lucky, Sandy, because the other ninety-nine percent of the world has."

"Your Honor, Ms. Marshall is out of line. I object."

"He's right, Ms. Marshall. No more commentary."

"Sorry, Your Honor." Ellen looked suitably chastised, but again her point had been made; Julia noted some titters among the jurors.

Then the judge gave his warning to the jurors once again, thanked them, tapped his gavel, and dismissed the jury. There was a bit of end-of-the-day paper shuffling, a motion entered by Ellen, a question from the DA as to tomorrow's starting time.

The usual. The first day of the People vs. Thomas Innes was over.

And Bret McSwain still hadn't shown Leann Cornish's videotape.

The evening began with the nightly brainstorming session. Cam gave his take on the day; Julia gave hers. Needing support, Livie hugged her father, but Thomas seemed distracted. Julia told herself, *Well, of course he is.* Then again, Livie had sat there that morning and listened to testimony about her mother's murder, listened to Holman, her mother's lover, who believed her father had committed that murder. Just the thought made Julia's head swim. Livie shouldn't be subjected to this. Couldn't Thomas see that?

After the younger set left with Maggie, Thomas turned to Ellen. "When do I get to testify?" he asked.

"We already discussed this," Ellen said. "It's rarely a good idea for the defendant in a murder trial to take the stand. Thomas, you know that."

"But all these people, they get to tell their stories, which are lies. And I have to sit there and never say a word to defend myself?"

"I defend you," Ellen said.

"But, damn it —"

421

"She's right, Thomas," Julia put in. "Listen to Ellen. Honestly."

"I don't even remember what those two women were talking about today. I never saw either of them before."

"But they allegedly saw you," Ellen said softly. "And both of them testified at Matt Holman's trial."

"I swear to God I don't remember them. There were so many witnesses. . . . I do know one thing, they're lying. Samantha and I never had a public fight. I mean, hell, we never fought at home, either."

"The jury will decide if they're lying," Ellen said, but Julia barely heard, she was wondering how it was Thomas and Samantha never had a fight — anywhere — when he'd always admitted he knew Samantha was having an affair. Knew it and blamed himself for being so busy, gone so much. . . . Still, they *never* had an argument? *Come on, Thomas,* she thought, her nerves tingling under her skin, when she looked abruptly over to Cam. He was staring intently at her. He could always read her mind.

"Ellen, I think I should testify," Thomas was saying. "Don't forget, I speak in public a lot, I'm good at it. I think people should have a chance to listen to my side."

"Thomas, you're paying me a lot of money for my expertise. Don't waste that. You will not go on the witness stand."

He gazed at her, shook his head, said he had a few phone calls to make to Sun Valley, and he went upstairs.

"I'm sorry," Julia said to Ellen.

"Don't be. This always happens. Don't worry about it. Every defendant thinks if he just gets up there, everyone will fall at his feet."

"You're sure he shouldn't testify? I mean, Thomas is right about one thing, he does often speak in public, and he is persuasive, very charming."

"I am absolutely positive he should not take the stand."

Ellen stood up to leave then. It was time to meet Mason — he was staying at the Hotel Jerome, a renovated Victorian hotel, a mainstay of Aspen's silver-mining days returned to its original glory.

"I'll see you all in the morning," she said. "Early."

Julia walked her to the front door. "Between you and me," she said, "how do you really think it went today?"

"Aside from the photographs, I think it went well. It's too early to say. I told you

423

this before, a jury trial is a crapshoot. Want any more clichés?"

Julia sighed. "Sorry, dumb question."

"Yup. See you."

Cam was still at the table, reading a last-minute report about one of the next day's witnesses. And Julia thought, as she had before, how was it that they contrived to be alone together so often?

"She's going to spend the night with Mason," Julia said, sitting down across from him.

"I figured."

"Don't you think it's a good sign he came up to see her at work?"

Cam rubbed his jaw.

"You still don't trust him."

"I don't *like* him."

"It's pretty obvious."

"Good," he said. Then, "I'm outta here, too. Early to bed and all that."

"But you don't sleep."

"Not much." He gathered up a few papers, put on the sport coat that he'd worn in court that day. "See you in the morning."

"Wait," she said, feeling awkward, not wanting him to go, like a little kid trying to squeeze the last bit out of the day, she craved the last ounce of the sweet moment with him.

He looked at her for a second, then said, "Walk me out."

She pulled on a heavy sweater hanging on a peg by the front door. "Do you always go straight to your room?" she asked, hating herself.

He turned and stared at her. "Why?"

"Oh, I just wondered."

He studied her for a moment longer, opened the door, held it for her, closed it behind them. "Sometimes I go downtown and have a drink or two."

"Where do you go?"

"La Cocina sometimes. Or the Red Onion."

"Do you meet people there?"

A corner of his lip quirked. "You mean women?"

"No, no, I meant —"

"No, I don't meet anybody. I say a couple words to the bartender. Talk to a cop if one happens to be around."

She hugged herself and followed him down the porch steps to the sidewalk. It was dark out, a moonless night, and fallen leaves scurried before a sharp wind, dancing across the ground.

They reached his Bronco. She felt ridiculous, hanging around like a high school kid.

"Are you going downtown tonight?"

"Why, you want to go with me?"

"Oh, no, I can't."

"Right," he said.

"I'm sorry, Cam, I'm being nosy. Silly. I just . . . I just wanted to see you alone for a minute." There, she'd said it.

They stood facing each other, in the dark, the wind swirling off the mountain and plucking at them. She couldn't read his expression; his eyes were in shadow, his cheekbones, his nose, his lips — white marble curves with dark shadows. A strand of his blond hair lifted a little then fell.

He said nothing, but he put a hand out, placing the back of it against her cheek. His fingers were warm. She leaned into his touch, closing her eyes, giving into the small moment.

There was so much she wanted to tell him. She wanted to pour her heart out — her doubts, her fears, her needs. Thomas . . . and him. But she couldn't say anything. Not now, not here. In another universe, maybe. She felt sadness well up in her breast.

"I know," he said softly, reading her mind again, "me, too." Then he got in his Bronco and drove away.

★ ★ ★

Thomas was watching the evening news from Denver when she got back later from taking Blackie for his walk. The trial was prominently featured: opening day, video of both lawyers entering the courthouse, a distant shot of Thomas and Julia. On-the-spot reports from each Denver news program, and that didn't include CNN, FOX News, or any of the other national broadcasts.

"God," Julia said, coming into the bedroom. "Why don't they leave us alone? It's so much better in Canada and England. Pretrial publicity is against the law. This is a disgrace." She was irritated, not quite sure why. Something about Thomas, remote in hand, clicking away on every channel, one after the other.

He stopped on the NBC affiliate, which was showing sketches from the courtroom. Ellen, Bret McSwain, Judge Scott, Thomas . . .

"Not a bad likeness," he said. "Those sketch artists are pretty talented."

"Isn't there something else on?" she asked.

"I guess. Hey, did today go as well as I thought? Ellen won't comment to me."

"It went well, yes." She stared at him.

"Except for the police photos. Juries always want someone to pay when they see those kind of pictures, that someone being you at the moment."

"But we got past those."

"Yes. Livie didn't, though. She had to leave the courtroom."

"I saw that."

"Well?"

"Hey, look, didn't I plead with her to start college? I didn't want her here. But even her grandmother took her side."

He had a point.

Then he went back to his favorite subject of late. "I still think I should testify."

"Let Ellen make the decision."

"It's just so hard, sitting like a lump, listening to people talk about you, lie about you, and you can't say a word to defend yourself."

"I know. I know." She rubbed her face, suddenly tired to the bone, and then she looked at her husband. "Thomas, tell me the truth, are you scared about the trial? Are you worried?"

He flicked to another channel, where a solemn-looking man was standing in front of the courthouse, pontificating. "What good would that do?"

"You must . . . you must be upset,

Thomas. Tell me. Please, talk to me."

"What I am is pissed. I'd like to testify, damn it. This whole thing is so . . . so goddamn inconvenient."

"Inconvenient?" she said faintly.

"I'll get off, Julia. For chrissakes, I'm innocent. They can't convict me."

His assurance was monumental. She could tell him stories about innocent people caught up, wrongly imprisoned. Like Matt Holman, maybe. But she couldn't think that, because if Holman was innocent, that meant Thomas was guilty. No, she wouldn't go there. She sat on the edge of the bed, put her hand over his, and she said, "I'm sure you're right."

"I'll just be relieved when it's over. Behind me."

And she thought: *That's the first genuine thing he's said today.*

"The Sun Valley clinic is scheduled to open in a couple of months, and I plan on being there," he said, and he switched off the television set, turned off the lamp on his night table, and rolled over onto his side to go to sleep.

In the bathroom, washing her face, putting on moisturizer to combat the dry mountain air, brushing her teeth and listening to the deep rhythmic breathing of her sleeping husband, she wanted to cry. She put her hands on the edge of the sink and hung her head between her shoulders and couldn't stop thinking about his ridiculous statement that he and Samantha had never had a fight, public or private. How stupid did he think they were? And why would he say such a thing? It just made him seem . . . seem as if he was lying. And he'd only have one reason to tell such a transparent lie. . . .

No, do not go there, she reminded herself fiercely, and somehow she managed to drive the hideous demon back into the shadows.

She stared into the white porcelain basin and saw Cam's face. She always saw his face, especially when she needed reassurance or comfort. She closed her eyes and felt his phantom touch on her cheek. Heard his voice, low and raspy, full of hurt, too. Like hers.

She stood there like that for a time, then she turned the water on and swished toothpaste down the drain, watching the water swirl away. Like her life.

NINETEEN

Victor Ferris was dressed in sweatpants and his favorite Denver Nuggets T-shirt. His apartment was its usual mess — empty pizza and Chinese take-out boxes littered his granite kitchen counter and geometrically shaped coffee table. He was in the throes of the fictional Beckett trial, working up to the climax of the story.

He watched the TV coverage of the real-life Thomas Innes murder trial ceaselessly. He received daily inside-the-courtroom reports from Cam, so he didn't need to leave home, which was just as well, because he was late for his deadline. Not that his editor would berate him — as far as his publisher was concerned, he was the goose that laid the golden egg. And, besides, he often reminded himself, what self-respecting author would turn in a manuscript on time?

He sprawled out on his couch, remote control in hand; he watched local Denver news coverage, the national twenty-four-hour stations, even the Western Slope stations out of Grand Junction. Court TV was a great source for insider tidbits. He watched every talking head who discussed the trial, the hard-edged commentators, the kinder, gentler ones, the smart ones, the stupid ones. He watched that sharp lawyer-lady on FOX who'd had her face remade. She really knew her stuff.

As he watched, all night long, the courtroom scenes for his Beckett take-off murder trial coalesced in his mind.

His first witness would be Mike Hanson, the guy who'd been in jail all those years for the murder of Andrea Beckett. Of course, no one could mention that Hanson had been tried and convicted for the crime.

Carole Nichols, Beckett's defense lawyer, would cream Mike on the stand. Likewise the other witnesses the DA, Fred Hadley, marched in. But the crux of Victor's trial would be the nurse who had witnessed Beckett returning to the hospital the day of Andrea's murder, late for a surgery. With a cut on his hand. The nurse who, a couple of weeks ago in Victor's manuscript had been alive and ailing but was now dead — Victor had rewritten two entire chapters the morning of the real-life woman's death.

And, of course, her videotaped statement would garner all kinds of sympathy with the jury. Oh, yeah.

The videotape, Cam had informed Victor, was the one crucial piece of evidence worrying Ellen Marshall. So it would be the one thing worrying Carole Nichols.

Even though it was almost two in the morning, Victor was invigorated. He got up from the couch, strode through the mess on the living room floor, and locked himself into his tidy office. He sat in front of his computer, the blank screen no enemy now, lit a cigarette, flexed his fingers exactly three times, and got to work.

Diamond in the Rough

Luke stayed in the courtroom the first day of Beckett's trial. To see how things were progressing and to keep an eye on pretty Janet Beckett, who sat in the first row behind her husband, her face blanched, a shredded tissue balled in her fist.

He knew he was on the witness list for both the defense and the prosecution, because he had intimate knowledge of the previous case. Ei-

ther one could use Luke to his advantage, he supposed. As for him, he'd just give them the facts, the evidence. Whether or not Dr. Beckett was guilty, Luke was still sitting on the fence, unwilling to commit even to himself.

He listened to Mike Hanson, the lover, go over the morning of Andrea Beckett's murder. Same old same old. He knew this story word for word. The DA had the man sounding as if he'd been a saint. Luke eyed the jury. They bought every word.

Then, on cross-examination, Ms. Nichols asked Hanson so many detailed questions the guy got a bad case of aggravation. In the end, Carole Nichols cut poor Mike to ribbons, making everyone believe he was a hard-hearted gold digger.

Side out.

During the lunch recess, Luke spotted Janet Beckett standing forlornly by the courtroom door. He couldn't resist — his feet just walked him over to her.

"Hi," he said.

"Oh, hi. You're the detective, right?"

"Guilty as charged." What a fucking dumb thing to say.

"Are you going to testify?"

"Maybe. If they decide to use me."

"Have you had a lot of experience with trials?"

"Too much."

"What do you think, is this going well for Larry?"

"It's the first day, Mrs. Beckett."

She sighed, and he thought maybe she was going to cry.

"Hey, look, it's just started. No one knows how it's going yet. Your defense attorney is very good, though."

"She's supposed to be the best."

"Well, I wish you luck. Even though I'm on the other side."

"Thank you. Really. I appreciate it."

Poor woman. He'd love to cheer her up. And what if Dr. Larry Beckett actually was found guilty and went to jail? Then pretty Janet would need a whole hell of a lot of cheering up.

After court that day Luke meandered into Alice's for his evening libation. He told the guys what had gone down in court that day — they were always fascinated with the weird machinations of the justice system.

Then he drove home, too fast, the night hot and close, whistling by his *ears in his T-Bird. And all the time he thought about Janet. Was her husband guilty? What if he really had murdered Andrea? What if he was so friggin' smart, he'd fooled everybody? Even Luke.*

Tall, dark, good looking, doctor to the celebrities. Full of himself. Larry Beckett had been an arrogant prick years before, and he was still the same guy.

Capable of murder?

At home Luke took his gun and holster off, laid them down carefully on the cabinet where they lived. He'd had a burger at Alice's, so he didn't need to eat. Was there some ice cream left in the freezer?

Then the phone rang. Kind of late. Maybe it was Davie, still on that case — the knife murder. He picked up the receiver, dropped into his favorite chair, kicked his shoes off.

"Yeah."

"Luke?"

He froze. That voice. "Who the hell is this?"

"Son, this is your father."

"My father? Didn't know I had one anymore." His hand tightened on the receiver.

"Of course you have one. Just because we . . ."

"It's late. What do you want?"

"To talk, that's all. It's been so long."

"Like five years, Dad."

"Oh, no, it couldn't have been that long."

"The hell it couldn't."

"I heard your name mentioned on TV, son. About that trial there in Denver. The doctor?"

"Really."

"Something about you investigating the murder of his first wife some years back?"

"Yeah."

"Now they think this Dr. Beckett actually killed his wife."

"Your point?"

"Just making conversation, Luke."

"Well, I'm busy. I don't have time for conversation." And he hung up.

Fuck that old son of a bitch, he thought. After what he did to my mother. After the way he beat her. Broke her spirit and killed her. And beat me until I got big enough to face up to him. And now he wanted to make nicey-nice? Not bloody likely.

Luke sat there, jaw locked, his mouth pulled down at the corners, and thought about the pain that old man had caused, and then he got up and, shaking with anger, he slammed a fist into the wall. It hurt. Goddamn, it hurt. But he felt ever so much better.

The next two days of the Innes trial consisted of one hospital employee after another recounting, as well as they could recall — which wasn't very well — what had happened that long-ago day of Samantha's murder.

This was the grunt work that Julia had labored over for months. Repetitious but necessary. Nurses, doctors, cafeteria workers, front desk personnel, all took the stand. At least, the employees the prosecution could locate from twelve years ago, and those whose stories were vaguely plausible.

Julia listened hour after hour as McSwain got up in front of each of these witnesses, asked them the same set of questions: Where were you that day? Do you remember seeing Dr. Innes? When and where? Could he have been gone for any period of time during the hours between eleven in the morning to one in the afternoon?

Then Ellen would rise and ask each witness: Are you so sure about your testimony that you'd stake a man's life on your memory? Why didn't you come forward all those years ago with this information? Why didn't you contact the DA at the time and tell him Thomas Innes was missing for half an hour while you ate your lunch?

McSwain had prepared them, though. They all said Dr. Innes could have been gone, but no one had bothered to ask them last time, because Dr. Innes hadn't been a suspect.

One of the nurses, now retired and living in nearby Basalt, became irate at Ellen's insinuating questions.

"Do you really think I would have gone out of my way to tell the cops I didn't see Dr. Innes for a time between surgeries? Besides, I never thought about it. I never in a million years would have suspected the doctor of leaving the hospital, killing his wife, and returning to surgery. My God, sure, we all idolized him, but to even insinuate we'd — *I'd* — cover for him is outrageous. What kind of person do you think I am?"

"Precisely my point," Ellen said softly.

In his seat at the prosecution table, Bret McSwain glowered. He recrossed the nurse, playing on her adoration of Thomas Innes, and made her testimony pivot a little more in the prosecution's favor, but not much.

At the end of three days Julia couldn't see much advantage to either side. If pressed, she'd say Ellen was ahead, but you never knew what was going on in the minds of the jurors. Especially the impatient stockbroker, who shifted in his seat a lot, his face a study in boredom.

Cam was out of town, trying to chase down Rosalyn Dangelo, the anesthesiologist who'd been fired from University Hospital, according to Craig Winagle's story. Cam hadn't found out anything in Denver, had gone on line to a professional organization of anesthesiology, thought he might have located her working in St. Mary's Hospital in Grand Junction, Colorado. Name changed, but that might be due to marriage. If she could help their side, he'd try to recruit her. If not, he'd talk to her and leave.

Julia and Ellen had discussed the Dangelo woman. "If Winagle's story is true, then she's going to hate Thomas's guts. This Dangelo woman is going to want to get on the stand for the prosecution and ream him," Ellen said.

440

"On the other hand, maybe the woman will be a great witness for our side, discount every word Craig Winagle has to say."

Ellen cocked her head and lowered her voice. "We have to consider that Winagle is telling the truth."

"God, Ellen."

"Hey, everyone screws up once in a while, right? Maybe that incident was Thomas's one screwup. We just don't want some damn woman showing up this late in the game to corroborate Winagle's testimony. Unless she's some kind of a space case, she has to have heard about the trial. Believe me, if she wanted to get your husband, she'd have offered her testimony to McSwain a long time ago. I bet she wants to forget it ever happened."

Julia nodded. But she didn't forget Ellen's words — maybe Winagle was telling the truth. Maybe Thomas had screwed up, left that elderly patient paralyzed, stood by and allowed Rosalyn Dangelo to lose her job, her career. No matter how hard she tried to deny it, there was that ambitious, callous side to Thomas. She'd always told herself all great men were driven. But would he have destroyed two lives to save his own career? *Would he?*

"What did you tell Cam to do if this woman really is the same Rosalyn Dangelo from University Hospital?" Ellen asked.

"I told him to handle her with kid gloves."

The rest of the day Julia sat in the courtroom thinking about Rosalyn Dangelo — what if the woman decided to testify, but for the prosecution? What if Cam was only stirring up a hornet's nest by going to Grand Junction to interview her? Yet another person who'd crossed paths with Thomas Innes — another person out to get him. The list was growing.

Against Julia's advice, Maggie took Livie and Dennis to the Little Nell Hotel for dinner that evening. Of all places . . . The Little Nell was jammed with media. Livie and Dennis got back to the house and recounted Maggie's stock answer to every reporter who'd confronted them. Maggie had said, "Oh, go screw yourself." Livie thought that was funny. Ellen only blew out a breath and looked heavenward, and Thomas went straight to the garage apartment to have a chat with his mother. Then Julia's own mother phoned and wanted to know if this commentator from Court TV was right about some stupid point, and Julia had to beg her mother not to watch

TV at all. She promised to phone every evening from now on to fill her parents in on the day's proceedings. By the time she took Blackie out for a walk, she was frazzled. God, how she wished Cam would get back — Cam, who somehow had become her rock, her mentor, her friend.

That night she climbed into bed next to Thomas and said, "Are you sure about Craig Winagle? I mean, that he'll come off as a hanger-on, a loser who was jealous of you? I mean, Cam said he was —"

"Christ, Julia, will you stop? It's always Cam said this, Cam said that . . . you'd think the guy was a genius or something. So *what* if he misread the guy in New York? Ellen will tear Winagle up on the stand."

Thomas was asleep shortly after that, but Julia only stared at the ceiling, her heart pumping. She thought about Rosalyn Dangelo, about Craig Winagle and Leann Cornish and Matt Holman and Bret McSwain. She thought about Maggie and Livie and Ellen and Mason. Mostly she thought about Cam and longed for his return.

The following day Dr. Craig Winagle flew into Aspen and was called to the stand in the late afternoon. He told the story about Thomas and the surgery-gone-wrong. He was clear and concise and completely unemotional. Thomas came off badly. Ellen saw some of the jurors eyeing her client, a few frowning. The annoyed stockbroker looked interested for a change — bad news.

When McSwain finished with the direct examination, Ellen stood and moved around the table. She smiled in a friendly manner at Dr. Winagle. Handsome guy, an air of confidence to him, a ring on his finger. Married, then.

She went through the usual getting-to-know-you questions, then said, "You were a resident with Thomas Innes?"

"Yes, as I told the DA."

"Is being a resident tough? I hear it is."

"It's brutal."

"Is there sometimes a little bit of competition between residents, Doctor?"

"I'm not sure I understand the question."

"Oh, sure. Let me rephrase, then. Like who gets the best review from the head of residents. Who gets the best slots at the best hospitals. You know, a little friendly competition?"

"Oh."

"Is there any of that, Dr. Winagle?"

"Well, I suppose. Sometimes."

"And did Thomas Innes come out of his residency with good reviews, good offers?"

"I believe so."

"And this despite what you say was a bad mistake?"

"Yes, I suppose."

"And is it fair to say Thomas Innes has gone on to become an international expert in the field of orthopedic medicine?"

"Yes, that's fair." Reluctantly.

"While you remain in your hometown in —"

"Objection! Your Honor, this is insulting and prejudicial," Bret said.

"Sustained. Ms. Marshall, please."

Ellen smiled and said, "That's all I have, Your Honor."

That night was Friday. While Maggie played hostess to her granddaughter and Dennis in the apartment, Ellen and Mason had dinner with Thomas and Julia. They ordered in; Ellen couldn't do much about his mother or daughter, but no way was she letting Thomas out on the town during his trial. Cam's absence was telling. Julia looked lost, as if she were waiting for him to walk in any moment.

He was on the hunt, Julia told everybody. "When he hunts, he always gets his man. Or woman in this case." Then she added, "He's probably back by now."

Ah-ha, Ellen thought. So she knew his every move. And she wondered if they spoke by cell phone when he was gone.

"Did he get hold of the Dangelo woman?" Ellen asked.

"I don't know. I'm sure we'll hear in the morning," Julia said.

So maybe they didn't talk *every* day.

"How long are you staying, Mason?" Thomas asked, and Ellen pulled her attention back to the group.

"Till Sunday."

"I sure wish your visit could be more of a social thing. Do you golf?"

"Whenever I can. But I'm lousy."

"Too bad . . . Oh, well, next time you're up here, we'll get out for a round anyway."

The menu that night was Italian. Rigatoni stuffed with portabello mushrooms, shrimp pasta, and antipasto. From Campo di Fiori, a locals' favorite. Ellen noted that the table was set quite nicely, a good bottle of wine, Julia's wedding silver and china and cloth napkins.

Did Julia launder and press the napkins, for God's sake?

Ellen went back to the Hotel Jerome

446

with Mason. Left Julia with the dishes. She felt rotten about that, but Julia had shooed her away. Too bad Cam wasn't around to help her clean up.

"You were good today," Mason said when he unlocked the hotel room door. "I watched this morning."

"All those boring people from the hospital. Of course, there *was* one of the DA's star witnesses, Craig Winagle. I handled him okay." She yawned. "But wait till it really gets interesting. Leann's videotape."

"I won't be here."

"I know." She took off her blouse and hung it up in the Victorian armoire. Folded her slacks.

"Come here, little lady," Mason said.

He kissed her, and she felt herself melting. It was so good with him most of the time. Maybe he'd never raise a hand to her again. Maybe that incident was an aberration. He wasn't like that. An abuser. No way. She'd just pushed too damn far; the Pope would have been tempted to swat her, for Lord's sake. Mason was like this, big and warm and handsome, strong hands on her hot skin and dirty words whispered in her ear.

And they had all night.

On Saturday morning she left him to

sleep and drove to the Innes house for a short work session. She felt great, relaxed, refreshed.

Cam was there, back from his jaunt to Grand Junction. "Yeah, I found her," he said. "Name's changed to Silvers."

"And?" Ellen asked.

"She wants absolutely nothing to do with testifying. Said she only wants to forget that part of her life."

Ellen nodded. "I figured as much."

"But what did she say about Craig Winagle's story?" Julia asked.

"Not much," Cam said, and Ellen knew immediately he was being evasive. She'd get him alone and find out what Rosalyn Dangelo Silvers had really said. And she'd bet it wasn't good for Thomas.

She did finally catch him as they were leaving the house.

"What did Rosalyn really say?" she asked.

"Hey, I didn't want —"

"I know. Julia. But you can tell me now."

"She agreed with Winagle's assessment of the incident. Said she'd had a total breakdown because of the poor old man who was paralyzed. Swore it wasn't her fault. She was so undone; she said she didn't even care about being fired. Took

448

her five years to recover and start getting on with her professional life."

"Ugh."

"Not pretty."

"And she blames the incident on Thomas?"

"Like I said, she really didn't want to talk about it, but yes, that was the impression I got. Thomas screwed up during the surgery."

"Great."

"Yeah."

"Okay, she's of absolutely no use to us. Just the opposite, in fact. You sure she won't make trouble, contact McSwain now?"

"Man, she's so shy of that whole memory, she almost fainted when I introduced myself."

"Thank God. Well, let's hope you're right. Look, I have to run, but do me a favor, don't let Julia weasel this info out of you, okay?"

"I'm not about to tell her."

"Good, good. Okay, I'm out of here."

"Got a date?"

She saw his scowl. He wouldn't even say the name "Mason" aloud. "Yep, a date," she said, and she hightailed it back to the Jerome.

That afternoon Mason said he wanted to drive the forty miles down the valley to Glenwood Springs. He wanted to soak in the fabled Hot Springs pool. Kick back in the October sunshine.

"You ever been in the pool?" he asked Ellen.

"Me? No. Never had time."

"Well, we're going today. It has curative powers that the Ute Indians discovered. Did you know that?"

"No. But, Mason, I don't have a bathing suit."

"I called. You can rent them there."

"In a size four petite?" Ellen quirked a brow.

"Of course," he said.

The Hot Springs pool sits in the valley of the Colorado River, right next to the river. It's big, really big. The length of three Olympic pools put together. At one end there's the "hot" pool, smaller and much warmer. At the far end of the big pool are lanes for swimming laps. In between, especially on weekends, are hundreds of children playing and splashing with balls and water toys.

The hot pool was more sedate. She and Mason found seats on the shallow stone steps leading down to the water. Half submerged, they lolled in the almost-too-hot, sulfur-scented pool. The autumn sun was hot on their backs; the dark sulfur water hot on their legs.

"Idyllic," Mason said.

"Very nice. How long do we have to sit here?" she asked.

"Jesus, Ellen, will you relax?"

"I relaxed last night, didn't I?"

"I'm not sure you'd call what we did relaxation."

She tilted her head up to the sun and leaned back on her elbows. "It's hard to get the trial off my mind, that's all."

"Screw the trial."

"Okay, for an hour or two."

On the ride back to Aspen, in his silver Mercedes, she felt drained from the intensely hot water. "That's supposed to be good for you?" she said. "I'm dead meat."

"Me, too."

"Want to go out tonight? Someplace special?"

"Sure. I have to leave tomorrow, you know."

"I know."

"Don't sound so disappointed. You knew I was only here for a few days."

"I know, but —"

"Why don't you come to Washington

451

sometime? I'll show you around."

"Oh, Mason, I never have time."

"I always have to give in, don't I? Why is that, Ellen?"

"Mason, don't."

He was quiet for a time, but she knew the signs. He was building up a head of steam. A pleasant afternoon and now this.

"And tell me, Ellen," he finally said, "how come you're so damn confident you're going to get Thomas off? That doctor, what's his name? . . . *Winagle*, right? You want the truth? He destroyed Thomas."

"That was nothing, Mason. And I totally rehabilitated Thomas's reputation when I cross-examined. Sorry you missed that. Regardless, the trial's not over because of one man who has it in for Thomas. I have plenty more up my sleeve, don't you worry."

Mason snorted.

"Damn it," she said, then she clamped her mouth shut, and they rode the rest of the way in silence.

Things did not improve at the hotel.

"So," Ellen said cheerfully, "where should we go for dinner?"

"I'm too tired to go out," Mason said.

"But it's Saturday night. It's your last night here."

"Let's just get room service."

"We could walk downstairs to the restaurant here."

"What part of 'I'm too tired' don't you understand?"

He was surly. She was sick of trying to placate him and his moods.

"Fine, we'll get room service. Whatever."

She turned on the television set and plumped cross-legged on the bed to watch the latest coverage of the trial, if there was any on the weekend.

"Christ, Ellen, don't you get enough of that crap all day long?"

"It's my job."

"Well, it's not mine."

She clicked the TV off and threw the remote down. "Can you tell me why you resent my profession so much? I mean, it's as if you're jealous of my job. Of my success. Give it a rest."

"Jealous, right."

"You never give me any support, do you realize that?"

"Is that what you want from me, support? Forget about it."

"Then what *should* I want from you? What do I get out of this relationship? Sex?"

"Is that all you think we have? Sex?

Christ, you can be crude."

She got off the bed and placed her hands on her hips. "Oh, for God's sake, you can't even fight the right way."

"I can't? I can't fight the way you want me to?" He came over and stood above her, his face taut with anger. He frightened her when he got this way, and Ellen hated to admit being frightened by anybody or anything. She stood her ground.

"I'm going back to Julia's," she said, pushing him out of her way.

He made a noise in his throat and grabbed her arm, yanked her so hard she swung around, losing her balance, falling against the corner of a dresser. Sharp pain flared in her cheekbone and she cried out.

He stood over her, breathing hard, but she'd turned ice cold. Holding her cheek, she got up and glared at him. "Excuse me, I'm going into the bathroom. Please get out of my way."

His face twisted with uncertainty. "Ellen . . ."

She held her free hand up, shook her head. Went into the bathroom, closed the door, and locked it.

She peered at her cheek in the mirror — a magenta mark, which would swell and bruise. The bastard, the bastard. She wet a washcloth and held it to the area.

How could she face a courtroom with a black-and-blue lump on her cheek? What kind of defense lawyer did that make her? She wanted to cry, to sob and scream, but she clenched her teeth and refused to let out a sound.

She huddled in the bathroom for a long time, sitting on the tile floor Indian style, thinking, thinking. What in God's name was she going to tell everyone? And Julia. And *Cam*. Shit shit shit.

Then she heard Mason's light tap on the door. "Ellen?"

"What?" Furious, disgusted.

"Please come out, Ellen. I'm sorry. Please."

"No."

"Ellen, come on. Don't be like this. At least let me apologize."

"Leave me alone."

"No, I can't. Ellen."

He sounded sorry, he really did. He hadn't meant to harm her. Not really. She'd spun around and lost her footing on the carpet. And she'd been cruel. She could be cruel, she knew that. Her big mouth.

"Listen, Ellen, hey, I'm sorry but, don't get mad now, but I really have to take a leak."

She almost laughed. She stood up, turned the old-fashioned brass knob, pulled the door open.

"Ellen?" His eyes were red, his mouth quivering.

"Take your leak."

"Okay. Okay. I'm sorry, but I had to . . . Look, I'll just be a second."

When he finished, flushed the toilet and washed his hands, he came out to face her.

"I'm so sorry," he said again, reaching out tentatively to touch her wound.

She jerked her head away. "Don't."

"No, please, let me." Then he bent and kissed her sore cheekbone. She only half turned away from him. "I'll get you some ice," he said.

"That would be nice," she said coolly.

He left and returned shortly with an ice bucket full. Solicitous, loving. He wrapped a towel around some ice cubes and held it against her cheek. "There," he said softly. "Now, sit down, lean back, there, like that. And hold the ice on your face. Twenty minutes at a time. Off and on again, every twenty minutes."

He sat next to her on the bed and stroked her free hand. "It's just a little bruise is all. I'm sorry, Ellen. It was an accident."

"What about the next accident, Mason?"

"There won't be another one. I promise. Oh, God, Ellen."

He kept stroking her hand, turning it over, making whisper-light circles on her palm. She held the ice pack to her cheek and closed her eyes, trying so hard to hate him, but she could feel her heart opening like a flower. Giving him absolution. Against her will, but giving it nevertheless.

There won't be a next time, a part of her brain said. To be answered by another part: *If you believe that, Ellen Marshall, you are one stupid woman.*

TWENTY

When Ellen walked in the front door on Monday morning, the first thing Julia saw was the purple lump under her eye. Covered with makeup, but standing out like a beacon. She knew instantly what had happened. *Damn that man.*

Cam was not in town — he'd driven the sixty miles to Rifle to try to interview Leann Cornish's daughter. He had an itch, he'd said. Had one since interviewing the nurse and then watching her make the videotape.

For Mason's sake, it was lucky he wasn't around. Cam would have done something awful to him.

"Mason did that, didn't he?" she said to Ellen, who was picking up some papers to take to court that morning.

"What?"

"That." She pointed.

Ellen touched her cheekbone. "Oh, that."

"Don't tell me you ran into a door. I've

heard that too many times, Ellen."

"It's nothing."

"It doesn't look like nothing."

"It was an accident."

"Oh, for God's sake, he hit you again, didn't he?"

Ellen looked so stricken for a moment that Julia didn't have the heart to pursue the matter.

"He's gone back to Denver."

"Yes."

"Good."

"Julia, it's not what you think, really."

"Oh, yes, it is."

"Let's just drop it, okay? We have a trial, or did you forget?" she snapped.

Julia thought, *Wow,* talk about someone's defense mechanism working full time. She didn't say another word.

The media was gathered, as usual, in front of the courthouse. Livie, Dennis, and Maggie came in a separate car. But Julia, Thomas, and Ellen entered through the back door, to avoid the ravenous hordes. Unfortunately, today there was one lone reporter lying in ambush for them.

"Ms. Marshall, Ms. Marshall, a comment?" he said, chasing after them and thrusting his microphone forward.

Julia took charge. "Not today," she said.

The reporter stopped for a tick, craned his neck, then Ellen was past him.

"What the hell was that?" he asked, the mike turned off.

Ellen didn't hear him, but Julia did. Later, she was astonished how fast the lie formed on her lips. "Ms. Marshall and I went hiking over the weekend. She fell and bruised herself," she said quickly. "It's not very dignified, but it's not very newsworthy, either."

"She fell, huh?"

"One of those slippery scree fields. Excuse me, I have to go."

She had difficulty concentrating on the trial that morning. All she could think of was the swollen bruise on her friend's cheek. She thought again how fortunate it was Cam had gone off to Rifle. Although he'd be back later, and of course he'd see the bruise right away. He'd know.

She forced her concentration back to two more prosecution witnesses from the hospital staff as they were sworn in and took the stand, but she barely heard their words. After McSwain finished with each of them, Ellen chipped away at their testimony, leaving everyone with the impression that no one was truly positive about what they'd seen or hadn't seen so many years ago.

In Julia's opinion, the defense and prosecution scores remained even.

Judge Scott called the lunch recess early. That afternoon McSwain was finally going to call Rick Krystal and then present his ace in the hole, Leann Cornish's videotaped statement.

"Do we have a setup for the tape?" the judge asked the court clerk, the lady with the ponytail.

"Yes, sir," she replied.

"Okay, lunch. See you back here at" — he shot the cuff on his robe and looked at his watch — "one-thirty."

Julia waited for Thomas and Ellen in the hallway outside the courtroom. She was nervous — the tape was the one piece of evidence she was seriously concerned about. They had their defense mapped out; still, Ellen needed to be on her toes. Now was not the time to be distracted by a black-and-blue face.

Cam turned onto Interstate 70 outside of Glenwood Springs, heading west along the Colorado River toward Rifle. Through juniper-studded hills and into winding Six-Mile Canyon, on the slopes of which fourteen firefighters had died in a wildfire a few years ago. Then the valley widened out, and on both sides of the river ranchland spread for thousands of acres up into the high country. Beautiful country, mountainous here, but, as the miles passed, giving way to the great mesa lands of the West.

It was an easy drive from Aspen to where Marcy Cornish lived with her boyfriend on a small ranch.

On the phone Marcy had refused to speak to him beyond a tight-lipped retort that he was trying to vilify her dead mother. That the whole defense team was disgusting. That her mother had just died, for the love of God. Couldn't they leave her alone?

Well, he was here to take a face-to-face stab at her. Leann had become a mystery to him — the more he chewed over the woman's behavior in the months prior to her death, the more puzzled he became. Unless, of course, she really had been trying to cleanse herself of the lie she'd lived with for so long. Which Cam wasn't entirely buying — a damn itch he just couldn't seem to reach.

For six months he'd used his mental fingers to push all the pieces of her possible motivation into place — and they fit just fine, if she'd been telling the truth. The trouble with that solution was twofold: First, why hadn't she accused other staff members who'd been instrumental in her firing? And second — a real big second for Cam — he still believed Matt Holman had done Samantha, still believed there was no way he could have been so goddamn wrong.

He drove and he pondered the problem. *Leann, Leann, what motivated you? Why, even as you were dying, did you have it in for the doctor?*

Cam had learned that Marcy Cornish lived on a family ranch run by her boyfriend, Colin. They lived together next to a hay barn in a mobile home. While this Colin spent much of the autumn rounding up cattle from public grazing lands beyond the ranch, Marcy trained horses — jumpers and eventers. From her appearance at the preliminary hearing, he recalled she was a tall, attractive girl, bigger-boned than her mother had been but with the same fine features and a gorgeous mane of blond hair.

He drove along a rutted dirt drive toward the barn, parked by a couple of pickup trucks and horse trailers. He spotted Marcy Cornish on the far side of the barn. She was in a fenced ring teaching a lesson — a rider cantered over the same jumps several times, Marcy calling out instructions.

He got out of his Bronco, which fit in just fine with the pickups and trailers, sauntered over to the ring and leaned against the top rail. While he watched her work, Marcy studiously ignored him. Pretty girl, he thought again, obviously knew her stuff, not that he could tell one end of a horse from the other.

It was warmer down here in Rifle, 3,000 feet lower in altitude than Aspen. Crisp fall weather. And it was always more dry in the western reaches of the state. He smelled the dryness, sagebrush and alfalfa, horse and cow manure. He watched dust rise under the horses' hooves, felt it in his nostrils and on his sun-browned arms.

The lesson finally over, Marcy walked slowly to where he leaned on the fence. She was wearing a sweat-stained baseball cap, her blond hair pulled through the hole in the back. She took the cap off, mopped her brow with a forearm. Tough girl.

"What do you want now?" she asked belligerently. "Nobody invited you here, mister."

"I have just a couple questions." He took off his sunglasses, met her gaze squarely.

"First you hound me on the phone, and now you just show up. Will you please leave me alone?"

He remained motionless, casually leaning his arms on the fence. "It won't take long, Marcy," he said, his tone even. "A man's life is at stake here. You could give me a few minutes."

"That man's life *should* be at stake. He murdered his wife."

"Why do you say that?"

"Why do I say it? Because my mother told me."

"And you believed her."

"Completely. She'd never lie. She never lied to my brother or me. She never lied to anyone."

"I want to understand your mother," he said. "Help me here."

She shaded her eyes by tugging on her cap. She shifted her stance. Impatient. Uncertain. Finally she said, "Look, she was a wonderful mother. She raised us all by herself. She was a great nurse. What else do you need to know?"

"What about her personality? Tell me something about her."

Marcy sighed. She was loosening up. "I suppose you'd call her pretty reserved. Very passionate about her job." She shrugged her shoulders and dust motes rose, dancing in the light. "I'm not going to tell you anything bad about her — there was nothing. You're wasting your time."

"Did she ever talk about Thomas Innes to you? I mean, before she decided to accuse him?"

"No," Marcy said. Too quickly? he wondered, or was he misreading the girl's impatience?

"Did she get along with the doctor?"

"Look, I don't know. She worked with lots of doctors. She didn't talk to me about them."

"Okay, Marcy. Can I leave you my card just in case you think of something else you want to tell me?" He unfolded himself, reached in his jeans' pocket, and handed one of his business cards to her. She had strong brown hands with short dirty fingernails, sinewy forearms. All that riding, he supposed. "Call me any time."

"I have nothing to say, don't you get it?"

"Sure, I get it." He put on his sunglasses and walked to the Bronco. He now knew one thing for a certainty — Marcy Cornish was definitely holding something back.

Former Aspen Valley Hospital dietician Rick Krystal took the stand immediately

466

after the lunch recess. He was a big man, beefy, wore a black beret on his shaved head, a dark tweed Italian blazer, sleeves pushed up, a collarless white shirt beneath it. Italian loafers, no socks.

McSwain got him to recite his name, address, former employment at the hospital. Then, "On the day of Samantha Innes's murder, did you see Dr. Innes?"

"Yes, I did."

"Where?"

"At the back of the hospital, coming down the trail that leads over to Meadowood."

"You saw him on the foot trail?"

"Yes, I did."

"Where were you?"

"In the kitchen. There's a row of windows looking out at the hillside."

"At approximately what time did you see the doctor out back?"

"It was after the lunch trays had come back from the rooms. Around one, one-thirty in the afternoon."

"Why didn't you tell the police this?"

"Hey, no one asked."

"You didn't think about coming forward with this information?"

"Not really. I mean, this other guy, her lover, got arrested and that was that."

"Thank you, Mr. Krystal. That's all I have."

Ellen cut to the chase on cross. "Mr. Krystal. Did Dr. Innes come to you that April about a mistake made on a patient's dinner tray?"

Krystal shrugged. "I don't remember."

"Let me help refresh your memory. You served surgery patient Brenda Nielson chicken and potatoes and green beans, when her diet was supposed to be liquid. Dr. Innes pointed out that this mistake was serious, possibly life-threatening, and if it occurred again, you would be terminated."

"Objection," Bret McSwain barked. "Relevancy."

"Your Honor, I'm trying to establish Mr. Krystal's motivation."

"I'll allow it. But get to the point, Counselor."

Ellen turned back to Krystal. "Do you recall this episode now?"

"No."

"Okay, then, do you recall being reprimanded by Dr. Innes?"

Krystal shrugged again.

"Yes or no, Mr. Krystal?"

"It was twelve years ago."

"Yes or no?"

"No, I guess."

"You *guess*. Well, I have here a statement to *refresh* your memory, Mr. Krystal. From a man named Daniel Ortega, who worked in the hospital kitchen with you. Do you remember Mr. Ortega?"

"No." Sullenly.

"He remembers you." She went to the defense table and picked up some papers. "This is his statement." She read: " 'Dr. Innes came into the kitchen. It was late at night. He was mad. He told Rick he'd just given one of his patients solid food when she was on a liquid diet. He was yelling. He grabbed Rick's arm. I thought they were going to get in a fight right there. He said the woman was vomiting and she'd pulled out some stitches, and she'd have every right to sue the hospital. The doctor was madder than hell. He threatened Rick and said he'd get him fired. It was a scary scene.' "

Ellen laid the papers down and pivoted to face Krystal. "Do you remember Daniel Ortega now?"

"No."

"Speak up, Mr. Krystal."

"*No*."

"Your honor," Bret said, rising. "Combatative."

"Sustained."

"Now, Mr. Krystal, how did you feel about Dr. Innes after he reprimanded you?"

"I don't remember."

"Yet you remember precisely when and where you saw the doctor out of the hospital window?"

"Yes."

Ellen said nothing for a beat, then, "My goodness, your memory is selective, isn't it, Mr. Krystal?"

"Objection!" Bret said.

"Sustained. Really, Ms. Marshal," the judge said. "The jury will disregard Ms. Marshall's last statement."

"That's all I have," Ellen said. "Recross, Mr. McSwain?" And she smiled sweetly.

Whew, Julia thought. Ellen was in top form; she'd just destroyed Rick Krystal's testimony. And Cam — it had taken him a month to locate Daniel Ortega, but he'd found him and gotten the man's statement.

Now Ellen had to neutralize Bret's final witness. But this one would be much harder, a hell of a lot harder.

The courtroom was darkened, the many blinds drawn. The VCR made no noise, but the sound and the quality of the video-tape were less than professional.

470

On the screen was Leann Cornish, in the living room of her home, telling her story. The tape was in color, of course, but the colors were not true; her face was a greenish tinge.

She looked awful, emaciated, eyes hollow, scarf covering her head. But she stared directly into the camera and spoke strongly. She told her story, exactly the way she'd told it to Cam. Of course, Julia had seen this video before, and she'd heard Cam's own taped interview so many times she could practically recite it word for word.

"I saw Dr. Innes through a back window at the hospital," the former nurse was saying, "and he was hurrying down the path from the Meadowood subdivision, where he used to live. I met him right outside the back door, the one that leads to the cafeteria. There's a shaded sitting area out there, a few decorative boulders, you know, for landscaping. The path goes up over the hill into the subdivision, and there are a couple of picnic tables." On the tape Leann could be seen shrugging. Julia could just hear Bret McSwain coaching the woman for this session, reminding her to be as detailed and exact as possible. "Anyway, I had to ask Dr. Innes a question about a patient, something about an allergic reaction to a particular medication. He seemed a little out of breath. What stuck in my mind, especially later, was the cut he had on his hand. It was on his right hand, on the outside ridge by his little finger. I asked him if he wanted a Band-Aid, and he said he'd get one. I think he said it was no big deal, he'd been taking a break, sitting on one of the rocks, and cut himself.

"Then, in surgery later, but no more than fifteen minutes, I'd say, he was kind of nervous. I saw his hand shaking. That wasn't at all like Dr. Innes. He was always very calm. No matter what, he was in control. The nurses used to call him the Ice-Man."

Leann was not in the least bit self-conscious on the tape. She came off as sure of herself, almost gracious, near death but extremely credible. Despite having seen the tape over and over, Julia closed her eyes for a moment, took a deep cleansing breath, and tried to hold her anxiety at bay. Yes, she'd seen the video a lot, but this was the first time the jurors had seen it. She tried to gauge their expressions, but the courtroom was too dim.

"I realize everyone wants to know why I waited so long to tell my story. It's because

472

I'm dying, and I want to set the record straight. I couldn't do it before, because I needed my job. I knew Dr. Innes could get rid of me in a heartbeat if I was any kind of a threat to him. I was a single mother with two small children to raise. I couldn't lose my job. But I also really couldn't believe he was guilty for the longest time. I thought about that day over and over, and I knew I'd seen Dr. Innes hurrying down that path from the direction of his house. I saw the cut on his hand. I saw him shaking in surgery right after that.

"I knew all that and I knew he told the police he'd been in surgery all day and never left the hospital. I mean, everyone thought he was on the premises all day. I just couldn't believe he'd do such a horrible thing. Even after someone else was arrested, I kept thinking that Dr. Innes couldn't have done it — he was a healer, not a murderer. But I saw him. God forgive me, I saw him and I've kept this terrible secret for years and years.

"I hope this tape isn't necessary. I hope I can testify in person. But if I can't, please believe me. I'm telling the truth, so help me God."

Gray flickered on a darker background and the tape was over. In the courtroom lights came on, and everyone blinked in the sudden daylight.

Bret McSwain stood and moved to the jury box. He waited a proper interval after Leann's words, designed, Julia was sure, to show his respect. Then he spoke: "Leann Cornish died three weeks ago. As you can see, she wanted very much to be here to testify in person, but she knew the possibility she wouldn't be able to appear.

"She was duly sworn in before she made her statement. There were three persons there representing the court, a representative of the defense, as well as her own attorney. You are to treat the videotape as Leann's testimony and to give it equal weight to testimony from any other witness.

"Ladies and gentlemen of the jury, Judge Scott, my honorable opponent, I respectfully rest my case. Thank you."

Another interval of silence stretched out, no one wanting to disturb the somber tone of Bret McSwain's summary. There was no doubt Leann's statement was powerful. A lie but nonetheless powerful. A vengeful woman trying to reach back from the grave to destroy Thomas.

Finally a faint murmur rose from the spectators, a rustle of movement.

Judge Scott called for a recess. "Fifteen minutes," he said, and he banged the gavel and disappeared into his chambers.

Ellen spent the short recess pacing in the hallway outside of the courtroom, rehearsing. She and Julia had discussed their strategy long and hard. Which witness should immediately follow Leann's videotape? In what order should they present their witnesses? On whose testimony should they rest their case?

Julia stood by the stairs, so anxious her skin was crawling. Thomas was in the men's room, a deputy guarding the door. As he'd passed them in the hall, he'd only shaken his head, saying nothing. For once, something had gotten through those barriers he'd so carefully erected since his arrest. Julia would have been thankful for the breakthrough if the situation had not been so gravely detrimental to his case.

Finally the bailiff came out into the hall and announced the court would be in session in five minutes, and everyone started filing back into the courtroom.

"Okay, folks," Ellen said. "Curtain's about to come up."

Court in session, Ellen stood, straightening to her tallest, looking very professional in a smoke-blue pantsuit, a white blouse, and a silk scarf around her neck. Clunky high heels, her glasses. The minute she started talking, you forgot her lack of stature.

"Your Honor, ladies and gentlemen of the jury, I ask you to bear with me for a minute. As must be obvious, I cannot cross-examine Ms. Cornish. You need to know that Leann Cornish resigned last year, on June the third, from her job as chief OR nurse at Aspen Valley Hospital.

"She was forced to resign because of several incidences that could have turned out disastrous if not caught in time. Dr. Thomas Innes, along with Dr. Jeffrey Bathke, an OB-GYN, asked the hospital administrator to request this termination." Ellen looked befittingly grave, sorry for the poor nurse. "That Leann Cornish was terribly ill during this period is not at issue here. She made crucial mistakes and was subsequently asked to resign. With this in mind, the court has granted me permission to read the statement made to the police twelve years ago by Nurse Leann Cornish."

Ellen moved to the defense table, picked up a set of papers, and returned to face the jury. She adjusted her glasses and read in a loud, clear voice: "Dr. Innes was at the hospital all day. I'm positive he never left the premises, much less the OR."

She dropped the papers to the table, turned slowly, deliberately, back to the jury. She removed her glasses; the task seemed to stretch out for a long time in the silent courtroom.

Finally she spoke. "You have now heard Leann Cornish give two versions of the same day. Both sworn to as the truth and nothing but the truth. If you —"

"Objection," Bret said. "This is not the time for a closing argument, Your Honor."

"Sustained."

Ellen nodded her head. "Nothing further, Your Honor."

And that was the end of the fourth day of the Innes trial.

Cam returned from Rifle that evening. He walked in, said hi to Livie, gave an off-hand salute to Maggie, who was watching the TV and a trial report, and strode directly to the dining room. Julia was scanning a hospital employee's file; Ellen was on the phone with hospital administrator Patrick Askew.

"Hi," Julia said, her breath snatching as always when he appeared. "How did it go?"

He smiled sardonically. "She hates everyone who hurt her mother, sticks to her story that Leann was a saint, says there's no way her mother lied. If Leann says Thomas Innes killed Samantha, Marcy believes her."

"I wonder why Bret hasn't added her to his witness list," she reflected.

"My guess? Marcy probably refused to testify. McSwain doesn't want an uncooperative witness. I mean, she just lost her mother."

Ellen hung up, turned. She started to say something and then fell silent.

"What the hell?" Cam said, staring hard at her face.

"It's nothing." She subconsciously reached up, touched her cheek, and hastened to add, "I'm so damn clumsy."

"Don't give me that shit."

"Cam," Julia tried.

"Mason. That son of a bitch," he said.

"Cam, no, honest, I was —"

"Don't, Ellen, don't waste your breath."

"Look, he's gone back to Denver," Julia put in. "Cam . . ."

He turned away, ran a hand through his hair. "For chrissakes, Ellen," he muttered.

"Are you through?" Ellen said sharply.

"Are you through taking out your wounded soul crap on me?"

"Come off it, Ellen."

"Listen, you two —" Julia began.

"I'm fine, get it? I'm okay. Drop it," Ellen said, cutting her off.

Cam sank into a chair. Dennis had stopped typing, and was sitting motionless, trying to look very small. Livie had come to the doorway from the kitchen and was staring at the group. Maggie had put the TV on mute.

In the abrupt silence Ellen seemed to gather herself. She raised her voice and said, "Okay, everybody, scene over. Let's get back to work. We have a defense to present tomorrow."

Everyone in the room started breathing again. Julia watched Cam, though, not sure how well he'd recover. Every time he looked at Ellen, he'd be reminded. And what would he do to Mason when he returned to Denver?

What had he said to her? That it was a good thing he was off the police force, because sooner or later he would have done something unforgivable.

She sat across the table from him, the file open in her hands, and she was actually afraid for him. She wished she could talk to him, help him see that Ellen was not his responsibility. She wished she could help him calm down. But everyone was there, including Thomas, who had just now finished his nightly phone calls to Sun Valley and come down the staircase. And Ellen was so right, they had a case to try tomorrow, and a lot of work still to do tonight.

Cam must have decided to put his anger aside, because he was collected enough when he gave them his report on Marcy Cornish.

Ellen listened, asked a couple questions, her fingers unconsciously going to her cheek.

"I keep thinking there's something more I could get out of her," Cam said.

"Like what exactly?" Julia asked.

"Wish I knew."

"If I were to subpoena her, she'd be a hostile witness. And she wouldn't say any more than she already told you. There's not much sense in that," Ellen said.

"No."

"You never put someone on the stand who might surprise you. This Marcy Cornish could be a real loose cannon," Julia put in.

Ellen nodded in agreement, then turned

to Cam again. "But you still think there's something there?"

"Yeah."

"Um, well, don't waste your time on her for now. Let's go over the witness list again. Patrick Askew is all set for tomorrow. And there're our hospital witnesses to refute Bret's crew. . . ."

Ellen reviewed the list for another few minutes before they all retired to the kitchen for leftover chili. Thomas seemed cheerful, his denial back in place like a coat of armor. Tonight, Julia envied him. Oh, did she envy him.

"How did Leann's videotape come off today?" Cam asked.

Julia thought a moment, then said, "Credible. Even after seeing it so many times, if I were a juror, I'd find her very credible."

"Jesus Christ," Thomas said, "what about the statement she made to the cops twelve years ago? Wasn't anyone listening to *that?*"

"I'm only looking at it from a professional point of view, Thomas," Julia said. "That's our job. I never said she was telling the truth on the tape."

"Still . . ."

Then Maggie. "Well, Cam" — she held

481

up a tortilla chip she'd been using as a spoon in her chili — "if *I* were on that jury, I would have seen straight through the woman. And I thought people in Aspen were so sophisticated. Huh. It just goes to show —"

"Never mind Leann, we're moving on," Ellen said. "From now on, it's our case."

"But she lied on that tape," Thomas said, his voice full of amazement. "I can't get over it. I never will get over it."

"People lie. Witnesses lie," Julia said. "It happens all the time."

"Can't everyone tell she lied?" Thomas said.

"Not everybody," Cam said quietly.

Julia stared at him, but Cam's remark evidently bypassed Thomas, and her husband went on to ask about the DNA test results on the Buddha.

"Nothing yet," Cam said. "I'm hoping by the end of the week. Keep in mind that the standard FBI tests came up empty. The DNA was too degraded."

"Well, if they can get results with their newfangled tests, I'd like to see them come back before the end of the trial," Ellen said. "If not, if there's a chance they can get viable DNA, I may have to consider asking for a continuance. That's not something I want to do. So, Cam, maybe you could find out where all this stands?"

"I'll phone my guy."

"Good," Ellen said.

"Why?" Thomas said.

"Why what?" Ellen.

"Why don't you want to see a continuance of the trial?"

Julia answered. "Well, for one thing, the jury gets pissed. For most of them, time is money. And they want to take it out on someone."

"Me?" Thomas said incredulously.

"Who else," Cam said, going back to his bowl of chili.

Nervous about tomorrow, Ellen retired to her room early. Thomas went to have a nightcap with his mother in the apartment, and Livie left with Dennis the minute her father was out of sight. Walking, now that it was too cold at night to ride the motorcycle. Sometimes Livie borrowed Julia's car to go downtown; sometimes she borrowed Maggie's.

Only Julia and Cam were left in the house.

How did she keep managing to be alone with him? Causing herself anguish but unable to stay away. Often, she wondered if Thomas noticed, but, amazingly, he seemed either not to notice or not to care. Regardless, she found herself seeking out Cam's company at every opportunity. She wondered if he, too, contrived to arrange time alone together. She wanted to believe he did.

"So, how was court today?" he asked as they settled across from each other over the cleared-off kitchen table.

She rolled her eyes.

"Yeah, Leann's tape."

"It was almost worse than I thought it would be. Even with her previous statement, it's going to be hard to overcome."

"What's with Ellen?" he finally asked.

"You know as much as I do."

"What the hell did the press think?"

"Oh, God, I thought for a moment Ellen was screwed today. Anyway, I came up with a story, something off the top of my head about going for a hike this weekend, and Ellen taking a fall."

"Very good. And quick."

"Hey, don't get the idea I'm an enabler, because that isn't why I did it. I did it for Thomas. I did it because we already have enough media insanity surrounding this trial without the reporters going after Ellen and making her look like a battered woman."

Cam frowned. "Well, whatever, her boy-friend should have his balls stuffed down his throat."

"Oh, and you'd like to be the one to do it?"

"A figure of speech."

"Nice one, too."

"Look, if you think I'll go after him again, you're wrong."

"Am I?"

"I am *not* your Luke Diamond. Stop getting us confused. I'm real. He's an over-blown figment of Victor's imagination, and a piss-poor one at that."

She shook her head and smiled. "Don't worry, I don't get you two confused."

"Yeah, sometimes I wonder about that. And I suppose you told Ellen about Luke Diamond."

"Actually, I did."

"Christ."

"I think she said something like 'What a kick.' "

He ducked his head, then looked up. "Oh, man, Julia . . ."

He'd said it again, her name, a supplica-tion. Her insides turned to liquid. "I'm sorry if you didn't want her to know."

"Oh, I bet you are. But what the hell?"

He stood and took his black leather

jacket off a chair back, shrugged it on. "It's late," he said.

"Will you be in court tomorrow?"

"I'll try."

She wanted to ask him if he was there, would he sit next to her, but she didn't dare. Instead, she said, "Well, it'll be over soon."

"The trial?"

"Yes. Maybe a week or so. You know, I feel like my life's been on hold for months. I can't go forward, I can't go back. I just have to wait for the whole thing to end."

He took a step toward her. "Have you figured out what you'll do if . . . ?"

"You mean, if my husband goes to jail?" She gave a short laugh. "No, I don't know what I'll do. It can't happen. It just can't."

"I hope for your sake he's found not guilty. I mean that, Julia."

"For my sake? Not for his?"

He fixed his eyes on her, those pale blue eyes that were like hollows through which the sky showed. No faraway gaze now. He was studying her face, close-up, devouring her as if he'd never see her again, as if he had to memorize every feature.

"For your sake, Julia," he repeated.

"I'll . . . miss you," she whispered, her throat tightening. "You've been a good . . . friend."

His expression changed, the lines hardened, his jaw clenched. He looked abruptly dangerous. "A friend," he said. He shook his head, walked to the door. He stopped there, a hand on the knob, half turned. "I am your friend, Julia. Don't forget it. If you ever need me . . ."

"Cam . . ."

"It's late," he said, opening the door, stepping through into the night, closing it behind him.

TWENTY-ONE

The next morning Julia could see that Ellen was focused. She looked terrific in a gray gabardine pantsuit, a black silk knit top underneath. A string of pearls today, no scarf. Pearl-studded earrings. Businesslike but feminine. The proverbial pit bull in pearls.

When the jurors filed in, Ellen made a point to smile at them, nod to them, especially the impatient stockbroker.

Judge Scott appeared; the formalities were accomplished. Day five began.

Cam was not in the courtroom, not sitting next to Julia, not there to support her with his presence. She missed him, missed the warm sensation of his leg so close to hers, and the occasional brush of his shoulder. She couldn't believe she even thought of such things under the circumstances, but she did. Often. Far too often. But as much as she yearned for his presence, she knew he had work to do — which did not stop her yearning.

She listened attentively, sitting forward on the bench, as Ellen addressed the court that morning. "I call Patrick Askew to the stand."

Askew came in the main door from where he'd been waiting in the hall with the other defense witnesses. Julia didn't have to turn around with the rest of the spectators to observe his entrance. She already knew he was tall and pear-shaped. When he passed by her seat, she saw he was wearing a beige tweed sport coat a bit too tight for him. He was a blue jeans type man, and probably hadn't worn the sport coat in years.

He was sworn in and took his seat in the witness box. He was high-strung to begin with, and today he looked doubly nervous; she'd told Ellen what an A type personality he was, so Ellen was prepared.

"Good morning, Mr. Askew," Ellen said pleasantly.

"Good morning."

"Please state your name and address for the record, Mr. Askew."

He so stated.

"And now, please explain what your position is and how you knew Leann Cornish."

"I'm the administrator of Aspen Valley

Hospital. Leann Cornish was an OR nurse."

"Okay, Mr. Askew, now please tell us, in your own words, what happened between you and Nurse Cornish a year ago last June."

Despite his fidgeting in the witness box, Askew turned out to be a good witness. Julia breathed a little easier as he described the forced resignation of Nurse Cornish. She had prepped him well.

"So there were several complaints about Ms. Cornish?" Ellen asked, hammering home the point.

"Oh, yes."

"Could you have thoroughly investigated the doctors' complaints before asking her to resign?"

"I could have. I felt it wasn't necessary. My responsibility, first, is to the patients. There was no reason to believe the doctors would make up such a story. And, then, she was so ill. She'd had surgery. She was undergoing both chemotherapy and radiation. She was in no condition to work."

"What was Ms. Cornish's reaction when you asked her to resign?"

Askew began to fidget again. *Careful, Ellen,* Julia thought. God, how she wished she could be up there asking the questions.

She trusted Ellen without any reservation. Still . . .

Ellen repeated the question, and Askew finally said, "Leann was naturally upset, and I guess you might say she was angry. She cried. She begged me to let her keep her job. It was pretty darn awful," he said, his voice fading.

"Did she know which doctors had gone to you with complaints?"

"Oh, yes, she knew."

"Did you yourself tell her?"

"I didn't have to. But she knew. She even cussed Thomas out by name."

"That's all I have," Ellen said, appearing satisfied, and Julia felt her muscles loosening.

Bret cross-examined the hospital administrator, but he got nowhere. Patrick Askew stood firm on all counts, especially on his belief that Leann knew Thomas was behind the complaints about her performance.

Thank you, Patrick, Julia thought, *thank you.*

Ellen's next witness was a nurse who'd worked with Leann twelve years ago. She stated that the day Samantha was murdered had been extremely busy, and she didn't think Dr. Innes had been late for any surgery. She testified to his skill and caring. Her own son a couple years back had undergone shoulder surgery, performed by Dr. Innes, who'd been fantastic.

In cross, McSwain pounded at the woman, asking how she could possibly have followed Thomas Innes's every move that fateful day, but the DA only went around in circles. If anything, he made the woman's testimony more profound, when she said, "Good Lord, it was the kind of day you're so busy you don't even get to go to the bathroom or grab a candy bar. Surgery after surgery after surgery."

Julia recognized Bret's expression as he thanked the witness and dismissed her — maybe no one else saw his scowl, but she knew him too well. Oh, yes, he was angry.

Ellen then called Dr. Romano, the retired anesthesiologist from Durango. He also swore that Thomas had not been late for any of his surgeries; and he was sure Innes had never left the hospital.

In cross-examination McSwain asked, "Did you see him every moment?" Dubiously.

"Well, no, of course not. But the surgeries were scheduled one right after the other, no time in between, so he couldn't have been gone," the doctor said.

"No bathroom break? No lunch break?" The DA put his hands in his trouser pockets and half faced the jury, raising a brow as if to say, *Come on, pal, we all know you went to the bathroom and got something to eat.*

"God, no. I think I grabbed a PowerBar on those days. And sometimes, not even that."

"Your Honor," McSwain said, turning his back on Romano, "I have nothing further for this witness. He's excused." Julia recognized the tactic — by addressing the judge, Bret was insinuating the man was such a liar he was not worthy of another question. Maybe the jury got it, maybe not. Still, she felt a twinge of admiration for her former boss. And it *was* hard to believe these doctors and nurses had not taken a minute to use the rest room or grab a snack.

Ellen's next witness was a PA, a physician's assistant, who'd been a nurse twelve years ago and was still employed at Aspen Valley Hospital. He testified to Dr. Innes's skill, his care of patients, his presence either in the emergency room, OR, or pre-op all that busy day.

Bret McSwain tried another assault with the bathroom-and-food routine, and Julia was afraid he was finally scoring points. He kept comparing a busy day at the hospital to a busy day in the courthouse — no one could possibly account for anyone else's whereabouts every minute.

A couple more nurses took the stand after that; the testimony was starting to get repetitive. The jury was losing interest. She was not surprised when Ellen cut her witnesses short.

Judge Scott called for the lunch recess. Julia, Thomas, and Ellen had sandwiches in the empty second-floor law library, while Maggie took Livie and Dennis home for lunch. Then Julia and Ellen went to the ladies' room, and Ellen reapplied makeup over her bruise, which was starting to turn yellow and green. *Lovely,* Julia thought.

That afternoon Ellen called two doctors to the stand. Both testified at some length that Thomas Innes was a talented surgeon and that his success rate was phenomenal. Ellen had them describe a couple surgeries he performed, which were now classic repairs written up in the *New England Journal of Medicine*. They even provided slides and X rays. One of the female jurors began subconsciously rubbing an elbow, as if she had sympathetic pain and was considering surgery — with Thomas.

McSwain crossed, asking the same question of each doctor, questions he'd prepared well ahead of time.

"Doctor, what is your relationship with Thomas Innes, professionally, I mean?"

"He's a colleague."

"But is it true he refers patients to you when he's too busy to take them on?"

"Yes, that's true. Sometimes."

"Is it accurate, then, to say you've gained financially from your association with Dr. Innes?"

"Well, I'm not sure I'd put it like that."

"Then I'll rephrase. Do you make money from patients referred to you by doctor Thomas Innes? A yes or no will suffice."

"Yes, I suppose you could —"

"Thank you, Doctor. That will be all."

The point was made. *Not bad, Bret,* Julia mused, but Thomas had still come off as a god among surgeons.

The fifth day of the trial was over.

"Where are the results on the damn Buddha?" Ellen asked that evening.

Cam held his hands out. Empty.

Ellen worried her lip. "I'm going to have to make a decision here. Whether to forget about the DNA or ask for a continuance. Big decision."

"I think delaying things will be counter-productive," Julia put in. "We're really moving now. We've got the momentum."

Ellen agreed.

"I'll call my friend again, see if he can't nudge the FBI lab," Cam said. "Like I'm the only person waiting for results."

"Okay, okay. It's not the worst thing that could happen," Ellen said. "The jury knows Holman was there. They don't know Thomas was there. That's what counts."

"Are you going to put Holman back on the witness stand?" Cam asked.

"No. I don't think so. I could, but my instincts say to leave well enough alone."

Strategy, strategy. Like a general fighting a war, they had to envision their enemies' moves, get their own defenses into place, deploy their forces when and where they were needed.

"Well," Ellen said, rising from the dining table, stifling a yawn, "I'm hitting the sack."

"Yeah," Cam said, but he was looking at Julia — as he always was.

The sixth day of the Innes trial began with Claudia Dessaro, a former friend of Samantha's, who now lived in Denver.

She'd come up for the trial, ready to testify.

"Ms. Dessaro, tell me about the conversation you had with Samantha Innes, approximately a month before her death."

Claudia was beanpole thin, with weathered skin, short hair going to gray. "I knew about Matt Holman. Samantha told me. And I'd been in the bar with her the day she'd met him. I believe it was the Saturday after opening day on the mountain. Anyway, that following spring she was going through a really bad time with Thomas. She had a little girl, and she was alone so much of the time. Thomas worked very long hours. Ridiculously long hours. He didn't pay any attention to her or their child at all.

"Samantha was very attractive. I wasn't surprised when a man came on to her, and I certainly wasn't surprised when she had the affair."

Ellen moved directly to the attack. "Tell us what she said to you that day a month before her death."

"She admitted she was having the affair with Matt. Mr. Holman, that is. She told me she really liked him, but he was a ski bum and bartender at night, had no money, not much of a future, basically. She said he kept telling her to leave Thomas, and she was going to have to end it with Matt because of that. She was quite upset, actually."

"Okay. Let's back up. Did Samantha say exactly why she had to end the affair?"

"Oh, yes. She said she had a feeling Matt wanted her to get a divorce, get lots of alimony, and then she could support him."

"Your Honor," Bret McSwain said, rising as if bone-weary. "I must object. This is hearsay."

The judge ducked his head, peered at him over the top of his reading glasses. "This is a person who was involved in the conversation, Mr. McSwain. I'll allow it."

Ellen asked, "Did this upset Samantha?"

"Very much. She told me she had no intention of divorcing Thomas."

"She said, unequivocally, that she was not going to divorce her husband?"

The woman looked directly at the jurors. "That's exactly what she told me."

"Your witness, Mr. McSwain," Ellen said.

After a moment McSwain half rose and said, "No questions." He sat down and studied a file as if the last witness had bombed out for the defense.

After the lunch recess the parade of

character witnesses for Thomas began.

"He fixed my knee . . . my shoulder . . . my wrist . . . my ankle." "He took excellent care of me." "He was wonderful to me." "He was always calm and pleasant." "He really had the best bedside manner of any doctor I've ever seen."

On and on. Bret couldn't do a thing with these witnesses, because if he tried to tear down their testimony, he came across as the bad guy. So he rarely cross-examined.

Julia and Ellen had discussed this testimony. Ellen had argued that it might strike the jury as self-serving. Thomas this, Dr. Innes that. The jury might ask themselves, *Was he really that terrific?*

But Julia convinced her that the accolades were necessary. She listened to the witnesses now and she watched her husband. She could see his profile, and she recognized his smug smile, faint but obvious to her, at the praise he was hearing.

Did the jurors see that smile?

Court was adjourned early that afternoon. The jury and spectators filed out, and Judge Scott wanted to know how many witnesses Ellen had left.

"Only one, Your Honor. It shouldn't take too long."

"Then you'll be done tomorrow?" he asked.

"Definitely," Ellen said. "I'm waiting for DNA results from the FBI lab. But since I'm sure what they'll show, I don't believe the results will impact the jury's decision. I'd like to have them, but I won't delay the trial if they're not ready."

"I don't know why you're bothering with them," Bret McSwain said.

"Now, now, Mr. McSwain," the judge admonished. "Save all that righteous indignation for your closing arguments."

That evening the atmosphere at the house was surreal, everyone, including Maggie, very quiet. Julia kept thinking, was the trial really going to end tomorrow, after all these long horrid months? Then she thought about Cam. No matter the verdict, he'd leave town. For good.

The only issue discussed after dinner was Marcy Cornish — should Cam take one last stab at her? Ellen said, "Hey, it can't hurt, right? The one thing bugging the hell out of me is Leann's motive in all this. Even if we never get it in front of the jury, I'd sure like to know."

"Yeah, so would I," Thomas said.

Then Ellen joked, "And besides, Victor Ferris is picking up your tab, it won't kill

500

him to pay for one last trip to Rifle, right?"

Cam smiled thinly. "He hasn't complained yet."

"Well, he's getting a goddamn book out of this deal," Thomas said, "and at my expense. He shouldn't complain."

Everyone wanted to retire early. Even Livie, who turned down an offer to watch TV with Dennis. She was too nervous, she said. Julia found herself waiting to take Blackie out for his walk. She knew she was trying to catch Cam alone, hoping he might walk with her. But by the time she got Blackie's leash and put on her coat and gloves, Cam had left. She went out front and couldn't help looking up and down the street, just in case his car was still there. But it was gone.

On the last day of the trial the first thing Ellen did was enter into evidence the DNA test results that they'd gotten in weeks ago.

She spoke directly to the jury: "I have from the FBI forensics lab in Virginia the results on DNA testing from the bedsheets." She held up the documents and walked them to the clerk of the court to admit into evidence. "Definitive results," Ellen said, "Matt Holman's DNA and Samantha Innes's DNA on the sheets.

There was no other DNA. That puts Mr. Holman at the scene. That does not put Dr. Innes at the scene."

She laid the papers down on the table, stood a moment, back to the jury box, then pivoted to face them. "This is irrefutable scientific evidence, ladies and gentlemen, which you must take into account in your deliberations."

There were several more items of evidence to be entered into the trial records, and then Ellen's last witness. Dr. Deanna Gregg, an oncologist from Denver who had treated Leann Cornish for breast cancer. They had saved the woman for last, because they wanted to leave the jury with this particular doctor's testimony. Barring an unforeseen happening, such as Marcy Cornish spontaneously confessing to Cam that she knew her mother wanted to harm Dr. Innes.

Dr. Gregg was around forty years old, a little heavy in the hips, with short waving blond hair and a sweet face. She was sworn in and stated her name and address. Told the court that she was an oncologist at the Sally Jobe Cancer Center in Denver.

"You treated Leann Cornish, correct?" Ellen asked.

"Yes, I diagnosed her originally and went

through the entire three years of her illness with her."

"She had surgery?"

"A mastectomy, yes. And a lumpectomy on the other breast a year later."

"She had radiation?"

"Yes. A six-week course."

"And chemotherapy?"

"Twice."

"But none of these helped her, is that correct?"

"Unfortunately. She had a particularly virulent type of estrogen-sensitive tumor."

"So she was quite ill during the entire three years before she died?"

"Not so much the first year, although the chemo was very hard on her. But after that, she was quite ill, yes."

"So sick she shouldn't have been working at a sensitive job such as head operating room nurse?"

"Objection. Your Honor, relevancy," Bret McSwain said.

"I'll let her answer," Judge Scott said.

"I'd say that it would be hard to work full-time while undergoing chemo."

"Please tell the court how a person feels when undergoing chemotherapy."

"Judge, I object," McSwain said. "This has nothing to do with —"

503

"It goes to Leann Cornish's state of mind when she made the videotape," Ellen said.

"I'll allow it."

Ellen re-asked the question.

"Well, the effect of chemo varies greatly in each individual. Loss of hair, that's obvious. Fatigue, anemia, nausea, lack of appetite are the most common physical effects. Depression and anxiety can be mental effects," Dr. Gregg said.

"Would you say, Doctor, that a person undergoing chemotherapy, who is sick to begin with, would be physically and emotionally impaired?"

"Objection," Bret said. "Relevancy."

"Calm down, Mr. McSwain. I'll let you continue, Ms. Marshall, but let's see your point pretty quick here."

"Thank you, Your Honor," then to Dr. Gregg, "Would Leann Cornish be impaired, in your professional opinion?"

"Yes, she would be."

There was a rustle in the rows of spectators.

"How exactly?"

"She was depressed and very angry. Some people accept their illness with grace, and some don't. Leann was one of the latter."

"How would this have affected her decision-making?"

"Well, I can't say for sure, but people who are depressed and angry usually don't make good decisions. And chemo can cause mental aberrations in some people."

"Thank you, Dr. Gregg. Your Honor, the defense rests."

The DA cross-examined. "You're making a blanket statement about cancer patients, Doctor, involving their mental state."

"Well, a generalization, yes."

"Then you have training in psychiatry?"

"No, I'm an oncologist."

"But you generalize about a patient's mental state. That's very interesting, Dr. Gregg."

"I've dealt with many, many cancer patients. I don't just deal with their physical illness, I also deal with their emotions."

"But you're not a psychiatrist."

"No, I'm not."

"Thank you, Dr. Gregg. That's all I have."

"Re-cross?" the judge asked.

"Yes, Your Honor," Ellen said. She remained seated, a ploy to show how comfortable she was with this witness, how much she trusted her. "How many patients do you generally treat in a year, Dr. Gregg?"

"About a thousand," the doctor said, well prepared.

"So, let's assume three thousand in the years you treated Ms. Cornish. Is that fair to say?"

"Yes."

"How many of these patients had emotional problems?"

"All of them, Ms. Marshall."

"So you've had a fair amount of experience dealing with emotionally disturbed women?"

"Oh, yes. More than most psychiatrists have, I daresay."

"Thank you, Dr. Gregg. That's all," Ellen said as Bret rose, indignant, to make an objection.

Cam made another trip to Rifle that morning. A light rain glistened on the road, spattered on his windshield. He wondered if Marcy Cornish would be out riding in this weather. And if not, would she be home? And would she let him in the house?

He would have phoned, but he figured she wouldn't talk to him. It was better to just show up like before.

He turned onto the long ranch road, wondering how the trial was going. Wondering how long the jury would deliberate, what their verdict would be.

And what Julia would do — whichever verdict the jury returned.

Regardless of the official verdict, he had his own ideas, his own suspicions. And it was like a knife in his gut that Julia was married to a man who was, quite possibly, a murderer. He must have asked himself a thousand times over the past months what he should tell her — how much he should tell her — if her husband was found not guilty. Jesus, how could he turn his back on her and just leave? On the other hand, if he laid it all out, she could only think one thing, that he was a sick-minded, jealous prick. Because if he really believed Innes was a killer, then why hadn't he told her months ago?

Yeah, he thought, *and just why haven't you?*

He shook off the same questions he'd been beating himself up with and forced his mind onto the problem at hand, another bone he'd been chewing on for too long — Leann's motivation. Why try to fuck over a man even as you were dying and, you'd think, had more important things to consider than trying to get justice for a dead woman you didn't even know very well?

The rain was coming down harder as he pulled up next to the barn. No one was riding; the ring was empty. A pickup was parked by the mobile home. Someone was there.

"Oh, God, it's you again," Marcy said at the door.

"Listen, I'm beginning to think your mother might have been right," he said. Not lying, exactly, merely trying a new slant. "It's the last day of the trial. This is your only chance to make a difference, Marcy."

"I have nothing to say that I haven't already said."

"What if you could be the one to prove Innes was guilty?"

"Oh, please." But she hesitated, thinking. Standing there on the threshold, not letting him in but not telling him to leave, either.

"It's getting personal now. I want the truth, and I don't care how the cards fall. Marcy, you know something."

"I told you what I know."

"Elaborate, please."

"My mother," Marcy said finally, "was a very angry woman at the end. She wanted to get the doctor, yes, it's true. It was . . . I don't know, like a mission."

"Why him? Why not the other doctors who registered complaints about her?"

"Because." She hesitated again. "Because she idolized him. She idolized him from the day he moved to Aspen. She talked about him . . . a lot."

The rain pattered on the tin roof of the porch, dripped off the eaves. He said nothing, waited. His breath made white puffs in the damp air.

"Can you imagine how awful it was when she was fired? She lost everything. And, to make it even worse, he did it. She didn't care about the other doctors. I mean, Thomas Innes was her idol, not the others. And I think that's what killed my mother. Not the cancer but him."

On the drive back to Aspen, Cam went over Marcy's body language, her words, every nuance. She'd told him plenty. Explained why her mother had ratted out Innes after so many years. Marcy had reinforced Cam's belief that Innes had done his wife. Leann had kept his dirty secret and he'd betrayed her. She'd tried to pay him back, even if it had to be from the grave. Yet Cam sensed there was still something Marcy wasn't saying. Something . . .

Well, whatever he'd missed wasn't going

to impact the trial. Still, he'd failed to get to the bottom of Leann's motivation. He'd failed at a lot of things, he'd been wrong about a lot . . . Holman and Innes. It looked more and more as if he'd helped put the wrong guy in prison.

His windshield wipers swished, the gray scenery slid by. He drove on autopilot, his mind elsewhere.

He was glad as hell the trial was going to be over today. He'd be able to return to Denver, get back into his routine. Forget about Holman, forget about Innes. Mostly forget about Julia.

It was the proximity that tortured him. Seeing her but unable to be with her, to hold her again, to kiss her. One kiss, one embrace. He could still feel where she'd touched him; as if a brand were burned into his skin.

Yes, he thought about Julia, and he thought about how he was such a loser. She wouldn't want him even if she were free. He had trouble with commitment, and she was all about commitment.

Funny, he could see himself so clearly through the Luke Diamond character. His fears and denial, his violent streak, his abject cowardice when it came to a meaningful relationship. The scars his abusive father had left on him.

He could see it all so clearly, but he still didn't have the guts to face down his demons, and the price he paid was loneliness.

He neared Aspen, saw the clouds lifting, the rain ending, sun breaking through layers of mist that blew in tatters from the high peaks. And his mind turned again to Marcy. Damn, there *was* something there. If Leann were alive, if he could just talk to her again . . . But she was dead. Only her videotape remained as her witness. Trying to visit a kind of divine retribution on Thomas Innes.

He parked near the courthouse, walked up the stairs to the front door, then up two more flights, and let himself into the courtroom.

He spotted Julia sitting in the front row and felt the familiar blow to his chest.

Bret McSwain's closing argument was clear and well thought out. Somewhat long, Ellen thought, watching the jury intently.

"Here we have the motivation and the opportunity for Thomas Innes to murder his wife." He ticked his reasoning off on his fingers. "She was having an affair, which she apparently flaunted in public,

511

she was going to leave him, which meant he'd have to pay alimony and child support, and she had just had sex with her young lover in their marriage bed.

"He lived a couple minutes from the hospital, so that he was able to take a quick break, dash home, and discover his wife still lolling in bed, her lover having just left, her lover's scent on everything that was his. They argued, and at some point he hit her on the head with a heavy, fourteen-inch-high Buddha, sustaining a cut on his hand in the process. But he didn't have time to see to the cut until he returned to the hospital. What he hadn't counted on were the two witnesses to his return — Rick Krystal through the kitchen windows and Leann Cornish, who was actually looking for him. Who even commented on the cut to his hand.

"You've heard that Thomas Innes was nervous in surgery, unlike his usual manner, and he was instrumental in getting Leann Cornish fired, because she'd witnessed his return to work from his Meadowood home.

"There is only one verdict you can return to balance the scales of justice, ladies and gentlemen of the jury. Please return with a finding of guilty to the crime of second-degree murder. Let both Samantha Innes and Leann Cornish rest easy in their graves. Thank you."

Long-winded, Ellen thought again. She could see the jurors shifting in their seats — they knew all this.

"Ms. Marshall, your closing argument," Judge Scott said.

Ellen stood up, moved around the table to face the jury.

"I won't retry the case in my closing argument. You've heard all the evidence. For each point Mr. McSwain brought up, there is clear evidence refuting it.

"But this is the most important point: Thomas Innes is a healer, not a killer. He is a well-known surgeon. You've heard how talented he is. He has a wife and a child, an established clinic. He is an exemplary member of his community. If he were the rabid murderer Mr. McSwain believes him to be, what about the last twelve years? His wife of eight years, ladies and gentlemen, is very much alive."

Titters from the spectators. Two of the jurors smiled. Now Ellen had to be careful. To neutralize Leann's statement but not to come down too hard on the dead woman, which would only turn the jury against her.

She drew a mental breath and plunged

in. "Leann Cornish's videotaped statement seems like a serious piece of evidence, until you realize how sick she was, how a poisonous chemical flooding her body skewed her emotions and decision-making capabilities.

"You can understand, we can all understand, why she wanted to lash out, blame someone. And the timing — over a decade had gone by before she decided to speak. *After* she made a statement to the police that Dr. Innes had been in the hospital all day. *After* she lost her job. Even though she'd supposedly known Dr. Innes was guilty for all that time. She went to the DA only *after* she was terminated.

"In the end, you will decide on Thomas Innes's innocence or guilt with common sense. There is more than enough reasonable doubt as to his guilt. This man" — she gestured at her client — "is no more guilty of murder than you are. Thank you. Members of the jury, Your Honor, I rest my case."

She turned and walked back to Thomas, who sat composed, his hands clasped on the top of the table. But she was looking past his shoulder to the first row of benches, to Julia, who gave her a smile of total confidence. And that, in itself, was worth these past six months. In the end it wasn't the acclaim or wealth you'd accumulated — though, Ellen knew, those things didn't hurt — it was your friends that mattered.

TWENTY-TWO

The waiting was the hardest. A time of agony, of trepidation, heart pounding, mouth dry, stomach sick. And no way to release the tension. Ellen giving only a few words to the anxious press, the Innes group all ducking into cars and trooping home to await the verdict.

"How long do you think it will take?" Thomas asked.

"As long as it takes." Ellen shot him a look. "The sooner the better from our point of view. Usually."

Livie hugged her father. Her lips were quivering. "Daddy," she said, "it'll be all right. I just know it will."

He fluffed her hair. "I know it will, too."

Dennis was still hanging around, although he could have returned to Denver, his end of the work done. As always, he tried to be as unobtrusive as possible around Thomas. Still, he held Livie's hand.

Cam had returned from Rifle and met

them at the house. He said he was going back to his room, change clothes, and go for a run; he would be back shortly, but he would take his cell phone with him just in case.

Julia wished she could go with him, leave, forget for a second, just a second, that seven men and five women were deciding her husband's fate.

"Is anyone hungry?" she asked. No, nobody was. No one could eat or rest or read or watch TV or do anything but wait for the phone to ring.

Even Thomas revealed a case of nerves, pacing, his brow furrowed. Everyone but Maggie was afraid to speak to him, the pariah, the one on whom judgment would fall. And even Maggie chose her words with more care than usual.

Ellen retreated into her room; she'd been through this before. But Julia hadn't, not in a criminal case, and certainly not for a member of her own family. Although she didn't feel like talking to a soul, she phoned her mother and father — more reassurance to them that the jury, despite the media sitting on the fence, would of course find Thomas not guilty.

"I don't care what they say on CNN,

Mom," she said. "I was there the whole time. I saw the jurors' faces."

She promised to phone the instant the verdict was in.

The day slid into dusk, an early autumn dusk. Cam returned, freshly showered.

"Do you want something to eat?" Julia asked.

"No, thanks, I grabbed something on the way over. How's it going?"

"Awful."

"Yeah."

"Did you get to see Marcy this morning?" Julia asked then.

"Yep. Got nothing much from her other than her mother idolized Thomas, and that's why she was so angry when he got her fired."

"She idolized him," Julia mused. "So it must have really hurt when he was instrumental in getting her fired."

"Must have," Cam said, but he didn't look convinced.

Their home phone line rang at seven. Julia grabbed it. "This is the clerk calling to inform you the jury has ended deliberations for the night and has been excused until nine tomorrow morning."

"Okay, thanks," she said, her voice choked.

"What?" Thomas asked.

"The jury's gone home for the day."

"Oh." He sounded disappointed.

The entire night stretched before them, possibly the next day, too. How would they all get through this unbearable waiting? How would she get through it?

Thomas finally went upstairs. "To hell with this," he said on the staircase. "I've got a clinic to get open, a dozen calls to make."

"Do you think that's wise?" Julia began. "I mean, everyone has to know what's going on in court right now."

He let out a disgruntled breath. "So you think I should stick my head in the sand?"

She shook her head. "Never mind. Make your calls."

"That's what I said in the first place," he muttered, and he disappeared up to their bedroom.

Julia turned to Cam when she heard the bedroom door close. She gave him a false smile. "He's just on edge. You know . . ."

"Sure," Cam said.

Ellen never came out of her room. She skipped dinner, and was most likely talking to Mason. Julia brewed tea in the kitchen and reflected on that. Ellen certainly hadn't said anything about ending the relationship. She'd go back to him, and sooner or later he'd hurt her again. Abusers always escalated, too. Julia knew that from the many cases she'd dealt with over the years. They escalated until the woman left or he injured her so badly she was hospitalized, and the authorities were called in. Or, sometimes, she ended up in the morgue.

She really had to convince Ellen to get help if she wouldn't leave Mason. But not now — Julia couldn't think about that now. She could only think about Thomas and the jury, each one of whom she felt to be so familiar. Most of them were probably in bed by now. What were they thinking? Would they sleep? Or would the burden of the decision keep them awake?

Maggie finally talked Livie and Dennis into a card game up in the apartment. And, once again, perhaps for the last time, Julia found herself alone in the living room with Cam. She was blindly leafing through a magazine, occasionally sipping her tea. She wanted to tell him how precious these moments were, how much she'd miss his company — even if he rarely spoke, she'd grown used to his presence. Blackie at her feet, Cam in the easy chair, one ankle crossed over the other knee, bare branches tapping on the windowpanes. Should she tell him how she felt? Tell him that as soon as the verdict was in — no matter which way it went — she was starting a new life? Either way, Thomas didn't need or want her. She was a wife in name only, a symbol. They'd both used each other in this marriage, for different reasons, yes, but whatever love there had been had died. And the awful thing was, she wasn't sure when that had happened.

She wanted Cam to know that. But if she told him, she'd sound pathetic. Or worse, uncaring that her husband was right now in their bedroom, alone and anxious despite his bravado.

No, she couldn't open that part of her heart to Cam. He would never understand. Only a woman would.

It was after eleven when he got up to leave. She walked him to the door.

"Get some sleep," he said.

"Like you will?"

"I don't count. You need rest."

"I'll try."

"This is the worst, I know." He looked down at her. "I wish I could help you."

"No one can help me."

"I know," he said softly.

She must've slept a little that night. She remembered a dream, so she must have drifted off. She got up at six and took a shower, feeling like hell. The anxiety starting again the second she'd opened her eyes.

Thomas was already downstairs, drinking coffee with Ellen in the kitchen.

"They'll come back with the verdict today, I know it," he said. "I mean, how long can it take? It's so obvious. If they can't see reasonable doubt, there's something wrong with them."

"Don't hold your breath," Ellen warned.

Somehow Julia got through the day. The minutes seemed to drag on forever, but curiously the hours flew. Everyone hung out in the main house. No one had much to say. And no one wanted to go out, not even to their car — the press lay in wait. After breakfast and cleaning the kitchen, Julia did housework just to stay occupied. Housework, mindless and rote, took her thoughts off the waiting.

"Will you stop?" Thomas said after lunch. "You're driving me nuts. You're driving all of us nuts."

She stopped vacuuming and stared at him. "I was just trying —"

"I know, but you can't do this to all of us."

She put the vacuum away and went upstairs to dust the bedroom and clean the bathroom, where she wouldn't disturb anyone. Blackie dutifully followed her, settling with a pleasurable groan at the foot of the bed on the down comforter. Julia almost shooed him off — Thomas hated the dog on the bed — but she thought, oh, screw it.

Cam didn't show up that day. She wasn't sure whether she was sad or relieved.

She considered taking Blackie out for a long walk, losing the press, maybe going to Cam's motel to see if he was there, but she didn't dare. What if someone saw her? Took her picture? What if the verdict came in while she was gone?

The phone rang at 4:40 p.m. Everyone in the house froze, stared at it for an endless moment, and then Ellen went over and picked up the receiver.

"Yes," she said. "Okay. Thank you." She placed the receiver quietly back in its cradle.

Julia was paralyzed. She felt acid rise in her throat.

"The jury's in."

"I told you," Thomas said.

"Don't be so satisfied," Ellen said. "Let's not get ahead of ourselves here."

"No." He shook his head. "It's not guilty. It has to be."

Julia and Thomas drove in Ellen's car to the parking garage next to the courthouse, while Maggie again played chauffeur to the kids. The reporters and cameramen crowded on the lawn in front, cables snaked on the ground toward vans with network logos on their sides. Everyone had heard — it was an old Western showdown on Main Street. The time of reckoning.

The three of them used the back door, but were still jostled by reporters, microphones thrust at them, voices yelling over voices. Several Aspen police officers appeared and held the throng at bay.

Cam was already in the hall outside the courtroom, waiting for them. He sat next to Julia; this time he even laid a hand over hers. "I heard from one of the cops," he said.

"You didn't have to come."

"Yes, I did." He paused, removed his hand. "How're you doing?"

"I've been better," she said.

The jury filed in. The judge entered, sat at the bench. The court clerk was standing and ready.

"Do we have a verdict?" the judge asked.

"Yes, Your Honor," the foreman of the jury said as he stood.

"Will the defendant please rise?"

Ellen came to her feet, motioning Thomas to do the same.

Julia couldn't bear it. She couldn't. She studied the faces of the jurors, knowing that if they looked directly at the defendant, the chances for a not guilty verdict were good, but the jurors were looking all over the place, some at the judge, some at the court clerk, some at Thomas, some at McSwain. She couldn't read them. Her heart thumped at her chest like a wild creature. Next to her Cam shifted on the oak bench, so that his thigh pressed against hers. She wanted to scream, to weep, to fall into his arms and collapse against his chest. But she sat there, her back ramrod straight, her eyes cast down, her hands balled into fists. The tall windows were open slightly. Outside it was cold. But she was sweating.

"May I see the verdict?" Judge Scott asked. The clerk took it from the foreman, handed it to Scott. He gave nothing away, not a flicker, until he was ready to read it out loud.

Dear God, get on with it! her mind shouted.

"In the above entitled action, the People versus Thomas Innes, on count one," Bill Scott read, "we the jury find the defendant not guilty in the second-degree murder of Samantha Innes."

Julia didn't hear a thing after the "not guilty." She gasped. She must have cried out. Her heart gave a painful lurch, then tears sprang from her eyes. Not guilty! Not guilty!

The courtroom was in an uproar, so many reporters dashing out all at once to use cell phones that there was a crush at the door. Thomas was grinning, giving Ellen a bear hug, lifting her off her feet and swinging her around.

Judge Scott rapped the gavel, calling the room to order. After several minutes and several more raps, everyone quieted down.

"I'm going to poll the jury," the judge said. "Please keep order in this courtroom until we are done."

He asked each juror, "Do you agree with the verdict of not guilty?"

Solemnly each juror answered, "Yes, Your Honor."

Judge Scott said, "Thomas Innes, you are a free man. You may leave the court-room. Jurors, thank you for your service. This trial is adjourned." His gavel thumped one final time.

Thomas turned to Julia then. "I knew it!" he boomed. "I knew it!" He leaned across the railing and hugged her. She hugged him back.

Directly behind her Livie was squealing with delight, jumping up and down.

"Daddy! Daddy!" she cried.

He came around the railing and hugged her, too. "Livie, baby, thank God, thank God."

Maggie was still sitting, a handkerchief clutched in her fist, biting her lip. Thomas leaned down and said, "It's all right, it's all right now. Hey, don't cry."

"A statement!" the few remaining reporters shouted, pressing close with the rest of the crowd.

"No, please, no statement right now," Thomas was saying.

"Just a word, Dr. Innes."

"Julia? Ellen? Can we get out of here?" Thomas said.

The bailiff escorted them out past the judge's chambers and down the fire escape stairs, but that didn't help much. Out back of the courthouse, they were waylaid. It was a madhouse. Thomas had an arm around Ellen on one side, Julia on the other. Livie and Dennis followed, Maggie clinging to Dennis's arm. A few cops showed up and tried to hold the crowd off with little success.

Where was Cam? Julia craned her neck to scan the growing crowd. But in this mass of humanity, she couldn't find him.

"You're going to have to say something," Ellen was trying to tell Thomas over the din. "They're not going away until you do."

"All right, for God's sake. Okay." Thomas freed his arms from Julia and Ellen, straightened his shoulders, stood erect, and cleared his throat. He stepped forward toward the swarm. "Please, everybody, now that this ordeal is over, please respect our privacy. All I'm going to say is I knew justice would prevail. I want to thank the jurors. And my attorney, Ellen Marshall. I owe you my life, Ellen. And my wonderful wife, Julia, who stood by me all this time and never doubted my innocence. And over here" — he gestured — "my daughter Olivia. And of course, my mother, Margaret. They've been here this whole time for me. I don't know how to thank everyone."

Julia swallowed; her face felt stiff. The crowd elbowed her. She tried to smile, but she couldn't. She searched the crowd again for Cam.

"Where's the car?" Thomas turned to ask. "Where the hell did we leave the car?"

"It's still in the parking garage. Let's make a run for it," Ellen said.

"Ms. Marshall! Ellen!" a few reporters called out. "A statement!"

Ellen smiled and waved and called back that she'd hold a formal press conference tomorrow, as soon as she got back to Denver.

Thomas strong-armed through the people, made his way to the parking garage elevator. When the door slid shut, the seven of them were alone, the sudden silence deafening.

"Goddamn, Ellen, I knew it! I told you!" Thomas crowed. He pulled Julia close, ebullient. "I'm a free man. Honey, what do you say to that?"

"I'm so happy for you. I knew they'd find you not guilty."

"Hey, Livie, kiddo, was there ever a doubt?" he said, pulling his daughter close and giving her another hug.

The elevator stopped, the door opened. The parking garage was cold and dim and reeked of motor oil.

"It's right over there," Ellen said, pointing.

Livie and Dennis headed with Maggie to her car, while Julia followed Ellen. She felt a kind of panic. It was over, her life was over. But a new one was beginning. Yes,

yes, there was no reason to panic.

But where was Cam?

Ellen used the remote to unlock the car doors. "Hope we don't get ambushed at the pass," she joked.

Julia cast around with a kind of desperation. Where was he? Then she spotted it, his Bronco, a couple rows over. And there was Cam, opening the door, ready to slide in, to drive away.

"Wait," she said, mostly to herself, and she took a step toward the Bronco, then another. She didn't give a damn about anything else. From two rows apart their eyes met, her pulse throbbed in her temples, the panic snatched at her. He was leaving. He was leaving. Then he gave her a rueful smile, a short wave of his hand, slid into his car, started it up, and backed out. She couldn't see him. She heard the squeal of tires around a corner, up a ramp. *Cam . . . no, don't leave me.*

"Was that Lazlo?" Somehow Thomas was at her side. "Hell, I wanted to thank him. He did a good job for me. Oh, well, I'm sure I'll catch him sometime." He took her arm, squeezed it for a moment. "Let's get out of here. Come on, Julia."

"Yes," she managed to say, "we may as well go."

Bret McSwain simply could not believe the verdict. He'd heard it with his own ears, heard the judge poll the jurors, he'd seen Ellen Marshall's grin of triumph, Thomas Innes's celebration of his freedom.

Again. The man had beaten the odds *again.*

He wanted to crawl in a hole, curl up, suffer in silence. He didn't want to witness the defense's happiness, any more than he wanted the simpering sympathy of his colleagues.

But he had to face the media. He couldn't stay holed up in Lawson Fine's office forever. He had to walk out into the light of day and face the music. Oh, God.

With great effort he did it. He strode out of the front door of the Pitkin County Courthouse, and he forced a smile, and he spoke words he'd never recall. Cameras flashed, video cameras whirred. Reporters shouted questions. He was calm, dignified; words spewed off his tongue, the requisite respect-for-the-worthy-opponent crap.

Then he excused himself, found his car somehow, and began to drive down the valley toward Glenwood Springs.

He hated Aspen. He hated its success, its

beauty, its power to overcome obstacles, its insider superiority. He hated the town, and this was why.

Jealous? a little voice trilled inside his head.

His cell phone rang as he was passing the Woody Creek turnoff. He answered it and was immediately sorry.

"Bret, Charlie Singer here."

Shit, Singer, the state attorney general. "Yes, sir?"

"What the hell went wrong?"

"Nothing went *wrong*. The jury saw fit to —"

"Don't give me that garbage. You didn't do your job."

"I respectfully beg to differ, Charlie."

"Now we've got a murderer walking the streets. A rich famous murderer."

"The people of my district judged the man not guilty. You know a jury trial is always a crapshoot." The old cliché.

"I expected a different outcome, Bret."

"So did I, Charlie. So did I."

He clicked off, threw the cell phone on the passenger seat, and drove into the setting sun, stuck in a line of commuter traffic, and that was when he realized his cheeks were wet.

Jesus Christ, he was weeping.

Diamond in the Rough

Luke Diamond was driving his T-Bird along Colfax Avenue on his way home when his cell phone rang. He braked lightly — he was going twenty miles an hour over the speed limit — and answered the call.

"Beckett just got off," the voice said. It was Davie.

"Well, I'll be damned."

"It's all over the news."

"I bet it is."

He did an illegal U-turn and headed back to the Federal Building, where the trial had been held. He might get to see the reporters make fools of themselves, as usual. The vermin. He might get to see pretty Janet, who had stood by her man for every moment of the trial.

He might even get to see Larry Beckett himself, stare in the guy's eyes and see whether he was happier at getting off or happier that he fucked the system. Oh, yeah, Luke would know.

It occurred to him that if Beckett were a murderer, he'd now be walking around free, and he could do it again. Although he probably wouldn't — too smart, too successful, no reason to kill anyone anymore.

Like his wife Janet? But, hell, they'd been married for years, hadn't they? And he hadn't offed her yet. Nah, he probably wouldn't, not after the trial. Maybe that would be the one good thing to come out of this fiasco.

Luke drove too fast along Colfax, dodging traffic, garnering an angry horn blast or two. Yeah, up yours, buddy.

Pulled up to the curb in front of the big white building with its semicircular wings, left the car in a no-parking zone.

They were all there, on the broad steps leading down to street level. A regular press conference, all the local channels had vans there, even several national stations were represented, the usual gaggle of newspaper jockeys and a few tabloid grunts. Reporters yelled and shouldered one another aside. And there was Larry Beckett, impeccable in a dark suit, pale blue shirt, and matching tie, Janet at his side, his arm around her waist. Oh, he was one joyous sucker, grinning, kissing Janet for the cameras, telling everyone what a wonderful defense attorney Carole Nichols was, how grateful he was to the jury, his family, colleagues, blah, blah. How he'd known the outcome had to be his freedom, because he was an innocent man.

"Now," he said as Luke stopped a few steps below, "if you'll give Janet and me some privacy . . . We just want to go home and relax. Get our lives back. Right, honey?"

"Oh, yes, Larry," she said.

Luke felt like puking. But he pushed his way closer, flipping his tin to get through. "Excuse me, Denver Homicide, excuse me." And the waves parted as if for Moses.

He finally stood nose to nose with Larry Beckett.

"Remember me, Beckett?"

"Sorry . . . ?"

"Luke Diamond, Denver Homicide. I investigated your first wife's death twelve years ago."

"Oh, sure, right. Well, too bad they didn't listen to you this time, Mr. Diamond."

"I promised Andrea I'd find her killer," Luke said.

"And you did, you certainly did," Beckett said, avuncular, sickeningly chummy.

"Did I?"

That gave Beckett pause. Then Luke saw a look cross his features, a split second of cunning triumph.

"Well now," Beckett said, keeping his voice low.

"I'm putting you on notice, pal."

"You're what?"

"You heard me."

"You're aware of the rule of double jeopardy, Diamond?"

"Yeah, I'm aware. I'm also aware of murder and the subsequent punishment."

"Fuck off, Diamond," he said, and he turned away, put a meaty arm across his wife's shoulders, and led her down the steps.

Luke stood and watched them for a time, feeling the slow burn in his chest, fighting it. Now was not the time. This was not the place.

He walked down to where he'd left his car, pulled the parking citation out from under the windshield wiper, *threw it on the floor on top of a heap of other tickets.*

He drove away from the scene, toward his apartment, let the wind blow across his face, through his hair.

He'd get Beckett sooner or later. Oh, yeah, he'd never rest until he did. The son of a bitch had admitted to him . . . fucking admitted . . .

Ah, well, Luke thought, passing a bus, then swerving back in to avoid a car making a left-hand turn. Ah, well, vengeance is a dish best served cold. Ain't it?

In the car Ellen, Thomas, and Maggie made plans for that night. Dinner at Piñons, a truly gourmet feast, champagne, a lot of Thomas's friends and colleagues, a lot of Livie's friends, too. "Hell," Thomas said, "the whole town is invited."

Julia hadn't the heart to celebrate, but she knew she had to change her clothes and put on her party face. There was no way out. She desperately wanted to join in the festive mood, but her mind was consumed with Cam's absence.

This was Thomas's night, his moment of triumph, and he deserved it. But she needed to tell him the truth, tell him how she felt — soon. But not tonight. God, no.

They drove home from the courthouse followed by the press. Aspen police held them at bay until, slowly but surely, they all disappeared for the night. They would be back tomorrow, Julia knew, but maybe then it would be easier to handle them.

"Goddamn," Thomas said inside the front door, "I haven't been out in ages." He rubbed his hands together.

The Innes party took over the restaurant, filling the bar and most of the tables. Luckily, it was a quiet night, still off-season.

Julia smiled and smiled. Accepted kisses, said the requisite things. Ate a little, drank two glasses of champagne, and felt promptly sick.

Ellen was in her glory. She'd be getting calls from all over the state after this. A victory was always good for business.

"What's the matter?" Ellen whispered to Julia once.

"Nothing."

"Come on."

"I'm exhausted, that's all."

"I'll be exhausted tomorrow. Tonight's for fun," Ellen said.

Thomas was having a ball. Surrounded by family and friends, eating, drinking, his face shining with pleasure and sweat.

What if the verdict had been different? Julia thought. What if, right now, she was home alone, Thomas awaiting transport to the state prison, Ellen getting ready to file appeals?

Even if Thomas had been found guilty, Cam would have returned to Denver. His job would have been over. And she wondered: How, exactly, would Victor Ferris end his book? The same, with the doctor getting off? Or maybe he'd end the story differently, with the doctor going to jail. Maybe Luke Diamond would find the last piece of the puzzle to prove who really committed the murder. Because there was always a murder in the Luke Diamond books.

And who was the woman Luke would fall in love with in this book? The doctor's wife or someone else?

She sat next to her husband and she smiled until her jaw ached, and when she felt she could, she said to him, "You know, I'm really tired. Would you mind if I walk home?"

"The fun's just starting," Thomas said. "Don't be a party pooper."

"You stay. Have a ball. I just need to get home. I'm really done in."

"Okay, honey, whatever. But don't wait up for me."

After saying good night to Livie and Dennis and Maggie, who gave her a look of disapproval, she walked home, the cold air feeling wonderful on her face. Past the *Aspen Times* office and Carl's Pharmacy, turning down the street toward her house. Walking in the dark, shoulders hunched, hands in pockets. Thinking about Thomas and Cam and what she wanted to do, what she needed to do. And they weren't the same at all.

The next morning Thomas slept late. Ellen got up early, hung over. "It was that Grasshopper," she groaned. "Thomas bought me a goddamn Grasshopper. Oh, God."

"You okay to drive? You can always stay here another day."

"Give me a couple hours, I'll be all right. And besides, I promised I'd hold a press conference. Got to get my moment in the sun while it's still shining. You have any Alka-Seltzer?"

"Ellen, I have to say one thing before you leave."

"Oh, God, don't thank me again. I'll vomit, I swear I will. You'll get my bill soon enough."

"No, it's not about that. Listen, you have to promise me you'll go to counseling with Mason as soon as he gets back to Denver."

Ellen peered at her through bloodshot eyes. "What on earth . . . ?"

"I'm dead serious, Ellen. I've seen too many women in your situation. It's dangerous. Either you get counseling or he's going to really hurt you. I'm not kidding."

"You're laying this on me now? When I'm hung over as hell?"

"Yes."

"Jesus, Julia."

"That's what friends are for," Julia said. "Promise me."

"Maybe."

"Do it."

Ellen waved a hand vaguely. "Not now."

"Okay, then tomorrow, make an appointment and keep it."

Ellen packed, loaded her car. She looked pale. She was wearing faded tights and a loose blue sweater. She kept drinking water and giving Julia reproachful glances through bloodshot eyes.

Julia followed her out when she was ready to leave. They hugged each other.

"Thank you," Julia said.

"Don't. I just did my job."

"I know . . ."

"Hey, as long as we're being so frank here, what about you and Cam?"

Julia looked away. "He's gone."

"Oh, okay, so that's that, huh?"

"I don't know."

"He's got a phone."

"Yes, but —"

"You going to break it to Thomas?"

"Yes."

"When?"

"Soon. I have to do it soon."

"Oh, like when I'm going to get Mason to go to counseling?"

Julia tried to smile. "Yes, that kind of soon."

"You dope. Go get the man if you want him."

"I have responsibilities, Ellen."

"Right, right."

"I'm married."

"I happen to know a really great divorce lawyer."

"Not yet."

"But you are going to leave him." It was not a question.

"Yes, yes, I am. I don't know exactly how or when, and I don't know what to do about Livie, but I have to leave him. I mar-

542

ried him for all the wrong reasons."

"Well, good luck. Let me know . . . well, you know."

"I will. And get that counseling."

"And just who in the hell needs counseling around here, Julia?"

TWENTY-THREE

"I've got a great idea," Thomas said the next morning.

They were eating breakfast, autumn sunlight slanting through the kitchen windows. Julia still felt bereft, glad for Thomas, but a terrible turmoil of emotions was ceaselessly clamoring in her head.

"I'm going into the clinic today," he said. "Then there's the weekend coming up, so" — he grinned at her, the old Thomas — "last night at dinner, Peter offered us the use of his cabin, and I told him I'd get back to him. But I've been thinking, I don't have any surgeries scheduled, and the clinic here is covered for obvious reasons, such as no one knew how long the trial was going to last." He grinned again. "The bottom line is I really don't have to deal with the Sun Valley project till Monday."

Julia looked up.

"What do you think? Just you and me, getting away from everything? We'll buy some groceries, a couple bottles of wine, drive up there. Peter's got plenty of firewood, sleeping bags, the works."

"Peter's cabin," she said. "Where exactly is it?"

"You know, up the Little Annie's Road, on the back side of Aspen Mountain."

"That's a pretty rough road, isn't it?"

Thomas waved away her objection. "No sweat. We've got four-wheel drive. Peter's sure we can make it."

"Oh."

"Won't it be good to get away from everybody? No television, no phone, nothing but us? A roaring fire in the fireplace, steak, wine, and cheese?"

"Well . . ."

"Oh, come on."

"It's just so . . . sudden. I was going to stop by the courthouse this afternoon, see where I stand."

He cocked his head. "Where you stand? You aren't thinking about your old job? Jesus Christ, Julia, are you crazy?"

"Thomas, look, I can't just let my career go. And I have to work. . . ." She wasn't quite ready to tell him that soon she was going to have to support herself.

He was staring incredulously at her. "You'd go back to work for that asshole, that McSwain? You must be kidding."

"Bret was doing his job, Thomas, that's all. He didn't solicit Leann, for God's sakes, *she* came to *him*. What was he supposed to do? Ignore her because I worked for him?"

Thomas just kept staring at her. Finally he said, "You know what? I don't want you going into the courthouse right now. I mean that. We'll talk about it over the weekend. And you're also forgetting one small detail: We'll be spending half the year in Sun Valley and half the year here. You couldn't have kept that job in any case."

She could have told him right then that she would never have left her job under any circumstances other than his arrest and trial. That she sure as hell never planned on spending six months at a time away from her home, that this was the first she'd heard of his plans — and how could he have assumed she'd meekly go along with this, anyway?

She looked down at her plate and told herself to cool it — none of this mattered any longer. By the end of the weekend both of their futures were going to change dramatically. She felt as if a flood were building inside her, and soon the dam was going to burst. How long could she hold herself together?

"Look," she said, rising to clear the kitchen table, "you're right, we'll take the weekend off, iron everything out up at the cabin."

"Good," he said. "You'll get the groceries, then? I really do have to go into the clinic today, at least touch base."

"Yes, I'll get the groceries. But what about Maggie? Should we ask her to come along?"

"*Mother*, and Livie for that matter, aren't invited. But you're going to have to break the news to them. Livie won't give a damn, she's got Dennis" — he scowled — "but you know Mom. It'd be better if you tell her."

"Um," she said, "okay, I'll talk to her. But at Piñons last night she said something about leaving for San Diego over the weekend."

"Well, she doesn't need us here for that. We'll just say goodbye before we take off," he said, tugging on his parka. "Everything's under control. I'll be back before six, and we'll leave for the cabin early in the morning."

"Sure," she said.

After telling Maggie about their weekend plans, Julia ran a dozen errands that day;

547

she'd either been at the trial or stuck at home with her nose to the grindstone for weeks now. Everywhere she went in town, people stopped her, congratulated her, asked about Thomas and Livie and how everyone had managed to survive such a terrible, unjust ordeal. The good news was that the media was nowhere in sight — though most likely they'd track down Thomas at the clinic for one last attempt at a formal interview.

Not Julia's problem. But she was concerned about Livie and the girl's future plans. Among everything else Julia needed to talk over with Thomas, she'd promised Livie she'd mention Denver University to her father. Thomas was going to be irate. He'd always wanted her to go to school in Ann Arbor, and he'd see straight through Livie's scheme to be close to Dennis.

"I'll take care of Blackie for the weekend," Livie had said, "if you promise to talk to Dad about me starting DU this January."

Blatant extortion. But it had worked.

At the post office Julia ran into Lawson Fines as she was getting out of her car. He was genuinely happy for her and Thomas, but said, "Hey, don't ever tell the boss I said that." He laughed. Then, "You coming back to work?"

"Well" — Julia sighed — "I'm thinking about it. I mean, I'd really like to. The question is, will Bret rehire me?"

"I don't know why not." Lawson shrugged. "He always liked you, and you conducted yourself very ethically during this whole mess. And besides, rehiring you would make him look like a real team player."

"I hope you're right."

"Give it a try. Call him on Monday. What have you got to lose?"

Lawson had *that* right. By Monday she wouldn't have a damn thing left to lose.

By the time she got home late that afternoon, Thomas was still at work, but Maggie and Livie were there, collecting Maggie's things from all over the house and apartment, packing her car, getting her ready to leave.

"You aren't taking off tonight?" Julie asked.

"What's the point in staying? My *granddaughter*" — she shot Livie a look — "is spending the weekend helping Dennis clean up that house for the owners, and you're leaving for the great outdoors. I can make it as far as Green River tonight and on to San Diego tomorrow."

"You're not even going to stay to say goodbye to Thomas?"

"Oh, I went by the clinic and said my goodbyes."

"You aren't mad, I mean, that we're leaving this weekend?"

"Not in the least. I've been here for months and I'm freezing half the time now. I'm ready to get home. But let's talk about Christmas soon. Maybe we'll all do Christmas this year at my house."

"Maybe," Julia allowed. "We'll just have to see."

Maggie left a half hour later, giving Julia a hug and crying on Livie's shoulder. "And for goodness' sakes, sweetie, don't go running off or anything like that with your fellow."

"Running off, Grandma?"

"Eloping, you know. We want a big wedding."

"Okay, Grandma, no eloping. But Dennis and I aren't *there* yet."

"You could have fooled this old lady," Maggie said, and she drove off, literally, into the setting sun.

"God," Livie said, rolling her eyes before she left to help Dennis with his house cleaning.

Julia went back inside and sorted the groceries for the weekend trip, dutifully packaging everything in Ziploc baggies.

She started dinner then, a crabmeat and wild rice casserole. Blackie had his own dinner and fell asleep on the throw rug by the back door. She felt shaky, as if she were still awaiting the verdict, holding herself together with thin threads. And no matter how hard she tried, she couldn't stop thinking about Cam, missing him so terribly her heart felt as if it were bruised.

At about six-thirty the phone rang and her pulse leaped until she realized there was no possibility Cam was going to call her. Why would he? It was Thomas on the line. He'd be at least another hour, he said, one of his patients had retorn an ACL skiing in Argentina and had just flown into Aspen to see him.

"Fine," Julia said, "dinner will keep." She hung up, turned around, leaned against the wall, and finally the dam burst.

It was Sunday morning, but Victor Ferris allowed no time off when he was working. Cam sat on one of the chairs in his office. He'd had to move a stack of books and an old yellowed manuscript before he could sit down.

Victor was dressed in orange sweatpants, stretched-out tube socks hanging off his toes, and a navy blue Broncos sweatshirt, sleeves cut off raggedly just above the elbows. His curly hair was standing on end and he was unshaven, his dark eyes glinting with excitement. A cigarette hung from his lips.

"Okay, now describe McSwain again, you know, when he got pissy."

Cam obliged.

"And Ellen. How did she stand? Hands on hips? Hip cocked? How many people were there as spectators? Mostly locals or mostly press? I want the *feel*, the *smell*. Come on, my man, give it all to me."

Cam tried his damnedest.

"The wife. Julia? You haven't said too much about her. She's important. What was she really like?"

Cam didn't want to go there. "Nice lady. Pretty in an old-fashioned kind of way, like she could be a World War II nurse or something in one of those Hollywood flicks." He paused for a moment, the image of her too overpowering to go on. But he couldn't let Victor see that. He shrugged and said, "Let's see . . . Julia. A lawyer, you already know that. She cooked for all of us. Ran all of our errands. And she must have spent eight to ten hours a day twenty-four/ seven working with Ellen and Dennis. If anything, I'd have to say she was the one planning the strategy. In the background, of course. Oh, and she has a dog, part black Labrador, funny-looking thing, missing one ear."

"A dog. I like that. Oh, yes. A dog, a misfit, mangled in a fight when he was a puppy. From the pound, one day to go before he got gassed. Then in comes the pretty lady, rescues him. In the nick of time. Good stuff.

"Now, tell me again, the scene in the courtroom when the doctor got off."

Dutifully Cam described everything Victor asked for as best he could. But, hell, Cam was no writer.

"Okay, okay. I'm seeing it. Hey, did I tell you I rewrote the end?"

"Actually, no, you didn't." Cam leaned back in the chair. "So, who did it?"

"The husband. At least in this draft he did."

"Well, well, Diamond screwed up big time, didn't he?"

"Gotta give him imperfections. Nobody's perfect. He's got to be sympathetic."

"Does Luke end up with the girl?"

"You know, it's interesting that you ask, I don't believe he does in this book. A bit of a change. We'll have to see during rewrites." Victor squinted as smoke wafted up to his eye.

"Poor bastard," Cam muttered.

"Hey, don't take it personal, Lazlo. This is fiction."

"Right. Fiction."

Cam's cell phone rang then. He held it up, checked the number — familiar. "Gotta take this, Victor," he said.

It was Frankie, Cam's cop friend from forensics. He listened carefully, felt his blood chill, asked only one question: "The results are positive?"

He listened for another moment, then clicked the phone shut, sat there for a split second, his mind spiraling down, down the vortex, to the center, the kernel of it all. The parts slid together, like pieces of a magical puzzle, forming themselves into a picture, whole and complete.

"Gotta go," he said.

"What? What?"

"You might want to hold up rewriting that end, Victor," he said as he strode out of the office, through the messy apartment, right past the elevator to the stairs.

He didn't even stop at his apartment; he got into his Bronco and started driving, west out of Denver, speeding up the ramp and onto the interstate.

Should he call Julia? Tell her that now he knew what had happened that long-ago day in May?

He wouldn't call yet. He had to talk to Marcy once more. Now that he knew, he had certain questions that had to be answered. Like what exactly was the relationship between her mother and Thomas Innes?

Because . . . Jesus, he still could barely believe it . . . Leann's DNA had been found on the Buddha.

Leann, in the end, a poor sick woman, but twelve years ago she'd been strong enough to bash Samantha Innes's head in. Jealous? Or maybe angry Samantha was betraying the good doctor, Leann's idol? Something like that.

He drove far too fast through the afternoon, up over the Continental Divide, down through Vail, Eagle, and Edwards, and on into Glenwood Springs and then Rifle. He was still speeding right up to the ranch road.

The weather had turned chilly, gusts of wind bending trees and whirling up dust devils. The horses in the fields stood, rumps into the wind. Pewter clouds gathered, lowering, on the peaks standing sentinel over the broad Colorado River Valley.

Marcy's boyfriend answered the door. Tall, skinny, blond, boyish looking. "You're that investigator that's been bugging her. Got that doctor off. So what more do you want with her?"

"Just a couple questions. It's important."

"Colin? Who's there?" Marcy, coming from the back of the house. "Oh, *you*."

"Marcy, please, two minutes."

"Can't you leave her alone, man?" Colin said.

Marcy glared at him, then shook her head in disgust. "Okay, two minutes, I'll give you two minutes, and then you leave me alone. Permanently." She folded her arms. "But if you've come to gloat over that verdict . . ."

"No, it's not that," Cam said.

"Well, then?"

He stood there in their living room and decided to tell her straight out. "Look, on a hunch at your mother's videotape session, I collected some hair samples from her bathroom and had them sent in to the FBI lab for testing. Your mother's DNA was found on the Buddha, the murder weapon, Marcy. Not the doctor's, not Matt Holman's. Your mother's."

Marcy's eyes widened and she started to say something, then shook her head. She was visibly shocked, but Cam had the feeling she was not surprised. How much did she really know?

"It's time to level with me. No one's going to jail anymore. Your mother's gone. Two men stood trial for Samantha's murder, neither one of them did it. Marcy, tell me everything you know."

She finally sat down on a worn sofa, put her face in her hands. Shook her head. "They had an affair," she said through her fingers.

"Thomas Innes and your mother?"

Head still bowed, she nodded.

"When Innes was married to Samantha?"

Another nod.

"Okay." He was thinking, his brain sifting through the facts.

"My mother was in love with him," she said in a strangled voice. "He told her he was going to leave his wife and marry her. Of course he didn't."

"Your mother told you this?"

"Only after she got so sick."

"But she never told you . . . about Samantha? That she was the one who used the Buddha on Samantha?"

Marcy's head shot up. "She couldn't have! She was a gentle person. A nurse, for chrissakes! My mother couldn't kill anybody!"

557

Cam expelled a breath. "Okay, okay, listen, your mother is well out of this. There's no point in worrying about that. But . . . one thing . . . did she ever say that the doctor knew the truth?"

"My mother didn't do it! I'm telling you, she couldn't!"

"Did Thomas Innes know?"

She turned her tear-stained face up to him. "I don't know. I just don't know anymore."

Colin sank down onto the sofa next to her, put an arm around her shoulders. "Get out of here, man," he said in a broken voice.

Cam looked at them for a minute, decided there was no point in torturing them any longer, and he left.

He got back in his Bronco, a little dazed, satisfied despite feeling badly for Leann's daughter. What a helluva thing to learn about your mother.

Leann and Thomas. He'd had a hunch, all right, but why hadn't he seen it? Maybe not twelve years ago, but he sure should have at least considered jealousy as a motivation for Leann's statement — then maybe he would have spotted the truth. Leann . . . so hurt and so jealous — Innes had not only deceived her, but then he'd gone and married Julia, a new, younger wife.

Hell hath no fury.

His thoughts veered to Julia. Married to the man who'd already destroyed two women. And Innes had to have been aware of Leann's crime, right from the beginning, he had to have known exactly who killed Samantha. He might even have been there when it happened. Probably was — because Rick Krystal had seen the doctor returning through the back door. Had Innes gone home to stop Leann from a confrontation, walked in on a brawl, maybe witnessed the murder? At the very least, he was an accessory after the fact.

Another, more disquieting thing struck him: The son of a bitch couldn't be tried again for the murder of his wife — double jeopardy — but Cam was betting an autopsy on Leann Cornish would show her death was not natural.

Oh, yeah, Innes had made damn good and sure Leann never took the witness stand, where she might have finally confessed, being so close to death, and she would have taken him down with her.

How had Innes done it? He was a doctor, he'd know. The old air bubble in the vein trick? Or maybe he'd smothered her. There was always morphine. Who'd notice a little too much morphine given to a near-death cancer patient?

The night Leann had died . . . Where exactly had the doctor been? Cam had been in Denver, found out from Ellen what had gone down. But Julia would know where her husband had been that night. Julia would definitely remember.

He drove back to Glenwood Springs and turned onto Highway 82, heading toward Aspen. Julia. With that man. Why in hell had he left her with Innes? Given her a smile and a wave and driven away. My God, what was wrong with him?

He knew, of course. Just as Victor knew why Luke never settled down with a woman, no matter how much he professed to love her.

Fear. Run-for-your-life, instinctive fear. Taught at his mother's knee. *If you love me, I'll hurt you.* Simple as that.

What a fucking coward he was.

And now Julia . . . Where was she? At home? She'd be okay at home. Maggie might still be around, and Livie was definitely there. Most likely Dennis was still hanging out, at least through the weekend.

Even though Julia had been with Innes these past six months, and he hadn't harmed her or, as far as Cam knew, threatened her, Cam still felt an urgency. He tried to tell himself it was okay, he was too close to the situation to be objective — but the sense of impending danger only mounted. He stomped harder on the accelerator, the wind rocking the Bronco, leaves skittering across the road. Ahead, in the upper valley beyond Aspen, the sky was turning black, a storm rushing in.

When he couldn't wait another second, he pulled out his cell phone. Eyes switching back and forth between the road and the phone, he punched in her cell number. It rang, once, twice, then an electronic voice told him he could press five and leave a message after the beep.

Shit.

Was it his phone or hers? The valley here was narrow. Was it the reception? She always carried her phone, always had it turned on. Where the hell was she?

He punched in their home phone number. If Thomas answered, Cam would sever the connection. But no one picked up except the answering machine. He didn't dare leave a message.

He passed a Range Rover in a no-passing zone, came up to the Aspen Airport, flashed by under a yellow light changing to red.

He'd left her with a man who was a callous bastard, an accessory to a crime, and if Cam's intuition was right, very likely a murderer. Cam had abandoned the woman he loved, waved, and driven away, and now she might well be in terrible danger.

All day Saturday, Julia had thought, *what a good actress I am.* She went for a hike with Thomas and they'd talked and admired the brilliant autumn foliage that spread on the mountainsides like golden mantles. They ate a picnic lunch on the hike then started back to the cabin. She was almost able to convince herself that their marriage was good, that their union would continue despite everything, that they'd return home together after this respite and live out their days as a contented couple.

She told herself she owed her husband this weekend, this time to relax, to put things in perspective, to finally enjoy the little things in life after the last six months.

It was all a lie, of course.

That night Thomas wanted to make love; how well she knew the signs. A knot grew in her belly as bedtime approached, as he put a last log on the fire. *Oh God,* she thought, *I can't.*

She made an excuse when he turned to

her, the sleeping bags zipped together, slithering around them. "Oh, Thomas, I'm really sorry. I got my period this morning."

So he kissed her and gave her a short laugh. "Great timing."

And she lay there, smelling the pungent wood smoke, her flesh shrinking, thinking of another man, while her husband slept guilelessly beside her.

Julia waited until Sunday morning to tell him. After breakfast, when he was replete, stuffed with eggs and sausage. She had to steel herself. This was the man she'd once loved. How to say it? "Thomas," she began.

"Hey, you know, I think it's going to snow," he said, standing at a window. "Come on over here, look at this."

"Thomas."

He turned around then, and tossed another log on the fire. "Good thing Peter has lots of wood."

"Thomas."

"What?" He was squatting now, poking at the fire.

"We have to talk."

"Sure, go ahead. Unless it's about that damn job."

She ignored his barb. "Thomas, I think

we need some time apart." My God, she'd said it, she'd finally said it.

He straightened and frowned, as if he hadn't quite heard her correctly.

"We need to think about the future, and maybe . . ."

"What do you mean?"

"What I mean is that we should try a separation." She swallowed hard.

"Look, I know these last months have been hell, but now it's over. Everything is back to normal."

She shook her head. Her hands were trembling. "It isn't that, it isn't the trial . . . or any of that."

"Then what the hell is it?"

"It's us, Thomas."

"What's wrong with us?"

"Maybe it's just me."

"Jesus, Julia, what's the matter with you? Everything comes up roses and you want a separation? If this is about Sun Valley and that goddamn job of yours —"

"It's not about the job, Thomas. It's about how I feel," she said softly.

"I was found innocent by a court, Julia, and you want to punish me now?"

"No, no, I don't want to punish you. I want some time alone, to think about things, figure out what I need to do."

"What *you* need to do. What about me? I'm your husband. I just went through hell on earth, and now you dump this shit on me?"

"I'll move out. You won't have to do —"

"You'll move out? What will everybody say about that? What about my reputation, goddamn it."

"Thomas . . ." She felt so helpless. He'd never understand; everything was always about him. Always had been.

"I don't want any money," she said. "I don't want anything."

"You bitch," he said.

"Thomas, please, let's not do this. Let's not be enemies."

He moved close and thrust his face into hers. "Listen to me, Julia. In my life there are two kinds of people — those with me and those against me. Maybe you'd better think about that."

"I don't want to argue."

"Well, then, we won't. You know what? I'm going out."

"Going out?"

"For a drive. Before this storm hits."

"Thomas, please."

He grabbed his parka and went out the door, slamming it behind him. Shaking, she sank down onto a cot, hearing him start up the Suburban, race the motor viciously, spin the tires on the dirt road.

He'd come back, she decided. He'd say he'd been thinking, maybe she was right. They'd talk. In the end they'd be friends. She could see Livie whenever she wanted. She'd buy a condo or a small house, she'd get her job back, and . . .

She got up, paced the small, one-room cabin, back and forth over the Indian rug on the plank floor, past the moss rock fireplace and the tiny kitchen and the chinked-log walls, back and forth, hugging herself. Thinking: *What am I going to do? What am I going to do?*

An hour dragged by, then another. The sky was growing darker. She could hear the wind whistling through the pine needles, rattling the windows, wailing in the chimney flue. Smoke puffed from the burning logs back into the cabin.

Where was he? Lost on the mountain? Had he driven away . . . left her here? No, no, he wouldn't do that. Not with a storm coming. He'd just wouldn't do that.

She went to the front window for the hundredth time and peered out. A dark line, like gray gauze, was coming toward her from up the valley, moving toward the Maroon Bells. The storm. Yes, it would snow.

And then her cell phone rang, the electronic double tone so bizarre up here in the cabin, that for a second she didn't know what it was.

She snatched the phone off the table and clicked on. She hadn't known if there was reception up here or not. Maybe it was Thomas. Or Livie . . .

"Julia?"

Her brain couldn't fit itself around the reality of his voice.

"Julia?"

"Yes," she finally got out. "Cam?"

"Where are you?"

"I'm at a cabin on the back side of Aspen Mountain. What . . . ?"

"Listen . . ." His voice faded out.

"Cam, Cam, are you still there?"

". . . Damn phone. Julia, listen. Is Thomas there?"

"No, not right now."

"What? I didn't get that."

"Not . . . right . . . now." She was practically shouting.

"But he's around?"

"Yes, but —"

"Okay, I want you to . . ." His voice faded again.

"What, Cam?"

". . . Very careful. I think . . ."

"Oh, Cam, I can't hear you!"

Then, suddenly, his voice so clear he could have been right outside. "Where was Thomas the night Leann Cornish died?"

Her heart seized up, then gave a great leap. "What?"

". . . The night Leann died?"

She couldn't breathe. She knew exactly where Thomas had been. It was the night of her planned seduction.

"Where was he?"

"He was . . . at the hospital," she said, knowing at that moment something irrevocable had occurred. "At the hospital," she whispered.

"Julia, please, I want you to . . ." Dead air, nothing.

"Cam?" she cried. "Cam!"

The cabin door closed with a quiet snick behind her. She whirled, the useless phone still in her hand.

"Well, well," Thomas said, his face devoid of expression.

Had he heard? She searched his face, the phone in her hand, standing there in the middle of a bright Navajo rug, the fire crackling. *Had he heard?*

TWENTY-FOUR

Luke Diamond never panicked, but Cam Lazlo sure as hell did. He headed straight to the police station in the basement of the Pitkin County Courthouse, ran down the stairs, and stopped in front of Gloria, the desk sergeant.

"Who's on duty today?" he said, breathless.

"Well, hi, Cam, thought you'd left. . . ." she began.

"Look, I'm back, and I've got an emergency, is the sheriff around?"

"Not on Sunday, but a deputy's on duty, out on patrol, though, and one Aspen police officer, but he's on a break."

Shit. "Okay, now, listen. Julia Innes is in danger somewhere up on Aspen Mountain, in a cabin. I'll find out exactly where. I need someone who knows the area to take me there. Now."

"Well, I —"

"There's a homicide suspect involved, and Julia's in danger. Get it?"

"All right, all right. I'll contact the sheriff. Hold on."

While she made the call, Cam tried Julia's house again. Finally Livie answered.

"Livie, where exactly is Julia?"

"Is that you, Cam?"

"Yes, now tell me, where exactly are your father and Julia?"

"Gosh, they're at a friend's cabin on Little Annie's Road, way up near the top. It belongs to Peter Fender, a friend of Dad's."

"Do you know exactly where it is?"

"No, I've never been there. What's going on? Where are you, anyway?"

"I'm back in Aspen, Livie. Listen, can you tell me how to get hold of this Peter Fender? I need to get up there."

"Why? Can't you — ?"

"It's important, Livie. Cell phone's not working, no reception."

"Okay, wait a sec. His number's probably in Dad's phone book."

He heard her leafing through pages. He waited, every second a small slice of torture.

"Okay, here it is, 555-8383."

"Thanks, Livie." He hung up.

"The sheriff wants to know what's going on," Gloria said.

"Tell him I need to get up to this cabin now, right now. I've got the number of the guy who owns it. But I need the owner to give directions to someone local."

"Um. That would be Jeb Feller," she said. "He lives in town and does a lot of jeeping."

"His number?"

He caught Feller at home, luckily. Explained the situation, gave Feller this Peter Fender's number. "Call me back right away," Cam said. "Better yet, I'll pick you up. My Bronco's four-wheel drive."

He met Feller at the roundabout on the west side of town. "I had to track Peter Fender down, but I got directions," Jeb said, sliding in beside Cam. "Now, will you tell me what's going on?"

When Cam was finished, the Aspen police detective said, "Holy shit," as they raced along Castle Creek Road, which led to the dirt track up the back side of Aspen Mountain. "Let me get this straight, Leann Cornish did Samantha? I mean, she must have if it was her DNA on the murder weapon. And you think Innes helped her death along?"

"You got it."

"Say you're right about the doctor doing Leann . . . how does that put Julia in danger?"

Cam spun out of a long winding curve and clenched his jaw. "Because I was stupid enough to tell Julia on her cell phone. Then we got cut off. But I think she wasn't alone. If Innes finds out I'm on to him, God knows how he'll react."

"I think I should clue the chief and the sheriff into what's going on," Feller said. "They'll want to send some backup."

"Screw that, we're not waiting for them," Cam said grimly.

"Fine, fine." Feller made a couple calls on his cell phone. From what Cam could hear, the reception was fading in and out even this close to Aspen. The mountains. No way was he going reach Julia again.

Feller talked on his cell and about five miles outside of town waved a hand to direct Cam where to turn onto Little Annie's Road.

Feller finally clicked off. "We've got some real doubters," he said.

"Fuck 'em," Cam said.

"It's going to snow." Feller gestured at the legions of clouds closing in. A solid gray line, swirling with flakes, sat in front of them, wider at the top, narrowing to a V at the bottom of the valley, a veritable wall of weather.

"Yeah, so what?"

"I guess you don't know this road."

"Guess not."

"Okay, fasten your seatbelt, folks, it's going to be a bumpy ride."

Cam turned to the left, crossed Castle Creek on a bridge, passed a few houses clustered at the bottom of the mountain. Then they started to climb, the road nicely graded here, a few houses, set prettily in the pines, then becoming scarce, the road more bumpy and narrow as they ascended, badly rutted. He shifted the Bronco into four-wheel drive.

He was now wrestling the steering wheel, foot heavy on the gas, sliding around corners, Feller bracing himself on the dashboard. And he thought of Julia, up ahead somewhere, alone with that killer. Cam shouldn't have phoned her, not at this isolated cabin, because now she knew — now she was alert and suspicious, and Innes would know.

Julia. Alone in the middle of nowhere with a murderer. How would Innes react? If he were rational, he'd realize she was the least of his problems. But if he panicked . . .

And how had Julia ended up in this situation? Blame none other than Cam Lazlo, coward, driving off into the sunset, leaving her behind with that bastard, because he was afraid to commit.

He'd suspected her husband all along. Why hadn't he leveled with her? Jesus. He'd just had the wrong victim.

"Hey, take it easy," Feller was saying, "better we get there in one piece."

He drove without regard to the road or to Feller.

"How far?" Cam asked.

"I don't know in miles, but say less than an hour now." Feller braced himself again on the dash.

Julia had no idea he was on his way. They'd been cut off. Maybe she'd be smart enough to keep her cool, maybe . . . What the hell was he thinking? He'd just told her Innes was a murderer.

He had a sudden flash of hope then, could almost see her manipulating an escape, driving down this very road, and she'd stop and jump out and so would he, and he'd grab her and hold her, and never let her go.

"Will you look at that," Feller said, motioning to the windshield.

Cam blinked away the fantasy. It had started to snow like hell.

Thomas had smiled, and that scared Julia more than anything else.

"Who was that?" he asked.

"Oh . . . oh, Livie . . . she thinks Blackie's sick."

"That's why you were saying his name?"

"Who? Whose name?"

"How stupid do you think I am, Julia? You think I didn't notice the cow eyes you two made at each other? For six whole goddamn months?"

"Thomas, I don't —"

"I saw all of it. I didn't say a word because I figured you needed your little games, and I knew you'd never have the balls to really do anything. Am I right, honey?"

She said nothing.

"But now, now, after all this is over, you want to leave me? I don't think so."

She was terrified. Her face must show it. And Thomas . . . he was like the predator who instinctively stalks the weakest animal in the herd; he recognized fear.

"I won't leave you, I swear. We'll work things out. I didn't know . . . I didn't know how you really felt." She was barely able to talk, her breath short, her muscles paralyzed.

"You've never known how I felt."

"I'm sorry. I'll . . . try . . . really, I will. If you'll . . . just tell me." Keep him talking, grovel, whatever it took. What was Cam doing? Did he even know where she was? He must be doing something, he had to. He knew she was in danger. He knew.

Time. She needed to stretch out the time. Keep Thomas talking.

"Did you love Samantha?" she asked, babbling.

"Samantha?"

"Did you really love her?"

"Yeah, sure, I loved her. At first. Then she fucked that young gold digger, and it really turned me off."

"Do you . . . love me?"

He glared at her. "What is this, confession time?"

"Yes." She edged toward the door. If she could somehow get outside. Run.

She could see through one of the windows beside the fireplace. It was snowing, big white flakes spinning out of the gray sky. Her heart knotted. Snow would make the road impassable. The cabin would be snowed in. She would be trapped.

The car. Where were the keys? Had he left them in the ignition? If he'd left the keys, she'd take the car. But she had to get past him, had to get out of the cabin.

"Did you . . . love Leann?" A stab at getting his attention.

His eyes became slits. "Leann?"

"You did, didn't you?"

"What the hell are you talking about?"

"You had an affair with her. And she was the one who hit Samantha."

"You're crazy."

"Were you there, Thomas?" She moved a little, her muscles tense, coiled. She'd only have a second. "Leann must have believed you'd marry her. But you didn't. That's why she wanted to get back at you."

"She was sick."

"I don't think so. Not twelve years ago, anyway. She was in love."

"It doesn't matter what you think."

Her pulse was pounding. "Did Leann really just pass away? Or did you help her along, Thomas? You were at the hospital, I remember."

"Shut up," he said, "just shut the fuck up, you don't know what you're talking —"

She lunged then, grabbing for the door latch, pulling at it, but the latch stuck for a moment, then came loose. Not before he was on her, holding her in a bear hug from behind. She kicked backward at him, felt a foot connect, but he squeezed her so tightly her ribs felt as if they were cracking, and black swam at the edge of her vision. She threw her body weight backwards, felt

577

him lose his balance. He pulled her over with him, hit the cot, was knocked sideways.

In that instant she was on her knees, scrambling. He caught her foot. Not a word, panting, fast breathing, a grunt as she kicked and kicked at him. Then he was on her again, bearing her down. So heavy. She struggled. Too heavy.

He pulled at her arm, yanking her up. "Let's go," he said.

"Where?" she panted. "They'll know!"

"They won't know jack-shit. You're about to run away, bitch."

He was going to kill her. Kill her and no one would find her body till spring.

She didn't waste her breath then. Got dragged outside. Snow hit her face, plastered on her skin, pattered on her clothes.

She let him pull her along for a moment, gathering her wits, gathering her strength. At least she was outside. Leaning against him as if she were spent.

Felt his hold relax infinitesimally, slick and wet from the snow. Then she jerked away, fast and hard, felt his hand slip, and she was free, running, stumbling, down the steep slope toward the trees, running, her breath flaming in her lungs, snow blinding. Running into the shadow of the storm.

Behind her his voice, yelling, "Julia! Julia, goddamnit!"

She made the trees and slipped, falling hard on the slick pine needle floor. Then she was half up, scrabbling to get to her feet. Over there — underbrush . . . She clawed her way, felt twigs and briers snatch at her clothes.

"Julia!" He was close.

Crouching in the thick underbrush, shivering, knowing he was going to appear out of the curtain of snow. Trying to catch her breath to run again.

Cam clutched the wheel, his hands like talons, his eyes fixed on the road ahead, body straining forward, willing the Bronco to go faster. Up and up, the road muddy, engine revving, bouncing over potholes, loose rock, the vehicle lurching from side to side, skidding out of control.

Julia, stay cool. Don't antagonize him, don't let him know.

What if he got there too late?

"Okay," Feller called over the grind of the engine, "look on your left. It should be coming up. Damn, I can barely see in this storm."

Around a switchback, the world closing in, the snow dancing crazily on the windshield, the wipers swishing back and forth, back and forth. A clearing ahead, sloping down. And a stand of spruce trees, tall and dim in the storm.

"There it is!" Feller shouted, pointing.

Yes, Cam could just make out the roof of a cabin under the trees, almost blotted out by snow. A small square log structure, a pile of split wood outside. He braked and slid sideways onto the dirt track leading down to the cabin, stopped short. There was the Suburban, and the front door of the cabin, open. Wide open.

He pulled his gun out of the glove box, slammed out of the Bronco, yelling, "Julia, are you here?"

Ran, sliding in the wet snow, to the open door. One look inside, eyes darting around. A fire dying in the fireplace. One of the cots shoved aside, pillows strewn about. A struggle.

Julia?

"No one here," he called to Feller.

"They're out here somewhere!" Feller shouted back, starting to look around.

"You got your weapon?"

"Hell, yes."

"All right." Cam wiped snow off his face impatiently. "You head down that way." He gestured with his firearm. "I'll go to the right. If you see either of them yell."

He stepped through the wet snow, gun leading, squinting, trying to see through the whirling whiteness. Tracks. There should be tracks. But he couldn't make out any. Around the side of the cabin, every muscle taut, ready for action.

Shit, it had been years since he'd done this kind of thing. But you didn't forget. You never forgot. The thrill and the fear, the adrenaline, were always lurking beneath the surface.

Past the corner of the cabin, sliding around to the back, scanning the trees below, the ground for footprints. So damn hard to see, sound deadened, the world contracted to the few yards surrounding him. He wiped impatiently at the snow with the back of a wrist.

Julia was out here somewhere.

He heard something then. Stopped in his tracks. Listened hard. A muffled echo. A voice? Another echo. Definitely a man's voice.

Crouching, he moved toward the sound, down the slope, his feet soaked, slipping, his pants wet to the knees.

There. At the edge of the trees, movement, a bright color shrouded by the snowfall, a shadowed figure moving stealthily.

The voice, faint: "Julia, get the hell out here . . . nowhere to go."

He moved faster now, the figure coming into focus, Innes in a red-and-black shirt. Standing there, peering into the trees, calling her name.

He would have used his gun. No problem. But if he missed and the round went into the trees . . . So he ran, slipping, righting himself, throwing himself on Innes, knocking him to the ground, twisting his arm up behind him, knee in the small of his back.

"Where is she, goddamn you, where is she?" he panted.

Innes grunted, heaving upward, trying to throw Cam off.

Cam pressed his knee harder into his spine, jerked his arm upward until the bone was ready to snap. "Where is she?"

"Don't know!" he cried out. "Haven't . . . touched the bitch!"

Cam jerked the man's arm even harder, heard him yelp in agony, ground his face into the snow. "Where the hell is she?"

"Don't . . . know!"

Feller came on the run. "You got her?" he panted, sucking air.

"Not yet."

"Dr. Innes, have you harmed your wife?"

"Who the fuck are you?"

"Detective Feller, Aspen police. You remember me." As he spoke he clicked handcuffs onto Innes's wrists.

Cam left them both, Innes on the ground, cursing, trying to rise to his knees, Feller standing over him. He made his way around some underbrush, into the tall, dark blue spruces, their limbs laden with snow.

"Julia!" he called. "It's Cam!" He yelled out till his voice was hoarse.

Finally, finally, there was a movement in the forest, a shadow detaching itself from the thick shroud of snow.

A faint voice. "Cam?"

He ran, saw her more clearly then, standing, moving, alive.

"Cam, oh, God." She threw herself into his arms. "You came. You came!"

"It's okay." He held her. She was trembling, shivering, soaked, crying. "We have him. He can't hurt you now."

"I knew you'd come. I knew you would."

He finally tipped her face up to his. "Are you hurt?"

"It's nothing."

He put an arm around her, led her limping back toward the cabin. Her hair hung around her face, wet strands, her flannel shirt and fleece jacket were wet through.

Jeb Feller was inside with Innes. When she saw them, she drew back instinctively. "No, I can't. I can't go in there."

Cam helped her into his car, turned on the ignition, flipped the heater to high, went back and got blankets from the cabin, draped them around her.

Her lip was split and puffy. She supported her left arm. She admitted her shoulder hurt. He didn't care. She was alive, she was okay. He held her. This time for keeps.

TWENTY-FIVE

Early May in Aspen. The leaves are budding in the palest shades of green, a delicate tracery embroidered on branches. Snow still covers the high peaks, and the chill of winter lurks in damp, shaded corners. Every morning the city sends cleaning machines up and down each street to wash away the winter grime.

People are out on bicycles. Walking their dogs. Jogging. The mountain sits forlorn and empty, its slopes leprous with melted snow. The high country will not reawaken until June, when it will be navigable to hikers and Jeeps.

Robins cluck and brood their nests. Hawks soar overhead. Bears awaken and emerge, grumpy, slow, and shedding. Coyotes howl back and forth across the valley floor to one another. Foals and calves come into the world up and down the Roaring Fork Valley.

On May 5, at nine in the morning, Judge Bill Scott tapped his gavel and called his courtroom to order. Case 83750, the

People vs. Thomas Innes, one count being the murder of Leann Cornish on October 10 of the previous year. And the other count, the attempted murder of Julia Innes that same month. Alternately, the jury might find Dr. Innes guilty of the reduced charge of assault on the person of Julia Innes.

Bret McSwain stood, ready to make his opening argument. He'd rehearsed his speech, his gestures, his facial expressions until he was word perfect. No mistake this time. No way would the celebrity doctor walk.

He'd even used Ellen Marshall as a consultant on the case. She'd refused to defend Innes on these charges, and she couldn't appear in court, of course, but Bret had run a lot of his strategy by her when he'd visited her in Denver several times, even taken her to dinner. Ellen was one smart cookie. Not to mention a very pretty lady. He'd sure as hell rather have her on his side than opposing him.

"I will prove," Bret said to the jury, "that Thomas Innes, with malice afore-thought, went to Aspen Valley Hospital on the evening of October 10 of last year, with the intent of killing Leann Cornish, who lay in a near coma. I will call as witnesses two forensic experts who examined her exhumed body, every nurse and doctor in the hospital that night, and you will return the only possible verdict, that of murder in the first degree.

"I will further prove, with testimony from the victim herself, that Dr. Innes attempted to kill Julia Innes, his wife, because she learned he had murdered Ms. Cornish. Again, you will return a verdict of guilty."

The attention of the jury was fixed on McSwain, and he experienced that powerful expansion of feeling, knowing he held people in thrall, he controlled their thoughts, he could lead them through the intricacies of testimony and the law, so that they would do his bidding.

This was the way a great actor felt, he thought. On the stage, the audience in the palm of your hand.

There would be no mistake this time around.

Outside the courtroom, in the hallway of the Pitkin County Courthouse, Julia waited. She was going to give testimony today. She'd been well prepped by Bret. He'd presented her with every possible question Thomas's defense attorney could ask. And she herself had come up with a lot more. She was prepared.

She knew she'd have to face Thomas in the courtroom. She'd only seen him once since that awful day. Cam had not wanted her to make the visit, but she knew she had to see her husband one more time.

"I hate the word *closure*," she'd said. "But I need to do this."

"I'll come with you."

She almost smiled. "I don't think so."

"What's left to say to him?"

"Things. We were married, Cam. I owe him a visit. One visit. Nothing more."

So she went to see Thomas in the Pitkin County Jail, because this time the judge had not seen fit to release him on a personal recognizance bond. He was in an orange jumpsuit; he looked thinner and pale. And very, very angry.

"Nice, Julia," he'd said. "Look what you've done."

"I didn't do this, Thomas," she said softly. "You killed Leann, you tried to kill me."

"I barely touched you. I just wanted you to listen to my side of things."

She put her fingers up to her still swollen lip. "You did this. You tried to kill me."

"Bullshit. Bullshit!"

"I'll have to testify, you realize that."

"A wife doesn't have to testify against her husband."

"I'm beginning divorce proceedings."

"Oh, great, that will really help my case."

She shook her head. He didn't get it. He'd never get it. "You'll give me a divorce, won't you? I don't want any alimony. Keep your money, you'll need it to pay your defense attorney. And for Livie."

"You are a class A, number-one bitch," Thomas said bitterly.

"No, I'm not. I'm not at all." She took a breath. "But I do want to apologize to you for one thing. I married you because I thought that what I needed was security. I was wrong. I'm sorry, Thomas."

"You've already got a goddamn boyfriend. Jesus, Julia."

"Our marriage was over before any of this happened. You know that."

"There was nothing wrong with our marriage."

"Oh, Thomas," she'd said sadly.

She'd left the jailhouse shaken and bowed down by grief. A kind of mourning, as if her life, everything she'd believed in, had died. And she had to shoulder a certain amount of blame herself. She'd married Thomas for so many wrong reasons. You can't escape your past, she'd thought so often.

Well, this time she was going to try.

She'd have to face him in the courtroom

today. She knew he'd glare at her, try to intimidate her. He'd been quoted by the media as saying terrible things about her. Hurtful things. That she'd been a cold, hard bitch who'd cared more about her career than him or his daughter.

Livie was out in San Diego with her grandmother Maggie right now. She'd been living in Denver, enrolled in a few courses at Denver University. But she was taking this time off for the trial. Even Dennis couldn't comfort her in the face of what had happened. She was going to start over, she'd said. She and Julia talked on the phone almost every day.

How could Thomas have done this to his own daughter? Whenever Julia thought about that, she would get furious, and despise him for what he done to her and to so many other lives.

Cam sat next to her now, holding her hand. He'd told her he wasn't going to leave her side until the trial was over. He'd taken time off from his job with Victor Ferris to stay with her.

She could hear Bret's voice rise and fall through the double doors. Then Thomas's defense lawyer, a top-notch attorney from Denver. Recommended by Ellen, actually.

Her heart beat fast, and she kept licking

her lips. She'd be on the witness stand; she'd be answering questions, her role reversed from prosecutor to witness.

Cam squeezed her hand. He knew what she was thinking; he always knew. He loved her. They were going to get married as soon as her divorce was final. The papers had been given to Thomas. He was balking, but eventually he'd sign them.

She was going to move to Denver. Cam's landlords were selling the bookstore and he'd been house hunting. She and Ellen were considering going into practice together, starting their own firm.

She and Cam had talked everything over, and just after the New Year, they'd taken Livie out to dinner. Both had asked her to stay with them, at least until she was finished college.

The Aspen house was up for sale for a ridiculously high sum, millions, and Julia had been renting a condo for her and Blackie until the trial ended. She couldn't bear to set foot in that house again. All she'd removed from the place were her clothes and some personal items.

The voices inside the courtroom droned on. She drew in a quavering breath, then another.

"Soon," Cam said, "and then it'll be over."

"Will it ever be over?"

"I'll do everything in my power to see that it is."

"What if Thomas gets off?"

"He won't."

"He'll hate me forever."

"His problem."

"Oh, God, let's talk about something else," she said. "Victor. The book. What's happening with it?"

"Well, he finally sent it in. His editor read it and loves it."

"He had the husband guilty of killing his first wife, right?"

"Yep."

"Why didn't he rewrite it the way it really happened?"

Cam smiled. "Because he said no one would believe it."

"And did Luke get the girl?"

"Nope. Victor couldn't bring himself to marry Luke off. He said it would ruin the series."

"Poor Luke."

"However" — Cam held a finger up — "he did offer the possibility of a serious relationship for Luke."

"With me?" she asked.

Cam grinned. "No, Luke can't have you. I saw you first."